The
ACTUATOR
— 1 —
Fractured Earth

JAMES WYMORE
AIDEN JAMES

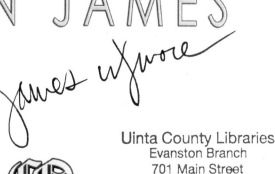

A Division of **Whampa, LLC**
P.O. Box 2540
Dulles, VA 20101
Tel/Fax: 800-998-2509
http://curiosityquills.com

© 2013 James Wymore & Aiden James
http://jameswymore.wordpress.com
http://aidenjamesfiction.com

ISBN 978-1-62007-318-6 (ebook)
ISBN 978-1-62007-319-3 (paperback)
ISBN 978-1-62007-320-9 (hardcover)

TABLE OF CONTENTS

Thanks to Aiden James. Your help and insights made this all possible.
For my mother.

~James Wymore

To James Wymore, for creating a concept that's been so deliciously fun to work with!
To Fiona, my love, my muse, and mentor... I love you forever.

~Aiden James

CHAPTER ONE

tanding next to a colorful rock outcropping from a desert mountain, Red McLaren watched the crew study the surrounding geological formations. The merciless morning sun forced him to carry his black leather jacket, and one might presume his holstered pistol was intended for the workers around him. But, as a Key Hunter, the weapon was strictly for protection. He'd felt something wasn't right since daybreak.

He brushed his dark hair from his face, trying not to think about what he'd miss when Xenwyn used the Actuator. Jon told him to not let feelings get in the way of the job. So Red kept his uneasiness to himself, despite his feeling he should be there with Xenwyn. He never called her Lisa Gull anymore.

"What's so important about these rocks that half the Untouched House had to come see them?" The MP named Jackson stepped out of the military van and joined Red.

Red nodded indifferently, knowing the answer, but preferring not to give an impromptu training course about Machine Monks to a guard who should have known already—one who just didn't listen during training. "Maybe they were just tired of being cooped up on base."

"Aren't we all," said Jackson. He pulled out a Kleenex from the driver's side door of the van and began dusting the red sand from his polished black shoes.

Red cracked a smile before returning his gaze to the Machine Monks. The group was crushing rocks with hammers and analyzing samples. "I hope they wrap it up in time for a decent lunch."

"While we're out, we should get some Chinese take-away," the MP said, chuckling.

"You can buy since you still owe me twenty bucks after last week's football game." Red grinned, and walked over to the edge of the bluff. His gaze followed the long road they'd traveled, cutting through Joshua trees, sagebrush, and sand. The closest Chinese restaurant was a good fifty miles away. The base was closer, visible where it nestled between two distant peaks. The Actuation would happen soon. As one of only two resident Key Hunters, he should be monitoring things from the control tower, instead of babysitting what was happening here. The next event would be coming soon. He sensed it.

He hated being out here where he would miss the excitement of the earth-changing event today. It gave him such a rush. How effective could he possibly be out in the field when his mind remained focused on only the Actuator site? Whether it was an addiction or just a Pavlovian response to the adrenaline of the change, he no longer cared.

Red could see the Actuator clearly in his imagination. Sitting on a round pad of concrete, the five foot square metal base had vents on the side like a large computer. Half the base had a console on the top where key holes appeared when they used the machine. The other half had a control and display panel rising up with various switches and readouts. One looked like an oscilloscope, another resembled radar. Nobody ever touched the controls. The Actuator worked autonomously. Above that, a large metal pole held three satellite dish shapes, which transmitted the signal. The pole rose to a round metal ball fifteen up, which looked like a lightning rod. Although despite many electrical storms over the years and the machine sitting in the middle of a one mile radius clearing, it had never suffered any damage.

One of the Machine Monks, a tall blond in jeans and a tan blouse tipped her sunhat back and walked over to him. "Almost time?" she asked. He and Veronica Turner had been friends for years. She preferred the nickname, 'Glass.'

"Yeah... I can feel it. Just like every other time," Red said. "Even from here."

"We all can," she said, shielding her eyes from the sun as she gazed toward the invisible oasis between two peaks. "Everybody on the base can, too. It's become the center of our entire existence."

"Not for Empty House."

"Well, it's not supposed to be," she said. "Not for us, either. But it is. The Actuator defines our purpose, and our perspective."

"It's a screwed-up way to go through life."

"Not really. Most people's lives center on their jobs. They think it's for the money to pay for homes and cars and food, but their actions revolve around the work they do."

"Not like us, though. They still go home to families and have barbecues on weekends…" Red's voice trailed off when they saw a white flash over the horizon where the base lay.

Glass gasped.

A sphere of energy blasted toward them from between the twin mountains. Something like an event horizon from the fifties, the blast traveled faster than sound, sparkling as it swelled across the miles. There wasn't time to speak or run for cover. The transformative power of the pulsing arc would find them. In a matter of a few seconds, the crest flushed over and through them.

Red's entire being shook from the familiar sensation, as his eyes were blinded by bright light and his ears filled with thunder. Placing his hands over his eyes and ears wouldn't help, since the sensation came from the electrical interactions with brain and nerves. The bitter mix of vinegar and caramel corn swelled his tongue and the scent of acetone and vanilla embraced his nostrils. Every inch of skin prickled and his muscles tensed.

The energy wave continued its magic, and the Machine Monks—including Glass—shook from what looked like intense euphoria. The bright light faded, and the rumble in his ears softened.

Glass said, "We shouldn't… shouldn't feel this… There's something…"

"Something's wrong," Red finished.

"What in the h–h… What's g—going on?" Jackson demanded in a new, grating voice. A low, guttural growl infected every word.

Red jumped in dismay. The MP had turned into a green-skinned monster. Surely, Jackson didn't realize he had a slimy pig snout and beefy tusks sticking out of his mouth. How fitting… a wannabe cop was now monstrously pig-like. It was hard for Red not to laugh, but fearing what would come next, he caught himself.

"How did the Actuator reach us from so far away?" Glass' arms were shaking and she tried to wrap them around her abdomen to get them to stop. The geological testing chemicals suddenly turned into glass vials of unknown alchemical liquids. The rest of the Machine Monks gasped and backed away from their animated tools.

"Look at my h—hands!" Jackson, the new orc marveled. He followed it with enthused grunts that grew louder as he saw his shiny shoes had become rough leather boots, sized to fit his far bigger feet.

"Calm down," Red said. It was a struggle to keep his face serious as he reached out to steady the MP. "It's probably just a glitch in the system. Jon's there and will probably figure this out any moment."

"That's eas... easy f-for you to say," Jackson graveled. "You don't look l-like... like a f-filthy pig."

"An orc," Red corrected him. He stepped closer and placed a tentative hand on the shoulder of Jackson's torn leather tunic. "Obviously, this is Xenwyn's work."

"That slut did this to me?"

"Hey! She's not a slut." Red hated what the soldiers on base said about Xenwyn, but this wasn't the time to school an ignorant base cop on a girl he knew quite well. "It must be a problem with the dampeners. Just hold on there, and Jon will have the key back in the Actuator in a few seconds. Then all of this will go away."

"He b-better, or...," the orc grunted. Jackson reached for his gun and found instead a heavy battle-axe strapped to a thick belt. "W-where's m-my gun?" He lifted the axe and began gripping it in a fit of anger.

"Stand down, soldier!" Red ordered. Recognition came into his muddy green eyes, and the slob of a monster brought his heels together while straightening his hunched back. "On this trip I out rank you. Is that clear? I don't give a rat's ass if you're a candy coated cookie man, you will help me get these Monks back to base. You can sort out your personal issues then. Again, do I make myself clear?"

The pigman nodded, though shaking. His teeth were a gritted fence of rage. Glass retreated quietly toward the other cowering Machine Monks.

Red cracked a smile. "Yes... sir?"

The orc snorted. In a fast motion he lifted the axe to attack. "I don't take orders from your kind!"

Red barely escaped the swiping blade, but having been through enough actuations, he knew to expect anything. Shaking his head in disgust, he reached for his gun and seemed only slightly surprised that he pulled out a crossbow instead.

The guard grunted as he spun around and leaped into the crowd of cowering Machine Monks. When he lifted the axe to slice through Glass, Red pulled the trigger. The small arrow sunk deep in the monster's back. Blood poured from the wound where it nicked the heart. The beastly man's hairy green arms began to shake. He fell, coughing out his last bit of life, as his axe clattered against the rocky ground.

Glass had one hand over her mouth, fighting the urge to scream as tears streaked down her cheeks. Red rushed to her side and she buried her head into his shoulder. "Why would Jackson attack me?" she cried. "We were friends, I thought!"

"It's what the Actuator made him," Red said, gently patting her back. "It wasn't his choice."

"That's awful," said Cindy, another Machine Monk. She pulled her pink knitted sweater tight as if she were cold, despite the sun's heated rays.

Red nodded. He knew Jackson, too. Although not close friends, they'd talked at more than a few social events. He hated having to kill him.

"Why'd you kill him?" another Monk– Owen— asked. Clearly, he was in shock. "Why didn't you just wound him?"

"It's my job to protect you all at all costs," Red said. He knew if anything had happened to Glass, Jon would never forgive him. "We protect the Actuator, then the Monks. He would have kept going. I've dealt with Xenwyn's orcs many times. They aren't rational beings."

"The machine just sucked out his free will?" Glass asked.

Red nodded. Why hadn't Jon put the keys in and turned things back to normal yet?

"Will he be alive again when they fix it?" Owen asked. He had shaved his head to accommodate his bald spot, but wore a goatee beneath black-rimmed glasses. *He should shave the beard, too*, Red thought.

"No," Red said. "He's dead. And I have to live with it." Now it was Glass hugging him.

"What do we do? Do we call the police?" The manic monk wouldn't calm down.

"No," Red said. "Everybody in the van... I mean carriage." The van was gone, and in its place sat a large white carriage with a team of six horses stamping in agitation. "We need to head back right away. I'll send somebody to pick up Jackson's remains once we know what's going on."

"We can't just leave him here!" Glass said.

"I'm not leaving him forever... let's get going."

"No. I want to know what you know, Red. Why didn't the Actuator turn us into monsters, too?" Owen demanded.

Red sighed, and held his crossbow aimed at Owen's legs. Instead of shooting a warning arrow toward his feet, he put it back into the holster.

"It depends on Xenwyn's mental model," he explained, while climbing onto the carriage. He was leaving with or without them. "She probably sees

Machine Monks as a separate classification of people than guards. It's all very complicated, and I just killed somebody. So, can we stop with the twenty questions and get out of here?"

Owen reluctantly nodded and the six Machine Monks climbed into the carriage, perching on wooden benches instead of comfortable seats.

"Thank you for saving me," Glass whispered, right before disappearing inside. "I'm so sorry this happened."

Red nodded. "Me, too."

Red levered off the brake and whipped the horses. The carriage turned around the green-skinned corpse and Jackson lay motionless. Blood sank into the sand, leaving Red to regret not listening to his instincts.

CHAPTER TWO

Red looked up at Glass's face. Even with her yelling, he couldn't hear well over the thunderous hooves of the horses. She said, "I just don't know why they haven't put everything back yet." She held up one hand to keep her wind whipped hair from hitting her in the face.

"I don't know." Red urged the team faster, even though it already felt like the ruts and rocks of this dirt road might crack the wooden carriage wheels. It had been a regular road when they drove out this morning. Owen kept trying to yell questions or comments up to the front of the carriage. Red ignored him and kept talking loudly to Glass. "There were supposed to be dozens of Machine Monks working the Actuator today. All of Dedicated House, one Empty House, and a couple from your house were all going to try and negotiate territory in the test zone."

"Do you think it overloaded the machine somehow?" A gust of wind brought desert dirt up and they both turned aside for a moment.

"No," Red said, wagging his head for emphasis. "We've done multi-user tests before without any problems."

"Seems like Jon would have recovered the reset keys by now." Glass wiped a tear from her eye. Red didn't know if it was from the wind or seeing a man killed right in front of her minutes earlier.

"Not if the dampeners failed," Red said more quietly. "The keys could be scattered all over the world." His voice dropped as his jaw tightened. An unseen vise gripped his heart. Red never killed anyone before. They'd trained him to, of course. When he signed up for this job, it was a very real possibility. However, in all his training, nobody ever told him how awful it would feel. Guilt battled with grief for control of his feelings. Each beat of his heart echoed in his ears the taint in his soul. Jackson didn't deserve to die because of an accident.

And Red didn't deserve to be the one to kill him.

13

He wanted to blame Xenwyn and her silly fantasy world for changing Jackson into an orc. It would be like blaming an owl for hunting mice. The base recruited Xenwyn for her obsession, same as all the Monks. She didn't know the dampeners would fail. Nobody did.

"It's not your fault," Glass said, putting one hand on Red's shoulder.

"But it's me who has to live with it."

"You saved my life," she said, rubbing his back gently. "Thank you." He could hear the conflict in her as she forced the words. He recognized her struggle with survivor's guilt as she wondered whether her life was worth more than Jackson's.

"You're welcome." He nodded. When he found Jon, he knew his boss would tell him he did the right thing. Somehow knowing wasn't enough. He needed to hear it. He needed Jon's declaration of absolution. Jon was the head Key Hunter and Red's mentor. Red had no other parent or superior he respected or cared for. Though, Karla Newell was the base commander. Red's loyalty always lay with Jon.

They fell into silence as the base neared.

The dampeners, once sophisticated speakers on top of tall posts positioned around the testing site, now looked like stone defensive towers. A crenelated stone wall replaced the razor-topped chain-link fence that used to surround the two mile diameter area where they conducted experiments. As the base, which attached to the testing ground on the far side, drew near, they saw the buildings had all been transformed into medieval architecture, both gothic and fantastic.

Where the road entered the base, they saw huge wooden gates had been broken down, and even above the commotion of the carriage, they heard the sounds of distant screams and chaos. Blocked from view by the wall surrounding the citadel, they began searching for clues about what might be happening.

Red slowed the horses as they went through the broken doors. Except for the occasional glimpse of somebody rushing across the street or slamming heavy shudders, they couldn't see what had everybody running. When they finally brought the carriage to a halt in front of the main row of barracks, Red jumped down.

He recognized Markus Beechen darting into a nearby alley and called out, "Mack!"

Red moved cautiously into the space between stone walls. He saw the taller, stronger man ducked behind a column. Red went over and asked,

"What's going on?" Mack glanced back at the carriage. "Better get those guys off the street. It's not safe."

Red didn't hesitate. He signaled the rest of them to follow him into the small alley. He put his jacket back on, despite the heat, while the others worked their way in behind.

"Now what's so dangerous?" Red asked again.

"Orcs," Mack said. He had on a gray muscle shirt, which prominently displayed the skull tattoo on his shoulder. "The guards out in the field all turned into orcs. They've been marauding through the base, killing anybody they find."

"Won't they find us when they see the carriage?" Glass asked.

"Everybody out!" Red ordered. He checked the road in both directions before crossing to the recreation center, which now looked like a medieval cathedral. Everybody followed. Red pulled back his crossbow and loaded another bolt. One shot wouldn't be enough if a whole group of orcs found them.

"It gets worse," Mack said.

"Worse than a band of orcs killing everybody they find?" Cindy demanded, pushing her glasses up on her nose.

"Commander Newel is a—" A terrible crash sounded outside, cutting him off. Red rushed to the door in time to see a flamethrower ignite the horses and carriage in a single, terrible conflagration. Then massive reptilian claws swooped through the fire and scattered the carriage into flying pieces of burning wood. The horses burned where they landed, dying in a ball of light.

Red jumped back to avoid a fiery wheel as it bounced up the steps and into the hall where the Machine Monks now cowered. When Red looked back, he finished Mack's sentence. "Dragon."

Covered with coppery scales and bigger than a whale, the gigantic wings lifted the mighty titan into the air. Her serpentine tail traced the graceful flight.

"I think most of the orcs died fighting that thing," Mack said.

"What happened out there?" Red demanded. "Where's Jon?"

"I don't know," Mack said. "Everything seemed normal except they put in more Machine Monks for this test. All systems checked out, so they started the Actuator. We all put in our ideas and the machine started churning, but instead of dividing up the test area like before, the machine transformed everything into this fantasy. Jon went after the keys as soon as he saw something had gone wrong. The rest of us stood around like idiots, looking at the Actuator. It had twenty-five key holes. I've never seen it with so many, of every shape and size, covering the flat console. All those key holes, but Xenwyn's was the only change we could see. The Actuator looked like it was on overdrive, spiting white lightning out in every direction."

"Did Jon find the keys?" Glass asked.

"I don't know. Before he came back, the orcs came over the wall and started chopping up Machine Monks. We all scattered. They chased us, but only the fast escaped. They probably killed more than half. I wanted to fight one, but I didn't have any weapons and they were hacking people into bloody messes." Mack's face registered a lop-sided smile. "It was kind of cool.

"Anyway, we all ran across the test zone. Just before we got out, the dragon came down, burning and eating orcs like it's a buffet. We scattered once we cleared the gate and spread out. Several Monks ran out into the desert through a hole in the wall. Once they got outside the base, the dragon just let them go. I decided to take my chances here. That desert is way too big to make it safely across on foot. Besides, I don't like the sun."

"I'll go find Jon," Red said. He turned away before wagging his head. *Could Mack really think it was cool to watch people being slaughtered?*

"Where?" Glass asked.

"He'll be at the office sooner or later. You all stay here and keep inside. Once I have Jon and anybody else I can find, we'll meet back here."

"There's a cellar where the bomb shelter used to be," Mack offered. "It might have some supplies. I didn't go down there yet because it was locked."

"I'll look for the key to it," Red said. He knew where the key should be. He just didn't know if it and the keyhole would match now. Those kinds of details were always a little fuzzy when they tested the Actuator if they didn't prepare the Machine Monk for it on purpose.

"It's too dangerous," Cindy said, holding onto Glass for support. "We should all stay here."

"Until what?" Red asked. "The government sends help?"

"Yes."

"The whole world looks like this," Red said, trying not to be too harsh.

"Not exactly," Mack said. "I know somewhere out there are places I made."

"You know that how?"

Red knew Mack was a Machine Monk of the Dedicated House. His specialty was horror. With how bad Xenwyn's supposedly innocent fantasy world had turned out, he didn't even want to think what it would be like if Mack's obsessions were unleashed on the world.

"You can feel when the great conversation happens. The Actuator gets in your head and reads out your thoughts and feelings. You can feel it asking you questions, even sense the words sometimes. It probes your ideas until it understands your will. Then it draws all of that out and turns it into electrical waves. You just know when it's happening."

"So where out there is your…" Red didn't know how to say it tactfully. He didn't want to let the revulsion he felt show. He'd seen the kind of depravity the Actuator generated in test sessions with Mack. Monsters and psychos of all kinds were in regular attendance. "If you felt it happen, do you know where it is?"

"New Orleans for sure," Mack said. He took pleasure in watching Red cringe from the news, rubbing his large biceps. Red gritted his teeth, taking a deep breath. He knew Mack loved nothing so much as fear and darkness incarnate. "I spent a lot of time thinking of zombies. Transylvania too, of course. I'm pretty sure there are asylums all over the world I touched and several haunted houses. Not sure where those all are, though."

Suddenly, a sick realization brought Red to lean against the stone pillar. "You mean the whole world is not just Xenwyn's fantasy, the whole world is a patchwork of every type of obsession the Machine Monks have been developing?"

He'd been inside the test area during many Actuations. He'd seen aliens, killer robots, sea creatures, samurai, werewolves, cowboys, and every other creature invented in the imagination of human beings come alive in the testing zone. Those were all controlled tests. If they were free now to roam the world, he could only imagine the havoc the entire human population suffered.

What have we done?

"I guess so," Mack said.

Red felt numb and dissociated. His forehead went cool. He recognized the symptoms of shock. However, he had to suppress it. He couldn't afford to be overwhelmed right now, so he went back to what he did best. "Do you at least know your own key?"

"Of course. It's a skull like this." Mack struck a pose, showing his beloved tattoo over flexed muscles. "A Voodoo witch doctor has it in New Orleans.

I've been on a zombie jag lately. I wish I was there with a chainsaw right now."

"Shut up!" Red commanded. "You're sick. Those are real people you turned into undead, mindless corpses. We have to save them, not cut them down for entertainment."

"Sorry," Mack said, shrugging. "I was just doing my job."

"Well your job now is to keep the rest of these people safe." Red scanned the road and the sky. Seeing nothing, he slipped onto the dirt road, keeping to the shadows, expecting a fire-breathing dragon to drop silently in at any moment and destroy them all.

CHAPTER THREE

Jon Van Allen sat in the wooden chair, his head against the heavy table his desk had become. No matter how many times he tried to think of something else, he couldn't stop replaying the Actuation over and over again in his mind. He'd done the safety checks personally.

The wild card was and always had been the Actuator itself. It operated on principles outside of normal human understanding. They played with fire every time they used it. *Who were they to risk the world on a few dampeners? What gave any of them the right to tempt fate by using a machine capable of transforming the world?*

His mind flashed to the wave of holographic energy as it projected from the machine. It started slow, as if somebody blew air into the bubble and wanted to begin delicately. The umbrella emanating from the tower engulfed the Machine Monks and stopped, holding them in a pulsing cocoon of light. Once they finished 'talking' to it, the shimmering bubble began to expand.

That moment, perhaps two seconds after the expansion, Jon knew something had gone wrong. As the range of the Actuation front expanded, Jon saw with horror that there weren't multiple areas. Only one idea, Xenwyn's medieval fantasy, spread through the entire test area. Jon had moved toward her, to get the key. However, the Actuation didn't stop at the dampeners. Normally, they kicked on and created interference waves, which disrupted the energy and stopped it from moving beyond the designated test area.

Jon watched again as the wave rushed past them, leaving behind tall stone towers and then racing away. The Machine Monks all stood dumbfounded. Jon knew none of them had expected this. With mouths open and eyes wide, they just stood there dumbfounded. Then the slaughter started.

Someone opened the door, yanking Jon from his reverie. Jon kept his forehead on the desk and said, "I failed."

"I talked to Mack," Red said. "I saw Commander Newell, too."

The freak and the dragon, Jon thought.

Jon said, "Somebody sabotaged the dampeners. I checked every one before the test. The readings were optimal, but somehow they never turned on."

"Why would anybody do that?"

"I don't know. It wasn't an accident. I know that much."

"What are we going to do?" Red asked.

Jon knew Red wanted him to jump up and announce a big plan, but he couldn't do it. His soul ached. For the first time in his life, he wished for death.

"I don't know what to do," Jon said. His voice echoed back in his face from the nearby desk surface. "The whole world is changed. They don't even know why. Almost seven billion people and we turned their lives into hell because we didn't know when to stop playing with fire. Half the Machine Monks are dead. I watched them get cut down by orcs. But then the dragon took most of those out."

"Not all of them. One was mine. I killed Jackson." Red's voice broke and he sighed, revealing the weakness Jon had tried so hard to train out of him. "He attacked Glass and I shot him in the back."

"Glass?" Suddenly Jon sat up and looked at his faltering assistant. "Is she okay?"

"I have her with the others at the rec center. Did you see Xenwyn?"

"She's alive," Jon said as the image of Glass came to him, offering the first moment of relief. Jon felt guilty for letting it in.

"What are we going to do?" Red asked again.

"If the rest of the world is like this base, half of them are dead already," Jon said, standing up. He shuddered as a chill went through him. "Three billion people are probably gone." Habit held back tears he couldn't let free. He deserved to cry for eternity. "Whatever percentage of that is my fault, it's a huge number. Millions. More than Hitler killed in his entire life. How can I live with that?"

Red looked at Jon with his brow knit. It wasn't loathing. Could it be worry? Jon saw disappointment then. Red had come looking for hope. He needed reassurance. Jon couldn't give it to him. If they had the keys right now and put them in the machine, the world would still never be anything close to right again.

Finally, Red took a deep breath and said, "Mack says his key is in New Orleans. We could start there."

Jon closed his eyes and took a deep breath too. He needed something to work for. He needed a goal. Keeping Glass safe would be his mission. He'd never feel he deserved her love, but he could keep one person on this broken planet from dying.

"First we get the key here," Jon said. "Xenwyn is reliable if nothing else. Her key is always the same magic wand. We probably can't use it yet, but we need to get it. We need to gather as many of the Machine Monks as we can, too." Jon spoke without emotion, as if reciting a long passage of the law. Only duty propelled him.

"Mack said some ran off. He said the bomb shelter is still intact."

Jon pulled a knife from the desk and put it in his pocket. Then he opened the now wooden closet and grabbed a crossbow like Red's before strapping on a sword. Red picked up more crossbow bolts and tucked them in his back pocket.

Jon said, "We split up. You take the south half. Check every building. Send anybody you find to the rec center, but don't travel in groups. When we're all back there, we'll move to the shelter."

Red nodded and turned to the door.

"One more thing," Jon said. Red looked back. "It wasn't your fault you had to kill Jackson."

Red nodded, taking a deep breath. "Hardly seems to matter now, in the face of all this."

"You need to know that because I think there will be a lot more killing before we're done. None of it is on you. You understand me?"

Red turned and went out the door. Jon knew just saying the words couldn't relieve Red's guilt. Everybody on the base was culpable.

Charged with a mission, Red threw his every thought into it, blocking out everything else. He scoured the buildings, carefully hiding in the shadows around the open places. He found Dragon Star sitting on the mat of the Empty House meditation room, cross legged and breathing softly.

Red's shoulder's sagged as the scene reminded him how empty he felt. What he wouldn't give to be an old, wise Korean with the self-discipline to meditate after the whole world had just been turned into a patchwork hell.

Dragon Star opened his eyes without moving and said quietly, "I am glad to see you, Red McLaren."

"Have you seen anybody else since the... accident?"

"I am all that remains of my house," Dragon Star said with a sigh. His real name was Choi Yong-kyeong. Red remembered when everybody used to call him Mr. Choi, but when he let it slip that Yong-kyeong translated to Dragon Star in English, the nickname had never left. He tried to complain humbly how it didn't suit him, of course. But in a base full of Monks renaming themselves things like Xenwyn and Glass, he had no hope of recovering his original moniker.

"We're meeting at the rec center," Red said. He wanted to sympathize. He knew Dragon Star would take this tragedy as a personal failure, even though Empty House couldn't possibly be responsible for the craziness inflicted on the Earth.

"My students have all perished," Dragon Star said. "I must avenge them." Red couldn't believe someone rising from a posture of tranquility could utter those words with such conviction. Then he saw the determination in Dragon Star's eyes.

"There will be time for that later," Red said. "Please just join us in the rec center."

Dragon Star stood up, wearing a full tae-kwon-do body suit. "I will defer to your leadership, for now."

"Thank you," Red said. He realized he had no authority. If somebody refused to listen, Red couldn't do anything about it. "Do you know where any of the others are?"

"I have only seen Jenwyn." Despite his excellent English, Dragon Star still struggled with Z sounds. He pointed to the hallway. "She is in the back."

"We aren't supposed to travel together," Red said. "Too easy for the dragon to spot us. You go ahead and I'll talk to Xenwyn."

Dragon Star bowed formally. Then he went to a closet and pulled out two katana, with blue handles, and scabbards. He strapped them onto his back with a black X-shaped belt and then moved out to the main road.

"Xenwyn?" Red called as he moved toward the back.

Suddenly a huge bug buzzed into the room. Red jumped back, swatting at it instinctively.

"Hey!" a tiny, high-pitched voice screamed.

Red's eyes went wide as the foot tall insect slowed in front of him. When it stopped, he saw a fairy. The small human form attached to the fast moving wings, was Xenwyn.

"Xen?"

"Don't say a word or I swear I'll kick you straight in the eye," she ordered.

Even moving fast and in low light, Red could see the iridescence of her wings. Purple clothes wrapped around her body, leaving the pink skin of her bare feet and arms showing. Her long silvery hair floated around in the air currents her wings made. He half expected some kind of tinkling or glittery dust, but detected none.

"What happened to you?" Red couldn't help grinning. After everything else, seeing her like this made him want to laugh. Honestly, he thought she looked adorable.

"What does it look like, genius? Did I hear you say we're all meeting up somewhere?"

"At the rec center. Then we'll head to the bomb shelter. Do you know where your key is?" He put his hands in his pockets to help resist the urge to reach out and touch her.

"Yes. It's in my apartment, unless that stupid dragon took it."

"Commander Newell?"

"She almost ate me...," Xenwyn said. "I flew away when the orcs attacked. I tried to sneak away when the dragon came, but she chased me like a cat after a laser pointer."

"Okay, you head to the rec center and I'll go get the key."

"No way," Xenwyn said. "I'll go after the key."

"It's my job," Red said.

Ignoring him, Xenwyn buzzed out of the front door, leaving a trail of yellow light.

"Stubborn brat!"

Red had liked Xenwyn for some time, but like all the Dedicated House, she was so obsessed with her world that she hadn't even noticed him. Right now, he thought she'd gotten a little of what she deserved.

Jon decided they couldn't wait any longer for Xenwyn. "Red, you lead the group. It's only about fifty feet. We'll be better off if we just take it fast and quiet together. Once we get there, kick the door in if you have to. I'll take the rear."

Mack said, "I wonder if Owen made it." The unhappy Machine Monk had decided he had better chances on his own while Red was gone and left soon after.

"Not likely," Jon said. "Our best chance is to stick together."

Mack opened his mouth and Tina raised one hand, but Jon stared them down. They backed away. In a situation like this, Jon wasn't about to listen to nonsense.

"Stick to the shadows on the far side of the road," Jon continued. "No matter what, don't look back. Just get in the shelter. Got it?"

Everybody nodded. Cindy clutched Glass' arm. Jon looked Glass in the eye. He wouldn't say it, but he needed her reassurance. He needed to know she understood that he had to be rough right now.

She winked. If he didn't labor under such stress and guilt, he would have let it melt his heart.

Red checked the road and the sky. Jon put one hand on his shoulder. When Red turned, Jon spoke softly in his ear. "No matter what, I need you to keep Glass safe. Please."

Red nodded. Jon knew this defied the order to put the job above feelings that he had been drilling into Red for years. He knew the situation had driven him to hypocrisy. Yet Red, thankfully, didn't say a thing.

Red rushed down the stairs and across the dirt road into the shadows the afternoon sun cast down from stone buildings. True to his orders, he didn't stop, but ran straight for the shelter.

Jon signaled Glass to go early in the group. He kept them all going, leaving only a few feet between as he sent them off. As the last few prepared to go, Jon grabbed a tall shield from the wall and slid his leather clad arm into it.

As the last Machine Monk departed, Jon descended the stairs and moved into the street. A piercing screech echoed from the buildings. He looked to see the dragon roar as it swooped toward them.

CHAPTER FOUR

ed physically held Glass back as they watched the copper skinned monster swoop in from the sky. His instincts screamed for him to rush out and help his friend against his orders to keep her safe. Though honestly, he didn't know what he could possibly do. He watched Jon check their position twice as the massive behemoth flapper her wings and brought her hind feet down on the ridge of a steep wooden building.

"We need to move off the street," Red said, unable to tear his eyes away from the scene as it unfolded. *Would Jon even be able to scratch that thing with his little sword?*

Jon held back behind his shield, waiting for an opening. Red saw one clawed hand swipe at his mentor. Jon easily sidestepped it, reaching out with the sword and bouncing it off the armored skin. A few pieces of scale fluttered to the ground. Jon stepped up to try for the dragon's neck. However, Commander Newell recoiled, spewing a jet of flame from her throat. Smoke leaked off the sides of the tight cone as burning fuel blasted Jon.

Glass screamed.

Red held her tighter as they watched, transfixed. Fire from the colossal dragon drenched Jon. Gasping for breath, they both sucked in sulfurous ash and choked. The great metallic red beast flapped its wings in place, spreading smoke in every direction and fanning the flames that had lit nearby trees and roofs, until two giant yellow eyes verified that Jon Van Allen was not getting back up.

"We have to go get him," she said with tears etching trails into the dirt on her cheeks.

"No, Glass" Red said, putting gusto into his words to try to sound brave. "He told me to make sure you were safe, no matter what."

"I'm safe now," she said, clutching his arm so tightly it hurt through the leather. They were under the ledge of what used to be an underground bunker. Now it was a stone walled cellar. No other building in the area offered as much protection.

"Go join the others." Red pointed down the dark stairs, illuminated at the bottom by a burning torch. He was scanning the sky, watching the dragon retreat. Occasionally the monster stopped and circled around if she saw anything move among the buildings below. For the most part, she was following a wide perimeter around the base she used to command.

"How did this happen?" Red asked himself for the hundredth time that day.

Red tried to see if there was any sign of Jon breathing. He glanced back up at the dragon's impossibly huge bat wings. When it was far enough away, he would sprint out to his friend. He knew each second was critical, but Jon was a big man and Red needed a few more seconds if he was going to drag the body back to this cellar. He hoped it wasn't just a body.

The instant the spiny dragon dipped past the first hill, Red sprinted forward to find his boss twisted in a heap under a shield. The metal melted at the edges under the intense heat of the dragon's breath. His legs and one arm stuck out. The leather boots, pants, jacket arm, and glove were burned off, leaving charred skin exposed and black fingers curled around the handle of a blood-stained sword. Jon had gotten a piece of the beast before it smashed him down into this fetal position.

Red couldn't help but wonder if Jon was being purposefully reckless. He had taken too much of the responsibility for this chaos on himself. *Why had he acted so rashly? It's almost like he wanted to die.*

Red kicked the still soft, metal shield, and it bent as it flopped away. Some of Jon's hair was singed. It smelled awful. There were a few welts from splashing agro on his face. But he was breathing, even if it was shallow. The hulking reptile had smashed down on top of him before blasting out the fire. Jon was only alive because he positioned the shield to protect his head and vital organs from burning.

For an instant, Red knew it was dangerous to move his mentor. If his back was broken, this would make it worse. But if he left him here, Jon would die. They hadn't found the base doctor and even if they could, the surgical equipment had probably been changed into medieval torture devices.

Red slipped his hands under the larger man's shoulders and began dragging him backward across the dirt road. That was when Red heard the dragon roar. Two trails where Jon's scorched boots dragged across the dirt marked their progress. But if that behemoth was coming full speed, Red knew they'd never make it like this.

He turned around and curled into a ball, twisting Jon's muscled body onto his back. In a single great press, Red lifted the mass with his legs. Hunched over, he carried Jon fireman style on his back. As he turned, he saw the red beast bearing down on them like a fighter jet.

Red pushed forward with all his strength and will, leaning forward to get a little more momentum from gravity. Each step made his legs burn with the effort. When he was a few steps from the doorway, a dark shadow blotted the sun behind him and Red knew his time was up.

A deafening roar shook them one second before a wave of heat blasted around them. Red couldn't look back if he wanted to. He just plowed forward. When his boots left the dirt and hit rock, he pushed hard enough to dive down the stairs.

Weighed down by Jon's body, he descended faster. Leaning even farther forward, assisted by gravity, he took two stairs at a time, all the while knowing it was nothing more than a controlled fall now.

With eyes burning from the ash and hands screaming with pain, he launched them both through the thick wooden door and tumbled to the rocky ground with the still burning body of his friend and mentor smoldering above him. The weight crushed the air out of him and Red had to fight to breathe.

Somebody bolted the door closed just in time to stave off another round of fire as the dragon belched a jet of accelerant down the stairwell. Unable to fit her massive head into the descending hallway, the giant reptile began thrashing the stones and earth above with her claws. Each swipe of the giant talons sent rocks flying and echoed like an earthquake inside the cellar. She was digging them out.

Red heard, but couldn't see, several of the machine monks scrambling to pat out any remaining fires on Jon's clothes. Then several of them together managed to slide him off to the side so Red could breathe again.

The monster's fury continued unabated. They knew that with each swipe she was tearing apart the stone stairwell and getting closer. The door wouldn't stop her from digging in and ripping them all apart. Then suddenly, it stopped.

"She must have seen somebody else," Glass said. They listened for the pounding fury to resume. But after a long minute, they dared to hope it might be over.

When he finally opened his eyes, Red could see his hands weren't burned as badly as he expected. The backs were red with the hair gone, but his fingers were fine. Singe marks marred the sleeves on his leather jacket. Although he never would have dreamed of using his friend as a human shield, the fireman carry had turned out to do just that. Jon had taken most of the blast from the fiery beast.

He turned to see Glass stuffing a rolled up tapestry under Jon's head. She was wiping his face with a damp cloth to reveal what was charred and what was just ash and dirt on the surface. The second blast had burned most of his back. Jon's legs were singed on both sides now. His arms fused to the clothes with cracked and bleeding black skin showing through in a few places. Red turned away and choked back vomit.

Could he have done anything different? Red played the scenario over in his mind, leaving the others to cut away the clothes and wrap the wounds in dry cloth. If their roles had been reversed, Jon never would have let Red take the second blast of fire. Of course, Jon wouldn't have had nearly as much trouble moving Red's body.

"Thank you," Glass said. She reached over and brushed away a lock of hair glued by sweat to Red's face. "He would have died out there if you didn't save him."

"Maybe," Red said. He couldn't imagine anything killing Jon Van Allen. If people were cars, Jon would be a tank. But he'd cracked recently. Would Red ever get his mentor back? Now that he had his breath, Red ignored his sore muscles and stood up.

There were eight people together in this underground chamber. A single torch near the door was all the light they had. Two other machine monks were helping Glass tend to Jon. One of them was Cindy Smith, Glass' mentor. The other one was Tina Westerfield, wearing a corset and an impractical skirt. Mack and Dragon Star wrapped pieces of fabric around their hands from the hot metal door handle as they tried to see if it could be possible to get out that way. When they managed to push it open a few inches, they saw rocks and rubble blocking the way. Luckily, they had another door out the back.

The last member of the group, Isaac, was going through the supplies. This had once been a bomb shelter. There was plenty of food, but when the world turned into a fantasy it had changed from the military rations designed to last fifty years into dried meats and fruit.

One more heave against the door pushed it another couple of inches. Then an oversized firefly zipped in, leaving a trail of sparks behind it. Several of the machine monks screamed. Dragon Star leaped forward with a katana, preparing to dispatch the invader.

"Stop, it's me!" a tiny voice cried out as the light dodged the blur of metal.

Red put up a hand. "Hold on, Dragon Star. It's Xenwyn." The elder lowered, but did not sheath his weapon.

"Sorry," Dragon Star said. "I didn't realize you'd changed yourself to be so small."

"Duh!" Xenwyn zipped around and popped him upside the head.

The room thundered again and new rubble smashed the door closed. The dragon was back, digging as furiously as before.

"I couldn't get to the key. Sorry I led her back here. I didn't have anywhere else to go," the tiny light said.

"She already found us," Red said. Then he surprised himself by laughing. The stress was getting to him.

"Don't laugh," Xenwyn said as she zipped over to a shelf and stood almost at Red's eye level. Her voice was so high-pitched, she had to yell to be heard. "If I couldn't fly, Commander Newell would have killed me by now. And this isn't my fault. The Actuator never changed the whole world before."

"It doesn't matter whose fault it is," Cindy yelled above the seismic booms that echoed through the room. She was usually such a quiet woman. "If we don't get out of here we're all going to be dead soon."

Mack, the largest of the machine monks, rushed to the far door. It opened into a hallway too dark to see down. Dragon Star tied strips of cloth torn from the green curtains to two spears and fastened the tapestry to them to make a gurney. They heaved Jon's body onto it as he moaned in pain. Dragon Star and Red picked up each end. Glass grabbed the torch from the wall mount, wondering just how long this thing would burn. The rest of them gathered whatever food, cloth, and other supplies they could carry. With Glass leading the way, they started down the damp hallway.

Xenwyn fluttered her butterfly wings toward the back of the group, trying to offer them a little more light from her phosphorescent body. Behind them, they heard one gigantic talon splinter through the wooden door and then rip it off the iron hinges. They rushed faster, Red and Dragon Star straining against the heavy load.

Suddenly the hallway was blindingly bright. Next they heard the crackle of a stoked fire. Then they smelled sulfur and smoke. The dragon had managed to get her head in and filled the cellar behind them with agro.

The seven people in the back, driven by panic, were physically pushing Dragon Star forward. Red stumbled once, but Jon's head rammed him from behind and he caught himself before he brought the whole group down in a dog pile. They all kept their faces forward, toward the good air, as the firelight behind them died.

"I see another door," Glass said. She pushed it open and the group piled into another dark room.

With the little light they had, they puzzled over several carriages arranged in rows. Horses began clomping toward them, attracted by people who might somehow alleviate the fear they felt instinctively.

"It's the lower level of the parking garage," Glass finally realized.

"Who puts a stable underground?" Red asked.

"It's just an oversight of the transformation," Dragon Star said. The two of them heaved Jon's body onto the back of the nearest carriage.

"I wasn't planning for the whole world." Xenwyn zipped up to defend herself. Her small voice was screaming. "I could have done a lot better if I was. I was only thinking about my part of the hot spot that we always used. I made the key, designed my own place in the world, and did everything exactly as I was trained. It's not my fault the dampeners didn't work. And I'm stuck playing Thumbelina!"

"I'm sorry," Red said. It was an automatic statement, not a heartfelt apology. "I know you didn't do this on purpose."

"I'm not the only one anyway," Xenwyn kept yelling. "There were other Monks there, too."

Another big *boom* echoed from the hallway behind them. Was the dragon actually tunneling through to get at them?

"We have to get out of here," Glass said.

"How?" Dragon Star asked. "Once we are out in the open Karla will pick us off in ten seconds."

"You called her Karla?" Glass asked.

"We were friends," Dragon Star said. "And a military title hardly seems appropriate now."

"No time!" Red untied the reins on the closest carriage. "I think I know how we can get away."

CHAPTER FIVE

Dragon Star whipped the driverless horses near him as he guided his own team out of the bizarre stable. A dozen horse drawn carriages burst from the iron gates of the multi-level stables and into the light at once. A loud noise started them all running, but once the dragon noticed the commotion and began to move their way, terror motivated the horses. One driverless pair took a turn too fast and the carriage crashed into a pile of wood, metal, and legs while one wheel rolled away on its own.

Two of the carriages had drivers and passengers. These split up and took different roads, both leading away from the Actuator. As Dragon Star whipped his team of horses to urge more speed, he glanced back through the window of the carriage next to him and saw Glass holding Jon's head in her lap. This was crazy. The Dedicated House Monks might have been used to living in a world turned upside down, but Dragon Star wasn't. This felt like he had died and been sent to a strange hell.

Dragon Star took his carriage down the main street, headed straight for the front gate. Red turned to take a side road. That boy was reckless. There was no point in taking more time to get away. So far nobody had seen the dragon leave the outer perimeter of the base. He hoped she would stick to that and let them go if they managed to get past the gate.

As the carriages, some covered and some open, rushed in every direction, Dragon Star saw the mighty beast turn toward the closest group of three. He regretted telling the others his name meant Dragon Star. But now, in seeing the rage and single minded thirst for power that typified the mythological beast, he hated it. His life had been a walk on the path to inner peace. Now the death of his students, his only close friends except Karla Newell, left him unable to remain passive.

The horses ran between the stone and wooden buildings for all they were worth, kicking up a huge cloud of dust with their thundering hooves. The gargantuan dragon tipped into a fast dive and landed unceremoniously on a whole group of unmanned carriages, reaching with one rear claw to catch the last one. The ground shook once. Then she was up and after the next pair of coaches, one street over.

Dragon Star hadn't voiced his concerns over this plan. It was risky trying to distract a monster like that while they rushed to escape. But so far it seemed to be working.

With blinding speed the great reptile vaulted a crenulated tower. In a single swipe of her tail she smashed both of those speeding vehicles into splinters.

Although the distractions were buying them precious seconds, Dragon Star knew it would still be close.

Leaping into the sky for a bird's eye view, the dragon gracefully turned back. She didn't land for the next one. Instead, she blasted it with fire from above and let the burning horses tumble to the ground as the flaming pieces of the wrecked car rolled over them and spread in every direction. She rapidly reduced all the carriages to rubble, never stopping to feed or exult in her victory.

When the two roads merged, Dragon Star's carriage had the lead. He could see Red behind him, squinting to try and keep dust out of his eyes and coughing. Dragon Star hated the thought of causing distress to anyone. Unfortunately, he knew there was no way to fix it now. He would have to live with the shame of not slowing his cart in deference to the higher ranked, though still younger, driver behind him. In the grand scheme of things, he didn't think that small shame would even register next to the greater burden they all bore now.

Suddenly, Commander Newell broke off her patterned destruction and headed toward them. Even at this distance, Dragon Star thought he saw her eyes squinting out of determination and rage.

"Yah!" Dragon Star called to his team. "Ba-li! Ka-ja! Yah!" He was too preoccupied to use English.

Dragon Star flipped the reins again, but he knew nothing he did could inspire more speed than an airborne predator bearing down on them. The last of the stone towers whisked by, leaving only a stretch of dirt between them and the gaping wooden gate ahead. Dragon Star tried to concentrate on the road, but it didn't really matter what he did. The horses were racing for their lives.

Dragon Star wanted to move to one side now that the road was wider. He wanted to allow Red to get out of the dust cloud his cart churned up. But he wouldn't risk losing even that much time. When the roar of the monster behind them shook the ground, the horses found just a little more speed. Looking back, Dragon Star knew they weren't going to make it. He watched Red pull his crossbow out and shoot a bolt at the titan behind. It hit, but nothing happened.

"We need something to throw!" Red yelled. Dragon Star saw Glass looking around the red velvet lined cab of Red's carriage.

Cindy pushed her glasses up on her nose while opening the storage box beneath one arm rest. "There's nothing here!" Xenwyn flew above the box, as if her faint light could help.

Then Cindy opened her purse. "I have some scissors!"

"If it gets close enough, throw them!" Red called. Dragon Star turned away. He knew scissors wouldn't stop the jet of fire. The dragon probably wouldn't even notice.

Suddenly Xenwyn zipped in a wide circle and burst out the back of the carriage. Dragon Star watched as she corkscrewed a few times to catch the titan's eye and then bolted sideways. As if unable to turn her attention from the shining distraction, the dragon twisted and followed the little fairy who had evaded her hunt twice before. At her best, Xenwyn couldn't fly as fast as the speeding carriage. The dragon could gulp her down and be back on course in less than two seconds.

Red tried to turn and watch. But unlike Dragon Star's team, his fevered horses demanded his attention as they tried to run out of their own bodies. Red had to constantly adjust their direction to keep them from going off the road.

Glass started to cry. Cindy covered her eyes. Xenwyn disappeared down a nearby street. The dragon crashed into a conical tower and brought the whole thing down as it kinked and dived in pursuit of the tiny light.

A huge cloud of dust and smoke rose as the thunder of another destroyed carriage reached their ears. As the dragon hovered higher, Dragon Star's carriage raced through the gate. Red's came through right behind it. The desert surrounding the base stretched before them beneath the blistering sun. Flat sand, broken only by tumbleweeds and cactus reached to distant rocks jutting up through the surface like creatures rising from the oppressive dirt to gasp for air. The dry scene yielded only to the road they charged down with reckless abandon. Everybody turned to see the dragon roar a last death threat. She spread her wings and sailed toward them, then circled back to clear up the remaining carriages still in her territory.

Dragon Star pulled back on the reins, but it took several minutes before the horses would yield and slow. Red finally moved up next to them so he could stop eating dust. When they did slow, Dragon Star could see the leg muscles of Red's team twitching. The faces of Isaac, Tina, and Mack were searching through the small windows of the carriage. For years every trip off the base had been under close supervision. Now Dragon Star, like them, felt as if he were escaping.

"Where to?" Dragon Star yelled across, in deference to the higher ranked man.

"Follow the road west to those mountains," Red said, pointing. "The horses need water."

Cindy turned to look out the window as hot air filled her lungs and dried her eyes. "Why did Xenwyn do that? We could have made it." As if on cue, Xenwyn zipped back in. She fell to the empty seat cushion, tiny chest heaving and exhaling, and stopped flitting around for the first time.

"You're alive!" Glass said. With the horses slowed, Dragon Star clearly heard the discussion in both carriages.

"Of course," Xenwyn said between giant breaths. "Would have been easier if you slowed down sooner so I could catch up."

Everybody continued to check whether the dragon pursued them again. However, they reached the rocky break in the sandy desert intact. As Dragon Star scanned the area for any sign of a stream, the horses began growling.

Dragon Star tried to pull on the reins, but realized they were no longer connected to the bits. An eerie quiet made them panic as they realized the wheels were no longer touching the road. Dragon Star tasted Korean barbecue beef over salted kimchee. Bright light made it impossible to see the road. He heard the thunder of a thousand drums. A veteran Machine Monk, he knew they'd crossed a border between two different Actuated areas. He relished the feeling. Despite his efforts to always remain aloof of suffering or pleasurable vices, Dragon Star's life centered around the Actuator. Any taste of the machine brought him a moment of deep fulfillment.

When Dragon Star looked at Red's carriage, he saw vertical tubes where the wheels had been. The horses melded together and were converted suddenly into plated metal sculptures. Soon after, they were a single jet engine. The carriage changed into a flying car and, suddenly, Dragon Star was holding a steering lever and throttle instead of reins. A windshield grew up in front of him and the wooden bench sunk into a captain's seat.

"What just happened?" Tina asked. Except for the whining hum of the engine, it was quiet.

"We crossed a boundary," Mack said. Dragon Star concentrated on figuring out the dozens of dials and switches, which had risen out of nowhere, without taking his eyes off the road dropping away beneath them.

"We need to land," Red said through the radio. He waved to Dragon Star who was much less comfortable with the current vehicle. They both started to slowly descend.

Red landed without much trouble, but Dragon Star's hover car hit the ground hard. As soon as they landed, hydraulic doors opened and everybody walked down the small loading ramps, leaving Jon lying on a long row of padded seats inside. Except for the red velvet interior, the carriages had completely transformed.

"You've got be kidding me!" Xenwyn screeched as she came out of the hover car. Her voice had a metallic tang. Her fairy wings were gone and the bottom half of her still small body turned into a square with wheels beneath it.

Cindy started to laugh and then clamped one hand over her mouth.

"This is not funny!" Xenwyn's speaker mouth intoned. "Take me back. Now!"

"We can't go back to the base," Red said. He held his head high, assuming the position of leader. But Dragon Star could sense he was riddled with guilt. He blamed himself even though he hadn't been near the base at the time.

"How did this happen?" Tina asked as she ran her hand along the sleek silver exterior. They looked like flying limousines now.

Nobody had an answer. Red picked up robot Xenwyn and set her up on the hood. He asked, "Maybe we'll get some answers if we pool what we know. What happened to the machine after the dampeners failed and everything was turned into a fantasy world?"

Despite having a face of metal with lights for eyes and a speaker for a mouth, Xenwyn exuded anger. "I did my drill exactly as planned. I made the changes for just my part of the test area, but the dampeners didn't stop the wave like they usually do. They all turned into stone towers. Next thing I know, the whole place is going crazy. People running around and yelling. Orcs killing people. They tried to blame me, but it wasn't my fault. Look, we're in another area. It wasn't just me."

"I believe you," Glass said. "Did you notice anybody messing with the field dampeners before the experiment?"

"No," Xenwyn said.

"Any guess who sabotaged it?" Red asked everybody. Nobody answered. He turned back to Xenwyn, "So what happened next?"

"The dragon came and killed the orcs. She chased me until I dropped the key. Then you know the rest."

"Only one student from the Empty House was there," Dragon Star said. "The rest were all with me until they died at Karla's hands." He felt bile rise in his throat at the memory of his four angelic Empty House monks. It was a cruel twist of fate for him to live when they had died. He would give anything for the reverse to be true. He clutched the blue silk handle of one katana. He had no choice now but revenge. This sword would pierce the dragon's brain before he left this life.

"What about the Untouched House?" Red asked.

"We had a team of three people at the Actuation," Cindy said. She was the only one in the group who looked apologetic. "I suppose now they're..." She sobbed once.

Red stepped back and sat down on the loading ramp. He ran his fingers through his hair. "Do any of you at least have your keys?"

The monks looked at each other. Several wagged their heads. Only Tina came forward. She held out a metal stamp used for wax seals.

Red took it and held it in his hand. "One? That's it? One key?"

"The key is usually integral to the world. It's symbolic and embedded in very fabric of the world itself," Isaac offered.

"Don't cite the training manual to me," Red said with a growl. He ran his fingers through his messy black hair and began pacing back and forth. "Twenty keys? They could be anywhere in the world. How could we possibly find them all to put things back? Xenwyn, did you find yours?"

She motored her mechanical neck back and forth to signal she had not.

"Do you two know where your keys are?"

"New Orleans," Mack said firmly.

"North Carolina," Isaac said.

Glass put one hand on Red's shoulder to try and settle him down. Black char from the dragon's breath got all over her fingers. She said, "We can figure out the territories."

"And the key for each one would have to be in that same territory," Red thought aloud.

"Actually," Tina added, "There are probably more." She pulled her pink cardigan sweater tight. "My specialty is history, and I'm pretty sure there are at least a dozen places affected that way."

Red's face began to match his name. "What?"

"Feudal Japan, ancient Egypt, French regency, the golden age of piracy—there are several key periods of history when..."

"Stop," Red held up one hand. "Does this key shut all of those down?"

She tipped her head sideways and scratched her nose. "I think so."

"So there are twenty or so keys, but each one could be in any number of places." Red started to laugh.

"The dragon has my key," Xenwyn said.

Suddenly, red laser bolts fell from the sky. Dragon Star's hover car burst into flames, forcing everybody to jump back and scream. Dragon Star's instincts caused him to draw both katana. But he put them right back, knowing they would be useless against lasers.

"Into the car!" Red yelled. He jumped toward the driver's seat as six people tried to find a way to share four seats with a comatose man and a small robot. More laser fire tore the earth up near them.

"They're in flying saucers," Cindy said as she pushed her glasses up for a closer look through the window. "Little football shaped ships that are fat in the middle and pointy at the ends, just like in the old movies."

Red pulled back on the stick and pushed the throttle as far as it would go. Dragon Star's stomach turned. This insane world was the opposite of the inner peace he had spent his life pursuing.

CHAPTER SIX

A s Red raced past a tall mountain, he banked the hover car and dove into a crooked canyon. "Find a gun or something," he yelled. Dragon Star shuffled through the knot of people crowding the cab of the car until he could look over the controls.

"I do not think there is a gun," he said. Red weaved the flying vehicle left just in time to dodge a red laser blast as it set the tree in front of him on fire. He was starting to think a horse drawn carriage might be better. Looking out the window, Dragon Star said, "There are three of them. But this canyon may be more dangerous."

"If I leave this trench, we're sitting ducks," Red said as he dipped and turned right.

"Take it easy," Glass said from behind. She was trying to use her body to protect Jon's head as it jostled around.

Red ignored her as he lifted the nose up over a group of trees and then dived behind them. The chrome ships with red lights racing around their extended middles followed patiently. Instead of blasting lasers off in every direction, they carefully hovered above and behind, waiting for good shots. When the ravine began to open into a delta at the end, Red banked right. He knew they had no chance out in the open. Trying to stay close to the rocky ridges, he doubled back and pressed on the throttle again, hoping for more speed.

The saucer which had been furthest behind easily hopped over the ridge and blocked their path. Red cranked the stick left, but their momentum carried them in a wide arc and the alien easily blasted the bottom of the car. One of the rear lifters failed and the back of the car began to sag. They lost speed and altitude as the machine began to drag one corner and force them to turn.

Trailing smoke, Red pitched the front down and aimed for a small copse of dark pines. Then they crashed into the dirt. Red kept the nose up until the impact jostled them all forward involuntarily.

Rubbing her neck, Cindy said, "Why doesn't this thing have seatbelts?"

"Everybody stay in here," Red said.

He popped the side door up and the loading ramp down before drawing his pistol, discovering it had turned into some kind of ray-gun. He trained it on the disc shaped ships as they landed in a triangle, fencing them in against the steep rocks behind. The red lights that had been spinning around the outside of each silver ship came to a halt as they landed. When stairs rolled out the bottom of each flying saucer, aliens began to descend amid bright yellow light emanating from inside the crafts. These captors were slightly green with large heads and big, round eyes. After three of them came down carrying big guns that looked like super soakers, though Red was positive they were much more deadly, a human came down behind them. The group of aliens approached slowly.

When they stood about fifteen feet away, Red fired a warning beam. The blue lance echoed off the rocks behind him. He did it mostly to see what the gun would do. He was glad it looked potent. "That's close enough." The aliens stopped advancing, waiting for orders. The human stepped forward.

A timid voice asked, "Is that you, Red?"

Red moved out into the open and dropped, but didn't holster, his ray-gun. "Brian?" He was wearing a blue shirt with some "A" shaped insignia over the left pocket. Red forced a smile. "It's good to see you." It was sincere, in light of the three Martians training orange and blue rifles on him.

"Thanks," Brian said. He put one hand out to indicate the aliens could stand down. Red let out a big breath of relief when they lowered the guns. Brian had dark rimmed glasses and brown hair cut straight across the front. "What's going on?"

"Commander Newell is a dragon now. We just escaped. But she won't let anybody near the Actuator. Jon is seriously wounded. Can you help?"

"I, uh…" Brian looked back at the three companions he was with. "Not really."

"What? Why?"

"I'm not really in charge. I'm just one of the crew. I could ask the captain."

"You made a fantasy world where you're not even the captain?" Red asked.

"I'm not leadership material. I'm just a science officer."

"Who are these guys?"

"Those guys are security. These are just fighter pods. The mother ship is further north."

"Who's the captain, then?"

"Captain Neman is really great. He was the one responsible for the treaty with the Martians so that we all work together now."

"Do you think he'll help us?" Red asked.

"Maybe," Brian said. "He's pretty busy, though. I'm sure at the least he'll give Jon medical attention."

"What about the key?" Red asked. "Tell me you at least have the key."

"The captain has the key, of course," Brian said. "But don't bother asking for it. He'd die before he gave it up."

"Can you at least tell me what it is?"

"Of course. It's his trademark gold gun. It has a special fusion…"

Red cut him off with a hand. "How far to this mother ship?"

"About three hundred miles that way," Brian pointed northwest. "It's past what used to be Area 51, but the pods can only carry two people. We could take you and Jon there and come back for the rest. Fair warning, Captain Neman will expect you to join the crew if you ask him for help."

"This is your dream? You just wanted to be a crew member?"

"It's better than I even imagined," Brian said. "People listen to me and we go on great adventures of discovery."

Suddenly an unseen voice broke in. It was a woman's voice, distorted by electronics. "Officer Brian, the captain requests a mission status update."

Brian touched the A on his chest and spoke into the air. "The site is secure. There's no danger. Their ship is damaged and they have one wounded. I know them. They're good people."

"The captain says he'll send a shuttle. Check in when it arrives."

"We don't want to join your crew," Red said.

"Why not?" Brian asked. "The mother ship has everything you could ever want."

"We need the key," Red said. "We don't have time to play Space Opera."

"I don't think you have a choice," Brian said. "The captain…"

Red nodded. Then he jumped forward, wrapped his left arm around Brian's neck, and pointed his pistol at Brian's temple. The aliens snapped their rifles up again. "Drop 'em or he's dead," Red called out.

The Martians turned their big heads back and forth, looking at each other. Brian yelled, "Do as he says!"

Blinking huge black eyes, the aliens put their guns down.

"You three back off. Dragon Star!" Red called. The Korean man quickly descended the ramp and collected the guns. He handed one to Trina and another to Mack. The rest of them came out of the broken car, too. Jon's gurney had transformed into a hover pad which Glass and Cindy easily guided out into the open sun.

"Don't do this," Brian said to Red. "It's not too late. I know you're under stress, but I can smooth things over with the captain if you let me go and give the guns back."

"Can't do that," Red said. "This is serious. We broke the world. And we have to put it back."

"Why?" Brian asked. His wide eyes and sustained smile showed he hid no duplicity. Red let go of his neck and stepped back, the pistol still trained on his chest.

Red couldn't believe what he heard. "Why? Because it's our fault."

"But it's better like this," Brian said. "It's more interesting and exciting."

"It's chaos," Red said. "There are dragons and aliens running around killing people."

"Aliens don't kill people unless they are ordered to," Brian said. "They could have destroyed your car with you in it, but they brought it down safely on purpose."

"That's not the point," Red said. "This is wrong. Dozens of people on the base have died from that dragon. Really dead. Never coming back. Those aliens used to be people. You used the machine to change them against their will into something they aren't. Don't you see how that's wrong?"

"They like it," Brian said. "Just ask them. Besides, who put you in charge of fixing the world?"

"I'm not," Red said. "I'm just trying to keep it together until Jon can fix it."

"How does that make you any less of a lackey than me? At least I'm doing what I wanted."

"I don't have time for this," Red said. He pointed south with his free hand. "What's that way?"

"Cowboys, I think," Brian said. "They never cross the mountains, though. They don't mix well with aliens. We were on a routine border patrol when we saw you."

Red turned to Tina. She was brushing some dirt off the front of her skirt and retying the corset so it wasn't as tight. "Any chance these cowboys would be your doing?"

"No," she said. "Westerns were Karl's specialty. But we haven't seen him since the Actuation."

"Karl was a lot more reasonable," Red thought aloud. "Okay, everybody in the flying saucers."

"What?" Brian said.

"We need to borrow your ride," Red said. "Tell captain what's-his-name we'll be coming for that key. Hopefully by then you'll see some sense and help us."

"I'll never help you. This is an act of war against the alliance. You'll be shot on sight next time."

"Blah, blah, blah," Red said. "Brian, this is bigger than your childhood dreams. You need to move past all of that."

"I'm giving you one last chance," Brian said. His eyes were twisted into a sneer that was unnatural for his face. Clearly he wasn't interested in Red's higher ideals.

Red saluted with his ray-gun and ran over to join the groups boarding the small flying saucers. As he left, he heard Brian touch his communication badge and start reporting the situation. Once on board, Red cranked the stick back and used his foot to increase the lift. The pod lifted quietly up on unseen waves of energy. Ignoring the hundreds of readouts and flashing lights on the dash, Red carefully twisted the control stick and the saucer rotated. Then he slowly moved them south. Glass had Jon on her lap. With three people and only two seats to a saucer, Red wondered how the others managed to crowd into the other two pods.

"I always hated Brian," Xenwyn said into the radio. "He thought he was so smart, but he's really just a huge geek." At least she was small enough to fit between the seats of whichever ship she was on.

"Wow, he weighs a ton," Glass said through much effort to keep Jon upright on the chair and not open any of his burn wounds. "This sitting on laps thing really isn't all that romantic."

Red concentrated on keeping the ship moving steadily up and south. He couldn't see behind them, but he knew the other two ships were having trouble when he heard them smack together in mid-air. Over the radio he heard Dragon Star yelling, "Watch out. Move to the side."

Red laughed. There was no way they would make it out of here if the alliance was sending trained pilots after them. He pushed the stick faster, risking more speed.

"We got company," Cindy said through the radio. "They aren't close yet, but they're gaining fast." Red saw some yellow blips on a circular green screen that seemed to confirm what she said.

"Faster!" Red said. He pushed the stick all the way forward. As the ship darted across cactus and sage brush covered desert, a loud crackle was heard over the radio.

"We've been hit," Dragon Star said. "But not badly. Should we shoot back?"

Red scanned the controls. He didn't know how to shoot back. "Go ahead and try."

A red laser lanced over the top of his saucer and incinerated a Joshua tree several hundred yards in front of them. "Stop! Stop!" Red screamed. He hadn't come this far to die from friendly fire. "Hold your fire. We're just going to end up killing each other and saving them the trouble."

Suddenly he heard a violent creaking sound. The ship began twisting and bending. "What the..." The radio cut out before Cindy could finish her sentence.

The familiar white light filled Red's eyes as loud static pounded his ears to ringing. He tasted blood and cherry candy. It faded, leaving him looking at his black jacket, which was now a black duster. He pulled out his gun to see it had become a revolver with some kind of metal tubes and a geared firing mechanism.

The seats dropped, making Red's stomach flip flop. Then the saucer above them contorted into a football shaped balloon. The engines flipped behind them and became a huge propeller. The cab converted to a gondola. Suddenly air was rushing past them and Red could hear Cindy shouting across to them. "Are those spears?"

Turning back, Red saw their pursuers had stopped following them before they crossed the unseen border. With red lights spinning around the middle, they hovered in mid-air. The lasers they shot changed mid-flight into barbed metal projectiles. "Harpoons!" Red had to shout to be heard above the engine chopping the air with the propeller. "Don't let them hit the balloons!"

Cindy turned the ship's wheel, which had morphed out of the control stick, and her airship lurched to the side. Two metal shafts whistled past her and then fell out of the sky. Red moved to the rail of his ship where the harpoon gun was mounted. He had to step carefully to avoid Jon's body. Aiming at the only flying saucer of the four not blocked by his ship's propeller, he pulled the trigger. Pressurized air launched a metal bolt that whistled out. When it crossed the border, it turned into a red laser and gained speed, winging the attacking ship. Trailing smoke, the saucer began to spiral down toward the ground.

The Machine Monks who had the confiscated alien rifles looked at the bizarre contraptions they had become with curiosity. Wires, tubes, and gears seemed to mesh in an almost incomprehensible way. Finally, Dragon Star pointed one at a pursuing saucer and fired. A metal pellet shot out, propelled by some kind of flaming gas. When it reached the boarder it turned into a blue bolt of energy and blasted one of the ships. The other two Monks began shooting their strange rifles as well.

Soon the harpoons were falling short of all three zephyrs as they continued to evade, and the aliens broke off the pursuit. Apparently they weren't willing to cross into the primitive area.

Red watched the other space ships split up. One went after the damaged ship and the others doubled back to pick up Brian and the aliens. "I don't think we're in a western," Glass said, pointing at the balloon.

"This sucks!" Xenwyn screamed. Red looked across to her ship to see she was a dwarf. One of her arms was a hydraulic prosthetic and she was wearing goggles with green lenses. "Why didn't I make myself a queen this time instead of a stupid fairy?"

Red's attention was diverted when Jon moaned beneath them. He opened his eyes in pain, and then they glossed over before he passed out again. The floor of the gondola wasn't much bigger than the small ship's interior.

"He can't take much more of this," Glass said.

"We just need a safe, out of the way place to regroup," Red said.

"There!" Xenwyn pointed with her normal arm. People from all three ships scanned the area she indicated.

"I don't see anything," Red said.

"Those goggles must be telescopic," Glass said.

Cindy slowly drifted her balloon closer so the others could communicate with less difficulty.

"There's a big, wooden building next to a dirt road," Xenwyn said. "There's at least one other balloon parked there and several horses tied up."

"Let's go see what new hell we've discovered." Red ran his fingers through dark hair as it blew in every direction. Then he turned the wheel to point the airship in the direction Xenwyn indicated.

CHAPTER SEVEN

lass tried to enjoy the moment of peace as the balloons quietly carried them over mountains and trees. As they descended, she clutched Jon's head in her lap, watching each labored breath. Distracted, she yelped when Red vented too much of the hot air out the top and the whole thing lurched down. She turned to see Red's frustration as he cranked the burner up to get more lift. Still, the gondola fell fast and hit the ground hard. Jon moaned. Glass expected the brown canvas bag above them to fall down and smother them, but it only rippled before regaining its shape. After setting Jon down, she helped Red pick himself up off the deck. Glass pulled the throttle back to stop the propellers, which were trying to push the gondola across the weedy dirt and threatened to overturn the whole ship.

Once they stopped hopping and dragging through the dirt, Red jumped over the side. Glass reached out and grabbed a rope. Then she tossed it over the edge so he could stake the whole ship down. After watching the first ship try to land, the others had opted to hover low and wait. Red had them throw down their own ropes so he could stake them as they slowly vented heat and landed softly.

Glass was grateful when her mentor, Cindy, jumped out as soon as they landed and came to check on Jon. Glass left her unconscious hero in Cindy's care and walked over to join Red.

They were next to a three story, wooden building, which sat at the end of a line of about twenty smaller structures. It had been painted at one point, but now she could only see peeling and cracked wood surrounding dingy windows. The red sign hanging off the front of the building from two short chains was the only thing they kept up. It said, *The Steam Whistle*, and featured a picture of the same.

"You two go in," Cindy said, pushing up her glasses. "The rest of us will wait here."

Glass felt uncomfortable in the corseted bustle dress, which had appeared when they crossed the last border. The pink and white checks were nice enough, but after years of sticking primarily to comfortable clothes, Glass didn't like the restriction. She also hated her sandy blond hair, which had been pulled up into a bun. She followed Red around to the wooden deck in front. His new boot heels clicked on the wood below. Glass didn't know why Cindy had sent her with Red, but she respected Cindy's advice.

He pushed open the swinging saloon doors. There were a few empty tables and one with three men playing cards. She followed Red over to the bar tender who only acknowledged them by nodding.

Red asked, "Do you have rooms we can rent?"

"You don't look to be from around these parts. Let's see your money."

Red pulled out his black leather wallet, revealing purple money featuring a steam boat instead of a face.

"That'll get you one room for one night," the man said.

Glass asked, "How big is the room?"

Red glanced at her sideways and opened his eyes wide. She nodded, silently agreeing to let him handle the negotiations.

The proprietor said, "One bed. One dresser."

Red put his money away. "I have ten people. One needs a doctor. Is there any way we can work it off?"

"The doctors up the way," the man nodded in the direction of the small town Red had seen on his way in. "Unless you have a horse or something to barter, you'll need to find lodgings elsewhere."

"Barter," Red said. "What about an airship?"

The men playing cards grew quiet as they suddenly tuned in to listen. Glass felt some relief at no longer having to endure them staring lecherously at the curves this dress emphasized. The bar tender looked skeptical. "You have an airship? Let me see it."

Red nodded to the window where one of the ships could be seen through the sheer white curtain. Dragon Star, now dressed in some kind of brown cloak, was driving another stake into the ground for extra anchorage. Glass sensed the man wanted to run outside and look it over, but he played it cool. "That old thing? It's worth six months room and board for ten people."

"What kind of a fool trades his ship in for a room?" one man at the table said.

"You stay out of this, Tom," the owner said with a finger up in a threatening manner. "This ain't your business."

Tom thought better of being banned from the only saloon in town, and turned back around.

"I have three of them," Red said.

"Three airships?" Tom couldn't help himself.

"But I don't need six months of lodging," Red said. He did some quick thinking. "I want rooms and food for ten people for three months. I also want ten guns, two horses, and some cash to pay the doctor."

The barkeep went over to the till and popped it open. A bell rang as he looked through the cash. "I can't do more than six guns. The doc owes me a favor. I'll give you three months and you can use my two horses and carriage as long as you're in town."

Red looked around. Tom was physically in pain, keeping his mouth shut. Glass knew the barkeep was ripping them off. Red didn't seem to care.

Was he really going to take the deal?

Before Red sealed it she interrupted, "That and four hundred dollars. And we get to park the other two ships in your yard as well."

"Deal," the man said with a crooked smile before they could ask for more.

Glass could see Red shifting his weight back and shoulders dropping. He no longer had to hide the exhaustion of this insane day. Red shook the bartender's hand.

"You'll be needing some crew for that ship," Tom said.

"Not planning to hire drunken gamblers for that job," the barkeep said. With a gleam in his eye and crooked grin he spun around, too elated by the deal to care about insulting his only customers.

Glass waited by the bar while Red went out and brought the group in. They decided against taking Jon up the narrow stairs, opting instead to bring a cot down from the one of the rooms and lay him in it against a wall of the saloon. The barkeep sent one of the gamblers to fetch the doctor.

While Glass tended to Jon, the rest of the group shared two loaves of dry bread and cheese the barkeep had produced.

Near sunset, she helped Red assign a rotation of two people to watch the ships at all times. He gave them each two pistols and whatever strange contraption the confiscated alien rifles had turned into.

He said, "I'm given to believe these balloons are very valuable. Don't get out of the gondolas until somebody comes to relieve you. Be friendly to the locals, but if they get serious, don't hesitate to pull your guns. Fire into the air if you need help, but don't shoot the balloon."

Then he went up to one of the rooms and didn't come back down for ten hours.

Glass chatted with the other Machine Monks. They were all exhausted as they grumbled about their clothes. Eventually, they wandered up the stairs in search of beds, except Dragon Star and Mack who had the first shift guarding the airships.

Glass changed the dressing on Jon's burns. When the doctor arrived, he offered her some grease, but she politely declined. She accepted the painkillers and managed to get Jon to swallow one with some water.

The air in the saloon grew cold with dark. Glass pulled a shawl Cindy gave her tight around her shoulders before putting her cool hands on Jon's cheeks and forehead. She hoped it would offer some small comfort against his fever.

She couldn't get the image out of her head of the dragon smashing down on him and then blasting the whole street with fire. She wanted to go to him. But he bravely stood up against the huge beast in order to protect them all.

She had loved him for so long in quiet. She thought he cared for her, but he always took his responsibility so seriously. Glass thought they had plenty of time. Their dedication to the Actuator always took first place. Now he lay before her on the brink of death and all she felt was bitter regret. So much wasted time.

"Morning sleepy," Glass said as Red ran his fingers through his hair.

Glass was sitting next to Jon, wiping his forehead with a damp rag.

"Were you up all night?" Red asked.

When he found a bowl of questionable fruit and more bread out on the counter, he settled on a browning apple.

"No. Cindy and I took turns," Glass said. She was glad to see that Red had pulled himself together. Until Jon was better, they all depended on him. "The doctor will be back later to check on him. I think he has a fever." She tried to look dignified, praying Red wouldn't see her school girl crush. She was a Monk from the Untouched House, after all. They weren't supposed to get overwhelmed by emotions. "Now that you're up, we can finally start the meeting."

"Meeting?"

"We need to figure out as much as we can about what happened and come up with some kind of a plan. The good proprietor of this fine establishment reluctantly agreed to give us some paper and ink. He agreed to find us a map, too."

"How much did you have to pay for that?" Red asked.

"Nothing. He's had potential buyers looking at the ship all morning. I think he's just so happy you gave it to him for a song and a dance that he was glad to throw in a few extras."

Red nodded. She could see he still didn't care what the ships were worth. They could make do with two of them. "We're having this meeting here?"

"With the owner doing business outside, we have the place to ourselves," Glass said. "Have a seat and I'll go round up the crew."

"Crew?" Red sat in her chair.

Glass headed to the stairs, but she stopped at the corner and looked back at him.

Sitting alone with his mentor wrapped in gauze and clearly in more pain than primitive medicine could ease, Red curled up and rested his head on Jon's.

He said, "I'm sorry, Jon. I did what I could. I should have been the one to take the sword and distract that dragon. Then you'd have some hope of sorting this all out."

Jon rolled over and panted a few breaths before going back to unconsciousness. Glass wanted to run back to him. But she held back. "Get better fast," Red said softly. "We can't fight that dragon without you."

As the rest of the group came down, Red moved his chair closer to one of the green felt covered tables. Cindy pulled out a map and some paper. She pushed up her glasses and held a lead pencil, pointing to the paper to indicate she was ready.

Glass said, "I think we need to start by recording as much as we know about what happened that day and keep a record of all the machine monks we know about. It's an unhappy job, but it's all we have to go on."

"We have two of the house leaders," Red said. "Let's start with them."

Cindy wrote, *Untouched House*, in neat script across the top of the page. She smiled after putting her own house first. She wrote her name and then Glass'. Then a group of three names and a group of six names.

"We know for sure five of them didn't make it." She put a small x next to two of the names from the group of three and half of the group of six. "The

49

rest of them scattered after the orcs attacked. We don't know where they went. The Untouched House was dedicated to understanding the world as it was. We were charged with being able to put things back the way they were. And I think Glass can do it."

Glass blushed. She knew nobody could possibly understand the whole world the way it was. There was just too much. It was too complicated. She appreciated her mentor's confidence, but her job had been to fill in holes for the other groups. As she saw everybody's eyes on her, she felt inadequate. She could never put it all back how it was, but she didn't want them to lose hope.

She said, "I can only restore places, not people."

"That's why we need the keys," Xenwyn blurted.

She was standing, but still shorter than everybody in chairs. Glass gave a tiny sigh of relief when everybody turned their attention elsewhere.

"That's true," Red said.

Next Cindy wrote, *Empty House*. Beneath that she wrote, *Choi Yong-kyeong*, and four other names. They all looked at Dragon Star. He was sitting backward in his wooden chair, and staring gravely at the floor stained in a camouflage pattern of dried booze and dirt.

"Like I told you, they're all dead." He spoke between deep heaving sighs. "They were all four sitting in meditation when it happened. They never flinched despite the chaos. I stepped outside to see what was happening when Karla destroyed the whole building and whipped me aside with her tail. I hit the wall and passed out. When I woke, I went back to Empty House. That was where Red found me. I brought these to remember my honored students." He didn't move. But everybody knew he meant the two swords he carried. They'd been strapped to his back on the base, but due to all the changes they were now hanging one above the other from a strap on his left. He drew one sword, showing it had become curved with serrations along the back. "I will destroy Karla with these swords or die trying."

"Don't make any rash oaths," Red said.

Cindy put an x by each of the other four names.

Dragon Star said, "The Empty House was charged with having clear minds so that the machine and all the affected area could be a blank canvas should the need arise. Now that it affects the whole world, our discipline has no place."

"But we are glad for your help anyway," Red said. "And we may still need your skills with the Actuator."

Dragon Star didn't look up. Cindy wrote, *Dedicated House*, above, *Elizabeth Darling*, and, *Zach Medici*. She put Xenwyn next on the list of thirty names. With only eighty-five people living on the base, they all knew everybody else.

"We should probably write down their specialty and, where possible, the key," Glass said.

Cindy put, *fantasy – magic wand*, next to Xenwyn. She began filling out the rest of the chart. Sci-fi, western, cyberpunk, historical, vampire romance. Red began to wag his head. Glass knew the list, of course, but seeing it written out served to remind all of them how very screwed up the world was at the moment. At the bottom Cindy wrote, *Historical – wax seal*, and put a check mark next to it. They had one.

"What do we put next to Elizabeth's name?" Cindy asked. "She used to be Victorian and Regency. But by the end…" she trailed off. Everybody knew Elizabeth had changed since she got involved with Zach.

"Steampunk," Glass said. "We're in it right now."

"I thought this was western," Red said. "Brian said it was."

"No," she said. "Those airships aren't from any western."

"So western isn't historical, and Steampunk isn't western." Red laughed. "Are there any of the machine monks from the Dedicated House that we know who didn't make it out alive?"

Several of them called out names of former friends and people they loved with hushed tones. A few choked back sobs as Cindy marked each one.

"Xenwyn," Red asked, "how many of these people actually used the Actuator?"

She again told the story of how the dampeners had failed. Then she stopped. "Wait, why weren't you there yourself, Red?"

"It was a standard test. Jon was the Key Hunter. I was escorting Glass and her group off base that morning."

Xenwyn nodded. She cited from memory as many of the people she knew who had used the machine after the field dampeners failed. Cindy marked each one with an O. When the list was finished there were eighteen confirmed people who had used the Actuator and four they weren't sure about. Some of the monks who had used the machine were confirmed dead already.

"So we have to find those keys without their help," Red said.

"Uhhh…" It was a low moan coming from behind Red that slowly built into a recognizable word. "Ow."

They all turned to look at Jon. He tried to sit up, but slowly settled back. Perspiration was already beginning to form on his forehead.

"You're awake," Red said. Glass rushed over by Jon. She started wiping his brow again and helping him lift his head. Despite the pain he felt, she knew he would recover now. *At least the fire didn't burn his face.*

"Barely," Jon mumbled. "If you aren't going to give me any pain killers, you could at least get me some alcohol."

CHAPTER EIGHT

Red listened intently as Jon managed to speak quietly. "Did you find out who sabotaged the machine?" Jon paused to turn on his cot and relieve his stiff muscles. He rolled back when the pain was too much.

"Not yet," Red said, dropping his eyes.

"So itchy." Jon started to move one arm to scratch the other, but the skin cracked and he flinched in pain. "Can't move, Can't scratch."

"The doctor said the first two weeks will be the worst," Glass said. "If you hold on that long you'll start to feel better."

"Doctor? Where?" The wooden feet of the cot scratched the dirty floor as Jon tried to move to one side.

Glass used a handkerchief to wipe his head as she said, "We're in a territory southwest of the base."

"We have to go back," Jon said with his eyes closed. He was mentally forcing himself to stay still. "Have to get the Actuator before the saboteur."

"Why?" Red asked. He leaned forward, straining to hear each quiet word. They all knew if anybody was going to fix this mess, it was Jon.

"Not done," Jon said.

"Well Commander Newell has it well protected now," Red said. Going back there now wasn't the right choice. "I doubt anybody will be taking the Actuator from her any time soon."

"Don't play…" Jon's voice trailed off.

"What?" Glass asked softly.

"Where's Zach?" Jon was panting now.

"Somebody get some alcohol to help with the pain," Glass said. With the bartender gone, Cindy took it upon herself and started rummaging around behind the bar.

"We don't' know where Zach is," Red said. "But we know he didn't use the Actuator."

"Didn't use it?" Jon panted between sentences. "That's good. He's letting go of the obsession. The only way to beat an obsession is to let it go."

Red nodded his agreement. The other machine monks were suddenly pre-occupied with the table or something in their hands. None of them wanted to hear such advice.

"Don't play her game," Jon said. He paused as Glass put a large bottle of whiskey to his lips, giving it to him a few sips at a time.

"Don't play the dragon's game?" Red asked after a few minutes. He needed more than riddles.

Jon nodded. "We have to hurry." He finished the brown liquid. "Can't beat an obsession from inside. Don't' play her game."

"What's her game?" Red asked.

He could feel Jon ebbing too soon. They needed more information. Red needed directions. He couldn't keep pretending to lead these people without some idea of what they should do.

Jon's eyes opened for a moment as the alcohol began to course through him. Red held his breath, waiting. Jon sighed as the tiniest edge came off the pain. Then he closed them and fell back, heavy against the cot.

Glass set his head down softly and then handed Cindy the empty bottle. Everybody shifted their chairs back toward the table. Red was the last one to turn to face the group.

Glass started again, "So what should we do now?"

"Jon said we should go back and take the Actuator as soon as we can," Dragon Star said.

"That's definitely our top priority," Red said. He kept his voice strong, to cover the fear inside. How could they possibly fight that dragon? It had been all they could do to get away. "But I think we have a much better chance against that dragon once Jon has recovered."

Everybody nodded their agreement. He let out a breath he held in anticipation of anybody going against his only plan.

"What about the saboteur?" Glass asked.

Red thought about it. "If the dragon hasn't killed them already, then we should assume she's still keeping the Actuator safe for now. Maybe the saboteur is happy with how things are now."

"So we just sit and wait for Jon to get better and hope he can kill the dragon next time?" Cindy asked. She sat on a barstool. "How will the next time be any different than the last?"

"Because we aren't going to be playing her game next time," Red said, borrowing wisdom.

"What does that mean?" Xenwyn asked.

"I don't know," Red said. "But it won't be long before Jon is better, at least enough to tell us what he meant." Red knew it was a weak position. But it was the only position he had. An awkward quiet fell. Everybody kept looking at each other, unsure how to proceed.

Xenwyn finally broke the silence. "We need Pete."

"What for?" It was Tina. "Pete's just a drunk."

Red wished he could ignore her obviously display of emotion.

"You're mad because he jilted you," Xenwyn said.

Red saw her posturing to show off her prosthetic arm and thick muscles.

"Enough," Red said. He didn't need any silly drama right now.

"Pete knew everybody on the base the best," Xenwyn said. "He wasn't a Monk or military man, but he knew everybody and he was there when everybody was using the Actuator. He'll have a good idea of what happened. I was a bit distracted, trying to stay alive and all, but he will know what happened. He might even know who the saboteur was."

"But how do we find out where Pete is?" Glass asked.

"That's easy," Xenwyn said. She walked around the side of the table where she could see everyone without tip-toing. "He left the base with Hanna."

"Hanna? The Goth girl with tattoos?" Glass asked.

"Hanna the vampire enthusiast," Cindy clarified, pointing to her chart.

"You're sure Pete left with her?" Red asked.

"Positive," Xenwyn said. "Didn't you all know Hanna was Pete's newest fling?" She scratched her flesh arm with the smooth part of the hydraulic on the other one. Red decided a geared up dwarf was Xenwyn's least attractive form.

"I never liked her," said Tina.

"Hanna was sometimes hard to deal with," Glass agreed. As Red looked around the group he realized Glass and Cindy were probably the only two women on the base who hadn't been involved with Pete at some point. He hadn't been close friends with Pete, but they'd gotten along well enough. At least Pete never dated Xenwyn seriously.

"If Pete's with Hanna, we could get her key at the same time," Red said as he looked at the list. "But where would they have gone? Transylvania?"

"Honestly, don't you read?" Tina asked.

"Of course," Red said. "But I couldn't possibly read enough to keep up with all of you. I haven't read much vampire stuff."

"The Pacific Northwest," Glass said. Several of the women sighed when she said that.

Red rolled his eyes. "At least it's closer than Europe. It would take forever to get across the Atlantic in one of our balloons and who knows what they would change into when we got there."

"A giant bird pulling a flying chariot?" Xenwyn guessed. Red watched as several Machine Monks rolled their eyes. "Hey, at least part of England is mine. Camelot is alive and well right now."

"Let's get to work on the map," Red said.

Cindy pulled a tan page to the top of the pile. It had sepia writing on it. It wasn't a great map. But it had most of the Western United States, some railroads, and a few American Indian Reservations marked.

Red put his finger down, in the Southwest. "So we're here?"

"Well, since your finger covers almost a hundred mile diameter on this map, that's pretty close," Cindy said. She took the charcoal pencil and put a nice dot to the left of his finger. "We're here."

"And the base?" Red asked.

"Here," Glass offered.

Cindy marked it with another dot. She lightly sketched the borders of modern day Nevada, Utah, Arizona, California, Idaho, Oregon, and Washington. The base was in Southern Utah near the Nevada border. They were now at the tip of Nevada where it met California and Arizona.

"That's remarkably accurate," Red said.

"Untouched House," Cindy said. "We study what the world is. Or at least what it was before."

"We need to draw in the territories we know," Red said. "Around the base is fantasy with dragons and orcs and such."

Cindy put a light circle in that area and wrote, *Fantasy*, in neat script above it. "Brian's Sci-fi is here." She sketched another circle around Nevada's famous Area 51 site.

"Hopefully it will be a very large area," Red said. "Those saucers are a lot faster than the balloons."

"So we just need to get across Nevada into Oregon," Red said.

"Probably all the way to here," Cindy lightly drew a small circle around the peninsula at the top of Washington state. She wrote, *Vampires?*

"Of course," Red said. "And who knows what is between the two. We won't all go, of course. I think maybe just three of us in one of the airships."

"I will go," Dragon Star said.

"I'm in," Mack said. "I knew Hanna pretty well. Our obsessions overlapped. We were dating up until recently. We had a falling out, but she'll talk to me."

"Why did you break up?" Glass tried to sound upbeat, but it felt awkward to Red.

"You don't have to tell us if it's too personal," Cindy said.

"I don't mind," Mack said with a laugh. He had a broody visage. Red knew he liked talking about things which made everyone else uncomfortable. "I told her real vampires should be all Bram Stoker, not sparkly like Fae. That's why she started hanging out with Pete, to punish me. Like I care."

"Are you sure she'll want to talk to you?" Red asked.

More drama. Just what he didn't need.

"I'll apologize." Mack nodded. "She'll take me back." He exuded confidence, a weakness in Red's opinion.

"Okay," Red said, happy a plan of action was forming. "Since you had the overnight watch, get some sleep now. I'll gather supplies. We'll leave at dusk. Wherever we're headed, we'll attract less attention if we travel at night. While we're gone, Cindy will head up a search. The rest of you need to look around this Steampunk place and try to find the key."

"It's probably in England," Glass said. "Elizabeth loved London."

"Look anyway," Red ordered. "But don't get into any trouble. We'll take three pistols and a weird rifle. That leaves four pistols and two rifles here so you can keep a watch on the other airship and Jon. With any luck we'll be back in a week, and Jon will be well enough to help develop a plan to take back the Actuator."

The meeting began to break up. Even though most of them didn't have any specific orders, they began moving upstairs or outside.

"I'd volunteer to go with," Xenwyn said holding out her gear enhanced dwarf arm, "but I don't know what I'd be in vampire territory. Some kind of homunculus bat, probably."

"I think we'll manage," Red said. He smiled at her. She paused to fiddle with her green goggles, but when she noticed, she smiled back.

"I can't help but notice we're not really doing what Jon said." Glass turned to Red once most of the group had moved off. "He said we need to go after the dragon fast."

"I heard him," Red said, grateful she hadn't brought this up during the meeting and started a schism.

"Then why are you going after Pete?"

"Because we need him to help us find the other Monks and keys," Xenwyn interrupted.

"Shouldn't we be trying to figure out a way to beat that dragon first?" Glass asked.

"Maybe," Red said. "But right now we only have one key. Unless we get more, there's no benefit to having the Actuator. Besides, I don't know how to fight the dragon."

"With a sword. With an army. With magic. All the usual ways," Glass said.

Red looked at the table. Then he looked at Xenwyn before turning to answer Glass. "I'm not that guy. Jon's the expert at medieval weapons and military strategy. I'm just the assistant. He only put me in when people like Saul were actuating NASA missions and such."

"You don't give yourself enough credit," Glass said.

"You got us all off the base and safe," Xenwyn added.

He felt his cheeks flush, but in her current dwarf form, he couldn't think about anything like that now.

"We don't have time to wait for Jon to heal and fight the dragon," Glass said. "The world is in ruins. People are dying. Lots and lots of people. We have to fix it as soon as we can. And what about the saboteur? If Jon's right and they manage to get the machine before us, things could get even worse."

"It would be a lot easier to get the machine from them than from the dragon," Red said. "It's true. The best move would be to take the Actuator back as soon as possible, but I don't know how. Even if I could kill the dragon somehow, we don't have anything to do with the Actuator once we get it unless we have the keys. That's what Jon would do. That's what he will do when he's better. He's obviously delirious. Until he's well, I'll concentrate on recovering as many keys as possible so that when we do get the machine back we can start cleaning up some of this mess."

"But people are dying all over the world," Glass said. "Right now."

"I know." Red stood up. "Maybe billions. And none of them know why or how to stop it. Aliens, orcs, vampires... No matter what the Machine Monks thought their worlds were, the only one who got what he expected is Mack. All that training, and nobody considered the real world consequences of their obsessions. We've plunged the entire planet into an unending horror."

Xenwyn turned and walked away. Red heard her sniff before she stomped up the stairs.

Red wished he hadn't said it. He probably shot down any chance he had with Xenwyn. Still, maybe he didn't want to like someone lost in a dream world. He looked at Glass. "Nobody else even knows why the world is like this. They are all lost in confusion. We're the only ones who can change it back. But even if Commander Newell was dead, we don't have the keys to change it back now. So there's nothing we can do for those people yet."

Glass wiped tears from her eyes and stood up next to him. Red realized her training, among all the Machine Monks, had given her the deepest appreciation for the world as it had been. She knew better than anybody how much had been lost. He moved forward and hugged her.

"I can't put it back either," she said. "The world was just too complicated. I... Even if we get the keys in, it won't work. I don't know enough."

"It doesn't matter," Red said, turning to the side and looking at Jon as he held her. "You're the best we have. How good you are is good enough. It's all we have to give back to the world."

"Just hurry," she said. "Thinking about so many people suffering... it makes me die inside a little more each day."

"Can't have that," Red said. "I promised Jon I'd keep you alive."

CHAPTER NINE

This is going to be epic," Mack said, as he lowered a leather satchel full of dried fruit and jerky into the gondola of the airship. He took a moment to enjoy the sunset.

"I would prefer if we could actually see where we are going," Dragon Star said. He loosely tied a leather strap around the rifle so it wouldn't move around as the airship flew.

"There's a waning crescent moon," Mack said, pointing. "It'll give us light for the first few hours."

Mack loved the idea of departing at sundown. Not only did the red clouds look like blood smeared across the sky, but he always welcomed the embrace of a dark night. He'd enjoyed racing off the base in a horse drawn carriage. He thrilled as they streaked through the sky in a flying saucer. None of that would come close to the nearly silent motion of a dirigible through the cold black.

"We should take both balloons," Mark said, noting the absence of the third. "That way if something happens to one, we won't be stranded. And it's not like they have any use for it here except to guard it." He secretly hoped to be alone in the air so he didn't have to listen to the other two chattering the whole time about every stupid, little thing.

At least Red thought about the suggestion. Jon never would have, Mack knew. Red said, "Good point. But, if Jon recovers before we get back, I want him to have access to one. Plus, we have no idea what this thing will turn into along the way. I think we'd be better off staying together."

"The bartender did offer the others the use of horses as part of the bargain," Dragon Star said.

"And where are any of the rest of them going in the meantime?" Mack asked.

"It might be better if we had more firepower." Red went back for another gear-enhanced rifle.

As the mountain teeth slowly devoured the sun, the three men climbed into their ships. Mack couldn't help smiling. His plan had worked. The other two were going to ride together. He didn't care that it meant he wouldn't get a break from steering. He stayed up all night by choice, preferring to sleep in the dreary light of the day.

Mack smiled at the rest of the people who had come to see them off. He didn't really care about these people, of course. It just seemed appropriate for them to be adoring him as a hero. He knew they didn't understand the real greatness in a dark hero. Still he accepted their wishes for good fortune, shaking hands and thanking them. His will for the Actuator to change the whole world seemed to be paying off. He wouldn't tell them that, of course. None of them would be capable of making big sacrifices to get what they wanted.

Then his moment of exultation came to an end when Cindy, Isaac, and everybody else turned to look at the other ship. Mack looked over and saw Xenwyn, the ugly little dwarf, pull Red almost over the side of the rail and kiss him on the cheek. It was a short kiss that left them both blushing. Mack almost gagged. Everybody knew Red liked her. She was just being dramatic to draw off some of the attention. Little vixen.

"Let's go," Red said. Isaac pulled the other ship's stakes up as Dragon Star increased the fire in the balloon. Their airship rose quietly up and to the west as a favorable wind lifted them into the sunset.

So enamored by the silly little kiss, Glass and the other women watched it float away. Had they really forgotten about Mack? It made him mad. *Well, who needed them anyway?*

Mack pushed the lever to increase the heat in his own ship. It lifted, straining against the stakes pinning it to the ground. At the sound of fire and movement of the craft, everybody turned back to Mack. Isaac had to pull harder on the stake because the sideways motion of the balloon stressed it. He was too weak to get it free on the first pull. Mack despised weakness.

"Be careful," Glass said, waving one hand. At least she knew him well enough to know he didn't appreciate gushing smiles.

"Always am," Mack nodded.

With Tina's help, Isaac finally freed the last stake. The balloon lurched as it began to rise and chase the other one into the sunset.

"Good luck!" Cindy called from behind. Mack noticed Xenwyn was still looking at the other balloon instead of him. He didn't care.

Mack waved once more before turning his attention to the ship's wheel. He corrected slightly to get back on course. The other balloon seemed to be moving faster for some reason. He laughed when he remembered the propeller control. Mack didn't want to turn it up because the small steam engine on the propeller was so loud. He gave up his coveted silence in order to keep up with the others. He didn't like being behind them as they floated over the boring orange desert sand. The back of their dirigible looked like a giant butt floating through the sky. And not an attractive one. If he could, he would pass them in the night.

Occasionally, a shift in the wind brought their voices to him, but Mack couldn't understand any of the words over the constant chopping of the propellers. He had imagined this trip to be floating through the dark of night in silence like a specter. Instead, the annoying steam powered propeller chopped inefficiently through the air as it slowly pushed the giant football shaped balloon. At least the small, crescent moon was in front of them with thin clouds slowly rising up and veiling it in a dark and mysterious way.

Mack's fat balloon still hadn't caught them when he saw the shimmer of white energy as their airship morphed. It looked like the tip had driven into a huge piece of cellophane, causing reflected moonlight to shimmer near the disturbance. Then the point of the balloon pushed through and the entire vessel began to shift and contort. The balloon deflated while the gondola lifted. The whole thing closed like a giant clam. Once the change into a silver flying saucer was complete, it blasted forward as if an invisible slingshot had suddenly released it.

Mack greeted the barrier with hands out to the sides and chin up. The moment of transformation fed his Machine Monk addiction. He lived for it above all. He relished the moment when light filled his eyes, the rumble of an earthquake shook his brain, and the taste of blood and maple syrup filled his mouth. He knew there was no light or sound or smell or flavor. The pins and needles all over his skin and through his large muscles were simply his brain trying to interpret the energy as it penetrated and triggered all his senses. But it was a rush like no other.

This time he knew it was coming, so he prepared his mind. During the Great Conversation when a Machine Monk talked to The Actuator, it constructed the change based on criteria the Monk's mind gave it. Despite the romantic ways the other—more stupid—Monks used to talk about it, Mack knew the Actuator was a computer at heart. Therefore, at the root of the Great Conversation was a bunch of 'if then' statements. Having seen the bulbous headed green aliens running around with Brian, Mack knew this area had criteria for making some people into monsters. Not classical, awesome monsters like Frankenstein. But aliens could be monstrous, too. Having carefully considered what he knew about Brian, Mack had prepared for this border transformation. He filled his mind with the thoughts of hunting and destroying as the elixir of Actuating energy went through it.

When the static cleared, Mack saw the world only in shades of red and green. When he looked down at his hands and saw hard black claws, a jagged smile cracked the exoskeleton of his insectoid face. Mack had become a predatory alien with saliva stretching from one row of razor sharp teeth to the other when he opened his great maw.

He'd seen the controls the last time they came through Brian's sci-fi bubble. So those didn't excite him now. He glanced at the radar and velocitometer to make sure he was racing along behind the others. Once he felt sure everything was in order, he began moving around in the cramped cockpit.

Every motion of his arm clicked black exoskeletal plates against each other like eccentric medieval armor. He turned his head to discover he had a huge range of motion with his neck. His spine naturally scrunched over now, like a hunch back. When he moved his legs, something behind him smacked an empty chair. He swiveled his horse-like face around to verify he had a long, multi-jointed tail. It took some practice to get the hang of it, but he could even control it on purpose.

"Everything okay?" Red's voice broke in on Mack's mirth. Of course those dweebs wouldn't even have tried to do anything imaginative with the change.

Mack pushed the red communication button with one of his black thumbs and it lit up. "Aauga," came out of his raspy throat.

"What?" Red asked. "I couldn't understand."

Mack made a few sounds with his throat, realizing this form didn't have a tongue capable of complicated sounds. When he pushed the button again he just moaned, "Uh uh."

"Keep an eye on your radar," Red said. "With any luck Brian's friends won't notice us. At this speed we'll be across Nevada in a few minutes."

Mack saw three red blips show up on the round radar monitor approaching from their right. Red's ship was ahead of him in green. Based on how far apart they were, Mack knew Red couldn't yet see the ships closing in on them.

Mack pushed the button and tried to say there were already space ships coming after them. It came out like clicks and moans.

"I think we have some interference on this line," Red said. "Do you see anyway to change channels?"

Mack wagged his mandibles. They were in a space ship and Red wanted to look for a different walkie-talkie channel?

Mack leaned his heavy body across the back of the plush red pilot's chair so he could reach the controls with both claws. He found the weapon system and rotated the dial so the cross hairs faced behind him. This was simple to anybody who had ever played a video game in the last ten years. So obviously Dragon Star hadn't been able to do it before.

Before the pursuers reached the small ring around his green dot in the center of the screen, Mack began blasting away. He wasn't about to give that oversized pimple the first shot.

Brian's group began to spread out when they reached the line on the radar. So Mack knew he'd guessed right about it being the outside limit of his range. Using his other hand, he began bobbing and weaving the speeding vehicle to preemptively dodge the incoming lasers. As he knew they would, red bolts began shooting past him and off into the night.

"Are you under fire?" Red asked through the radio. Mack didn't bother to respond because he knew his current form couldn't possibly say, 'Duh!'

Despite the lower dexterity of pinchers, Mack kept the saucer jerking from side to side in random lurches while blasting cover fire in every direction behind him. Obviously, they knew some kind of trick he didn't, which gave them the advantage of more speed. But he had an advantage, too. He didn't fear death.

In a bold move, he suddenly banked the vessel hard to the right. His guns shooting out the back hit the ship edging up on his left and sent it spiraling down to the sand below.

"Surrender now," Brian said through the radio. "Or you will all be killed."

Before Red said something forgettable, Mack pushed the com button and roared a wicked battle cry. That shut Brian up.

In the moment of distraction, one of the saucers clipped Mack's. He grabbed onto the seat with both claws and his mandibles as the ridiculous vehicle tumbled end over end and dropped from the sky.

Mack discovered a side benefit of an exoskeleton when the whole thing crashed into the ground upside down. His hands ripped apart the chair he'd been holding onto and his body smashed into the ground. If he'd been human, it would have been fatal. In this alien form, he just popped his neck and back joints before standing up. It hurt, of course. But Mack enjoyed a little pain now and then.

All the lights went out inside the ship and the door opened. Since the ship landed upside down, the open hatch led up to the star filled night.

Mack heard Brian talking to his green-headed friends outside. He swished his tail back and forth, as he heard more voices outside. It made a hypnotic clicking sound all up and down the length of the jointed black exoskeleton. He imagined it would be like popping his knuckles.

Then Brian called in to Mack, "Don't move or we'll shoot."

CHAPTER TEN

ed knew they shouldn't have taken two ships. Now Mack's ship had crashed into the side of a sandy hill and two of Brian's new friends were circling them. The smartest tactical move would have been to push their lead and race for the other border of Brian's territory. The odds were overwhelmingly against Mack surviving that devastating crash. These stupid ships didn't even have seatbelts, but Red couldn't do it. He couldn't leave Mack behind.

Dragon Star, now piloting the ship so Red could shoot, slowly brought the vehicle down for a soft landing. Red kept blasting cover fire in every direction to keep Brian at bay. However, the guns shut down automatically when they came close to the ground. Rather than snipe them from the air, Brian had chosen to land nearby.

Red hadn't taken two steps toward Mack's shipwreck before Brian leaped from his flying saucer. They had ray guns trained on each other from the first second. Neither pulled the trigger. Red tried diplomacy. In his most reasonable voice he said, "Mack's in that ship. We have to see if he needs our help."

"Nobody could have survived that crash," Brian said. "I told you if you came back we would be enemies."

"We're not your enemies," Red said. He shoved the ray gun back into his underarm holster and straightened his black jacket. "Look, I have to go see if we can save Mack. If you're going to shoot me, fine. But I doubt your space alliance condones such actions." Red started walking toward the smoking wreck. The hull seemed intact, but it had a huge dent and crack where it landed.

"Don't move or we'll shoot!" Brian yelled. Two of his Martian playmates had come out, one from each flying saucer.

"Brian, you have a man down, too. Shouldn't you be going to check on the other fallen ship?"

"He radioed in. He's fine."

"Well Mack didn't. He's probably not." Red turned to walk toward the wreckage when a purple blast of energy lanced the ground in front of him. A rock exploded. Red turned in time for most of the shrapnel to hit his jacket.

"I said freeze!" Brian was shaking now. Red could see mania in Brian's eyes as he knitted his brow and aimed across the ray gun at Red's chest.

Suddenly a black blur arched out of the downed vessel. Red thought a minor explosion had ejected some pieces trailing black chemical smoke. A low rumble seemed to support the assumption until the smoke dropped back down to the ground between him and Brian. The rumble was a guttural roar. The pieces were a black, bug-like alien.

Brian and his crew turned their guns on the black, alien monster. Brian's eyes went wide and the tip of his ray gun shook.

The horrible creature roared again, revealing spit lines stretched between teeth sharp enough to make a shark jealous.

Brian fired at the creature, hitting one shoulder with the purple blast. One of the exoskeletal plates exploded, sending a firework of light trails off to one side.

The monster laughed. Brian whimpered.

"Mack?" Red asked. As soon as he said it, he knew it to be true. There hadn't been static on the line. Mack had turned himself into a monster when they crossed the border. Now Red wanted to shoot him, too.

The predatory insect began to laugh in rhythmic grunts as it swished its tail with nauseating clicks that ran up and down the length of the jointed appendage. In a sudden blur, the Mack-monster leaped forward and pinned Brian beneath clawed feet and pincer hands.

"Let me go!" Brian screamed. "Shoot it! Open fire!"

Mack rolled to the side, using Brian's body as a shield. Fortunately for Brian, his companions didn't act quickly. Mack grunted a few times, splattering Brian's face with sticky saliva. Eventually Red realized Mack couldn't talk so he decided to do it.

"Give us the key, Brian."

"I told you, the Captain has it." Brian's eyes kept wincing closed as the black mandibles threated to bite his face.

"He is lying," Dragon Star said. He came down the loading ramp wearing the same goofy red shirt as Brian, but holding one katana. "No Machine Monk would give an Actuator Key to a stranger who didn't understand it."

Red nodded. "You're going to die now, if you don't tell us the truth."

Mack clamped down a little harder with his pincers and clicked his mandibles one inch away from Brian's nose. Brian screamed, "Okay!" With tears running down the side of his face, Brian kept his eyes closed so he wouldn't have to look into the icy black orbs of the monster torturing him. "I have it on my ship. It's just an RFE."

Red opened his eyes wide and tipped his head. "It's what?"

"Resonant Frequency Emitter," Brian said. "Stop hurting me! I'm bleeding!"

Dragon Star retreated back up the ramp, still holding his sword like it could somehow deflect energy blasts. Red jogged over to Brian's ship, ignoring the Martians who trained their rifles on him. The red lights still raced in circles around the outside of the three undamaged saucers. He found a storage compartment to one side of the wide control panel and popped it open. Inside he found a metal, tube shaped device as long as a TV remote with several buttons along one side and four prongs sticking out of the top. He shoved it into his jacket's interior pocket. When he came down the ramp, he took the rifles from the aliens and motioned them to move away.

"Why didn't you just tell me it was a light sword handle?" Red asked.

"It's not, you idiot. Don't you ever watch TV? How could you not recognize an RFE when you see one?"

"We'll take this ship, too!" Red called across to Dragon Star, ignoring Brian. The Korean man bowed and then went inside. "Mack, you're with me this time!"

The black insectoid rumbled something. Red didn't know or care what it was. He just went back in and sat down at the controls. A few seconds later, the big black monster stomped up the ramp. Red pulled the handle back and moved the throttle forward. The ship raced up into the night sky before the door finished sealing, bringing a light draft. With his other hand, he aimed the ship's weapon behind them. Until now he'd never realized how practical the round shape of a flying saucer could be, allowing movement and aiming in every direction unimpeded. He blasted the last of the round aircrafts, hoping it would only disable the ship and not kill anybody inside. By then Dragon Star's ship was up and the two of them streaked through the night like shooting stars.

Whenever the ticking of the alien form behind him began to annoy Red, he remembered Mack would probably be dead and they wouldn't have Brian's key if Mack had stayed a human. He still couldn't imagine why anybody would want to be such a vile monster. In retrospect, it made perfect sense. Mack lived for horror. This black insect shape was as much horror as he could get from Brian's space opera. *Heaven save us all from Dedicated House Monks.*

Red took a wide path around the center of the region where he knew Area 51 used to be. He didn't know if Brian had special consideration for the site rumored to house evidence of the government hiding real aliens. Possibly Saul had transformed Area 51. Red liked Saul. Compared to the other Machine Monks, Saul's relatively normal interest in real space colonies, or hard sci-fi, would be refreshing.

While most people would find the idea of a government base hiding evidence of aliens to sound ridiculous, Red believed it. After all, he'd worked for years on a similar hidden base housing the Actuator only a few hundred miles away.

Not knowing for sure what Brian or Saul had done to the site, Red decided against the gamble. No other flying saucers had shown on the radar and they were making good time now. So he led them around the perimeter of the media-hyped military base. Then they continued north across the barren landscape. Brian hadn't changed Nevada much. Instead of typical sandy desert with mountains of rock breaking through, it now had craters to resemble Mars or the moon with mountains breaking through the crusty sand. For all Brian's hype, Red thought the small change reflected a lack of imagination. To be fair it represented just one sample. Probably Brian had affected changes in jungles and other areas all over the world, which looked more exotic.

"Still clear," Dragon Star said from the other ship. "How's the cargo?"

Mack grunted at the insinuation. Red turned away so his monstrous companion didn't see him smile. "All fine here, too. Any guess where the next boundary is?"

"No," Dragon Star said. "I found a display against the far right which brought up a map of the local area."

Red located a square monitor and touched it. A map lit up, a small blue dot indicated their present location. "Excellent," Red said. "I think the stereotype about old people not being able to use technology is unfair and undeserved."

"I'm not that old," Dragon Star said. Red heard a kind of humility in Dragon Star's voice, and remembered in Korea they valued elders instead of youth. "The map ends about two-thirds of the way up the state of Nevada, just past Reno."

"That's probably where the boundary is. We should be there soon."

"Maybe we should fly lower?" Dragon Star suggested and asked at the same time.

"In case it turns into another carriage or something which can't fly," Red nodded. "Good point. We should probably bring the speed down, too."

He eased the throttle switch back and gently pressed the stick forward to bring them closer to the ground. With the ground so flat, it seemed safe to fly low. Then he shook his head. Red knew nothing would ever be safe again as long as the world remained fractured.

Mack's tail began clicking faster with anticipation.

"Maybe you should just try to stay human this time," Red said over his shoulder. He knew it would probably be pointless. The obsession of a Dedicated House Monk didn't allow logic to temper it. "We don't know what to expect, and if you turned into an orc or something out of control it could go wrong." A wave of guilt flushed over him as he remembered shooting Jackson between the shoulder blades to save Glass. He wondered if the haunting image would ever leave his mind.

He kept his voice conversational, but Red didn't try to hide reaching his hand into his jacket and pulling out the ray gun. He already knew it would be ineffective against this armored black alien. He just wanted Mack to understand.

Mack growled, but he didn't move. So Red kept the gun out as they waited for minutes and miles to go by. With the moon down, he barely noticed a forest as they approached it.

Even at reduced speed, the ship carried them fast. Red had no time to react before the change hit. White light, the rumble of static, and the taste of lemon cake with spicy barbecue sauce blasted him in an instant. His skin felt like a hundred nails had scratched along his arms and all down his back.

Cold wind blew into his face as the ship disappeared and left them exposed. They rapidly slowed, landing on a grassy meadow. The ships were gone. Red's gun had vanished and he held a mirror in his hand. Dragon Star had one, too. He had his white outfit back, but no swords. Mack stood hunched over like an old man, then he straightened up and stretched his arms. As soon as he raised them, he flinched and turned to one shoulder.

Above his beloved skull tattoo, an ugly black scab cracked where Brian had winged him. Red watched Mack touch the wound, then flex his arm and smile. *He thinks that's cool?* Red noticed Mack didn't have a mirror.

The hand mirrors looked like the kind women use for makeup. Mounted on wood, the oval mirror had a leather wrapped handle.

"What is this place?" Dragon Star asked.

As if to answer, a pack of wolves nearby began tearing the night apart with their howls.

CHAPTER ELEVEN

As the wail of wolves filled his ears, Dragon Star turned in every direction. He squinted, searching the trees for any sign of the animals. With the moon now set, the shadows gave no help to his eyes, still adjusting to the deep darkness.

He watched Red trying to put the mirror into his jacket pocket, but failing. The jacket, like the rest of Red's clothes, had become soft, brown leather. He looked like a mountain man. The interior pocket was too small to hold the top of the wood framed mirror, and putting the long handle in made it likely the mirror would just fall out.

Dragon Star noticed his own clothes had become a coarse, beige robe with a braid of leather tied around the middle. The absence of his katana didn't bother him. The swords would come back at the next border. Besides, if nobody had weapons he felt confident his tae-kwon-do would carry him through any fight.

"We should make a fire," Mack said. He had tied bones running up and down the front and back of him like a barbaric armor. Naturally, his arms remained bare. Dragon Star found the strength without training to be laughable. Muscled arms meant nothing if you had no discipline to use them. Yet this buffoon kept his shoulders bare as a challenge to everybody around him, and now he had some kind of dark ceremonial garb. Dragon Star couldn't think of a Machine Monk more different from himself. They were the yin and yang of Actuator users.

"Wolves do hate fire," Red said, looking at Dragon Star.

Dragon Star respected Red as a leader. Red never used his position to exert his will, and he constantly looked for advice.

Twirling the mirror in his hand, Dragon Star said, "I do not think there is time. Also, I do not think these are normal wolves."

Red looked at his mirror, too.

"So why don't I have a mirror?" Mack asked.

"You didn't have a gun or sword," Red offered.

"I do not think they are weapons," Dragon Star said.

They moved closer together to examine the two devices. Another howl echoed in the chill air. Red and Dragon Star looked at each other with pinched brows. When he looked over his shoulder, he saw Mack smiling. Dragon Star wondered, *Was Mack so out of balance he enjoyed being viewed as prey?*

Dragon Star looked over the mirror before handing it to Mack. A thick oval of glass with silver painted roughly on the back left black smears at the edges. The wood reached around in five places as if a clawed hand grasped the pane. The handle, wrapped with leather, had two silver beads dangling from the tied ends.

"What does it mean?" Mack asked.

"I think we will soon find out," Dragon Star said.

Five huge canines slinked out between dark tree trunks. With red, gray, and black fur, their hackles raised as they slowly pawed forward with bared fangs. Big as black bears, these wolves had more muscle around the chest and shoulders than normal animals.

Red held the mirror in front, as if it were a knife. Dragon Star took his mirror back and tucked it into his belt. He stretched his neck and knees, assuming a defensive stance. His attempts to appear non-threatening were lost on Mack.

"Here puppy, puppy!" Mack clapped his hands together. He had a big dumb grin on his face.

The wolves stopped advancing a few paces away, standing next to each other like linesmen on a football team. Occasionally one of the beasts at either end would break off, make a quarter circle around one side, and then return. They clearly meant for the group of men to stay put.

Dragon Star began breathing purposefully. He cleared his mind, focusing on the movement of the monsters before them. Strangely, he felt no fear. He wouldn't have been ashamed to feel it. In that moment of clarity, he knew the loss of the other Empty House Monks had left a hole in his heart. His purpose, snatched in a moment of insanity, left only anger and disgust.

"What is this place?" Red asked quietly.

"I like it," Mack said.

If he had been an Empty House Monk, Dragon Star would be smacking him in the back of the head right now. "He means, how has this place been changed?"

"I know what he means," Mack said.

"Well do you know the answer?" Red asked.

"It's not mine," Mack said. "It's not Hanna's, either. If it was, those would be werewolves."

One of the oversized creatures then began to change. Standing up from beneath the black wolf as if the pelt had been nothing more than a costume, a bronze skinned man beneath a black wolf hat raised up. He wore a chest plate made of lashed wood and had a feather tied to his long hair where it came out beneath the hood.

"Maybe it's one of Hanna's," Mack said, unphased by what they saw.

Dragon Star bowed in greeting. The American Indian bobbed his head, to return the gesture. The other wolves began growling more. The red one in the center barked once.

Red lifted the mirror and his other hand to try to indicate they wanted peace. Then the gray wolf on the end transformed, too. This one turned into an older man with deep wrinkles in his face. His gray wolf hat had spots where the hair had rubbed off, as if he'd worn it for many years.

Dragon Star bowed again, but the old man didn't notice or care. He had a blue plaid shirt on, through which he scratched his chest.

"Hello," Red said. "We're just passing through. We need to head north of here."

"The way of death," the old man said. It wasn't a prophecy. Just something he stated with his raspy voice as if talking about the weather.

A black bird swooped between the two groups, drawing the attention of men and beasts. It twisted behind the group of three men, and landed softly on the ground. Red and Mack ignored it, concentrating on keeping eye contact with the pack before them. The three remaining wolves spread out so they were each staring down one of the intruders. Dragon Star turned and glanced at the bird. Suddenly, a body of leather and human skin sprung up beneath the black feathers, which grew down into long hair.

With lightning and thunderbird symbols beaded onto a leather blouse, the woman before him had a familiar face. A small medicine bag hung on a leather thong around her neck. He said, "Nancy Storm. It seems we have unknowingly wandered into your land."

Red and Mack twisted their heads to look at her, then snapped them back to the wolves.

"Nancy!" Red said. "Good to see you. Any chance these are friends of yours?" His pinched voice tried to mask the tension. "I was explaining that we're only passing through. We just need to get to the northwest. Any chance you can put in a good word for us here?"

Nancy kept her mouth straight even though her face seemed to be smiling. "I cannot do that," she said. "All who enter these lands must undergo the trial of their spirit or be destroyed."

"What?" Mack said. "Come on, we were just chatting last week at a party in Saul's apartment, remember?"

"I remember," Nancy said. "I remember you asked me to go back to your place, Mack."

Everybody turned to face Nancy now, leaving the wolves to their backs.

Mack said, "I stand by that. You're definitely hot. And seeing all this now, I'm sure we could get along just fine."

"I think you were just trying to make Hanna jealous."

Dragon Star again had to repress the urge to smack Mack upside the head.

"No way," Mack said. "She's got nothing on these werewolves of yours. If I'd have known you were into these monsters, I'd have dropped Hanna long ago."

Nancy didn't answer him. Her face didn't show if she felt complimented or insulted. Red said, "Look, Nancy, we are trying to put things back the way they belong. We just need your key. And we could use your help. The Actuator made a huge mess out of the world. People are dying. There are only a few of us who even know what happened. We need your help to fix it."

"The way things were was not right, either," Nancy said. The smile had gone out of her face. "My people and our traditions have been pushed aside for centuries while the white man builds oil refineries that blight the earth and roads which scar it. My people have been pushed back and put down and forgotten until they hardly exist. The old ways have been lost."

Dragon Star had one eyebrow up as he listened to Nancy. She usually spoke only in single, pleasant sentences. He'd always respected her for it, considering she alone among all the Dedicated House Monks had a quiet spirit. Now he knew the Dedicated House was a curse to all Machine Monks and it corrupted even those who had inner peace. All his respect for this woman fled as he heard the obsession poured into this long tirade.

"Our teachings and our traditions have been trampled beneath the heavy boots and iron machines of the foreigners who invaded our lands and desecrated our holy sites. Our men, they emasculated with alcohol. Our children, they tempted away with video games and movies. The few who remained true to the old ways have dwindled into poverty on reservations."

She raised her hands to the stars and spoke with even more conviction. "The one good thing the white man has done is to create the Actuator. Through it, our ways have been restored. The wilderness of our reservations has become fertile land and the loyalty of our people has been changed into literal manifestations of the great stories. We will not help you undo the only good thing to happen to our people in three hundred years. All who enter these lands must be tested. If you join us, you may live. If you fail, you must die like all the bad people who have polluted our lands for so long."

"See?" Mack said to Red, "That's hot, right?" The wolves behind them growled. This time it wasn't a threat, it was to protest whatever person or force held them back.

Red smacked Mack's bone shirt with the back of his hand. "Nancy, we've been your friends all these years. You know we're not responsible for the injustice done to your people. Can you at least just let us go?"

"It is not a choice," she said. "The rules of this place are set now. I cannot change them without using the Actuator. And I would not change them if I could. So many of the world's people live like zombies, dead inside to all that is important."

"I agree with her there," Mack said. "Killing zombies is the right thing to do." He turned to Nancy. "I wish you'd told me all this before. We really could've hit it off."

She ignored him, again. "This is a place of cleansing. Only those who have strong spirits may leave it alive."

"What do we have to do?" Dragon Star asked. He thought he knew where she was going with this. He'd seen some of her Actuations before. If nothing had changed, he did not fear the test. While he didn't agree with the penalty of death for those who were out of touch with spiritual things, he agreed with her in principle. Most of the world had lost touch with the spiritual matters, something they should hold in high and sacred regard.

"All you have to do is discover your spirit animal and change into it," Nancy said. "These wolves are the keepers of this forest. The human taint is not permitted here. Simply transform into your totem and you are allowed on our lands. Fail to change, and you will die right here, right now."

CHAPTER TWELVE

M ack wasn't sure he understood exactly what Nancy was asking. He really did find her incredibly attractive. He especially respected her choice of a raven for her spirit animal, or whatever. Anything related to Edgar Allen Poe impressed him.

Red's face had gone white. Mack could have guessed their new leader would take this all too seriously. Red took everything too seriously. Standing in the dark of night surrounded by wolves and shape-shifters, Mack felt a kind of exhilaration. The idea of some esoteric trial made it all the more interesting.

Dragon Star went over to talk to Red. A crash course in Empty House philosophy, no doubt. Mack put on his biggest smile. He flexed his arms, knowing girls really liked them, and moved closer to Nancy.

In a breathy voice Hanna had always found seductive, he said, "I really love this place. Honestly, I can't believe we lived so close to each other for years and I never knew how deep and interesting you were."

"You seemed interested enough at the party last week." This time she did smile. Girls always loved being flattered.

"I was genuinely interested," he said. He shifted to her left, up wind, so she could get a whiff of the musky cologne, which served him well over the years. "But honestly, if I knew this..." He turned and swept one hand dramatically, indicating the wolves and the dark trees. "I would have been after you so much sooner."

Seeing Dragon Star talking to Red, Mack caught a few of the old Korean's words. "This is not a time for pride or favorites. Think of your true self and find an animal with traits to match it. Do not try to be an eagle or a tiger. Be honest with yourself and find a real reflection of your soul in the animal world."

"You're not just going to be a dragon?" Red asked.

"That name is very far from my true nature," Dragon Star said.

"What do you think I am?"

"Nobody else can tell you that."

Mack turned back when Nancy said, "You are not afraid of the trial?" She had the half smile of a fox. Mack knew all this animal totem stuff had to be incredibly important to her. All his charms would only work if he first passed this silly test.

"Not really. I've accepted the dark side of my nature long ago. Same as you."

"Then show me," she said.

Mack thought for a minute. *What animal would she be most impressed by? Should I become a raven like her?* He probably would have chosen a wolf from the beginning except there were plenty of wolves here already and he preferred to stand out in a crowd. *What is the most ferocious, monstrous animal?*

As he mused about anacondas and crocodiles, he watched Dragon Star step back from Red. He pulled his weird robe out so he could sit cross-legged on the soft grass. Placing one hand on each knee, the old man closed his eyes and began to breathe slowly.

Every human and wolf watched as the black hair and dark skin slowly collapsed. A bubble grew up from beneath the beige fabric. Then the fabric became square. One end rose higher. Horns sprouted. A moment later, man and clothes disappeared, leaving only a large goat.

The wolves stopped growling for a moment. They began to sniff the air. Saliva rimmed their long snouts as a new desire gripped them. Suddenly a desire stronger than enforcing the code of the realm fought with their purpose. The wolves wanted to hunt and eat this goat.

Mack wagged his head. With a name like Dragon Star, how could he ever turn into a goat? Mack could imagine himself as a big horned sheep, because of the ram horns on demons. Even then, it didn't even come close to his top ten list.

Nancy held up a hand to the wolves. They turned their attention away from the easy meal and began growling at the two remaining intruders again. Mack had seen plenty of videos of wolf packs tearing apart huge animals. He knew these hulking, steroid-taking versions could end a man's life in seconds. He respected them for it, too.

Red sat down, copying Dragon Star. He still had the mirror in his hands, so he took a moment to look himself in the face. Mack resisted the urge to laugh. If Red had never tried Oriental meditation before, why did he think it would work for him now?

Mack turned back to Nancy. "Can it be any animal in the world? Or only animals from Indian mythology?"

Mack could see Nancy's face turn down. She actually wanted to watch Red? She turned and said, "I cannot tell you how many things are wrong with what you just said. I'm not from India. Clearly, if you look around, it's not just a mythology now. And we don't care where your animal is from."

She turned back to Red. Mack didn't like losing her attention, but he knew he could get it back when he made his change. He just needed a really frightening animal.

He watched Red look into the mirror, then put it away and close his eyes. Red didn't try to assume the full stance the way Dragon Star had. He sat with one knee up and his arm resting on it with the mirror hanging down. Leaning back against his other hand, Red took deep breaths. Mack thought it was more of a relaxation thing than a serious meditation.

Red stayed there a long time. Mack thought it had all gotten boring. He didn't know what would be going through Red's mind. Red probably thought he could find some kind of key hunting animal. Mack didn't let it bother him as he ran through his own list of animals. He really liked scorpions, but he'd already had an exoskeleton today. He narrowed it down to a tarantella, a silver-back ape, and an anaconda, when something interesting finally happened to Red.

Just like Dragon Star, his body began to shrink inside the clothes. Only this time, his jacket shrunk with him. Nothing bubbled up. Instead, the mountain leathers sprouted fur and turned dark. In a few seconds, the masked face of a raccoon looked up at Nancy.

She smiled her approval. Then one of the wolves grunted. Red bolted to the side and went up the nearest tree.

All eyes turned to Mack, as he felt it should be. The tarantella was out. He realized he wanted something big to put those obnoxious wolves in their place. A two thousand pound gorilla ought to do the trick.

Mack looked at Nancy and winked. She tipped her head to the side. When he finished this change, she was going to like him, he knew.

He didn't want to sit down and look submissive like the other two. Instead, Mack kinked his neck to both sides and stretched his muscles. Then he bent his knees and put his knuckles to the ground. He reached inside himself to the monster he had always nurtured there. He thought of King Kong and tapped into his inner fierceness.

Nothing happened.

Having transformed hundreds of times under the power of the Actuator, Mack expected this to be the same kind of thing. He waited for the light and sound to fill his mind. The growling of the wolves seemed to grow in intensity. One even broke into a bit of a whine. They strained against whatever unseen natural laws of this area restrained them.

"African animals," Mack said, as if it explained everything.

The smile in Nancy's face dropped. She said nothing, though Mack read a kind of threat in her lack of words.

"Don't worry, I got this. Hey, can I get a look at what's in your little necklace bag thing? Or is it private?"

"I will show you if you make the change."

Mack went back to the snake. It had been his first impression when she suggested a spirit animal. It represented everything he liked, from the Garden of Eden to the Vikings' Jörmungandr. If a raccoon represented Red, a snake had to be right for Mack.

For good measure, he sat down. He closed his eyes. What else had they done? The mirror! Maybe he needed one of those.

"Do you have a mirror?" Mack asked.

Nancy looked at him. "A mirror? What do you want a mirror for?"

"They both had one. Red was holding it at the end and looked in it before he changed."

"Mirrors will not tell you who you are," Nancy said. "They only show you what you already know."

Mack nodded. He closed his eyes again. He tipped his head from side to side, feeling his spine flex. He imagined it growing the length of his legs. He remembered the fanged mouth of the alien he had recently become and attached it to the long row of vertebrae in his mind. He knew this would work in an Actuation. He knew, deep down, he should be a snake.

He envisioned his massive jaw unhinging as he swallowed those annoying wolves one at a time. He imagined himself so large that nothing could feed him but his own tail.

Once he felt sure he had become a snake, he opened his eyes. He saw his hands.

"Did it work?" he asked, looking up at Nancy. *Had he changed back already?*

"No," she said.

"Are you sure?"

"Yes." More growling, fierce anger radiated behind him.

"I can do it," he said. He turned inside himself. What had Dragon Star said? Don't be proud, look for what you really are.

Mack looked inside, struggling to find his true core. He thought of ghosts, zombies, vampires, and werewolves. Was that it? Did he just have to become a wolf?

He had actually been a werewolf many times. He concentrated on his face growing long and hair sprouting from his strong arms. He connected with the full moon and the loss of control compelling him to hunt friend and foe with an insatiable hunger. The mewling of the pathetic beasts behind him annoyed him. He would start by silencing their insufferable noise.

Mack jumped up and turned to face the wolves. He would rend them with claws and fangs. He would destroy them. But they didn't cower before an alpha. They grew angrier, clawing at the ground and snapping their saliva coated teeth.

Mack looked down at his body. Nothing had changed. What was going wrong? Why hadn't he turned?

"I am sorry, Mack," Nancy said. He turned and saw she meant it. A small tear formed beneath one eye. He knew, even if she wanted to, she could not undo the Actuation. "I am so sorry."

CHAPTER THIRTEEN

From the tree, Red watched Mack trying again and again to change. A survival instinct had urged Red up into the branches, but he could still think as a human. His own moment of spiritual introspection taught him something about himself. He was a scavenger. Unwilling to commit to the mental discipline and single mindedness required of the Machine Monks, he had always lived vicariously on the side. He didn't regret the decision. He liked being a part of the Actuations without being mentally dedicated to a single ideal. Thus, he spent his career picking at the pieces of other people's ideas.

He wasn't a vulture. He had his own ingenuity and purpose. He was a hunter, but not big game. He hunted for the little pieces, which often turned out to be big in the grand scheme. He embodied the raccoon.

He appreciated Dragon Star's advice. Until now, Red had never seen the power and purpose in the Empty House. He never understood their goal. He hated the idea of being empty of thoughts. Now he knew better. He knew being empty of thoughts allowed them to focus with unbridled clarity on a single idea. It put all the power of an undistracted mind onto any feeling. Therefore, something usually ignored, like one's spirit, could be carefully examined. Red wished he had known these things about himself before.

The moment of self-realization distracted Red from being properly worried about Mack. When he saw Mack jump up and physically challenge the dire wolves, Red knew things were going very badly.

The snarling monsters advanced now. The American Indian men stayed behind, watching as if this was the natural course of nature and they had no desire to divert it. Despite his dire circumstances, Mack had a dumb grin on his face. Could he be so lost in his world of horrors that he would be glad to die at the claws of monsters?

Red didn't know if he should or could change back into human form now. He just knew he wouldn't let Mack face those wolves alone. Red leaped from the tree. He didn't know if Nancy had any kind of psychic control over the wolves. He knew she couldn't change the rules of this bubble she had made. It seemed like a bad idea for a raccoon to land in the middle of a clearing of wolves and humans. So Red aimed for the only thing he could reach from the tree branch and jumped toward Nancy.

As the three wolves spread out, pinning Mack between them, Red landed with a dull thud on Nancy's head. Her calm face twisted into anger and wrinkles as four tiny hands became hopelessly entangled in her previously straight black hair. Nancy turned around, reaching up to try and grab the large mammal. Red bit one finger and chittered. For a moment, it distracted the wolves. All Red's instincts told him nothing could be worse than for three giant canines to be looking right at a raccoon.

Into the void made by the distraction, a goat charged. Nancy began to say something to warn the wolves, but Red scratched her face and she stopped mid-word, turning it into a half scream.

Red watched Dragon Star in goat form rush between two of the wolves, past Mack, and butt his horns full into the side of the far wolf's head. The distracted wolf, twisted its muzzle the other direction, unable to stop the force of the charge.

Nearly thrown free, Red shifted so his belly stretched over the top of Nancy's head, not unlike the wolf hats her male companions wore. He twisted his feet into her hair for grip, and then scratched her face again. He bit her fingers once more as she twisted around to try and rid herself of the great pest. As she began to kneel, Red's eyes landed on the medicine bag hanging below her face and bouncing off her chest as she twisted. Suddenly his key hunter training kicked in. He knew that bag either held the key or was the key.

As she came down, Nancy leaned forward to try and smash Red against a rock with her head. Already moving toward his new goal, Red leaped forward. Grabbing the bag with both small hands, he bit hard in to the leather thong and snipped it with his teeth. His tangled feet brought most of her black hair around in front of her face when he jumped. Nancy misjudged and smacked her own head into the rock.

Yanking out the hair he couldn't take time to untangle from his feet, Red rushed across the ground. No matter what his intentions to help Mack, in this form he could spend his whole life and not buy more than one second's distraction from the huge monsters. So he ran for the trees, trailing the leather thong from the bag and black hair on his back paws.

From the safety of the clearing, he turned to see Mack and Dragon Star facing the three wolves and slowly backing toward the trees. Mack had a long gash down his not-tattooed arm and he wasn't grinning anymore. Red saw the wolves constantly turning to look at the blood dripping from Mack's arm onto the grass below. Dragon Star had turned back into a human, though he didn't look any more formidable against the predatory beasts.

Red knew it was time to change back. He wasn't sure how to reverse the process of introspection, which had enacted the first change. He just thought of being human. He didn't realize it had even worked until he looked down and saw the medicine bag had become much smaller and his other hand held a mirror. He absently tucked the bag into his mountain man jacket, next to the metal tube thing he'd taken from Brian.

As Red ran up to join his crew, he saw Mack hiding behind Dragon Star. Knowing Mack to be anything but cowardly, Red rapidly assessed the wolves would not attack Dragon Star. They were trying to find a way to sneak past and bite Mack without touching or hurting the Korean guard. Now using only Tai Chi, which he used to teach on the base, Dragon Star danced back and forth. He didn't even attempt to fight or counter the wolves. He just moved his body between them and their prey.

Red stepped in, blocking one wolf from sneaking around the side. His heart raced as the giant maw came close to him, but snapped shut before it reached his arm. Taking courage, Red joined Dragon Star in the careful retreat past the first row of trees and into the dark forest.

Red found he used sound to detect the wolves before sight beneath the umbra of thick leaves. Suddenly, he heard Mack cry out. To his credit, it wasn't a scream.

Red turned to see one of the wolves had gotten through from behind. Clamped around Mack's thigh, rows of terrible teeth dug deep into the flesh, bringing out so much blood they could see it in the dark.

Red swiveled and hit the beast in the eye with his mirror. Immediately, the wolf let go and retreated. A fountain of blood erupted from Mack's femoral artery. Mack clamped his hand over the wound and put pressure on it.

"Wow, the stuff's slipperier than I thought," he said.

Dragon Star continued his dance of defense, glancing over occasionally to Mack. Red began whipping the mirror around to hold the wolves at bay. They couldn't retreat now. They stood poised on either side of Mack.

"There are four of them now," Dragon Star noted.

Red didn't bother to count, watching his two wolves and keeping a hand or mirror in front of each.

"Give me back my medicine bag, Red McLaren!" Nancy's less than melodious voice approached a screech as her raven form turned back to human behind the harrying wolves.

"I'm a bit busy right now." Red twisted the mirror to block a thrusting nose.

"You cannot stop the wolves. They are not normal animals. Sooner or later you will grow tired. You had no right to take that. If you do not give it back, I will kill you myself."

"Sorry. I really don't have time to discuss it."

"Aaaargh!" A wolf had all of Mack's foot in its mouth. It snapped the sharp teeth down again and again, cutting through his leather shoes and mangling the flesh inside.

Dragon Star shifted to kick the wolf's face. "Now there are five."

"If you stop the wolves I'll give you the bag," Red said.

"I cannot," she said. "The only way to stop them is if he changes to his spirit animal."

Mack moaned. Red knew it would be impossible to affect a transformation in these circumstances.

"Transportation!" Dragon Star declared.

Red wasn't in the mood to make a joke about off topic conversations. One of the wolves nipped his hand, sending a streak of pain up from his smallest finger.

"The mirrors are not weapons," Dragon Star said. "They are vehicles!"

If Red had a free hand, he would have slapped his own face with his palm. Of course they were the vehicles. If they were weapons, Dragon Star would have had two.

"How do we use them?" he asked.

"Fast!" Mack cried out.

"You cannot use them," Nancy said. Her voice hesitated.

"The reflection," Red declared.

Dragon Star pulled his out and began looking at the world through the reflection. "There is not enough light here."

Red pulled Brian's metal stick out, hoping one of the buttons emitted some kind of light. There were a few strange sounds, but nothing happened.

"Give me the bag now," Nancy said. She reached forward to grab Red's jacket while his hands were full. Red twisted to the side and she fell in front of the wolves. The wolves stopped, barking, deferring to her until she could get back up.

Red backed up and put his head next to Mack's, holding the mirror in front of both of them. He angled it so the clearing behind them showed and with a few stars, he could see the tip of a distant mountain. "See the middle peak?" he asked.

Mack nodded. Then they both disappeared.

CHAPTER FOURTEEN

A cold wind whistled across the rocky mountain peak. Uncountable stars lit up the sky in every direction, even to the sides below them. Red didn't spend more than one second on the scenery.

"Too many stars," Mack said. "Not dark enough."

"Keep pressure on that thigh," Red ordered. He laid Mack's head down and lifted the leg up, looking at the other foot. The wolf had gnawed it to hamburger. Blood dripped off it, but without removing the pieces of the shredded leather shoe, it would be pointless to wrap it. Red grabbed it by the calf and lifted that leg, too. Lacking any rocks or wood nearby, he propped both legs over one of his knees and kneeled on the other. "I think we're going to need a tourniquet on that thigh."

"Those wolves were cool, though, right?"

"If you say so, man." Red knew Mack was in shock. "So tell me about the animal thing. You could turn into a big black alien today, but not a simple animal."

"I'm not a snake," Mack said. He started panting. "I'm not an ape or a snake. I thought I was. I thought…"

"We're still in Nancy's reservation area," Mack said. "You could still change. Maybe into a lizard or something that can heal limbs."

"I'm not a snake. Maybe a scorpion."

"Great, go with that. Try to be a scorpion."

"Too much pain," Mack said. "Pain's good. But too much… can't think to…"

"We need to get back to our ships," Red said. "We had supplies there."

"No tourniquet," Mack said.

"Can't help it. Sorry." Red pulled a strip of leather from the hem of his jacket. It tore easily where the needle had perforated it in a line at the bottom seam. He threaded it between Mack's blood covered hand and leg, then tied it once and pulled.

"Ugh," Mack said. "Not so tight."

Red pulled it tighter. "Don't take your hand off yet." Red took off his jacket and shirt. The wind bit into his skin, especially where liquid blood touched him. He shredded the linen shirt into wide strips and began wrapping the leg. The first pass he went right over Mack's hand. The second time he said, "Okay, take your hand off."

Mack didn't move his hand. So Red quickly knocked it away and rapidly wrapped the linen around the leg before tying it as tight as the tourniquet. He put Mack's hand back over the already soaked bandage.

"So forget about animals. What kind of monster do you want to be in the next place we go?"

Mack mumbled and closed his eyes.

Red reached over and gently slapped Mack's cheek, leaving red lines of blood. "No sleeping. Stay with me here."

"Cold." Mack's eyes fluttered.

Red pulled his leather jacket over the puddle of blood to cover Mack's chest.

"I think you really had a shot with Nancy," Red said. He pressed his own hand over Mack's to increase pressure. "We're seeing Hanna soon. She'll be jealous."

"Death cool…"

"No, it's not!" Red yelled to shock a reaction out of Mack. "It's not cool!" His voice echoed softly.

Dragon Star suddenly appeared by them, holding his own mirror out.

"I have a tourniquet on his leg," Red said. He still had both of Mack's legs elevated. His bare chest stung from the cold.

Dragon Star rushed over to Mack and shook his face. "No sleeping. You'll miss all the scary zombies coming up that mountain."

A single howl, very near, made them all flinch. Then more voices turned it into a chorus of doom. Soon a pack of wolves began approaching from every side. Red saw more than ten of them. His own mirror, with Brian's toy-like key was in the pockets of the jacket covering Mack.

"Get back!" Red screamed at the beasts.

They didn't even flinch.

Red felt Mack's leg muscles go slack over his knee. The blood stopped dripping. The wolves stopped advancing.

"The wolves left after you two disappeared," Dragon Star said.

"How about Nancy?"

"She did not seem happy. She will follow us here if she can."

Dragon Star began CPR, pressing hard on Mack's chest. Each time he stopped to breathe air into Mack's lungs, he took a quick check for a pulse. Red slowly slid Mack's legs off him and stood up. He wrapped his arms over his bare chest as a poor protection against the freezing air. He wanted his jacket back, but he didn't dare.

The wolves watched with kinked heads. Red wondered if they tracked people by their heartbeat and the confusing sound of Dragon Star pumping blood through a dead heart kept the monsters curious.

Eventually Dragon Star stood up. Red saw tortured eyes and a clenched jaw as sweat poured down his companion's face.

Through labored breath Dragon Star said, "He passed on."

The wolves retreated down the mountain.

"I've lost another one," Red said. He put his bloody hands up to his face and wished for tears. The stress wouldn't let them come.

"We did not make this place," Dragon Star said. "We did everything we could for him."

Dragon Star picked Red's jacket up and held it out. Red pushed his hands through. He put Brian's key back in the pocket by Nancy's bag and threaded the wooden bar buttons through the leather loops to hold it closed.

"Why so much death?" Red asked. "Why?"

Dragon Star didn't answer. They waited a long time, looking from Mack's body to the stars. Eventually Dragon Star broke the silence.

"These worlds the Dedicated House created were never meant to be real." Dragon Star put one hand on Red's shoulder, speaking warmly into Red's ear so a quiet voice could still be heard in all the wind. "They believed they were nothing more than fantasies. They never had to worry about the real life consequences before. The bad things in their stories were always meant to be overcome. Monsters were symbols for trials. They did not think real people would be turned into orcs or aliens."

Red picked up cold dirt from the ground, rubbing it on his hands and wrists to mix with the blood before scratching it off. "These aren't fantasies. They're horrors. All of them."

Dragon Star nodded. "Had I known the Actuator could have really done this much damage, I would never have agreed to be a part of it."

Red nodded. None of them had known. It had always been contained. It had always worked properly before. "What do we do now? Should we bury him?"

Dragon Star toed the ground with his leather moccasin. Red knew he thought how it would be impossible to dig a hole in the rocky peak. "He loved the night. I think he would want to stay there. We should not wait much longer if Nancy is trying to pursue us."

"She probably has a mirror." Red nodded. "Where are we?"

Dragon Star shrugged. He searched the stars for Polaris. "That way is north."

"Think these things can get us all the way to where we are going?" Red waved the mirror.

"I think we have to be able to see our destination in the reflection. With the curvature of the earth, even from mountain peak to mountain peak, it will be about 20 miles."

"That's still faster than Brian's flying saucers." By the light of the stars, Red searched for the farthest mountain he could see. "Sure wish we knew where Nancy's area ends."

"More than one jump away, probably."

"You see that tiny mountain, poking up between the two peaks of the closer range?"

Dragon Star nodded.

Red went over to look at Mack one last time. Mack's eyes were open, his head turned to one side. Red reached over to close them with his fingers, but stopped. He pulled his hand back. Mack would want them open because it's weirder. Crazy fool.

"Good-bye." Red pulled out his mirror, located the distant peak, and disappeared into the reflection.

Several jumps later, Red stopped. This lower peak had tall pines, which gave way to even taller redwoods below them to the west. In the dark, the gargantuan trees looked like a platform you could walk across all the way to the horizon. To the west, Red saw a large range of mountains, much taller and more pronounced. He knew they were the Cascade Mountains, running north nearly to their destination. The reservation started at the Sierra Nevadas. Since then, they had been hopping between volcanic mountains.

Red found a wide upshot of rock and walked over to it. He put his hands on the gray surface and leaned close, taking rest from the relentless wind which threatened to freeze him at every peak they had been on.

As usual, Dragon Star appeared a few seconds later.

"Over here," Red said. He waited for the robed man to come down and join him. He couldn't help but think how much easier this terrain would be for a goat and a raccoon. "You really can just go at the same time as me," Red said.

"I defer to your leadership," Dragon Star said.

"That's not necessary," Red said. "I'm not really the leader. If anything, you should be the one running things."

"If I am in charge, then we will go right back to the base and I will kill Karla or die trying. That is what I swore. That will be my fate. The only thing preventing that is you, as I am honor bound to follow."

Red took a deep breath. "I don't want any of this. I don't want to be in charge of anything. I don't want to be the one stopping you from your revenge. Who am I to be trying to change, much less fix the world? Everywhere we go people seem to like it this way. And they don't care if everybody around them is dropping like flies. I never signed up to be the leader, Dragon Star. I wanted to be a Key Hunter. See some cool stuff. Play in the fantasy worlds. I can't believe how this all turned out."

Dragon Star took some time to respond. "You are the only one who can. So you must. It is right to put the world back. People out there have no idea why their world has been turned into a nightmare. We cannot do anything for the dead, but we can bring some relief to the living. This is an honorable mission."

Red nodded. He knew they had to keep going. It wasn't like he could find a nice place to settle down and leave everything broken. "This realm of Nancy's has been going on for quite a while," Red said.

"I expected it to be smaller," Dragon Star nodded. "We have covered several hundred miles already."

"Let's hope she got everything from here to Vampire town," Red nodded.

Dragon Star laughed. "Maybe we should stop and find some wooden stakes."

Red smiled, but then it faded. "That's actually a really good idea. We keep going off into unknown areas, but sooner or later we know we will be up against Hanna in her Vampire Romance world. Do stakes even kill those kinds of vamps?"

"I do not know," Dragon Star said. "The rules of the realm will be whatever Hanna made them to be."

"Worst case scenario, we bring them some extra firewood," Red said.

He moved to a nearby spruce and found a dead branch, broken down from winter snow. He snapped it off and stripped the smaller branches away. Then he broke it so he had a piece as long as a hammer. He handed the rest of the branch to Dragon Star and went over to the tall rock they'd sheltered behind. He began rubbing the dry wood on the rough surface, slowly grinding it down to a sharp tip. Dragon Star followed his lead. They each made two. Dragon Star tucked his into his leather belt. Red held them with his extra hand, since his jacket pocket didn't have much more room.

To be honest, Red really enjoyed the simple task. He liked the physical exertion without adrenaline for a few minutes. His mind could relax and concentrate on the repetitive motion of his muscles. When they finished, Red looked at the sharp tips of his primitive weapons. "I really hope I don't have to kill anybody else." He still saw the crossbow bolt sinking into the thick vest on Jackson's green back. It brought a whole new wave of guilt, made worse somehow by Mack's death. He hated himself for it. And he hated the prospect of more. Regardless, if a colony of bat-winged monsters descended on them, he knew there would be no other choice.

Dragon Star nodded and put a hand on Red's shoulder. "Should we get some rest? We can start up again tomorrow in the daytime."

Red wanted to rest, desperately. He wanted to turn into a raccoon and curl up under a nice bush. He could even see such a bush down the slope of the rocks jutting up behind him. "No," he finally said. "Who knows what kind of craziness we'll have to deal with in the day time. Better to get by it in the night. And the sooner we can get back to Jon and the others, the less people will die all over the world."

"Okay. But consider your health."

Red laughed. The very concept of health seems pointless and funny. They walked back around the side of the rock so they could see to the north. The plethora of stars still illuminated their world. From this vantage, Red couldn't see any manmade thing. "You know, it's easy to forget how much of the world is still wilderness," he said absently.

Dragon Star nodded. "The danger comes when we let our spirits become manmade, too. People forget they are part of nature."

"You know, you're a really deep guy."

Dragon Star mumbled something like, "A thousand words." Then he pointed to Polaris again.

Red asked, "Which peak should we jump to now?"

With a shrug, Dragon Star said, "You're the leader."

Red rolled his eyes and pointed to a distant peak poking up from the vast sea of redwoods like an island. "Same time," he said.

Dragon Star nodded as they tipped their mirrors. Red still vanished first.

CHAPTER FIFTEEN

Thunder shuddered through Red's body after he appeared on one of the Cascade mountain peaks. He'd opted for one of the smaller peaks because it seemed farther than the big one looming to the east of them. With all the strange activity now, he knew he'd made a better choice.

Dragon Star materialized soon after. Each time it happened, Red noticed a faint shimmer, as if they really did pop out of the mirror's reflection.

Turning to get his bearing in the dark, Red had to watch for a while before he could believe his eyes. The taller mountain range to the side of them shot a flaming red rock into the air. The huge burning boulder lit up the night as it soared through the sky and then landed in a lake many miles to the north. The sound of splashing water and steam still reached them even this far away.

Red watched the mountain, searching for any sign of catapults, arms, or other means by which the massive projectiles launched. From this distance, he couldn't see anything.

"Look," Dragon Star pointed.

To the north, Red saw two more great mountains. From this distance, they were little more than hills. They would have been candidates for the next jump if not for the fact that the closer mountain range continued to toss flaming boulders in their direction.

Red watched the latest fireball arc high in the air, trailing smoke, which looked light blue in the starlight. It flew to this side of the river and crashed onto the ground, bouncing once before embedding in the dirt and slowly burning itself out.

"What in the world?"

The south range again lobbed a great rock. Trailing fire, this one hit a wide natural bridge holding back the lake and dislodged tons of earth into the trembling water.

"I suggest we stay far away from whatever is going on here," Dragon Star said.

Red tipped his head to the side, scanning the far side of the river for any feature they could catch in their mirrors by starlight, unconnected to these strange volcanic occurrences. As he searched, he saw a river beneath the natural dam leading down to a distant city. A few twinkles of yellowish light indicated fires far off. "Do you know what town that might be?"

"Should be Portland, Oregon," Dragon Star said.

Red stared at it longer until a remarkably close rock landing filled his ears and shook his body. "It's too small to be Portland."

"Who knows what conditions the Actuator left them in?"

Red nodded, turning back to look for their next suitable target. "How about there?" He pointed to an angular peak off to the west of the active range.

"I think that is Mount Saint Helens," Dragon Star said. "And it looks like before it blew the peak in the eighties."

Red didn't regret not studying geography. He never could have predicted the need for it now. He didn't know why the famous volcano did nothing while these other mountains he'd never heard of were spewing rocks at the river. Actually, he didn't care. Tired and cold battled for his attention. All he needed was a fast way out.

"There," he said. He pointed to a smaller bluff closer to them and still west of the geological nightmare.

Dragon Star nodded and they pulled out their mirrors. Red thought this would go faster if Dragon Star would just say what he thought instead of always letting Red guess the right answer. Red caught the bluff in his mirror and waited for the transport to take him.

Nothing happened.

Dragon Star had been delaying on purpose, again. Red tried a few more times. "It's not working. You try it."

Dragon Star tipped his own mirror. Again, no change. They continued turning their mirrors to catch the light from different angles as several flaming projectiles crashed and thundered before them.

"Have we reached the end of Nancy's land?"

"I don't think so, or the ships wouldn't still be mirrors. Would they?" Neither of them knew. "Well what do we do now?"

"Maybe we walk." Dragon Star tucked his mirror into his belt on the side opposite the wooden stakes. Red turned and began clomping down the rough mountainside, as meteoric fires crashed down periodically in front of them.

When the trees opened so they had a full view, Red could see they had no choice. The lake extended up to their right and a broad river flowed off to their left. The only way to keep moving north would be to cross the wide land bridge. It wouldn't be a problem except the path of the burning projectiles seemed focused on the tall stretch of earth.

Before they reached the bottom of the slope, a raven dropped in front of them. Red knew before she changed, they weren't finished with Nancy.

"Give me back my medicine bag," chirped the bird as it grew up into the black haired woman.

"How did you fly here so fast?" Red asked.

"Do not be stupid. It is not the mirror which allows you to move from place to place."

Dragon Star nodded, "It is any reflection. The Actuator constructed these as a compromise."

"So you just had to find ponds and shiny rocks," Red said.

"Give me back my bag."

"Nancy, we have to put the world back. Why can't you see that?"

"No, you don't. It is better like this."

Red held up his pointy sticks. "No, it's not. You killed Mack. It's your fault he's dead. Don't you feel any remorse for that? He was your friend!"

"He could not see the truth. He could not see the way. I did not tell you to come here. You did that. It is your fault."

"You made this place," Red said. "How many people lived in this area and died because they couldn't find their spirit animal in time?"

"It is the old way coming back," Nancy said.

"No, it's not!" Red stepped forward, hands shaking with fury. "It's your imaginary world. The world was never like this. There was never a time people could turn into totem animals. And I don't know what is going on with those mountains, but that never happened either."

"It is the bridge of the gods," Nancy said. "They are fighting for the love of Wallulah." She pointed to Mount Saint Helens.

"No, they aren't! I mean, they are now because you made them. But they weren't before. This never happened in real life, Nancy. You made it happen during the Actuation."

"That was not my fault either," she said.

"I know," Red said. "You didn't know it would come true. But all of us, the people from the base, we are the only ones in the world who know what happened. Everybody out there is dying and living untold horrors, and they don't even know why. We have to put it back. We have to stop the insanity."

"This place makes sense."

"Maybe," Red said. "But what about the places Mack made? There are probably zombies eating people's brains right now in New Orleans. Look at Portland!"

He thrust his hand out and waited until Nancy turned to see it. "It is still there."

"It's supposed to have millions of people, and electric lights. Do you know what's happening there?"

"No," she admitted. "My land ends just before it."

"Good thing, too. Or we'd have millions of people in Portland either dead or running around as squirrels."

"Why do the mirrors not work anymore?" Dragon Star asked.

"Because you have to cross the bridge," she said. "There is no other way across the river."

"You made the bridge a barrier so we have to cross it while mountains are spitting lava rocks at us?" Red clenched his fist, unable to remain passive any longer.

"It is from the legends," she said. "I just wanted them to be true."

"What about the volcano?"

Nancy hesitated. "After the bridge is destroyed, she will erupt to show her anger at the mountains. It is my own addition."

"So you are saying these fireballs will break the dam, sending a flood downstream to Portland, just before Mount Saint Helens erupts again?" His mind began to spin. How many disasters had the Machine Monks reset out of some kind of misguided romantic interests? Would Pompeii erupt again? Were Chicago and San Francisco due for huge fires soon? He felt sure the Titanic would be re-sinking anytime now.

"We did not know it would become real," Nancy said. "But since it has…"

"Enjoy it while it lasts," Red said. "Because this will all end as soon as we can put it right. And if you want to keep it this way, you're going to have to kill me. Just like Mack."

Nancy turned her head down and remained silent.

"You should come with us," Dragon Star urged. "We need help."

Nancy wagged her head. "I will not leave these lands."

"Then get out of the way." Red marched around her, leaving enough space for him to react if she did anything. She didn't try to stop them. Once they were down the path, she turned back into a bird and flew away.

Now that they were near it, the natural bridge looked much larger. Hundreds of feet wide and a quarter mile long, the water filtered through it naturally to feed the river many stories below on their left. Thick mud covered the top, punctuated with dislodged rocks and rotting tree trunks. Red marched onto it, only to sink to his ankles in the dark sludge.

"This will not be easy to cross," Dragon Star said. A fiery rock crashed into the water far off, splashing them with freezing mist. "Maybe our totemic selves will find it easier?"

Red smiled. He had to admit he wanted to spend more time as a raccoon. He peered into the mirror again, looking at his own face. Dark bags under his eyes and growing wrinkles testified to the stresses driving him these last few days. He reached into the simpler part of his mind again, and shrunk down into a furry masked rodent. The second time, he found it easier.

Dragon Star bleated a little as they began picking their way across the muck.

Fear filled Red each time a burning rock came near them. This form held a natural, irrational fear of fire. He tried to use that fear to push him faster, only once stopping to hide under a tree trunk when a nearby bomb lodged in the soft mud. They waited for the exposed dome to burn down, and then began picking their way across the treacherous dam again.

Whatever consciousness Nancy had given the mountains, their reach seemed unable to hurt each other. When the titans noticed the animals on the bridge, they joined forces to prevent the crossing. Fortunately, at such great distances, they had terrible aim.

Twice on the way, one of the two quadrupeds would bleat or chitter a warning and both of them dodged an incoming stone. Several times, water, splashed by the projectiles, drenched the pair. A great wave tore Red's his small claws from the soft mud before pouring him over the long drop on the far side. Only by fortune did he manage to tangle his paws in a tree root sticking out the side.

When they neared the far shore, a pair of boulders crashed onto the bridge. The fire began to steam and Red watched as a trickle of water poured into the new crater. Then, it worked around the side and into the next new hole. These shots left the liquid only ten feet from running over the side of the dam. One more boulder and the flood would spill over the tall cliff. The water would rapidly erode the entire earth bridge and bring it down. Then a volcano would follow the flood. Nothing could prevent it now. Nothing except taking Nancy's key back to the Actuator.

They cleared the far side, scrambled onto dry land, and changed back into humans.

"Maybe we should have gone around to Portland instead," Dragon Star said.

The mountains had returned their attention to each other, with most of the fiery bombs landing on the shore and in the lake again. Red couldn't get the image out of his mind of the water sitting benignly in the center of the land bridge. He wouldn't have felt any less concern for a ticking time bomb. "Let's get some altitude so we can finally get out of here."

CHAPTER SIXTEEN

Two jumps later, white light and roaring static overwhelmed Red's vision and hearing. The scent of musky sweat and sweet honey assaulted his nose before filling his mouth. His chilled skin, cold after a long night, burned as searing heat crackled momentarily across his body. He welcomed it while wincing until the fire faded.

Too exhausted from a long night of living nightmares, Red couldn't even enjoy the transformation. The once welcome and exciting change now added stress to his life.

As the brightness faded and the dark slowly returned to his eyes, the buzzing gave way to complex rhythm. His mirror disappeared. In his hands, he felt a thick leather belt. That clue told him he occupied another horse drawn carriage.

He pulled back on the reigns gently, to bring the team of horses down from a full sprint. A flutter nearby made him suspect his eyes hadn't adjusted completely to the dark road. Then, as the animals slowed, he realized the flutter came from the leaves of tall redwood trees, reaching high into the sky and blocking the stars with their dense foliage. As he slowed, Dragon Star's carriage rumbled by, narrowly missing a collision on the narrow dirt road. Slower at recovering from the change, Dragon Star brought his team to a halt a quarter mile further up. Red urged his own horses forward.

Coming slowly on Dragon Star's carriage gave Red a chance to examine their new transportation closely. Unlike the carriages they started out in, these were luxury vehicles with glossy black wood paneling and plush red velvet interiors. Brass gilding surrounded the curved cars over thin, efficient wheels. The teams held only black horses, equally dressed up in both ornate and gothic trim, which culminated in red plumes cascading back off each horse's metal faceplate to join their plaited manes.

The carriage windows rose to an arched point. The brass plate behind the door handle lent the final clue. "We're in Hanna's territory," Red said. He pointed to the telling plate. Dragon Star nodded when he saw the brass shaped into an ornate bat.

"Perhaps we should rest now," Dragon Star suggested.

Red nodded. "In vampire country, night is the most dangerous time to be on the move."

After so much guessing, it felt good to know something about the place they entered. He stood from the spring-mounted driver's seat to find his wooden stakes had fallen to the footplate by his now knee-high, black boots. He scooped them up and held them in the same hand as the reins as he climbed down the one tall step on the side. Small rocks poked through the thin leather soles of his boots. Pulling the reins forward, he patted each of the horses on the neck as he walked by. These were massive Clydesdale horses with white tufts by their hooves and sinewy neck muscles like steel cords beneath soft fur.

Now that he dismounted, he could see his outfit. His jacket had become a black-on-black brocaded tuxedo with white puffy lace at the wrists and frills down the middle. A fob-watch chain went from pocket to pocket. The velvet pants had elastic below the knee where they met his shiny boots. At least the boots had a row of silver spikes down the outside.

Once Dragon Star descended, Red immediately wished they had traded outfits. Dragon Star wore a floor length black jacket, split in the back like a duster. It looked like thin suede over a blood red button up shirt and black pants, which tucked into his ankle high boots. He had swords in red scabbards on each side of his belt. Beneath each handle, a wooden spike rested neatly in an auxiliary holster.

"You planned ahead," Red said.

"What do you mean?" Dragon Star feigned innocence as he raised his eyebrows.

"Look at that holster. That's not an accident of the change. You were ready for it."

"No reason not to be prepared." He smiled and patted his own lead horse on the neck.

Red looked for somewhere to tuck his wooden spikes. Except for the inside pockets, fitted neatly around Brian's RFD and Stacey's medicine bag on one side and his pistol on the other, he couldn't find a single belt or nook. These clothes wouldn't conceal anything.

He pulled out the pistol. It had become a small flintlock, single shot muzzleloader. He knew from training with Jon, these things were only accurate within a foot if your target stood fifteen feet away.

He tossed the spikes back onto the driver's foot stand and led the horses forward to a tree. "Do you think we should try to get off the road to hide?"

Dragon Star looked back at the now distant peak of Mount Saint Helens. "Probably. Although nobody with any sense would be heading down this road into Nancy's land."

"Still best to be safe."

Red led them through a couple wide openings in the tall trees. The umbrella above so completely absorbed the sunlight as to leave little growing on the ground. They counted on distance alone to secret them. Finding a few large trunks near each other to park behind, they put on the brakes to keep the horses from wandering.

"We do not have any feed for the horses," Dragon Star noted.

Red looked behind him into the carriage. "We have most of the food and supplies we packed into the airships. Several pistols and rifles, all single shot now. Some food, water, and first aid, too." His voice trailed off and he swallowed hard.

"I do not think any amount of gauze and tape would have saved Mack," Dragon Star said. "Those wolves were not natural. Even if we could kill them with guns, more would come. Eventually, our ammunition would be gone and they still would have taken him."

"I know," Red said with a heavy heart, as he backed out of the cab. "Why couldn't he just figure out his spirit animal?"

Dragon Star shrugged. "He spent his whole life trying to become something unnatural instead of finding what he really was. I do not think he had a totem, because his thoughts were always forced out of balance."

"Because of the Actuator?"

"Maybe. Or that is what drew him to it."

Red furrowed his brow before turning to the carriage. "There's no room to lie down inside these." He reached back in for a blanket and unrolled it on a sparse patch of clover.

"You will wrinkle your nice suit." Dragon Star gave a winning smile.

Red laughed. "I hope so. There's a blanket in yours, too, I assume."

"I can sleep sitting up just fine." Dragon Star went into the small carriage and closed the door.

Red could still see him through the window. Red thought stress and sadness might keep him awake on the unfamiliar ground in a cold night. However, exhaustion took him before he even had time to remember shooting Jackson in the back.

But he remembered in his dreams.

A vague, diffused light left Red unable to guess what time it might be when he finally woke. Dragon Star had brought out a blanket and now sat cross-legged in meditation with the long tails of his leather coat spreading out behind him. Red would have been impressed if the kink in his neck would let him care about anything else.

As quietly as possible, Red pulled out a canteen of water with felt covering the metal and little gold tassels dangling off the edges. It had been an oil treated canvas water bag when they packed it. He didn't waste time worrying about the different forms and shapes as he drank deeply from the cool refreshment. A basket, previously packed with apples, now overflowed with blackberries. Breakfast ended with biscuits, which now took the place of bread they'd packed.

"I'm ready when you are," Dragon Star said quietly, without changing his stance.

"Can you watch me psychically with your eyes closed, or do you peak sometimes?" Red asked.

"If there were elephants marching by, I could still hear you."

"Maybe when we leave this place you'll get your chance to find out if that's really true."

Dragon Star opened his eyes. "Are you not planning to go back through Nancy's territory?"

"If I didn't have to cross that dam again," Red said. "One more rock landing in the wrong spot and the whole thing will come down."

"I saw the same thing," Dragon Star said.

"But those mirrors are super-fast. Maybe we can come in from the side south of Portland?"

"Maybe." Dragon Star stood up.

Red had another flash of jealousy when he saw the swords and stakes only for a moment before the swooping coat completely concealed them. "This isn't the modern day vampire romance we expected."

Dragon Star nodded his agreement. "This is more gothic, Dracula-type stuff."

Red tossed his pistol in the back with the other antique weapons. He tucked the shorter wooden spike into his free vest pocket. The other he held in his hand. The wooden stakes had changed, too. Carved oak with lathed tips and ornate silver rings near the top, they'd become much more interesting. The rings even had small crosses etched into them.

"What is the difference?" Dragon Star asked.

"In the new version, Vampires are just super-models with lots of money and charm. Their skin iridesces in the sunlight and half of them are good guys looking for eternal love. The old school is much darker. They're the children of Satan with power to control people's minds."

"They all feed off blood?"

"Yep."

"How can there be a good version of that?"

"I don't know," Red said. "But from the look of things, we won't have to worry about sorting them out."

"At least we will know what to kill," Dragon Star said.

"Every human with wings or fangs." Red finished eating and began slowly leading his team back toward the road. Would he have to kill again? Would he have to kill Hanna? He thought how she was always so loud at parties and full of strange trivia. Despite her affinity for blood-suckers, nobody had been surprised when it didn't work out between her and Mack. He was the quiet, broody type. She had been more outgoing. He had big muscles and a sarcastic smirk. She had medium blond hair and dressed neatly. If you didn't know her well, you'd never know she was into the undead.

Thinking of Mack made him want to crawl back into the carriage and never come out. Instead, he did what Jon had trained him to do. He turned his mind over to the mission and blocked out emotions and negative thoughts. They needed Pete and they needed Hanna's key.

Once they pulled out onto the dirt road, they mounted the driver seats for the carriages. The dirt roads had more pits and rocks than straight sections. Although most of the ground seemed only damp, they rapidly learned the low parts turned to mud.

Slowly weaving along the awful road, Red asked, "How far do you think we have to take this road?"

"At this pace, it could be all day." Dragon Star kept looking up at the mammoth redwood trees rising to a great canopy of leaves above them. The base of one tree he passed extended wider than his carriage was long. He said, "Truth is stranger than fiction."

"Not anymore." Red said as he laughed. It cut short when one tire hit a sharp rock and bounced him so high he came off the padded seat for a second. "Thanks to the Actuator, the whole world is strange now."

Red tried to steer the horses along the less broken parts of the road. They didn't respond to micro-management. Each time they failed to take his direction, he ended up in a jarring bounce. He started to suspect the horses of doing it on purpose until he noticed Dragon Star looking around, completely unconcerned by the chaotic ride.

"Look at that." Dragon Star pointed with his eyes.

Red lifted his view. The trees rose so high he couldn't see the tops. Judging by the thickness of the tree trunks, they went as high again as what he could see. Red smiled. Only Dragon Star would be able to dissociate from the weird condition they were in to look at the trees.

"That's kind of cool," Red said.

"They are old. Thousands of years old. If we never put the world right, they will continue to grow. If we get all the keys and somehow manage to return the world to the way it was, these trees will never have noticed the difference."

Red let the older man's thoughts distract him from the uncomfortable ride. Once again, he found himself wishing for the zen which could carry him through so much stress and craziness emotionally intact. Once again, he found a new respect for Empty House.

CHAPTER SEVENTEEN

After a day of bouncing over rocks and holes in the road, Dragon Star no longer felt any interest in the trees. They stopped twice for food, and to rest their backsides. He kept to himself because he knew Red had been in a foul mood all day. Unable to raise the young leader's spirits, Dragon Star retreated into his own mind. He used the time to practice meditating among the distractions. Eventually, he stopped that and tried to watch the road. He found if he kept an eye on approaching disturbances, he could prepare his body for the jarring effects. A few times, he stood up, and absorbed the shock with his knees. By late afternoon, he felt battered and sore all over. Red's mood infected him.

"When we get there, I might put a stake through Hanna's heart just for putting us through this," Red said.

Dragon Star didn't take the bait. They left the redwoods over an hour ago and moved through smaller trees now. A light rain fell from the overcast sky. One drop landed in his left eye, causing him to wince. The ground had turned to sloppy mud, slowing their progress even more. Now they couldn't see the rocks, but the carriage still bounced over each one with a jarring rattle. The wheels sloshed back into the thick goo. Ugly brown dirt clung to the white fur tufts near the horses' hooves. These carriages seemed up to the task, but Dragon Star would never understand how people could travel this way. Several times, he thought of unstrapping one of the horses and riding it instead. Unfortunately, he didn't have a saddle.

"We should look for shelter," Red said.

"We do not have any food for the horses," Dragon Star reminded him. "If we can, we need to get there before nightfall."

"Get where?" Now that the trees had thinned, Red saw they had dropped into a small valley with mountains on both sides.

"Northwest." Dragon Star pointed to the right of the lowering sun.

The path led them northeast now. Despite the winding, it carried them generally the way they wanted to go. Twice they passed forks in the road leading off to small hamlets. Red chose to avoid those places. They had the road to themselves all day.

"Any idea how much farther?"

Dragon Star took a deep breath to force down his annoyance before speaking. "Maybe we will get a better idea once we get on top of the next mountain."

When they crested the next rise, the only break in the trees showed their path winding down the hill. The oak and pine trees, too dense to travel between, left their path unprotected from the cold and increasing rain. As the slope moved west, they saw the distant ocean. Near it, a tiny dot stood atop an overhanging cliff.

"Looks like a castle," Red said.

Dragon Star didn't answer him. From here, they saw the dark clouds over the ocean crackling with tiny white forks of lightning. With the wind blowing in their faces, they couldn't possibly get there before the storm. The horses stamped their hunger and irritation.

With the carriage still moving, Red opened the door and moved inside. With his knees on the bench and his arms hanging out the front window, he kept hold of the reigns. Dragon Star smiled approval at the attempted innovation. However, after travelling only a few hundred feet, Red stopped again and exited the carriage.

Before he mounted, Dragon Star said, "Maybe we can tie the reigns from one carriage to the back of the other. Then only one of us has to drive at a time."

Red nodded and put up a hand. Dragon Star tossed him the wet, leather strap and watched as Red tied it to a bar across the back. Then Red motioned for Dragon Star to take the first break in the carriage as he remounted the driver's seat.

Once inside, Dragon Star took off his long, leather coat and gave it to Red through the window. "You will probably want this." He handed back Red's brocade jacket, which had soaked through.

"Thanks." He pulled it on over his wet clothes and fastened it tight. The horses were already moving forward. Dragon Star watched Red urged more speed out of them as they descended the hill, until a big rock almost sent him flying of the driver's seat. "Anything back there I could use for a hat?"

Dragon Star fished around in the supplies. He moved the nearly drained canteen and a box of hard crackers aside. Finding a basket with fruit tied in a checkered cloth, he put the blackberries into the basket and handed the fabric up to Red. Red tied the fabric over his mess of dark hair, using one hand to block the rain.

Pulling his swords free of the sheaths on either side, Dragon Star sat back on the padded bench. The interior had much softer accommodations with better springs to absorb shock. With the steady patter of rain on the upper wood paneling and the rhythmic wheels bouncing first in the front and then the back, he found he could relax. He closed his eyes, and rested.

A loud flash and terrible thunder split the night and brought Dragon Star from his reverie. It had grown dark outside and the rain increased to a constant buzz on the roof.

"Time to switch," he called up to Red. No answer. He called louder, "Time to switch!"

Red pulled the horses to a stop, cranked the brake, and jumped over the side like a man recently brought back to life. Dragon Star opened the door, and Red entered with streams of water dripping off him. Red handed over the coat without a word, probably to avoid shivering when he spoke. He reached for the wet rag on his head, but Dragon Star put out his hand. "You keep it."

Once he mounted the soaked driver's bench, already feeling the cold penetrate deep, Dragon Star called back, "Any idea how far?"

"No," Red said. "Can't see anything unless the lightning strikes."

A fork of light split the sky to the right of them, temporarily showing gnarled trees in silhouette.

Over the next hour, Dragon Star tracked the horizon with every crack of thunder. He found the ocean and narrowed in on the cliff overhanging it. A few times, he even saw the castle. Over frozen, loud, and redundant hours, the image of the distant structure grew slightly larger.

Eventually the trees thinned and left plowed fields. Then the road had deep ruts with no rocks. The mud gave way to cobble stones when they entered a small town. Wooden buildings occasionally hid small lights inside, but nobody was foolish enough to be outside in this deluge.

Dragon Star knew every bolt of electricity might be the last thing he ever saw. It didn't bother him as he urged more speed out of the horses. He felt the animals behind tugging their resistance now. The horses didn't like being pulled along like nags. The storm didn't help their demeanor.

When the castle loomed only a mile ahead, he slowed the horses and stopped.

"What's wrong?" Red called up from inside. His voice cracked, still bleary after being jolted awake.

"We are near," Dragon Star said. As the lightning illuminated the tall, dark castle, Dragon Star wanted to stay away from it. Amidst the deluge of the cold and violent rain, instinct told him some of the shivering of his hands might be because of their creepy destination. "The horses in back are fighting us. Maybe we should find somewhere else to sleep."

"Where else?" Red hollered over the deafening rain. "Everybody locks their houses as we go by. This carriage can't keep the water out."

Dragon Star saw lightning reflect in the two inches of water running over the cobblestone road where deep puddles collected in the low spots. "I don't trust the castle." As he said it, he knew his instinctive worries could not hold up against the onslaught of the very real and dangerous storm.

Red mumbled something Dragon Star couldn't hear over the rain and popped the door open. He looked at the castle. Lightning destroyed a tree in a nearby field, which only failed to take fire because of the relentless downpour. "I see what you mean," Red said, "but there's nowhere else."

Casting one final look around, Dragon Star nodded his consent. His ears stung from the biting rain, and the hammering on his head and roaring in his ears gave him a headache.

Stumbling around the back, Red untied the other reigns and mounted the carriage. Dragon Star waited for Red to steer around and then fell into line behind. He knew Red hated his insistence on Confucian ethics, but relationships and respect were part of the natural order. Red needed to know Dragon Star supported him in every way, even if only by following through the rain. These small actions revealed the greater purpose in everybody.

Conveniently, Red's carriage broke some of the head-on wind, too.

During the last stretch, Dragon Star had his hand blocking as much rain as possible, trying to make out details of the tall structure. In the few beneficial bursts of lightning, he saw the castle front made of huge, gray blocks of stone with pointed tops on the windows. Except for the murder-slits around the corner towers, every window had black shutters pulled closed and locked. The heavy, wooden gates stood closed. Blood red tiled roof spires extended above each corner tower and several tall structures in the middle. At least the drawbridge remained down. Black flags with red bats twisted in the soaking wind on each side of it.

Huge ocean waves came from the disturbed waters, crashing against the seaside cliffs and adding saltwater spray to the assaulting rain. The smell of brine at least offered a welcome relief from the scent of wet horses.

The clopping of hooves changed when it echoed below the wet, wooden bridge. Red dismounted, fighting the horses to hold the reigns as he pounded on the wooden sideboard. The steady drum of rain on stone completely drowned out the sound of his hand on the spongy wet wood of the door. The last time he slapped the sidewall, lightning blasted the nearby trees. The roar further served to mute his knock. Freezing and frustrated, Red pulled a wooden stake from his jacket, turned the blunt side around, and used the butt of it to pound on the oversized door again. This time Dragon Star at least heard something.

After a minute, Red raised his hand to knock again, but stopped when a thin line of yellow light cracked between the two great doors. Dragon Star watched Red pulled his horses back, making room for the wide swinging gates. Two hunched over, wrinkled men in black, leather jerkins with the same stylized red bat on the front pushed the heavy doors slowly open. The rusted hinges screeched loud enough to hear above the downpour.

A long, stone hall stretched out behind the gate with rough fire braziers spaced out along each side. Black tapestries hung between most of the gothic lights. Another entry on the right stood ajar, letting drops of rain through the castle defenses.

One of the old men signaled for Red to bring the whole carriage in. So he snapped the wet leather line. The horses seemed more than happy to move into the dry space, shaking some of the water off their backs after they trotted through the gate. The same old man reached up timidly, with a feeble smile showing his toothless mouth.

Dragon Star's horses followed straight up, almost pushing the carriage from behind to get into the warm entry. Only by pulling them back hard could he restrain their enthusiasm.

Once Red dismounted, the man led his carriage through the side gate. The moment the rain stopped pounding on him brought immediate relief from the storm's abuse. Dragon Star didn't even try to stop the horses. They pulled in and started to follow right out the side, smelling hay and stables, which promised much needed food and rest. Jerking back to slow them,

Dragon Star reached through the window to grab his swords. He jumped from the still moving carriage and happily handed over the wet leather to the next geriatric door guard.

Dragon Star re-sheathed his weapons. He preferred his katana, but he could still appreciate the elegance in these long, slender blades the transformation gave him. The grip with a knuckle guard felt strange, though. He watched the ever-skeptical Red look out the side path to verify the stables connecting directly to the front hall.

Catching Dragon Star watching him, Red said, "We don't want to lose track of them."

"No," Dragon Star agreed.

Red pulled the wet medicine bag and electronic metal tube from his pocket. He didn't think the water could hurt them, but he wished he had thought to protect them from the elements sooner. He knew it didn't matter now, so put them both back.

The two spent several uncomfortable minutes dripping water on the stone floor of the hall. Dragon Star had to fight the urge to close the gates himself, desperate to be free of the cold and wet. He followed Red over to one of the braziers and joined in reaching his hands out to let the heat bring the blood back to his fingers.

Red pulled off the checkered, wet fabric and ran one hand through his hair, bringing a new patter of rain down on the floor below him to join the trickle already coming off his clothes.

Dragon Star pulled back his coat to let the heat begin evaporating more of the water from his soaked shirt. Trails of steam lifted off them when the two elderly men hobbled back in. They fussed with the gates for minutes until their arthritic hands managed to secure all the bars and locks.

Dragon Star felt a strong ambivalence toward these men. His instincts told him to revere the wisdom of the aged. They were close to their ancestors and near the time of ascending. But these two repulsed him as well. They reminded him more of mewling homunculi. He didn't like them rejecting the glory of their position.

The two moved up to them, hands clasped deferentially and bowed. Dragon Star returned the bow out of habit. Red, he noticed, didn't.

The two men turned to go down the long hall. Red looked at Dragon Star, then back at the two. One of the old men turned and bowed again. Dragon Star returned the greeting.

"I think we're supposed to follow them," Red said.

Dragon Star put one hand out. "After you."

CHAPTER EIGHTEEN

R ed followed the elderly gate attendants through a labyrinth of halls and rooms. He whispered to Dragon Star, "Good thing we didn't come late in the night and soaking wet, or walking this slow would really be uncomfortable."

Dragon Star nodded and gave a small laugh.

The slow pace afforded them plenty of time to look at the large banquet hall surrounded by torches and tapestries depicting scenes of torture. Red's soaked jacket hung heavy on his shoulders, dripping water down onto his boots so he continued to leave footprints for the entire journey. He went out of his way to avoid the plush area rugs when they encountered them. Like the tapestries, red trimmed them all and filled most of the patterns.

The place smelled primarily of soot, although a background smell of roasted meats made it much more agreeable. When the old men walked to a large promenade of stone stairs framed by ornate wooden bannisters, Red ran out of patience. "Do you mind if we just go on ahead here?"

The old man stopped with one foot on the lowest stair and turned to look at him. Then he turned back to the tall climb and let out a sigh of relief. Bobbing his head with a hollow grin, he motioned to the right and then moved his hand even farther.

"Right side, rooms on the right?" Red asked.

The kindly, pain-filled man nodded. His smile wasn't wretched if Red only looked at his light brown eyes. Red ascended the stairs rapidly, leaving Dragon Star to bow and catch up. Despite the torches, the damp air in the castle made Red's skin feel clammy. He found a hall lined with heavy wooden doors and pushed open the first one. A tall four-poster bed covered in quilts and animal skins took up the middle of the cold room. Ignoring the empty fireplace and chamber pots, Red moved to the small, wooden dresser. He found some generic beige clothes in there, which he assumed to be under clothes.

Dragon Star entered and said, "The next room looks like this one. Although the mural is better." Red saw a painting of a turbulent ocean with a black ship bobbing in the distant on the wall above the dresser. "Do you think we should stay together, in case they try something in the night?"

Red only thought about it for two seconds. "It's a castle. They probably have an army. If they want to hurt us, I doubt it matters which room we're in. It won't matter if we're together or if one of us is awake when they come." He knew exhaustion accounted for much of the rationalization.

A series of thunderclaps rattled the wooden shutters outside his window. The walls couldn't keep out the constant whistle and moan of wind.

"Probably true," Dragon Star said as he left, leaving only the grumbling storm as company for Red.

Red thought of calling him back, but decided exhaustion wouldn't let him keep a good watch anyway. He needed his mind to be sharp tomorrow when he met Hanna. Those platitudes carried him to change into the dry, coarse clothes from the dresser and burrow deep into bed. The steady drumroll of rain on the shutters lulled him quickly to rest.

Standing in a gray field of dying grass, Red stumbled on rocks every time he tried to walk in the silly boots. They felt fat and thick, so he couldn't place his feet without slipping on a rock. Nancy stood above him on the hill. She threw her black hair back as she laughed at him. Two fangs, stained with blood, peeked out of her wide-open mouth.

"It's your fault, Red McLaren," she said. "You killed Mack."

"I didn't kill Mack," Red said. Without taking his eyes off Nancy, he moved his foot to try to find a secure place to stand. "I killed Jackson."

"Jackson, Mack, and half the world." She pointed to his heart. "Was it worth it? For a couple of stupid keys, was it worth it?"

Red realized she wasn't pointing at his heart. She was pointing at the things he had in his jacket pocket. He reached in and pulled out a metal ring of old skeleton keys. The simple, iron pieces had been black once. Now rust covered the corners and seams. "These aren't the right keys."

"It's all your fault."

When he looked back at the keys the rust had turned to blood. In a black and white world, only the red on them had any color.

"I have to get all the keys," Red said.

Confusion made it hard for him to understand. Had he really killed Mack? He remembered lots of blood, and a crossbow.

"You'll never get all the keys," Nancy said, as she stepped nimbly down by him. She put one hand out in front. He knew she was going to push him. "They are scattered all over the world. You don't even know what they are or how many."

"I know some," he said. "I know there's one in New York. Or was it Washington D.C.?"

"You don't know anything." She smiled so the tips of her fangs showed.

Then, she pushed him.

Red dropped the keys as he slipped on the rocks. The gray world slowed down as he fell. He waited for his back to hit the ground, but instead he kept falling as if a pit had opened up behind him. Tumbling out of control into the darkness, he thrashed around in every direction, trying in vain to grab the ring of keys.

Red sat up in the cold bed of a strange room. How long had he been asleep? Minutes? Hours? He jumped out of the blankets onto the surrounding carpets. Then he walked off them onto the chilled stone floor. Noticing the puddle of soaked clothes on the ground where he'd left them, Red picked up the jacket and emptied the pockets. Returning to bed, he had the metal RFE, the medicine bag, and two wooden stakes. It didn't matter if they were wet. Too tired to think of any better solution, he shoved them under the pillow and curled up beneath mounds of heavy bedding until the heat took him and he drifted back to sleep.

Dragon Star didn't try to fall asleep quickly. With regular meditation he only needed a few hours of sleep. He changed out of his wet clothes, wearing only a long pair of shorts from the small dresser. He kept the sword belt near him on the bed. Putting one of the pelts over his shoulders for warmth, he sat up cross-legged in the bed.

The bumpy ride and torrential rain had kept him from clearing his mind properly all day. Now he finally sat in relative quiet and peace, but his mind wouldn't settle. A kind of buzzing nagged at the edges. He suspected the rain. However, in the past he knew rain usually made it easier to find his center. His nerves felt on end, as if he'd been in a room full of crying children all day. He went through several stages of relaxation, flexing and releasing muscles, then counting while breathing. When those failed, he tried concentration questions. Nothing would allow him to regain control of his feelings.

Refusing to sleep before he had some kind of mental balance, Dragon Star fought the exhaustion by letting his mind replay the recent events. So much had happened in such a short time. Finally, his mind latched onto the dragon. Commander Newell had burned down the building with his beloved students. Enraged, she destroyed everyone he cared about and all his life's work in a moment. With such a chaotic past, he had found peace on the military base, teaching the ways of the Empty House to Machine Monks. Their deaths brought him suffering he should never have had to face. It also proved his weakness. He should not love anything or anybody so much that it could make him suffer. Thus, she not only took away his purpose, she exposed his weakness.

Mack had been weak, too. Dragon Star played over the scene again when the wolves had been waiting in a circle around them on the mountain peak. Pumping the wounded man's chest over and over, he'd been thinking the whole time of his four lost students. He thought if he could save Mack, it would be something. Some life he could give back among all the death.

Once again, his passion left him open to suffering.

Dragon Star accepted the suffering of a broken heart as his just punishment now. He would carry another burden, like that of his fallen House Monks, in the regret of Mack.

The failed CPR didn't bring Dragon Star guilt. He had not caused those injuries. What haunted him was Mack's spirit form. At the time, Dragon Star knew his own form. Two of his four astrological signs were goats. And his own mother had called him an old goat nearly from birth. The guilt came because he knew Mack's spirit animal and failed to tell the young man.

Leading by example, he'd changed into his animal form with ease. Watching Red make the change felt like a victory. Mack was so confident. Too confident. Dragon Star hadn't wanted to see him fail. He only wanted to force the young man to face reality and really look into his own heart. Once he took the form of a goat, his mind was only half his own. Now, he knew he should have waited and helped Mack before changing himself. If Mack had been any of the Empty House Monks Dragon Star worked with, the test would have been simple. Dragon Star had not realized the extent of self-deception in a Dedicated House Monk.

The cocky boy had said snakes and scorpions. None of those were right. He flattered himself. His flattery was misguided anyway. Those animals didn't symbolize the darkness and power Mack craved.

Mack was a pig. His tie to American culture might dictate otherwise. For example, Dragon Star would have pegged Red as a monkey. A raccoon was pretty close to a monkey, though. Maybe if Dragon Star suggested a wild boar, Mack would have gotten it right and still be alive now. Would Mack have accepted the suggestion? Even knowing the answer, would Mack have been able to see the truth in himself?

Once he identified the imbalance, Dragon Star knew this had been the thing keeping him up. It didn't explain the strange feeling in his mind, like mental termites trying to chew the long strands of soft tissue from his thoughts.

Finally, Dragon Star let himself lie down. He heard the old man hobble in and take his clothes before he released his mind and allowed it to drift.

Cowering in a rickety carriage, Dragon Star dodged a clawed hand. It reached through the window and tore into the seat next to him. The two-inch nails pulled red velvet and white stuffing away before retreating out the window.

Then, the wicked claws came through a different window. Dragon Star dodged them again and again. Each time, more stuffing pulled loose and floated to the floor.

"Sit still, you little rabbit!"

Dragon Star dodged low as a spiked appendage rushed over his head from the front window below the driver's seat. He almost knew this woman's voice, made strange with venom and malice. He thought he might recognize her if he heard it again.

So he asked, "What do you want?"

It was a poor question, because it failed to note that wanting led to suffering. However, in America it expressed a common sentiment.

"I want your heart for dinner," the woman said.

"Hanna?"

He hadn't even seen her yet, but here she was, trying to kill him.

"Sit still!"

Dragon Star had never dreamed anything like this before. The noise of the rain on the outside of the carriage seemed to bore into his mind and unhinge his sanity. It upset him more.

Suddenly, he understood. The grasping hands were a diversion. The real attack was the sound, the rain, the fog—it dug into his consciousness and grasped at his thoughts, trying to seize control of his mind.

The next time her hand reached in, Dragon Star grabbed it and pulled. A fierce strength yanked him out of his seat. His arms both pulled out of the peaked window and into the rain. His head smashed up against the wall.

Pulled from his dream by a hypnopompic jerk, Dragon Star leaped up and ran into Red's room. Red thrashed restlessly on the bed.

Dragon Star shook him. "Wake-up. Red, you have to wake-up."

Slowly Red stopped thrashing and opened his weary brown eyes. It took five seconds before he recognized Dragon Star. "What? What is it?"

"Hanna. She is messing with our minds."

"How do you know?"

"Do you remember your dream?"

"Not really. The rain was pounding on the walls like a drum. I couldn't think. I couldn't get out..." Red's voice trailed off.

"It is Hanna. She is trying to mentally control us."

CHAPTER NINETEEN

D ragon Star waited for Red to absorb the news. The room remained dark and cold as thunder boomed outside, rattling the drenched wooden shutters.

"That horrible, little witch!" Red said. "She's trying to control our minds? You mean like a thrall?"

"I could feel her in my dreams."

Red shook his head before holding it with both hands. "How are we supposed to fight something mental?"

"Since waking up, I do not feel it as strongly. But it is still there."

"Are you sure it wasn't just your dream?"

Dragon Star didn't dignify that question with a response. "What do you want to do?"

"What can we do? We can't go forever without sleeping."

"We need to get out of here soon, then," Dragon Star suggested.

Red got out of bed, readjusting the loose shirt. "It's the middle of the night. Before we can go, we need to talk to Hanna and get Pete and…"

"She is probably awake now," Dragon Star said.

Red laughed as he pulled the things out from under his pillow. Dragon star had on a linen shirt just like Red's. They were both too large with long tie strings hanging down in front. Dragon star had his sword belt on. Red experimented with tucking the wooden spikes into his waist, but the material had no elasticity and he couldn't find a way to tie it right. Finally, he gave up and tied Brian's metal tube to the leather thong of Nancy's medicine bag. Then he put it around his neck and tucked the whole thing inside. The oversized tan shirt covered the huge necklace reasonably well.

"Do you think we should take the wooden stakes?" Red asked. "I mean, maybe diplomacy would be better. We are old friends after all."

Dragon Star rested his hands each on the hilt of one sword in a wide stance. He didn't intend for it to be an aggressive pose, but he felt on edge.

He suspected Hanna still probed at their minds from afar. He would never be comfortable as long as they were in this realm. "The Dedicated House Monks we've met so far didn't seem to remember we were friends."

Red nodded as he got out of bed. He held both the wooden spikes in his left hand. "Good point. Vampires are about power. Maybe she'll respect us more if we have some."

Dragon Star followed barefoot toward the door. He pretended not to notice the hair rise on Red's calves when his feet hit the cold stone. Dressed as they were, with no shoes, it would be hard to make Hanna see they had any real power. Obviously, she intentionally arranged it this way.

They continued along the fire-lit hall and down the curved stairs. When they reached the dining room at the bottom, he felt grateful for one of the plush area rugs between two broad tables to give their feet a chance to warm up a little.

"Welcome to Bathaven." They both jumped when a voice behind them suddenly broke the eerie silence.

Dragon Star recognized the low, gritty tone immediately from his dream. Red seemed confused until they turned around.

Perched atop a throne on a raised platform to the side of the dining hall, sat a tall woman with long, wispy blond hair in a blood red dress. It clung to her skin in a way unnatural for velvet. Black lace trim at the bottom rested above her knees, showing off her black leather boots with a dozen gold buckles each. She wore black, lace gloves, which climbed her arms like ivy, to meet the tight sleeves around her thin biceps. A tall, black collar framed her narrow neck and drew attention to two red scars over her jugular. Sitting with the light behind her, her face remained in shadow.

The image contrasted strongly with the dignified, business suited woman they'd socialized with for years. Dragon Star felt a sickness settle in his stomach. He couldn't understand the duplicity so many of his associates lived under. If she loved this dark horror, why had she spent so much of her time pretending to be an average, upstanding person?

"Mack sends his love," Red said.

Dragon Star sensed a deep sarcasm, which he appreciated in this moment, but loathed to indulge.

"Mack never loved anybody but himself," Hanna said with a scoff.

"That's not true," Red said. "He asked to join us explicitly so he could apologize and ask you to take him back.

"Too little, too late. What use would I have for another man? There are fifty of them around here."

"Are they all like your doormen?"

She tipped her head to the side. "They are all different ages, of course."

"Is Pete one of them?"

"Pete's here somewhere." Dragon Star could hear the hesitation in her voice. He suspected duplicity. He would always expect it from her now.

"We need to talk to him."

"I'm afraid he isn't available to talk just now. He's... tired."

"Tired?"

"He's not as young as he used to be. I think I took a lot out of him last time." She pouted in a coy way.

"He's too tired to talk?" Red asked. "We can wait until the morning."

"You underestimate me," Hanna said. Dragon Star tried to see through the shadows to detect if Hanna had pointy teeth. He could only see the outlines of her face and the backlit hair glowing gold.

"Hanna, what happened to you?" Red finally asked. "Only days ago we were all sitting around in the commons watching football and eating pizza.

"Football? Pizza? Could you think of anything more boring and pointless?"

"You seemed to like it then."

"Filling time." She waived her hand dismissively as she said it. "It's what all the Machine Monks did whenever they weren't in the Actuator. Trying to make the best of the mundane life and pretend you give a crap about anything else."

"Not all Machine Monks felt that way," Dragon Star said.

Another pang of sadness slowed his heart and let guilt threaten to stop it. Here, in the dark, before this deluded woman, he missed his students more than ever. Bile rose at the thought that so many Dedicated House Monks, responsible for the great mess the world had become, lived while his Empty House Monks perished in innocence. For the first time in years he had to intentionally subdue the anger threatening to overwhelm him. He unclenched his fists as he took deep breaths.

"You think the world might have been better if your house had been there for the actuation?" Hanna asked. "How pathetic. If Empty House had been in the machine the whole world would be erased now. Is that what you want?"

Dragon Star didn't answer. In his mind, he thought fondly of a world free of clutter and the endless toys of the wealthy. He believed in a simple life where nature and the bare necessities satisfied people so they could escape the stress of their burdensome lives and self-imposed difficulties. He knew she was correct.

Red said, "You don't understand Empty House. Neither did I, before. There's more power in it than you realize."

Suddenly, Hanna put up one hand and began to beckon Red with a slow, wonton finger. "Come closer, Red McLaren." The shrill of sarcasm dropped from her voice as she shifted to seductive lower tones.

Dragon Star watched without listening. He felt too much pain and sorrow to care about anything else. *How could all my life's purpose come crashing down so suddenly? What cruel twist of fate left me alive to suffer when my students moved on to their next incarnation?*

"You have a rugged handsomeness about you, Red," Hanna said. "I never realized how cute your dark hair was, even all mussed up."

"Thank you." Red stuttered, eyes darting to the sides with disbelief.

"I don't think we ever had a fair chance before. I was so pent-up. I lived my whole life split in two. I thought the way to balance was to walk on both sides of the line. And the only solution was to act prim and proper while secretly wishing to be powerful and bad. Do you like bad girls, Red?"

Dragon Star thought of the two women studying under him. They weren't so divided in purpose. They'd been focused and disciplined. They never had to pretend to be anything they weren't, because their principles kept their ideas simple and sure.

"I don't know," Red said. He looked to Dragon Star. Dragon Star knew his friend wanted help. He just didn't know what to say. It took all his effort to hold the grief at bay with intentional meditation, his chest heaving.

"I think you do," Hanna said. "You like someone with a little strength and power."

"Commander Newell had strength and power," Dragon Star said absently.

"What?" Red asked.

"She is a dragon now. But she had everything. She should have protected the Monks instead of attacking them. She should not have killed my students."

Red looked at Hanna. With the fire behind her, he couldn't see her face. But she sat forward on her chair with each hand grasping a carved bat at the end of the armrests.

"That is where we should be," Dragon Star said. "We need to kill that dragon." He could see clearly now. All these side trips were a distraction. He should never have allowed anything to get in the way of fast retribution. It would be the only way to balance his life now.

"Are you okay?" Red asked.

"I am fine," Dragon Star said.

"Well, you have a kind of charm, but Red's really the fine one here," Hanna said.

"None of this matters," Dragon Star said. He sat down on the nearby bench. "I have failed. Nothing else we do will fix that."

Red put one hand on Dragon Star's shoulder and looked at him until his friend returned his gaze.

Dragon Star thought those brown eyes reminded him of another of his students.

Red leaned over and whispered, "She's messing with your mind." Then he turned to Hanna. "Are you making him feel this way?"

As soon as he heard it, Dragon Star knew it was true. Distracted by Hanna, he'd neglected to keep his mind empty and she'd twisted his deepest feelings against him. He ground his teeth and clenched his fists again. Then he let it go. She would use that against him, too. He had to keep his mind clear.

"I think you'd make a nice prince, Red," Hanna said. If she noticed the change in Dragon Star, her voice didn't give it away. "Come closer so I can get a better look at those beautiful eyes."

CHAPTER TWENTY

ed let go of Dragon Star's shoulder and turned to face Hanna. *She really thought his eyes were beautiful?* He glanced at a large mirror on one wall, disappointed the low light prevented him from verifying her compliment.

"I think you might be the kind of guy I could get used to sharing with." Hanna stood and turned to the side so he could see her face and body in silhouette. "I'll need another throne, of course. But I have plenty of people for that kind of thing."

"With so many men, why would you pick me?" Red asked. His insecurities and lack of success with women seemed to well up. If this one really liked him, he wanted to see where that would go. He liked this castle, too.

"I was too repressed before to say it, but I've always liked you," Hanna confessed. She stepped down from the raised platform, tipping her backlit head to one side. Red remembered her face with a pert chin. Now her skin, unnaturally pale, contrasted with her blood red lips. She had a tight smile, which only occasionally broke into a laugh. "I have a huge crush on you, Red."

Red couldn't believe it. He'd always wanted someone to share his life. Hanna had always been nice. If Mack hadn't been entangled with her, Red might have let himself think of her this way before. "I really like your dress."

"Really?"

"And the boots. They go well with the gloves."

"Thanks! Most men don't notice clothes at all."

"I don't usually," Red said. He watched her move forward until only the wide, formal table separated them.

Dragon Star stood up behind him, but Red kept his attention on the alluring woman he'd overlooked for far too long. His feet moved forward toward the lovely creature beckoning him until a long table blocked his way.

He resented being pulled from the magical moment to choose whether he should waste time going around or look silly jumping over it.

"I think it's time you and I got to know each other better," Hanna said.

"Ask me anything."

Unwilling to remain apart from her, Red stepping onto one of the wooden benches, glancing at the table for empty space between pewter dishes and crystal goblets.

Hanna put one finger on her lips. "What is your darkest, most secret fantasy?"

Without a pause, Red couldn't remember any fantasies. He was enjoying this moment too much to drag up something imaginary. When he neared her, she put out one hand. He pulled it, propelling her into his arms. Leaning in slowly, he rested his lips against hers. She sighed in his arms. A kind of mental electricity burst through his brain. He'd never felt anything so disarming. There was nothing he would keep from her.

Suddenly, Dragon Star grabbed Red's arm and pulled him away.

"You forgot Xenwyn," Dragon Star said.

"The dwarf?" Red asked.

"Xenwyn is a dwarf?" Hanna broke into a deep laugh, throwing her head back. The sounds echoed through the hall. When she did, Red saw two sharp fangs where her canine incisors should be. "Serves her right!"

Confusion spread through Red's mind. He couldn't deny what he felt was a kind of dedication and love he'd never imagined possible. It was a warm elixir seeping through his veins and compelling him toward her as if attracted to a magnet. Yet he knew he shouldn't feel those things.

Only thinking of Xenwyn made any difference. He really hoped things might work out with her, if she ever managed to get back to full size. And Hanna didn't love him. She wanted to play with him the way a cat might tease a mouse before killing it.

"It's not funny," Red said, suddenly sobered. He wondered if Hanna could read his secret fantasy from his mind and she knew it already. He felt embarrassed and used. He compensated by snapping, "That's just one more thing wrong with the world."

"Take a number," Hanna said. His breaking free of her spell didn't upset her in the least. She didn't even seem surprised.

"We need your help," Red said. He wanted to say a lot more.

"Of course you do. But I can't think of any good reason to offer it."

Dragon Star interrupted. "We have been your friends. Now you have us standing here in the cold as if we were beggars you brought in out of the storm."

"Friends? You were all like Mack. You only liked me because I pretended to be one of you. None of you knew the real me. None of you even cared."

"Mack tried to get to know the real you," Red said. He hated negotiating with her now. Her presence nauseated him and he stepped back to get some distance. "After the last Actuation he wanted to come here and try to reconnect. According to him, the two of you broke up because you became interested in romance and he wasn't the right guy for it, but seeing how Gothic this place is now, I'm sure it would have worked out. If we didn't know the real you back at the base, it was because you were hiding it from us, not because we didn't care."

Hanna turned to the side so her straight nose showed against the glowing hair. "I guess I just wanted to be loved. But Mack doesn't love anybody but himself."

"That's why you took up with Pete?" Red asked.

"Pete was just a rebound fling. It's over now. Where's Mack? If he wanted to come beg me to take him back, why isn't he with you?"

Red paused, so Dragon Star stepped forward. "He's dead. Wolves attacked him and he bled out on top of a mountain before he could get here."

Hanna turned to look at Dragon Star. The reflection of fire made her eyes glow red for a moment. She looked demonic.

"Pity. I would have enjoyed throwing it in his face if he begged me to take him back. A weak mind like his would probably join all the others, simpering at my beck and call."

"That's what you wanted?" Red asked. "You could have made a piece of the world into anything and all you wanted was for men to do your bidding?"

"There's a lot more to it, of course. I have other realms, too. I'm much more complex than this Gothic fancy." Hanna laughed. "This was the closest one."

"We expected a teen heartthrob scene," Red confessed.

"After Mack, I knew it was all fake. The only thing that really matters is power. Love is just another way to get it."

"So bitter," Dragon Star said.

"Who are you to judge what I want out of life? I thought you were a Machine Monk and a Key Hunter, not the morality police."

Red said, "Then please give me the key and let us talk to Pete. Then we'll be on our way and leave you to your conquests." As he said it, Red held his hands out diplomatically.

Hanna's eyes fixed onto the wooden spikes still clasped in the other hand. "It doesn't look like you came here expecting me to play nice."

Red quickly changed the subject. "Mack is dead! Wolves tore him up. I held him in my arms as he bled out on the top of a mountain. Dragon Star performed CPR, but we couldn't save him."

"What a waste," she said. "I bet his blood was sweet, despite his spicy personality. He was never strong enough to really commit."

"That's not funny, Hanna."

"I wasn't joking." She straightened her dress. "Did you really think I was going to hand over my key and my pet because you walked in here with a sad story?"

"Your pet?" Dragon Star asked.

Hanna ignored him, stepping back up to the platform where her face disappeared into the shadows. "Do you think a couple of sharp sticks will hurt me?" She put out one hand and curled her fingers. Red felt his arm spasm, his fingers cracking painfully open against his will.

Dragon Star reached under his shirt and grip the handle of his sword. Red fought the strange force prying his muscles open. It felt like Hanna was crushing his hand from the inside.

One wooden stake fell from Red's shaking grip, making a loud crack as it bounced off the wooden bench and then fell to the soft carpet at their feet.

"What are you doing?" Red asked. His voice waivered under the strain of maintaining his grasp. "We haven't done anything to you." Sweat beaded on his chest as he struggled with the unseen force. *Was she in his head doing this? Could she control his hand from the outside?*

"You think I'm the kind of person to wait until other people act first?" Hanna almost laughed. She clenched her fingers into a fist. Against all his will, Red dropped the second stake.

"Where is your honor? Where is your loyalty?" Dragon Star asked.

Turning her attention on him, Hanna smiled. "I'm the object of loyalty now. I give it to no one."

"Then you will never have friends or love. How does darkness and blood make up for the only good thing in life?"

"You were never my friends. You only liked me as long as I lived in your world and played by your rules."

"It wasn't *our* world," Red said. He clutched his left fist with his right to try and reduce the pain. "That was *the* world. That was reality. This," he indicated the castle around them, "this is all wrong."

Hanna scoffed. "Right and wrong. How droll."

"This isn't a joke. Hanna, people all over the world are dying. Maybe billions of people are dead already."

She tilted her head. "What do I care about people? Does it concern you if plants or fish die?"

"You're not a vampire," Red said. "You're a person like us. You're deluding yourself if you think any of this is real. It's just another exercise you did in the Actuator. It can't stay like this."

"Why not?"

"We have to put it back."

Hanna laughed so loud it echoed down the halls. She stepped closer, sneering so light played down the length of her shiny fangs. "You think you can *put it back*? That's preposterous. The billion have died already. The world is adjusting to the new way. It will reach equilibrium again and then life will go on. If you *put it back* now, it will make it worse. People will start a new struggle to grasp for the power left unguarded by the loss of so many dead. Another wave of people will die because Red McLaren and Choi Yeong-kyeong thought they could put it back. You already saw you are powerless against me. I will not give you my key so you can do more damage and bring more death. You could never take it from me. So you will never be able to put the world back. And by stopping you, I will actually prevent more deaths, which you are too naïve to see."

Red staggered, dropping down to sit on the wooden bench. How could he have been so blind? Of course, she made perfect sense. People would already be adjusting to the new situation. Another change would make everything worse.

"She is controlling your mind again," Dragon Star said softly, patting Red on the shoulder.

Red knew neither of them would still be standing if they hadn't come here together.

Hanna stepped back and sat on her throne.

Dragon Star drew a sword and said, "You will give us the key." The firelight gleamed along the sharp edge of his weapon as he pointed it toward her face. "Or the last blood you taste will be your own."

CHAPTER TWENTY-ONE

Hanna screamed, "Guards!" Red wanted to cover his ears, but his hand still throbbed.

Dragon Star thrust forward with his sword, trying to pin her chest against the wooden throne. Before the blade entered, she disappeared in a cloud of black smoke, leaving only the echo of her piercing sound behind.

Red watched as Dragon Star pulled the sword free. He slashed through the swirling gases, only hastening the dissipation. For good measure, Dragon Star pulled out a wooden stake and stabbed the point of it into the noxious fumes as well.

"How did she do that?" Red asked. He felt an acute loss when she disappeared, as if the only person he could ever love had died. "One minute I was fine and the next she sucked the will to live out of me."

Before Dragon Star could answer, the stomping of metal boots filled the room. A dozen armored men with halberds and long swords marched in. They filled the room, covering every exit. Marked with the red bat on fields of black, the few faces not hidden by helmets made it clear they weren't prepared to discuss the matter.

"Drop your weapons," the armored man next to the stairs ordered. Red held up his hands. He watched Dragon Star struggle inside, trying to decide if he could take this whole group or not.

"Just do it," Red said. He respected the skills of the Korean, but he doubted they would be enough against Hanna's mind-puppets. Mostly, he knew he couldn't bear to watch another one of his friends die.

Dragon Star dropped the sword and stake. They clanged as they hit the stage. He raised his hands as well. Red averted his eyes, hoping against reason the guards wouldn't notice the other sword on Dragon Star's belt.

The soldiers efficiently moved in, creating a wall of weapons and armor. As they advanced, they pushed the two men toward the stairs. The group shifted once they moved out from between the tables and forced them behind the promenade. One of the geriatric old men waited behind the stone slope, holding open a black wooden door.

A smell of moldy, damp air hit them as the sharp steel moving toward the two urged them down the creaking wooden steps. With less light than the already dim dining hall, Red had to watch each step. The low ceiling forced him to bend at the waist in order to keep from cutting his head open on the roughly hewn rock. Unlike the castle above, this stairwell looked carved into the earth instead of constructed. Then somebody put wooden stairs in as an afterthought.

When they came out at the bottom, the ceiling raised just enough for Red to stand. A lone gas lamp protruding from one wall provided the only light. Metal bars on three sides each had gates entering into small cells. A dungeon?

"This is crazy," Red said. "We haven't broken any laws." Two swords reached out and threatened to stab him if he stopped moving. He passed the side doors, moving through the end gate into the largest cell. An older man lay on the ground, a thick, black metal cuff clamped and locked around his ankle.

Once the others were inside the cell, one of the guards pulled the gate closed and twisted an iron key. He handed it to another guard and said, "Take this to Lady Gregory."

"Key," moaned the man on the floor. Red looked down to see his frizzy, dark hair streaked with gray. The man looked sick as if every movement cost a great amount of energy.

Dragon Star opened his eyes wide and pointed at the guard leaving the small dungeon.

Key! Red nodded quietly. Then he squinted his eyes and looked down again. How would this man know about the key? "Pete?"

"Ugh."

Red dropped to his knees and rolled back the man's head. Through glossy eyes, the aged and weak face of Peter Thorstenstein returned his gaze.

"What happened to you?" Red asked. He began brushing dirt off the older man's shoulders.

"Han-na." Pete closed his eyes and began to snore. Red realized Pete couldn't leave this room even without the chain holding him in place. Dragon

Star pointed and Red looked down. Pete had two red holes on the side of his neck. Unlike Hanna's, these were new and raw. They both looked infected.

"He needs medicine," Red said to the guard who remained on duty. "Look at his neck. He could die from this infection."

The guard scoffed. "He's lucky. I only hope someday she favors me with that honor."

Dragon Star looked at the guard and back to Red. He didn't move or turn his body. From this angle, Red realized Dragon Star still had one sword and stake on his belt. He'd pulled the long shirt out to cover the handle of the weapons so it looked like the empty scabbard on the other side.

"Can we have our shoes back?" Red asked. "This stone floor is freezing. We'll probably get frost bite. We can't stay down here in these light clothes. And we need blankets or something to lay on."

"You get what Lady Gregory deems you are worth of," the guard said.

Red could still feel the thrum of rain outside. He knew he couldn't hear it. Yet the same gnawing buzz kept reaching into his thoughts. It distracted him, and made it hard to focus on anything for very long. He remembered they were here for Pete. He knew he should be angry or plotting an escape or something. However, his mind and emotions simmered in the background somewhere out of reach.

He felt tired. Watching Pete snore, emaciated on the floor, he envied the deep sleep.

Dragon Star remained in place, not moving or speaking. Red couldn't imagine the sheer determination it must take to do so. After a long stretch of horrific minutes, the guard finally leaned against the wall and began to look off to the side. Dragon Star silently undid his belt, slowly working the buckle to prevent the slightest noise.

Red allowed himself to be transfixed as he watched the excruciating drama play out. He prepared himself to jump up and scream in case a diversion became necessary.

With the accessory loosed, Dragon Star gently stepped toward Pete, secreting the weapons behind Pete's back when the man curled up on one side.

Once they were placed, Red stood and walked to the corner of the cage closest to the guard's line of sight. The man snapped his attention to Red as if he could hide the fact of his inattention.

"When do we get our bread and water?" Red asked.

"You get what—"

"The Lady deems we are worthy of," Red interrupted. "But when is that?"

The guard clammed up and looked toward Pete and Dragon Star on the floor.

"Can you at least ask somebody about shoes?" Red asked. "Can we have our own clothes back?"

"No," the guard said.

"What's your name?"

"My name is Matthew."

"So, how long do you have to stay down here and watch us, Matthew?"

"My shift is six hours."

"Whoa. Are you being punished, too?"

"I happily serve my Lady."

"Of course. But why? I mean, what does she pay you? We have guards on our base and I'm pretty sure we could offer you a lot more."

"Can you offer me eternal life?"

Red scoffed. "Eternal non-death, you mean. This is no life. Wouldn't you rather live one good life as a hero than endless years as a dog at the whims of a crazy woman? I mean, she's never going to let you be her dark prince. Why would she? Even if you get what you want you'll be here on guard duty, working for her, endlessly."

"If I'm lucky."

"I'd rather be dead," Red said.

"Maybe we'll both get what we want," the guard said with a scoff.

"Matthew, what did you do before, you know, the big change?"

The guard shook his head, as if he could shake the memories loose. "I worked at a hardware store. Customer service."

"Did you have a family?"

"No. A girlfriend."

"Where is she now?"

"I don't... I don't know. After the change, she sort of disappeared. I looked for her for days, but she wasn't at home or work. The phones and computers all stopped working. My car turned into a horse, so I rode it around looking for her. But nobody knew where she went."

"Anybody else go missing?"

"My family lives back East. But I couldn't call them. When I was searching several people said they had family go missing. All women."

"Only women went missing? Doesn't that seem strange?"

Matthew was opening up. Red began to hope he could talk some sense into this guard.

"Compared to this," Matthew said pointing to the dungeon bars, "nothing is that strange."

"That was just a couple of days ago, right?"

"Feels like another lifetime."

"Do you miss your girlfriend at all?"

"Once Hanna showed up, I knew it didn't matter. She made me a Bathaven Castle Guard, and promised my faithful service would be rewarded with eternal life. Nobody else ever offered me anything like that."

"And you believe her?"

"What else do I have? And besides, he's getting it. So why not me?" The guard indicated Pete with his eyes.

"He doesn't look well," Dragon Star said, feeling Pete's forehead to check for a fever.

"Probably takes some pain to make the change," Matthew said as his forehead wrinkled visibly beneath the helmet.

"What if I told you I can put this all back the way it should be?" Red said.

"What do you mean?"

"We know how to change the world back. That's why we came here. But Hanna doesn't…"

"Who's Hanna?"

"Your Lady vampire. That's what we called her before all this."

"She wasn't like this before? What was she like?"

"She was our friend," Dragon Star said. "She was kind and fun."

Red added, "We never knew she really wanted to rule a gothic territory as a blood sucking mistress of the night. Before she made this place she wore sensible shoes and business suits to meetings."

"She made this place? She made the change happen? How?"

"Yes and no. It's complicated. The point is, we need your help. If we don't get out of here, the world will stay like this. People aren't just missing out there. They're dying. Lots of people. Billions maybe. We have to put it back while we still can."

Matthew wagged his head. "She killed all those people to make this possible?"

"Liars!" Hanna's voice screeched down the entrance tunnel. The black, leather boots became visible before her red dress as she clomped down the stairs. "You fools! Did you think I wouldn't know when you messed with the mind of one of my men? Matthew, you're dismissed."

"I didn't help them, my Lady," Matthew said. "I never moved from my post."

"I said go."

Matthew dropped his shoulders and slowly marched up the stairs.

"Hanna, this is ridiculous," Red said. "Look at Pete. If we don't treat that infection he's going to die."

She glanced at the form lying on the ground. Pete's eyes fluttered open for a delirious moment before he fell back to fitful sleep. She said, "He is definitely going to die. I wish he'd hurry up already. Unlike you two, however, he will come back from it."

"Now you're going to kill us?" Red stepped back from the cold bars, to stay out of her reach as she slowly stepped forward.

"Eventually. But first, I'm going to drink your blood."

CHAPTER TWENTY-TWO

D ragon Star remained calm as Hanna moved toward the bars. He hoped she would pull out the key and open the gate. He wanted to spring up and attack, hoping to catch her unaware. She didn't take out the key. Instead, she turned into a cloud of smoke, which blew past the bars and rematerialized on the inside of the cell.

Red jumped back, putting himself between Hanna and Pete. Dragon Star stood up and stepped forward. He planted his feet wide with his hands clasped behind his back. "Take me first," he said. "I am prepared to die."

Hanna scanned the shorter, darker skinned man. Dragon Star let his mind flex so the tendrils of her constant attempt to invade and control him could reach inside. He would have felt less violated if her hands were inside his torso, poking at his organs. Still, he gave her enough to know he spoke the truth. He was prepared to die.

Red protested, "No, Hanna. This is crazy."

"Crazy?" she said as she turned on him. "Crazy is living the everyday life of a sheep. Crazy is spending every day studying and obsessing in order to get a few minutes of bliss when they give you a turn with the Actuator. Crazy is being one of the nameless masses who go through life doing nothing more than work and sleep and eat and breed. Crazy is thinking you can fix a broken world. Because the world was broken long before the Actuation. And even if you put the world back how it was before, it still won't be right."

"Killing us is wrong in any world," Red said.

"Not in this place. This is my world. And I decide what is wrong and right here."

"You can't decide that," Red said.

"I'm bored now," she said. Maintaining eye contact with Red, she turned her body. Then, in a sudden lunge, she twisted her neck and plunged her teeth into Dragon Star's throat. Dragon Star refused to flinch, accepting the pain. Blood sucked free of his jugular vein and dripped down onto his beige linen shirt. Only when her saliva dribbled onto his neck did he pull the last wooden stake out from behind his back and plunge it into her chest.

For a moment, when she opened her mouth to gasp, saliva and blood gushed out onto his shoulder. It spread a sickening warmth down his arm, highlighting the cold everywhere else. . Dragon Star held the wooden stake firm, pushing with all the strength her bite had not drained from him. He twisted the metal cuff like a drill and felt the tip crack two ribs apart and pierce deep into the strong muscle of her heart.

Hanna staggered and fell back, leaving open wounds in his neck. Dragon Star let go of the stake and clasped his hand over his throat. Red jumped up to check on his companion.

"I'll be okay," Dragon Star said with a wheeze. He clasped his hand in place—hard—to fight the slippery blood and seal off the holes. The pressure made it difficult to talk or breathe.

Dragon Star kept his eyes on Hanna. No blood came from the injury in her chest. Instead, a necrotic black circle formed around the wound where the spike ripped through her velvet dress. Hanna gagged once, but couldn't draw breath. Her face twisted into an ugly web of wrinkles as the pain of collapsing internal organs jerked her hands up over her torso and bent her waist into a fetal position. Her boots twisted unnaturally as she fell to the ground. A single breathy sigh escaped her bloody mouth before she seized once more and then went limp.

Red watched her for a few seconds before turning to Dragon Star. "I'm sorry you had to do it. You had no choice." Dragon Star heard Red's own guilt coming through, even as he tried to offer solace.

"I know," Dragon Star said. Speaking strained his neck to the point where he half strangled himself. He slowly sat down, leaning his back against one of the rough-cut walls. The blood cooled on his shoulder, sending icy shivers down his spine. He began mentally relaxing, slowing his own pulse by releasing his anxiety and stress.

Red came over, as if he could help. Dragon Star put out his free hand to stop Red. "Key," he whispered.

"Are you sure you're going to be okay?"

Dragon Star made a deliberate and slow nod. He watched Red start by attempting to find any trace of the key visually. Eventually the younger man began rolling the corpse from side to side, feeling around her waist. "It's not here."

Dragon Star began to count his breaths, slowing them down. He slipped easily into a light meditation now that Hanna wasn't constantly assaulting his mind and will. He made sure to take large breaths through his nose and past the constricted larynx, holding each one for two beats before exhaling through his mouth.

Something bothered him. He thought being locked in here with Hanna's body would cause him more stress than it did. Instead, something else nagged at him. He cleared his mind, letting his subconscious take over the breathing. One of the guards would come for them eventually. And they would bring the key. Dragon Star hoped they would wait until his neck stopped bleeding at least.

He reached out with his feelings, sensing raw emotion. Hanna's body left him weighed down by remorse and tension. Red drew loyalty and honor from him. Pete brought fear. Dragon Star had never liked Pete. He was a cocky playboy. They had nothing in common. But Pete had never caused Dragon Star any fear before. Now they both had Hanna's bite.

Dragon Star snapped open his eyes and said, "Red!"

Red turned instantly. "What is it? Is anything wrong?"

Dragon Star blinked several times before he could force the words out. "Get the stake."

Looking first at Hanna and then back at Dragon Star, Red said, "Pull it out?"

Dragon Star nodded. Then he looked at Pete's sleeping body. "We might need it again."

Red looked at Pete's neck and nodded, grimly. Halfway to Hanna's body he turned and looked back at Dragon Star. The middle aged Korean knew Red's eyes were on his bloodied hand.

Dragon star nodded again. With his strained voice he said, "You might need it twice."

When Red pulled the stake from Hanna's chest, he thought he heard air escaping. He expected blood or at least black puffy stuff from her skin to be on the oak column. Instead, it came out clean.

Red hated the feel of the silver band in his hand as he hefted the ultra-primitive weapon. He knew Hanna's twitching body would now join his nightmares alongside Jackson and Mack. Even though he hadn't killed her, his emotions still thought of her as a friend. Somehow, his mind couldn't think of her as anything but a victim in this horrific drama.

Now he faced the very real possibility of having to kill Pete. He loathed the thought of adding any more death to his account. He knew he couldn't kill Dragon Star. Not after all they'd been through together. He would leave the Korean here to become the new master of this castle before he ended the man's life.

When he looked up, he knew Dragon Star detected his thoughts. It wasn't the creepy vampire way Hanna tried to do it. Dragon Star just knew him and knew what Red would think. "Do not let me become one of them," Dragon Star said. His voice became pinched and strained under pressure. "Swear you won't let me become like her."

Red nodded. "I swear." He felt his stomach twist into knots. "But maybe if we get both of you out of this hellhole, you won't become vampires at all."

Dragon Star leaned forward as if he might stand up right then.

"Not now," Red said. "We're still locked in. I think it's taking Pete a while to make the change. We still have some time." Red took a deep breath. It was nice to have clarity of thought back.

Red moved Hanna's body over by Pete's, arranging them so it looked like they were taking a nap together. It was weird, but he hoped the guards might not notice she was dead right away. Of course, if their minds suddenly cleared, they might know anyway.

Red moved the sword so Dragon Star's free hand could grab it quickly. Then he tucked the wooden spike into the sleeve of his shirt where it rested along his forearm, reasonably well hidden.

"We'll wait until you stop bleeding," he said. "Then, if they haven't come down, we'll call for a guard."

Red didn't think Dragon Star would die from the bite. His companion just needed time for the wounds to close. That same time, however, would be allowing any infection to spread. Was it really just an infection? The red streaks on Pete's neck looked like the sign of an infected wound. However, Red didn't think it would be something antibiotics could cure. He knew how fully the Actuator transformed the physical laws everybody thought to be immutable before. He doubted any cure existed except getting out of this place and crossing the boundary into another realm.

Until then, they had to wait. Red looked around for anything to help make his companion more comfortable. He thought off pulling of Hanna's boots, but he doubted Dragon Star would want them. Finally, he said, "This is weird, right?"

Dragon Star smiled and made a raspy laugh. "If it did not happen to everybody in the world, nobody would believe us."

"That's what happens when you sign your life away and work on the base. You never get to talk to anybody else again."

"Do you miss it? Did you leave anybody behind?" With pressure on his throat Dragon Star's accent, though usually slight, seemed to come out more.

Red thought back to the life he left behind. It felt like a movie he'd seen a long time ago, not even really him. He usually tried to forget about it. Still, after the emotional rollercoaster he'd been on for the last few days, it didn't seem important to keep it secret.

"I didn't have a great childhood. Probably nobody willing to give everything up and live on a research base ever did. My parents were always fighting when I was young. Then one day my mother left. I know it's usually the other way around, but she had a history with rehab and I guess she figured she would lose a custody battle. She told me she wanted me to go with her, but it wasn't a choice. And if she stayed she expected it would get much worse."

"How old?"

"Nine."

"What did you do?" Dragon Star asked, closing his eyes. Red didn't want Dragon Star to slip into the same sleep as Pete. He knew a watered down story certainly wasn't enough to stay awake for.

"I told her I never wanted to see her face again."

CHAPTER TWENTY-THREE

ed felt a wave of guilt rise up every bit as strong as what he carried for killing Jackson. At the time, he hadn't understood what it would mean to tell his mother he never wanted to see her again. He might as well have killed her.

"My father was a paratrooper in the 82nd airborne," Red said with force. He made sure he saw Dragon Star's eyes flutter open before he continued. "He was a tough man, who didn't give any quarter or accept any excuses. I wanted to leave with my mother. I knew life with him would be hell.

"But you see, I was stuck. I didn't have a choice. She had to leave and she had to leave me. And now I know that was all his doing. He was just so fierce.

"Anyway, it was just a matter of survival. No matter what I really felt, she was the one who got to be free of him. I had to stay. Even at that young age, I understood his demand for ultimate loyalty. So it was a play for his favor. I didn't want to hurt her. But I had to keep living with him."

Red sighed, rubbing his eyes. "I knew he would like it if I chose him. I knew it would be a little easier if he believed I was on his side one-hundred percent. So once there was no other choice, I said it."

Dragon Star remained silent. Red knew he couldn't have kept talking about this if anybody else said anything about it. Now that he'd started, he wanted to see it through to the bitter end.

"I watched her eyes go wide and fill with tears. Her heart broke in front of me. I could read her mind. I know she thought I really had become like him. And since she hated him, she started to hate me, too.

"She never called or sent me a letter. I'd made my choice and she left me to it."

Red crossed his arms and tucked his hands under, to save a little heat in his fingers. "Anyway, there was no room for a teenager in that home. I was expected to be an adult, a soldier no less, from ten on up. High grades in school were expected. I had to join sports. We never talked or made plans. He just told me I would be a soldier like him when I grew up. And since it was an order, he fully expected me to follow it.

"But the older I got, the more I knew he had driven my mother away. I blamed him for what I'd said to her. I couldn't stand the strictness he demanded, waking up early every day and falling out of bed doing push-ups. All our nights out were to watch boxing or football. We only ever talked about sports and guns. He drank himself to sleep every night. I wanted nothing more than to leave and never see him again. So when I was eighteen and he was away for a couple of weeks on field training, I left. Just a few months from graduation, and I couldn't even stay to finish it."

Red paused to watch Pete shift his weight on the uneven rock floor. "I threw myself into anything and everything I knew he'd hate. I grew my hair out, took drugs, hitch-hiked from place to place. I couldn't keep a girlfriend for more than two weeks. I eventually ended up fighting with any friends I made. And when I got desperate, I started stealing. I mugged a dozen people, stole a couple cars. I didn't even know where I was going. All I knew was that I wanted to keep moving. At the time, I felt like I wanted to be free. But now, I know, I just wanted to find her. I wanted to see my mother again and tell her how sorry I was."

Dragon Star nodded. His knit brow gave way to wide eyes and an understanding nod. Red couldn't express how important that approving expression was.

"I didn't, of course. I got as far as Ohio when the police caught me drunk driving a stolen car. I punched one of them out. Then I took his gun. I stole his cruiser and ran into his partner on my way. Well, cops don't like that. So they had helicopters and twenty officers on me in two minutes. When they took me down, they dragged up everything I'd done for the past four years, including selling drugs, and slapped me with enough felonies to put me away for three lifetimes.

"I don't know how, but when my dad found out, he arranged for me to get an interview with Jon. Jon must have owed him a huge favor, because he brought me in and made me his assistant. I tell myself it was a good deal because even though I'll be living on a military base for the rest of my life, technically I'm not a soldier.

"At least Jon's nothing like my dad. And to be honest, I liked working on the base. It was a lot of fun before all this went wrong."

Dragon Star nodded his consent. He said, "I will take you over any ten soldiers."

Red took a deep breath. As much as he hated to admit it, he needed to hear that. He found himself wondering how different life would have been with somebody like Dragon Star for a father instead. He asked, "What about you? What brought you to the Actuator?"

"Not right now," Dragon Star said.

"Hurts too much to talk? Of course. Sorry."

"No, we just need to get out of here. Hanna or no, I do not want to sleep in this place."

Dragon Star slowly released the pressure on his neck. Red moved closer to try and detect any trickle of blood from the wound. Blood in various stages of wet and dry surrounded the lacerations.

He said, "I can't tell if there's any infection yet."

"It is too fast," Dragon Star said. His voice grew quiet as his cheeks tightened.

"We don't know that," Red said. "Maybe vampire bites are made to heal faster so they don't waste blood."

"Or maybe vampires heal faster."

"You didn't die. So let's get that key and get out of here. Then none of this will matter."

Red couldn't help imagining Dragon Star might just have some other terrible disease in a different place. He didn't want to think about it.

"It could take a long time," Dragon Star said.

Red nodded his agreement. "Then let's get going." He turned to the stairs. "Hey! Matthew! Anybody! She needs help! Help!"

A few seconds later Matthew returned. "What happened?" He grasped the bars, trying to get more information. From the back, he couldn't see anything.

"She needs help," Red repeated. "Where's the key?"

Matthew looked up at him. "I don't have it."

"Can you get it? Who has it? She doesn't have very long. I don't think she's breathing."

Dragon Star leaned closer, as if to listen to her.

"I'll be right back," Matthew said. He moved toward the stairs, looking at Hanna's body the whole time.

A few minutes later he returned. "There," he said.

A taller man with his face hidden behind a metal visor followed him in. Sword to the ready, he unlocked the door and pulled on the gate. "Back away from her!" He moved in, waving the sword at Red and Dragon Star. Red backed away. Dragon Star slid to the side.

The instant the guard swung his sword toward Red, Red saw Dragon Star grab the hidden weapon and leap forward. His precision thrust came down hard on the guard's neck, but failed to penetrate the chain mail beneath. The force of the attack knocked the man to the side, allowing Red time to jump in and wrestle the sword from the guard's hand.

The guard countered with a metal plated gauntlet, knocking Red upside the head. Fortunately, he fell too far to the side to make it a knock-out blow, and Red managed to recover.

Seeing Dragon Star rush through the gate and shove his sword tip in Matthew's face, Red copied and held the other guard as well. Sticking the point of the heavy broadsword into the opening on the metal mask, the tip rested only a hair away from one of the man's angry brown eyes.

"In the cage," Dragon Star ordered Matthew. He took the key out of the lock and tossed it to Red. Then he pulled his sword belt up from behind Pete and fastened it on, keeping his sword trained steadily on Matthew's nose.

"She bit you?" Matthew asked. "All our loyal service and she bites you one minute after you get here."

"Shut up," Red said.

The other guard put his hands up and leaned back against the wall. Red kept the sword up, but it bobbed up and down as he fumbled with the key. Once the manacle unlocked, Red moved in front of Pete, grabbing the man by the collar, and dragged him by his clothes out through the gate.

Red turned the black iron tool over in his hand. It had jagged teeth and the same stupid bat along the shaft. After years as a Key Hunter, this was the first time one of the Machine Monks used a real key. He stifled a smile.

"You'll never get out of here alive," the other guard said. "The Bathaven guards are all on full alert. A troop of fifty men is covering that door."

"Not likely," Dragon Star said, "or they'd be coming down here already."

Red helped Pete to his feet. Pete moaned, leaning against the bars of an empty cell for a moment while Red held him steady. Even dazed, they would make better time if Pete could walk. Dragon Star put one of Pete's arms over his shoulders and began walking out, leaving Red to cover both of the guards.

"She's dead!" Matthew cried as he turned over Hanna's body and saw the black hole where her heart used to be. Rigor mortis already claimed her so gnarled arms raised unnaturally into the air as he rolled her onto her back.

"You killed her?" The other guard lifted the face guard on his helmet to get a better look.

"Hurry," Red said as he locked the gate. He threaded the key onto the leather thong around his neck. With Dragon Star helping Pete, Red took the lead. Sword first he ascended the cold, wet stairs.

Listening for any sounds ahead of them, Red almost didn't hear Dragon Star say, "We should have taken their boots."

CHAPTER TWENTY-FOUR

ough hands pulling him from a delirious sleep brought Peter Thorstenstein back to a dim world of cold stone and metal bars. People were talking and yelling around him, but he couldn't understand the words. He felt distant, as if listening from far away. Leaning against the wall until somebody lifted him and helped him shuffle to the stairs, he felt the cold more acutely than any time in his life. He greedily clung to the man holding him, wishing to leech as much heat from the contact as possible.

Pete took every step deliberately, carefully placing each foot before shifting his weight as they moved up the stairs. An itchy pain ran up the side of his neck and made his teeth ache. A thumping and whooshing sound alternated in his ears. At first, he thought his heart was pounding loud, affecting his hearing. Then he realized it was something outside his body. He could hear somebody else's heart. At the same time, a chaotic web of vibrations bounced everywhere around him.

When he closed his eyes, Pete realized he could still see. He left them closed, yet still sensed the walls and the low ceiling. No color registered, of course. Yet, he could map out each of the stairs in the room. He knew how closely they followed the man leading up the stairs. For the first time in his life, he could smell the other two men in the close quarters. Their body odors drew his attention. He didn't have an opinion about their scent, but his mind memorized them like a blood hound, expecting he might someday be called upon to track them.

Pete remembered his name, but most of his life felt distant, as if he'd been asleep for decades and the dreams had replaced all his short term memories. He recalled his parents and siblings. He knew his friends and scorned lovers. He couldn't forget the base and the Actuator. However, none of that seemed important to him now. He felt like a phoenix rising from the ashes of a chicken. Nothing from that earlier life had any real significance compared to the greatness welling up inside him now.

Most of these thoughts came and went without much effort in the back of his mind. Halfway up the stairs, he knew he could walk on his own. He felt like he could fly if he wanted to. But instinct told him not to share that information. Continuing to shamble as the shorter man propped him up, Pete's whole consciousness blossomed into focus around one feeling. Hunger.

When they finally reached the door at the top of the stairs, Pete opened his eyes again. He felt a yearning in his stomach stronger than any urge he'd ever experienced. He no longer needed oxygen. He no longer craved sex as more than a recreation or tool wielded in the struggle for power. Instead, a thirst left his throat parched and every cell in his body contributed to the craving. Even having never tasted it, Pete knew the only way to ease the urgent need would be through thick, warm blood. He could sense the sweet nectar pumping through both of the men near him, and only by concentrating constantly did he kept himself from leaping on them unawares and draining their surplus life force.

"Stay back while I check for guards," the man in the lead whispered. He moved out around the side of the staircase hiding the dungeon door. Sword ready, he stopped behind a tall Corinthian pillar and listened carefully while searching the room. When he felt reasonably sure they were alone, he signaled with his hand and moved to the next column.

Pete suppressed the urge to laugh. These silly measures, flitting from post to post, would never conceal warm bodies from a vampire. Even now, Pete could see the heat of their body glowing deep red on wavelengths invisible to his prey.

They made their way around the great dining hall and started toward the wide entry they'd come in through. The braziers burned low now, not having been renewed. Pete made a mental note to make sure the staff knew this kind of oversight would never be tolerated under his reign.

Now that they were in more light, Pete recognized the men with him. Red had been fun to talk to during their time on base, if a little full of himself. They'd never been close friends, not that such a pathetic alliance would have sway over Pete now. Pete always found Dragon Star's self-righteous piety annoying. Even with Hanna's mark, Pete would take that one first. Now that she was dead, her mark meant nothing.

Red put out a hand as he reached the side door. "Check the front gate. I'll see if anybody is guarding the horses. Hopefully they didn't unhitch the teams or we'll have to leave on foot." When he pulled it back, the patter of rain grew loud and cold air blasted them in the face. Pete didn't shiver.

"Still no shoes," Dragon Star pointed to their feet.

Pete let Dragon Star help him lean against the nearby wall, then the shorter man went to check the gate as ordered. Pete kept up the farce with squinting eyes and labored breathing. He leaned hard on the wall, watching Dragon Star examine the levers and gears attached to the portcullis, now in place behind the heavy wooden gate.

While the others busied themselves with doors and horses, Pete reached out with his mind. He sensed fifty men in armor, stationed around the castle. All had weapons. Hanna had kept their minds well under control. Rather than deal with reasserting thrall on each one, Pete just tapped into Hanna's devices. Each of the men had something different they wanted and believed she might give them for their service. They had the strongest of misguided loyalties. Without revealing himself, Pete touched those same nerves. Like a virtuoso picking up another musician's instrument, he easily tuned them all to his will. They didn't even know Hanna had died.

When he found one in command who wasn't incarcerated, Pete knew he had to communicate. This worried him. Would the captain recognize a mental voice other than Hanna's? Pete took longer to feel this man's mind out. Predictably, he loved being in charge more than he loved Hanna. Pete cracked a small smile as he easily touched the connections between this man's pride and his will to dominate. Then Pete whispered a message into his mind. "Gather the guards. Do not let the prisoners escape alive."

"Where are they now?" the man's mind asked back, not detecting a new master. This would all be very easy now.

Still whispering to keep his mental voice nondescript, Pete thought back, "They are about to leave through the front gate by carriage. Don't let them see you until they come out."

The mental equivalent of a nod and salute floated in and out of Pete's mind. Now, he had to make sure these buffoons weren't ready before the captain mustered a troop outside.

With his tongue, Pete touched and caressed his fangs. Needle sharp, he realized how easy it would be to shred his own tongue or cheek if he wasn't careful while eating. Then he let out a small laugh. He wouldn't need to eat in the traditional sense anymore.

Pete heard horses clopping into the large hall, so he moved away from the wall and walked forward, purposefully teetering.

Dragon Star came back to him once the metal bars were up out of the way. "Just rest, friend. We will have you out in no time."

Pete nodded, but didn't go back to the wall. Something about the nearby fire made him uneasy. It blinded his ability to see the heat signatures of the men. When the first carriage of horses entered the big room, Dragon Star called up to Red, "We need the key for the gate."

"Of course," Red said. "It's probably the only key in this whole place." He pulled a leather thong from around his neck containing several objects Pete didn't care about. Pete watched the key, though. He would need it soon.

Dragon Star turned the key in the lock and handed the overcrowded lanyard back to Red. He took the reins before opening the door on the side of the carriage for Pete.

"Should we go back for the other carriage?" Red asked.

"We seem to have time," Dragon Star said. "And they are valuable."

Red nodded and headed back out into the rain. Dragon Star helped Pete up into the carriage. Pete fell to his knees and crawled in, keeping up his weak appearance.

Dragon Star led his horses back away from the gate to make room for Red. Then he climbed into the driver's seat. While he waited, he put his feet over the side to warm them on the heat from the fire.

Pete reached out with his mind and touched Dragon Star's. He kept his intrusion light, just looking for the mental state there. He found nothing. The clever Monk had somehow arranged his thoughts so nothing could be seen. *Was this guy so truly empty of feelings or ideas? Impossible!*

Pete found Red's mind easily. Red kept everything buried deep, focusing on the task at hand to prevent the bubbling issues from rising up. Pete didn't linger there.

His curiosity brought him back to Dragon Star. Being new to all of this, Pete had only touched the few minds in the castle. Of those, Dragon Star's was unique. Obviously, Pete had caught him meditating. It was a surreal moment. He'd never expected the Empty House actually to be devoid of thoughts. Yet here it was, as obvious as a mineshaft in the mental landscape of people in the castle.

Pete let it go, focusing instead on the men mustering outside the gate in the rain. His captain had well trained soldiers. Pete would reward him for it.

Stretching his perceptions even farther, Peter realized there wasn't another female within a mile of this castle. Hanna had some serious gender issues. Pete would remedy the problem as soon as he dealt with these two intruders.

"I think we're ready," Red said as he brought his horses to a stop. "The coast looks clear. We'll take the road to the nearby town and find someplace to stay."

Dragon Star nodded. "In the morning we should find Pete a doctor."

"And you." Red dismounted and pushed the gates open. Then he jumped back onto the driver's seat. "Let's go," he said to the horses. With a small whip, he urged them to stop protesting the cold rain and move out onto the road.

The two carriages accelerated over the bridge. Then Red pulled his horses to a stop. Twenty men with halberds and swords ready blocked the road.

The man in front said, "Get down and put your hands up!"

CHAPTER TWENTY-FIVE

With his feet over the warm ashes in the copper bowl by the stone walls of the castle, Dragon Star felt ugly tendrils beginning to probe the edges of his consciousness again. Still tired and weary, he automatically slipped into the meditation for which Empty House had been named.

The probing, so gentle, lasted but a moment and retreated. Even with the intrusion gone, Dragon Star found the idea of somebody probing his thoughts and feelings revolting. Was Hanna still alive? He'd seen the black cavern of necrotic rot where her heart used to be. He watched her rigor mortised arms reach up like claws when the guard turned her cold body over.

Dragon Star jumped down from the wagon and began working the gate. He exerted great force on the huge, wooden handles of the gear system to raise the portcullis. Concentrating fully on the satisfying exertion, he felt a familiar tickle in his mind. Again he drained all his thoughts, hoping the presence would push farther and possibly give a clue by what it looked at there. Instead, it disappeared again, just as quickly.

"I need the key," Dragon Star said as Red brought the second team into the entry hall. The younger man tossed the whole lanyard of Actuator keys. Dragon Star unlocked the gate and then lifted the wooden bar. The wind outside pulled the doors slightly ajar, venting some of the heat from the room. Standing on cold stone as the spray of spattered rain prophesied the misery before them tonight, Dragon Star felt old.

At just over forty, he wasn't as old or out of shape as Pete. But the Machine Monks often considered him on par with their parents. He took such a relationship as a compliment. However, it left him enduring some loneliness with few peers. But now, seeing Red overlook something simple like shoes over and over again, Dragon Star knew his age had begun taking a toll. A week ago, he had the best half of his life still in front of him. Today, he mourned the loss of shoes before a freezing storm.

Red gave the plan and whipped his horses forward. From the carriage behind him, Dragon Star watched Red coax his horses until they pushed the gate open. Then they plunged into the wet night. Just beyond the bridge, loud with clomping hooves, Red stopped. Dragon Star pulled back and to the side to avoid a collision.

The captain of the blockade said, "Get down and put your hands up!"

How could they possibly have known?

"We better do what they say," Pete said from the carriage behind him. When he heard Pete's voice, Dragon Star knew who'd been intruding on his psyche.

Pete began to open the door, but Red thrust one finger at him and commanded, "Stay put!"

As Pete waited in the doorway, Dragon Star tried to think of a way to get Red to give him their last wooden stake without alerting Pete he knew the truth of the situation. *Weren't there other ways to kill a vampire? Had Hanna really rigged it so only pointy sticks could destroy them?*

"He needs a doctor," Dragon Star said. "Hanna told us to take him to town and find a doctor."

"Who's Hanna?" The guard pointed his sword directly at Dragon Star's face. Dragon Star sized him up instantly. Without doubt, he knew he could take this pompous, over-dressed guard.

"Lady Gregory," Red said. His knuckles held the reins so tight that the cold made them white. "The Lady of the castle."

"That's a lie," the leader said with spit and reflected rain blowing off his lips. "She told us to stop you from escaping. Now come down off that carriage or we will kill you."

"That would be a waste," Pete said, choosing now to exit the coach.

"Who are you?"

Pete stepped forward, standing tall and regal despite the deluge soaking his torn and tattered clothes. "I'm the new Master of Bathaven."

With all eyes on Pete, Dragon Star waved at Red, trying to get his attention. Red didn't notice, and said to Pete, "You made a fast recovery."

Pete smiled and said to the guards, "These are my guests, if they will cooperate."

"We don't work for you," the leader said, moving his sword to point at Pete who now stood only a foot away from it.

Pete's face twisted into a wicked grin, with sharp teeth peeking out below his mouth. "You do now!" Pete threw up his arms and lowered his brow.

Suddenly, the guards all began to wince and moan as pain apparently coursed through their brains.

Soon they recovered. "We will serve the Master of Bathaven," the leader repeated, almost robotically. Dragon Star winced. He knew Pete had entered these soldier's minds and altered something.

Pete laughed as a fork of lightning thundered nearby. "Now, Red, do you want to be my guests or my prisoners?"

Red looked at Pete for a while before turning back to Dragon Star. Dragon Star held up one forearm and clasped it with his other hand, indicating the sleeve where Red had concealed the wooden stake. Red nodded back with heavy eyes and took a deep breath.

"We will accept your hospitality," Red said, "considering the inclement weather."

Pete snorted and began walking back between the carriages toward the castle. "Good, we have much to talk about. First I need that key, though."

Dragon Star watched Red dismount and put his hand to the leather cord around his neck. Then in a flash of anger, Red pulled the stake free instead. He set his foot against one horse's haunch and launched forward. He crashed into the unsuspecting Pete and both of them tumbled onto the floor of Dragon Star's carriage through the already open door.

"Yaw!" Red called. The lead horse, suddenly kicked from behind, and hearing the command, lurched forward and charged into the unsuspecting line of guards.

With lightning and rain for cover, Dragon Star didn't waste the distraction. Whipping his own team, he drew his sword and plunged into the chaotic wake. With guards scattering to both sides, the empty carriage rode through the line. Dragon Star followed right behind. Twice he used the sword to parry incoming halberds. Then they broke through the line and barreled down the bumpy road, throwing mud in every direction.

Guards chased them down the road until hope of catching up fled.

Dragon Star followed the runaway team for half a mile before the horses finally realized nobody sat in the drivers chair and began to swerve wildly. Then they came to a stop.

Dragon Star cranked the brake on his own carriage before jumping down. He had his sword out, ready to die avenging Red if Pete had done any evil to his companion.

"I think he's willing to listen to us," Red said with a dark grin. Red still straddled Pete, who lay sprawled back against the bench. The wooden stake was sticking out of Pete's chest where his heart was. The tip went in an inch where Red stopped, a firm grip around the ornamental handle. "One push and he's dead as Hanna."

Dragon Star nodded. "Should we go on to the town?"

"No," Red said. "Everybody around here is his puppet now. We've got to get out of this realm without running into any more potential thralls."

"I noticed a rough path a ways back heading west."

"Toward the beach?"

"You'll never make it," Pete spat.

Red wiggled the stake, twisting just a bit. Pete rolled his eyes back and shut his mouth. "The beach will be wet, but if we can ride along it, we might get out of here undetected."

Dragon Star tied the extra carriage's horses to the back again, and drove his own team up the wet path until he found the side road. Little more than two lines of mud between tall weeds, Dragon Star had to urge the horses twice to get them to venture up the bank and drag the wagon onto the rougher ground.

After a series of particularly loud and bright strikes, Dragon Star noticed the clouds above the mountains to the east didn't seem to grow dark again. The cold rain beat down like a typhoon for another five minutes while they slowly bounced and skidded down the too narrow footpath. When they finally reached the coarse beach, Dragon Star turned them to the south. Avoiding the softer sand, they rode along the firmer ground farther out from the crashing waves, their sound almost completely lost beneath the buzz of rain.

The storm waned again, with a hint of light growing where the sun rose. As the world grew quieter and lighter by degrees, Dragon Star could hear some of the conversation in the carriage below.

"Stop trying to mess with my mind, Pete. I'm trying to get through this without adding your name the list of people I killed."

"Don't be ridiculous. What would I want with a mind like yours?"

"Just shut up. I'm not going to tell you again."

"If you leave me here, we'll all be happy. You've already got one vampire with you. What do you need me for?"

"He's not a vampire. Neither are you."

"I am here. If you take me out of here I'll die."

"You don't know that."

"Even if I don't, I'll have a stake sticking out of me, that's bound to bleed a lot."

"This is not negotiable," Red said. "We need you to help us put the world back."

"What do I care about the world?" Pete said. "In case you haven't noticed, I'm better off here."

"That's not in your future. I'll kill you now before I let you stay here like that."

"But this place is a gothic horror. If you take me away, all those people will have no focus. They won't have anyone to tell them what to do."

"They'll figure it out," Red said. "Now shut up."

"Could you at least pull that thing back a little? Every bump it feels like you're going to skewer me."

"Sorry," Red said. "You're not yourself at the moment. Can't afford to give you any slack."

"And it hurts!"

"Suck it up."

Dragon Star felt the cold acutely. He suppressed shivering by keeping himself hunched over and holding the reins in folded arms. As the rain continued to lessen, a breeze seemed to blow all the way through him.

He'd tried to keep his mind empty to avoid Pete latching onto it, but the distractions were too many. Instead, he concentrated on his feelings. Besides the cold, he felt conflicted. He no longer feared Pete's mental intrusions. In fact, he felt a little bit jealous that Red would be taking all of Pete's attention.

Dragon Star reached out with his mind, suddenly touching a few hundred people to the east in the small village. They seemed to recognize and welcome him, like a long forgotten joke suddenly coming to mind and bringing a smile. There weren't many women among them.

As the sun began bringing some white to the black clouds in the distance, Dragon Star found himself preferring the rain. With an offshore wind carrying the storm out to sea, he knew he would need to get some rest soon. He felt hungry and tired.

"Oh no," he said quietly to himself and the storm.

With wide eyes and heart racing, he whipped the horses into a fury. Bouncing over rocks at high speed, he heard Red call up, "Hey, can we take it easy? I almost shis-kebabbed Pete!"

"No," Dragon Star said, whipping the horses again. It had taken most of a day to get to the castle last time. He didn't know if he had that much time left. "We cannot take it easy. How far to the boundary?"

CHAPTER TWENTY-SIX

A s the sun began claiming more of the storm weary sky, Red concentrated on holding Pete down with his legs and keeping the wooden stake steady with his hand. Once Dragon Star starting racing across the edge of the beach, the task had grown difficult. Red finally settled for letting the stake slide up and down between his fingers, hoping he would be fast enough to shove the point home if Pete made any sudden moves.

A few times Red had to brace himself when Dragon Star slowed the carriage to circle around large rock outcroppings. Other times they would veer into the softer sand to avoid fallen trees, sliding more than rolling the wheels through as they slowly sunk deeper and deeper.

Red began checking out the window. When a rocky cove blocked them completely, he called up, "Time to trade!"

"No time," Dragon Star said. However, a moment later he pulled back on the tethers and brought them to a stop. Red stayed in place while Dragon Star dismounted and the horses stamped restlessly on the ground. Red knew they were pushing these horses too hard. Half a night's sleep and one meal in the last day wasn't enough to revive them after yesterday's forced march.

He waited for Dragon Star to open the door.

Pete asked, "If we're trading shifts, can I at least get into a more comfortable position?"

Red ignored him. "You've gotten us through the storm, time to take a break."

Dragon Star nodded. He reached around Red to grab the stake firmly before moving his body onto the nearby chair so he didn't block the door. Red let go and stepped outside to stretch.

He said, "I think we might get a little bit of sun today."

Red watched Pete's eyes go wide as he looked at Dragon Star. "Looks like there's another rooster in the hen yard."

Dragon Star pushed down on the spike just enough to make Pete wince. "Then you better keep your mind and mouth to yourself and hope I do not decide to reduce the surplus population."

Exhaustion slowed Red down, but now he understood Dragon Star's urgency. The bite was making a change in the only person Red could trust. He winked and nodded. Then he jumped onto the driver's seat and started the horses moving forward. The same black rocks blocked their path, standing in defiance of the incoming waves.

Red veered up the hill on the east, threading closely between trees. Here he saw the cliff harbored a beach he didn't have time to enjoy.

Eventually, the cliffs pulled back and Red moved down to the sand again. Although the temperature wasn't comfortable yet, he felt better with the rain stopped and his thin clothes dried. Now he knew what it felt like hauling a truckload of dynamite. Sitting on top of two vampires, trying to move fast across unyielding land, he wondered if at any moment one of the monsters beneath might rise up and kill him.

If Pete held the stake in Dragon Star's heart instead, Red would be doomed. As it stood, he had to rely on Dragon Star to use his will to hold back what had taken Pete. Red felt the three keys beating rhythmically against his bare chest inside the shirt. Three keys. It wasn't much, but they had a start. If they could get Pete back to his senses, they might have a chance.

Boom! Thud.

Red watched something meteoric rip a trench through the ground in front of him.

Boom, boom!

A black cannon ball buried itself in the water off to his right and splashed mist over the caravan of speeding carriages. Another tore into the wet sand behind them, throwing up debris.

Red turned to see a black ship with red bats on the sails moving rapidly along the shoreline. Three more fire flowers blossom. A moment later, three more *booms* preceded the large artillery blasting at rocks and trees around him.

"You had them follow us!" Red yelled down to Pete.

"Not me," Pete said. "They're just doing their job."

"Liar!" Red began weaving side to side, trying to alter the pace and distance of the carriages as much as he could. One cannonball landed close enough to toss mud all over Red and the carriage. "Nobody knew we were taking the coast."

"Call them off!" Red said. "Dragon Star, if he doesn't call them off, we have no choice but to kill him."

"I swear it isn't... Okay! Ow! I said I'll do it."

Boom!

The cannonball blasted the carriage tied up behind them. The horse team in tow fell as the splintered mess behind them twisted off the wheels. The new weight pulled Red's team to a stop as they stamped and whinnied out of fear.

Red turned so his voice was clear. "Pete, if another cannon fires from that ship, you will have to die. We tried to save you. But this is your last warning."

"You can't kill a vampire," Pete said. "They are already dead."

"Care to argue with him, Dragon Star?" Red asked. "We'll be sitting ducks here."

"He doesn't want them to hit us," Dragon Star said with some effort. "He would die, too."

"Not likely," Pete said.

"New plan," Red said. "Pete, bring the ship in closer."

"Closer?" Dragon Star and Pete both said at the same time.

"We're never going to make it fast enough with these horses," Red said. "With this strong wind, we'll get farther on that boat." He pulled the horses to a stop and put on the brake, before jumping down and opening the door so he could see Pete's face.

"Bring us aboard that ship," Red said. "If you get us free of here and tell us what we need to know, we will let you go back to the castle."

"What about—"

"We keep the key."

Pete strained to look down at the wooden stake, which had already begun to turn his flesh black in a thin ring around the edges. He looked back up at Red. "You swear you'll let me go?"

"Once we're safe and you've told us what we want to know."

"Why can't you just ask me right now?"

"You figure it out," Red said.

Red stood on the edge of the ship's rail, watching the land go slowly by. As long as he didn't think about how the nauseous bouncing up and down of the ship over the waves, he could pretend it was the cold. After a tense movement onto the ship with Dragon Star constantly threatening the life of their new puppet master, the sailors finally had the black ship moving south along the shore. At least the sailors were just dressed in ragged sailing clothes and not some goofy uniforms like the castle guards.

Red glanced back at the door to the captain's quarters. Dragon Star stood watch over Pete in there, and Red had no idea what would happen. At Dragon Star's insistence, Red had blocked the door with a heavy wooden board so neither of them could get out easily. Standing here on the ship with two dozen sword-toting sailors, Red knew the board wouldn't make any difference. If Pete won, or the infection took Dragon Star completely, the sailors would be coming for Red. If they did, Red planned to jump over the side. He had Dragon Star's sword, but he knew better than to test his luck against a whole crew.

Red still regretted leaving the last carriage behind. At least Pete sent one of the sailors to take the horses back to the castle. Now when Red and Dragon Star returned to the rest of the group, they would have the new problem of coming up with transportation—along with everything else.

He held a glimmer of hope that this ship would turn into a jet airplane at the next boundary and fly them all home in luxury. Something told him none of the Machine Monks had actuated anything so useful. At least for now they were making good time. He just hoped they could get out of Hanna's gothic realm before anything permanently bad happened to Dragon Star.

Red's eyes went wide and he snapped his head toward the front of the ship. A familiar tingle of energy buzzed in his brain. The world rippled as if the cellophane surface of an invisible bubble had been pierced by the long pole sticking off the bow of the ship. The front of the ship plunge into the barrier, turning from black to white as the morphing energy took hold and twisted the very atomic matter to the Actuator's specifications.

The sea brine taste in his mouth changed to potato chips and grape jelly. His eyes filled with white static as the arrhythmic thunder blotted out all sounds. This time his stomach lurched, not because of the change, but because of the constant rise and fall of the ship. The whole deck seemed to drop three feet as his skin burned for one second.

When the change waned, red instinctively searched the world for differences. Although the deck lowered, they were still on a black ship. Red looked every direction, noting the crew's apparel had become more ragged. Several of them wore eye patches. One had a hook where his hand used to be. When red looked up at the still black sails, he knew in an instant what kind of realm they had crossed into. The bats on the sails had turned to skulls with ivory colored bones crossed beneath them.

Red actually smiled. This realm might be intensely dangerous, but at least he understood the rules. He looked down at his own clothes. Still barefoot, he had dark shorts under a large striped shirt. This would be one of Tina's realms. Historical fiction. Nothing was more fiction than a good pirate story. He just didn't know why there would be one off the coast of Washington. He did know they already had Tina's key. So at least he didn't have to worry about that.

Red pushed off the rail and began walking toward the captain's quarters, his feet splashing through water where somebody recently mopped it over the deck. The nervous feeling in his stomach never left after the change. Now he had to face the truth. *What would he find when he opened the door? Would Dragon Star be back to normal? Would Pete? Would they have some illness, or be dead?*

Red stopped his mind from imagining. There was no point in speculating how the machine would negotiate this one. He had to look and find out. He heaved the heavy board off the bars and took a deep breath.

Then he pulled the door open.

CHAPTER TWENTY-SEVEN

It took a moment for Red's eyes to adjust to the dim light in the captain's quarters. All the heavy drapes kept out the sunlight. He first saw the silhouette of people outside as he moved forward cautiously, leading with Dragon Star's sword to protect against he couldn't imagine what. Globes, telescopes, maps, and other maritime paraphernalia covered the table to one side and a shelf running around the perimeter. One body lay on the floor. The other sprawled across the hammock.

In the damp, dark room, Red saw both of them were dressed in the rough garb of buccaneers. Their chests moved slowly up and down. Unwilling to touch them until he knew more, Red stepped to the window and slowly pulled one of the heavy red curtains aside.

He saw Dragon Star on the floor. Pete, on the bed, had one hand over his heart. The wooden stake wasn't anywhere. He again verified they were both breathing. Then he said quietly, "Dragon Star? Pete?"

Dragon Star turned onto his side with a heavy exhale. Pete gave a small cough, raising his other hand to block his eyes.

"Are you guys okay?" Red raised his voice. "You're alive! How do you feel?"

Pete began to sit up. Red raised the sword. Pete moaned and sat back down, both hands on his chest now. Something between Pete's hands caught the light. Red stepped over Dragon Star's legs to get a closer view. A golden rod with a flattened skull at the end stuck up out of Pete's chest.

"What in the world?" Red lowered his sword and moved closer. He put his free hand forward to touch it.

"Don't!" Pete batted Red's hand away. "It hurts like the devil."

"Is that a key?" Red's hand went instinctively to the heavy collection of objects around his neck. The tighter new shirt didn't disguise them well at all.

"I think so."

Dragon Star roused and sat up. He rolled his eyes and laid straight back down with a moan.

"Do you feel sick?" Red asked.

Dragon Star nodded, one hand on his head and covering his eyes.

"Let me get a look at it," Red said. Pete slowly moved his hands apart, separating his torn shirt. Right over his heart, the shiny instrument stuck out of a black keyhole in his hairy chest. "Does your heart feel different?"

Pete nodded. "It's not right. It sounds like a clock in my head."

"Can you take out the key?"

"I don't know what will happen."

"What if somebody turns it?"

"I don't know! Who knows what crazy ideas these Machine freaks had?"

"This wasn't the Monks," Red said. "It's just the negotiations the Actuator makes."

"Well either turning or removing the key will kill me then. But we don't know which one."

"Then don't do anything for now. Do you still have mental control of the people running this ship?"

"No."

"Not that I trust you to tell the truth."

"I'm not a vampire anymore."

"Also what you would say if you still were. If you can't control the men, we have a problem. This is a pirate ship now. Those are pirates. They aren't going to take orders from an old man with heart problems."

"Cheap shot," Pete said.

"At least you're not dead... yet." Red moved over and checked on Dragon Star.

"I will be okay," the Korean said. "Just give me a minute to catch my breath."

"Take the sword and cover Pete." Dragon Star raised his hand to accept the weapon. Then he sat up and pointed it at the older man.

"I swear, I'm not a vampire. I don't want to kill you guys or control anybody. That wasn't me. That was what Hanna did to me. Honest."

"You'll understand our reluctance here," Red said. Pete nodded. "When I get back we'll have a nice talk and try to figure out if we can trust you or not."

"Where are you going?" Dragon Star asked. He stood up and moved shakily to one of the chairs by the cluttered table.

"I'm going to try and figure out what the men sailing this ship have changed into."

"Do you have a plan for where we go next?"

"I don't know. If the crew is amenable, maybe we'll sail all the way down the coast. We don't have the carriages anymore, so using the mirrors to get through Nancy's land is no longer an option."

Red pushed the door open and squinted in the bright morning sun. A group of pirates with flintlock pistols and heavy cutlasses moved in around him.

"Where's the captain?" asked a bare chested man with three gold hoop earrings on one side and a scar on his sunburned cheeks.

"He's sick," Red said.

"We want to see him," said a shorter man with a striped bandana tied over his bald head.

"What's the problem?" Red wished he'd kept Dragon Star's sword handy.

The first man answered, "We ain't got any orders, see? And we only take orders from the Captain."

"He asked me to tell you to take the ship south as fast as possible."

"South?" a dark skinned man at the helm called down from the wheel above them. "That's not a destination, is it?"

"Follow the shoreline to the south, and dock near Los Angeles."

"We don't take orders from you," said the man with the bandana. He raised a pistol. "We know you done something to the Captain. We ain't about to let you trick us into thinking you're in charge now."

Red put up his hands and backed away from the growing mob of half a dozen, which closed in a semi-circle toward him. "You got it all wrong. I'm with you. The captain's hurt. We've been helping him. You can see." He pointed to the door.

The group looked over, more guns drawn now so he knew Dragon Star's sword wouldn't help him at all. One of the late comers with black skin pointed a knife at him and said, "What's that around your neck?"

Red reached back and opened the door behind him. "I'll show you. Just wait here and I'll bring the captain out."

"Why can't we go in?"

"I told you, he's sick. Just give me a second and I'll help him come out." Red didn't wait for more questions. He spun in through the door and pulled it closed. For good measure, he dropped the locking bar into place, too.

"Here's your chance to prove we can trust you," Red said. He turned to see Pete sitting on the side of the bed. Pete looked up with a weary smile. "They want to see the captain and know you are alright."

"What should I tell them?"

"Just tell them to follow the shore south to Los Angeles."

"What about my... um, condition?"

Red looked around. He found a leather tri-corn hat with a feather. He handed it to Pete. "Cover it with this."

Pete gently placed the hat over his chest so the gold device didn't show. "I wonder if I need to wind it up."

"Not now," Red said. He helped Pete up. "Just look strong and angry."

Pete nodded as they walked over to the door. The men outside already rattled it, trying to force it. Red lifted the bar and the door threw itself open.

A loud commotion of men trying to push in stopped when Pete yelled, "Halt! Move out, dogs! Yer mother isn't in here so you can all stand back."

Red looked at Dragon Star who shrugged. He whispered, "Maybe don't overdo the smack talk."

The men backed away from the door. Pete moved forward slowly, making eye contact with each man as if he was measuring them. Red held his breath. One word and Pete could have them both strung up, or worse. Red never trusted Pete to begin with. He'd never been mean or vindictive, though. *Was it really just the vampire thing making Pete a sociopath before? Or would a crew of pirates at his command be another way to take some power?* Red started looking at the windows. Maybe they could jump.

Dragon Star must have had the same concern because he rose and lifted the sword to the ready. Red noticed it was a heavier sword now with much more curve along the blade and a broad knuckle guard.

"My first mate tells me you didn't want to take orders," Pete growled. Red rolled his eyes. He smiled and let himself breathe a sigh of relief. "I don't think I have to tell you what happens to a man what doesn't follow orders on my ship, do I?"

The crew wagged their heads. "We just wanted to know you was alright," one voice said from the back.

"Sure you did, and hoping to take my place if I wasn't. That's the next thing to mutiny. And I'll run through any man so much as thinks the word on my vessel. And I'll expect all of you to do the same. "Now trim those sails and get us south to L.A. as fast as a bird or you'll all be missing shore leave when we get there."

"Aye," several voices said in broken unison.

"Move!" The mob began to break up, only the original two men stayed behind.

"You have a problem?" Pete barked.

"I thought I was your first mate," the hulking, bare chested man said. "Seems you were unhappy with my work."

Pete stared off to the horizon, the rising sun to his back. "I misspoke," he said. "You are the first mate. And captain when I'm gone."

"Who's that then?" said the shorter one, pointing accusatorily at Red. Apparently he had plans to be the first mate next.

"Just our mission," Pete said. "He's the one taking us to the buried treasure."

Red rolled his eyes.

"Buried? Who would be fool enough to bury treasure? Only an idiot would do something like that."

Pete shrugged. "Sadly, he's been called that before."

"Now you're taking up with idiots and calling them first mate," said the short one.

"Are you questioning my orders?" Pete growled as his knees began wobbling.

Pete didn't have much left in him.

"Back to work, Shorty," said the bigger pirate. "Captain gave an order and you'll be following it. I'll see to it, Captain."

Pete nodded. "And don't disturb me until you can see the port!" He slammed the door and then began to tumble. Red caught him and helped him back to the bed.

When he pulled the hat away, they saw blood had trickled out of the key hole and smeared on the torn shirt and the hat's brim.

"What's going on?" Red asked.

"It is the stake," Dragon Star said. "It looks like a key, but it is really just the same stake. We need to pull it out."

"I'll bleed to death," Pete said, his wide face ashen to match his graying hair.

"Not if we staunch the flow." Dragon Star found a long wooden match and lit a nearby oil lamp. Then he held a small knife in the flame until it grew hot enough to glow along the cutting edge.

Pete's eyes went wide. "Just leave it in. Maybe the next change it will be gone."

"You know that's not true," Red said. He found a piece of rope and cut six inches off the end with Dragon Star's sword.

"What's that for?"

"For you to bite on," Red said. "We can't have you screaming and getting the crew jumpy again."

"At least you trust me now, right?"

"If we did not," Dragon Star said, "We would push that key in."

CHAPTER TWENTY-EIGHT

D ragon Star knew the black soot on the hot blade would leave a nasty scar. He held the blade into the flame longer while Red put the rope in Pete's mouth.

Pete spat it out. "That's disgusting! Are you sure we have to do this? What if turning the key is the right thing to do?"

Red shoved the frayed jute back in. "Dragon Star's right. It was a stake before. The Actuator wouldn't change the nature of the device. Pulling the key out is the right choice." He wound a strip of linen around his hand to make a nice compress, in case the blood didn't stop with the first burn. He looked up, signaling to Dragon Star. They were ready.

Dragon Star brought the blade over and held it next to the gold protrusion. With his spare hand, he gently took hold of the key. He glanced at Pete's eyes. They were wide beneath a wrinkled, sweat-covered brow. He loathed causing more pain, but knew it was the only way to save the man. "This might hurt a little bit."

After a lifetime dedicated to avoiding and relieving suffering, Dragon Star pulled the metal out of the black keyhole in Pete's chest. Before too much blood bubbled out, he pressed the tip of the blade, pointed side over the small end where the teeth entered to minimize how much of the blade he used.

Every muscle in Pete's body jerked as he let out a moan. A few seconds later, Dragon Star lifted the knife. The smell of seared hair and flesh filled the air.

A well of blood filled the keyhole and began to spill over. Red pressed the linen down to staunch the stream.

Dragon Star scorched the stain on the knife as he began heating it back up.

He said "We're going to have to put it into the hole."

Pete's eyes couldn't get any wider, but beneath the gag he said, "Huh?"

Red pushed Pete's head back down onto the bed with his free hand. "Just don't go in too far."

Dragon Star nodded to acknowledge the unnecessary advice. One small nick and Pete's heart would bleed out. No amount of cauterizing would stop it.

Once the sharp edge glowed red again, Dragon Star pulled it from the lantern and turned back to Pete. Red lifted the blood soaked fabric. Dragon Star put the hot tip in, searing the sides of the keyhole where he could. Blood poured out, rolling down the side of Pete's chest in a delta and staining the blankets beneath. Pete's moan rose in pitch and intensity.

"It's not working." Dragon Star pulled the knife free as Red clamped the wet fabric down again. "It takes too long and I can't put the tip in very far."

Red shook his head. "We need something flat. Maybe break the tip off the knife?"

Dragon Star paused.

"What is it?"

"Hand me the key." Dragon Star wiped the blood from the gold key onto Pete's shirt, briefly examining the teeth. Except for one kink moving back toward the bow, it was basically a square ended skeleton key. Dragon Star held it to the fire, turning it. He watched for any sign of the gold warping or melting. The skull he held it by rapidly grew too hot to hold and he had to drop it with a clang against the hard wood floor. Tearing a strip from his shirt, Dragon Star grabbed the key again and shoved it back into the fire.

Pete moaned again, his eyes rolled back in a kind of delirium.

Suddenly, a loud knock sounded. "You okay, Captain? What's going on in there?"

Red bit his lip. He reached over with bloodstained fingers and pulled the piece of rope from Pete's mouth.

"Fine!" Pete barked. He didn't sound fine.

"I'll be here," the man said. "Call if you need me."

Red put the soft bit back in and nodded to Dragon Star. Dragon Star began to think they should have waited until they got closer to their destination. But he knew the ship could change into anything any time. They had no idea what was next. They needed to fix this now.

Dragon Star gripped the fabric, holding the metal so tightly his fingertips still burned. Ignoring the pain, he gently positioned the key over Red's hand and nodded.

Red pulled the bloody rags away, smearing the trails before new ones formed. Dragon Star plunged the hot key into the hole. He moved it around, trying to touch every side surface as he went deeper in.

This time when he pulled it free, the blood filled the keyhole very slowly.

"One more?" Red asked.

Dragon Star wiped it again, heating the key until he thought the fabric might combust. Then he brought it over and plunged it into the hole again.

Pete didn't even flinch. His eyes had dilated. He stared off into space.

This time when he pulled the key out, Dragon Star didn't wait for the blood. He dropped the key with a clang on the floor. Then he tucked the small piece of fabric from his shirt into the hole.

Red put a new piece of linen over that. So far, the only blood on it was from his fingerprints.

"As often as I end up with blood all over me," Red said, "I should have been a surgeon."

"Or a butcher," Dragon Star said with a smile. He blew cold air on his fingertips to try and ease some of the burning.

"Think he'll be alright?"

Dragon Star tore a long strip of fabric from the edge of the bed cloth and worked it around Pete's back. Then he tied it tight around the compress so Red could let got.

Red poured water from a large pewter pitcher onto his hands, letting the excess fall to the floor. Then he put some in a metal mug and offered it to Pete.

"Tell me about your family," Dragon Star said. Pete stared at his face for a long time, not answering. Dragon Star patted his cheeks lightly to get his attention. "Where did you grow up?"

"I'm not like all you guys," Pete finally said. He took a few sips of water. "I had a great family." His eyes seemed to be coming back into focus. "I didn't sign away my whole life. They took it."

"Who took it?" Red asked.

Dragon Star thought back over the last few years. He really didn't know how Pete had come to be on the base. He wasn't a Machine Monk or military man. The job title of external consultant didn't really mean anything for people never allowed to leave.

"It wasn't anything I did or did wrong. I just had the wrong friends. I used to know the Andersons, before that cursed machine tore all our lives apart." Pete gritted his teeth between bouts of talking.

"You knew Arne Anderson, the creator of the Actuator?" Dragon Star asked. All the Machine Monks had ever been given was basic information about the man and a journal that read like riddles. *Could Pete really have known the inventor in person?*

"I was there when he built it."

Every Machine Monk knew the Actuator had a kind of personality. When the process started, it reached into your mind and extracted information to questions. The exact nature of the questions gave them all insights into the mind responsible for its design. But until now, none of them had ever had access to any information about the inventor of such a fantastic device.

"Why didn't you tell us this before?" Dragon Star asked.

"Because I like being alive," Pete said. "The government didn't recruit me to the base. They imprisoned me there. I had strict orders to keep my mouth shut or they would incarcerate me. The only person who knew was Commander Newell. She never asked me anything, though."

"What was he like?" Dragon Star demanded. "Was he full of deep insights?"

Pete nodded, then winced in pain. "He was like a butterfly, moving from one thought to another. He was a genius, of course. But he'd get off track so easily I could beat him at chess more than half the time. All I had to do was ask him about politics or suggest a word riddle and he'd start making mistakes left and right. Of course, if he kept his mind on the game through to the end, he could take me any day."

"And you liked that?" Red asked. Dragon Star didn't care to hear about Pete. He felt like an archaeologist who found an ancient treasure trove.

"It was a blast. One day we'd hang out at a coffee shop talking about which sub-atomic particles the universe could live without. The next we'd be planting trees in his back yard and debating the merits of various levels of governmental control. He never made me feel stupid. He could explain anything, no matter how complicated, so I understood and had a place in the conversation.

"Did I like it? Yeah. I loved it. It was the only time in my life I felt alive, when I was with them."

"Them?" Dragon Star probed. He suspected Pete might not be all the way out of shock.

"Agatha, his wife. The two were inseparable. You never saw two more different people. He was all science and absent-minded professor. She was a full-blown hippie, with flowers in her hair and everything. You'd think they wouldn't have anything to talk about, but they never stopped. Politics, philosophy, history. And they never made me feel like a third wheel. Sometimes I think they needed me. I was like a buffer, overlapping both of them so they had secure ground."

Red opened another curtain, studying how much blood Pete lost. Then he gave him more water. Dragon Star couldn't think of anything else. He felt like someone coming out of the desert into an oasis. He didn't want Pete to ever stop talking. "How did he build it? How does it work? Why did he build it?"

"Slow down," Red said with a laugh. "He needs some rest." He looked at Dragon Star with one eye half closed and a crooked smile. Dragon Star didn't care.

"I don't know how it works. He explained it to me once, but I was drunk and didn't really listen. It has something to do with resonance and matching spin on particles. That was only one part of the formula. The other, bigger part was getting a computer to understand what people want. He did it, though. Something about thinking in pictures and patterned recognition software. I'm sure he could have explained it to my understanding. But I was busy at the time and I didn't bother to ask."

"Busy?" Dragon Star stood up, indignant. "You were too busy to find out how the most amazing thing in the universe worked?"

"I've beaten myself up about it since," Pete said. "But I can't go back and fix it. I was able to tell them enough that they could make the dampeners. That's all."

Dragon Star felt disgusted. But he refused to let his emotions ruin this. He forced the judgment down and concentrated. "You said you know why he built it?"

"Yep," Pete said, with a half cough, half laugh. "They built it to save the world."

CHAPTER TWENTY-NINE

s Pete lay in the uncomfortable, sticky bed, he couldn't tell if he was going to die or if he just wanted to. Every click of the bizarre heart sent a tiny jolt of pain through his body. The regular ticking actually caused him concern. He never noticed his own heart beat before. Now he knew his brain had just adjusted to the *thump-thump* and blocked it out. The single, patterned flow of blood upset his mind.

That, and the burning of his chest made everything unbearable.

At least the hole felt clean somehow. It throbbed with pain all around the edges and top, but it didn't send that spike of pain through his heart like it did before. Pete had been through a lot of terrible relationships in his decades as a bachelor. Now, he knew Hanna trumped them all.

"Is there at least some rum on this pirate ship to take the edge off the pain?"

Red began looking around for a bottle. Pete liked him. Even when Red had pinned him to the floor of the carriage and put a sharp stick through his chest until it tickled his heart, Pete knew Red could understand him. They both lived on the base without being a Monk or soldier. Even though they weren't best friends, Pete trusted Red to walk the middle line between obsession and servitude.

Dragon Star stared at Pete now without blinking or glancing away. Pete hated the intense scrutiny. Early on, Dragon Star expected Pete to be his friend based only on their age difference with the other people on base. That had lasted about ten seconds. In better circumstances, Pete would just laugh and walk away, leaving the annoying Korean to suffer with his Actuatorial sycophancy.

Pete missed the days when people valued his input and talked to him like an intellectual equal.

"How were the Andersons saving the world with the Actuator?" Dragon Star repeated.

Pete knew his best play was to keep his mouth shut. One should always extract the highest price for valuable information. Also, he knew things he would never tell these two. Still, he needed them to trust him until they were somewhere safer and he'd healed. He didn't really know where they were taking him. Pete would just have to be careful about what he said. Lacking any better distraction to keep him from going mad with the clockwork heartbeat triggering pain in his burned flesh, Pete continued.

"They said humans were their own worst enemy. It's the prisoner's dilemma. The barrier between the world as we know it and utopia is human nature.

"Basically, everybody wants to live in a higher order with peace and mutual consideration. We all know it's possible. We all want it. But the reason we can't have it is because whenever somebody tries to set it up, it leaves a weakness individuals can exploit. The best benefit to the individual is to put the rest of the people down and lift themselves up above everybody else. That's how a few people become rich on the backs of the masses who are kept poor. That's how terrorists drive larger societies to spend fortunes on huge militaries. It's why one bad kid can bring a whole family down.

"But Agatha had this idea that if we could somehow skip the middle step where the people willing to sacrifice for the utopia were vulnerable to evil people trying to exploit them, everybody would be better off. The only losers in that situation would be the few who wanted to prey on the others anyway."

Seeing the narrative continue, Dragon Star sat back down.

"Arne caught on fire with that idea. He became intoxicated with the possibility of making a world where everybody could be happy. He kept talking about how human nature was the barrier to utopia. Then he started building the machine. Agatha and I both suffered with him gone. For the first time his mind didn't flit from idea to idea. He never swayed or got distracted. He talked about it constantly, but unlike before, he didn't listen to our answers.

"Without him it became awkward. I didn't feel right spending so much time alone with Agatha. But she stayed loyal to the end, believing with all her heart that Arne could build this insane machine.

"And he did. I never really believed he would. We talked about everything under the sun. He never went off and built any of it before. Not only did he build it. It worked."

Pete coughed and shifted his weight, looking for Red.

"I can't find any alcohol," Red said. "I'll have to go downstairs and look for it."

"What happened after they built it? Where are they now?" Dragon Star demanded.

Pete closed his eyes. These memories weren't good like the others. He didn't want to think about them now. And he realized he was talking without being careful. He had to be careful.

He said, "Too tired. I..."

Pete rolled over and closed his eyes.

By the time Dragon Star could get his mind back under control, Red had already returned with a bottle of foul smelling liquid. Finding Pete asleep, Red laid a blanket out on the floor and slept, too. Dragon Star had always been amazed at how fast Red nodded off. He may be reckless, but he burned hot. When he reached the end of his fuel, he went out in the blink of an eye.

Dragon Star knew he should try to get some rest, but his brain was firing on all cylinders. Why hadn't Commander Newell told them Pete knew about the creation of the Actuator? Why did the government imprison Pete on the base if not for information he knew?

Like all Machine Monks, Dragon Star always felt a closeness to the Actuator. It defined his purpose. Unlike the other houses, Empty House had always been a dichotomy. They sought to free themselves from all attachments and emotions. They trained to clear their minds so whenever they used the Actuator the test field became neutral in all respects. Dragon Star felt strongly how important such a task was, not only for the functioning of the device, but to the individuals. Yet the very fact of emptying one's mind for the purpose of the Actuator created a polarized idea. On the one hand, they were meant to be free of attachment and thoughts. On the other hand, they were feeding information into the Actuator. Using the machine was addicting. The energy of Actuation was a thrill to the senses. It represented the opposite of their goal.

So the Empty House was an oxymoron. Dragon Star's students trained in enantiodromia. They pushed all thoughts and feelings out of their mind in order to be overwhelmed by the greatest of feelings and most intense of thoughts. Thus, the end of all his meditations inevitably meant failure.

Dragon Star lived with the complex that no matter how well he trained his mind, it was motivated by the opposite desire.

Here, sitting cross-legged on the hard wooden floor, he watched Pete sleep fitfully. He knew he shouldn't be reveling in the new tidbits of information Pete gave him. Yet he could not deny his pulse racing and his brain burning to assimilate and analyze every thought.

Dragon Star always sensed a kind of benevolence in the Actuator. Until now, he had no evidence to support it. When he had the great conversation with the computer, he felt the device searching his mind. Just like when Pete had been trying to read and control his mind, Dragon Star knew what kinds of ideas and pictures the machine accessed during the upload of information before each Actuation. When the machine looked in his mind, Dragon Star always felt it was looking for ways to make the world better. Now he knew it to be true. While his understanding of computers was minimal, he knew the machine sought for good.

Dedicated House twisted and ruined it.

He clenched his fists. Always teaching it to make horrors and fantasies, they had reprogrammed the machine somehow. It had been searching for good, and they had taught it humanity wanted these escapist genres. How foolish they had all been. Instead of studying what the machine was, they jumped in and perverted it to what they wanted. Something elegant, built to bestow peace and love on the world, had been converted to bring death and horror.

Only when his thoughts turned to sadness could Dragon Star finally calm them. He still had a dragon to kill in vengeance for his students. But he'd long ago tucked that caustic passion away for later use.

He closed his eyes and let the meditation clear his mind. He realized without the Actuator, and with no hope of ever using it again, the meditation had returned to a pure state. It didn't have the taint of promised exhilaration as a reward. So with a new found integrity, Dragon Star cleared his emotions and slipped into an empty bliss.

Red jolted awake when somebody pounded on the door so hard it rattled the windows around the cabin. Despite the noise, it took a few seconds for his mind to remember everything they'd been through in the last few days. Even when he did, it took longer to put together why he was sleeping on the floor of a rolling ship. He remembered Nancy and Hanna, but it took a while to finally remember Pete and the pirates. He stood up before the second round of forceful knocking.

Pete moaned on the bed and shifted his weight. Dragon Star sat in his cross-legged meditation, but Red knew he was sleeping. In the short space between rising and moving into action, Red felt a flood of gratitude for Dragon Star being here. The man's solid mind had been the only anchor in this ineffable world.

Red remembered the bare-chested, over muscled man in his mind when the ham fists pounded the third time on the door. He knew they hadn't arrived in Los Angeles so soon. This could only be trouble. Dragon Star stood, too. He quietly lifted the sword and dropped it so it was in the shadows. Pete rolled over and opened his eyes.

Red shrugged and lifted the locking bar. If the pirates were determined to get in, there would be no way to stop them.

A crowd of men, perhaps the whole crew, left only a few inches free in front of the door. Not surprisingly, the earring-sporting oaf and his trigger-happy friend with the striped bandana were right in the front.

"I hope you have a good reason for interrupting the Captain's rest," Red said.

"Aye," the first mate said.

It had grown dark outside. Above the heads of the anxious crew, a smear of pink on the clouds behind them showed the sunset almost over. Red knew that color should be on his right if they were heading south. Instead, they were facing it full west. "Something stopping us from heading south?"

"We've been talking," the first mate said.

"I'll have none of that," Pete roared from behind.

"You'll have it because we are agreed," the shorter man said. He hadn't pointed the pistol at Red yet, but he'd primed it and kept shifting it from hand to hand.

"Agreed on what?" Red asked.

"We agreed we aren't going to Los Angeles," the big man said.

"And we won't go back to Bathaven either," the shorter one added.

"Why?" Pete demanded as he picked up his hat and stepped forward between Pete and Dragon Star.

"We won't go back to being slaves," the first mate said. "We don't know what happened to our families. But we know we can't get them back. So none of us wants to go back there and be controlled by the next vampire of the day."

Pete nodded. "I can understand that. But Los Angeles is in the other direction."

"We don't think we'll get there before something else strange happens. We don't know what it will be, but we aren't willing to gamble our lives for whatever fool reason you have to go to Los Angeles."

"We like it here!" several men said. "Wide open seas and freedom from all forms of tyranny."

The first mate wrinkled his bald brow and said, "You're welcome to stay on and captain the ship here. But we, none of us, are leaving these waters."

Pete said, "It's mutiny then?"

CHAPTER THIRTY

Pete stepped forward next to Red, staring in the faces of the ugly men. "We'd hoped you'd see it differently," said the huge man. The three rings in his ear wiggled as he spoke.

"How can anybody see it differently?" Pete demanded. "Am I captain of this ship or not?"

"Aye."

"And I trusted you as first mate."

"Aye."

"And did I leave you orders?"

"Aye."

"Yet here we stand. Tell me, what's the penalty for disobeying a Captain's orders on a pirating vessel?" Pete held the feathered leather hat over his heart, not willing to show any weakness. He wasn't playing a part or bluffing. In his soul, he knew he was the captain. It had fallen to him as surely as he was a vampire before. And though he remembered the change and the fact of being something completely different before all of that, he would not stand down. This was his vessel and he wouldn't let it go without a fight.

The men looked at each other uncomfortably, unsure what emotion to follow.

"The penalty be death," said the collaborator, shifting his bandana back with one hand and lifting the pistol menacingly in the other. "But you can't kill us all."

"Then I ask my question again. It's to be a mutiny, then?"

The pirates looked at one another, ashamed despite all their determination and recklessness. "We don't prefer it," the first mate said. "We want you to stay on as captain. It's not out of disrespect. But we ain't giving up our lives to anything other than the lure of treasure and the freedom of the open sea."

"Freedom?" Red laughed. "You can't sail north past Seattle or south beyond Portland. How is that freedom?"

"It's more than we had. And we won't risk it on some fool's errand," affirmed the short man in the back with scarred, black skin.

"We're asking you one last time, Captain. Stay with us and plunder these seas. There are ships out there and treasure. We've passed plenty of ports, too. What could possibly be better than that in Los Angeles?"

Pete nodded. He felt the tug of the sailor on his soul as if he'd been one his whole life. His clockwork heart seemed fine now. Surely the pain would subside in time. A captain would be well appreciated by wenches in every port. He'd get the lion's share of the gold. And the men wanted him. Nobody but Hanna had wanted him for a long measure of years.

Pete turned to Red, "I'm sorry, but…"

Slap!

With wide eyes, Pete realized Red had hit him in the face.

"You dare strike the captain—"

"Snap out of it, Pete," Red said. "We have an urgent mission. We're trying to save the world. Billions of people dying, remember? We need your help."

Pete noted with satisfaction the score of pistols trained on Red with itchy fingers waiting for the order to kill the interloper for this insult. A proper captain should set an example. Discipline was the key to running a tight ship. And if he ordered his men to take them now, Red would be powerless to stop him.

"You are not one of them," Dragon Star said. "Do not dishonor Arne and Agatha by succumbing to the fanciful creations of their machine."

Pete stepped back and took a deep breath, which sent pain cracking across his chest like a web of broken glass. Dragon Star was right. He'd had two friends in this world. Two people who had respected and loved him. He owed it to them to try and set things right. Besides which, he had unfinished business.

"Very well," Pete said. "I relinquish command. He handed his hat to the bare chested man. Every eye among the motley pirates expressed surprise. "I only ask that in exchange for my fine vessel you put us off in a port proper with some money and supplies."

"Aye," the large man nodded. "About face you dogs! Tack up the river to Portland and don't waste a single zephyr or it's the lash!"

Watching the black sails carry the ship away into the dark of night, Pete knew he would regret leaving the crew for the rest of his life. He'd only known them for a couple of days. But having touched their minds in a way few people understand, he felt he knew them all intimately. He'd seen their fears and hopes. He'd experienced their disappointment at losing jobs and families to the Actuation. He felt their loyalty. Despite knowing it came from outside them, they had chosen to embrace it for lack of anything else in their lives. They were the best and noblest people he had ever known. Now they sailed away from him between the stars and their reflection in the water, and he couldn't stop himself from taking huge, painful sighs. For the rest of his life he would miss them more than he missed the family he hadn't seen since childhood.

If everything else didn't work out, he would come back and join them. He didn't need to be captain again. He would be happy just to work alongside them, coaxing speed from the wind and collecting lucre to waste on riotous weekends.

He still had them in his thoughts when Red bought tickets for the next train at an old building covered in soot.

"There's a late train leaving soon," Red said.

They stood on the platform, on the outskirts of the town. Again, in the night they could only see a few dim lights. "It looks like a ghost town," Dragon Star said.

Pete didn't understand. "So?"

"That's how it looked from the other side," Red said.

"That's Portland?" Pete asked. "I thought it was a huge city with millions of people.

"It was," Dragon Star said.

"What's it now?" Pete asked.

"We don't know." Red strained as if he could make out some detail. "But most of those millions of people are gone."

"Let's not find out," Pete said. Something bothered him about it. As a former vampire and pirate captain, it felt odd to be worried about whatever dark and strange reality may lay there. A chill went down his arms and back.

The old-fashioned steam engine began building up pressure as it idled on the tracks. The engineer vented a bit of steam to blow the whistle and call the passengers. Red lifted the bag of food and knives the pirates had given them. Dragon Star held only his sword, now wrapped in brown paper to try and camouflage it as a parcel.

Pete followed them, empty handed. He tried to keep his breathing shallow and not exert himself much. He felt exhausted. He still had the gold key, but he felt like the pirates had taken some of his life force with them. Somehow, he had been a strong and commanding person with them near him. *Was it the crew or the ship lending him strength?* It didn't matter now. Both were gone.

The train smelled funny on the inside. Pete sensed the esters of hundreds of uncomfortable, sweaty people in tiny, little cabins with small windows. Clearly, they never aired out this train.

Red led them all down a cramped hallway to a short door. Inside were two beds, arranged like bunk beds. A small stool of a chair sat against the side by the tiny window. Pete reached over and pulled it open, craving fresh air more now than any time in his life.

"We're bound to go through several boundaries before we get all the way back," Red said.

"Assuming this train goes all the way back," Dragon Star said. Pete wished Dragon Star would stop staring at him. He knew the shorter man craved information about the Andersons. Pete could probably overload the Machine Monk's brain with it if he chose. But he wouldn't give it up easily. Information insured the two stronger men would keep him alive for the whole trip. Anyway, Pete could never tell them everything.

"I'm exhausted," Pete said. "Anybody mind if I take the bottom bunk? I think it would be hard to climb the ladder with my chest still not healed." The stupid thing still ticked like a clock.

Dragon Star looked off to the side. Clearly, the Korean man had hoped they'd have more time to talk.

Red seemed to notice, too. He said, "Fine by me. We'll have plenty of time on this trip. Hopefully."

Dragon Star bowed once and put out a hand to the low platform. "Go ahead."

"Do you want to eat first?" Red asked.

Pete wagged his head. "I just need to rest before I fall down." He gently removed his long brown jacket and rolled it into a ball to use as a pillow. Then he plopped onto the hard bed.

The other two stared at him like a circus freak, so he exerted more of his precious remaining energy to roll over and pull the thin wool blanket over his shoulder.

Pete slept all night and only left the bed twice the next day for food and the bathroom. He ignored the others, pretending to sleep. Even sore from disuse, his limbs still felt too tired to move.

They went through at least three boundaries. Two he was awake for, another woke him up. The one where he was in the bathroom was his least favorite experience of the lot. After the first, his heart went back to normal. Then it turned into some kind of robotic implant. After that, it finally turned back to his regular heart. He didn't know or care if there had been any changes in his sleep.

Each boundary, the train changed. Once it had gone quiet like they were floating above magnetic rails. Another time, in the dark of the night, Pete thought the vehicle might have turned into some kind of living thing. Luckily, it went back to normal before they had to get out. *Whatever normal was.*

In Los Angeles, they changed trains. The whole transfer happened inside a huge building, so Pete never saw what was going on outside. He heard several gunshots and something like an explosion. None of it affected the people inside the station.

The new train didn't have any sleeping arrangements. Red bought them first class seats, so Pete could at least recline. He had a nice window, which he promptly covered with a pull down blind and went straight back to sleep. Before nodding off, he looked down at his chest. His shirt had become a white button up, still ripped over the left side. He pulled back the bandage. Somewhere in the night, the hole in his chest had filled in. He still had an ugly black scar the shape of an old fashioned key hole over a knife shaped welt. But it didn't send spider webs of pain through his chest anymore. The beating returned to normal, too.

When Pete woke this time, a cowboy with a dirty, red bandana over his mouth and nose had a six-shooter pointing straight in his face. The bandit growled when he spoke. "Empty your pockets!"

CHAPTER THIRTY-ONE

Red couldn't believe their luck had lasted through more than a full day's journey and five boundaries. He didn't know off the top of his head which of the Machine Monks had been a fan of trains, but whoever it was, they were his new favorite. Nothing else could explain such a run of good fortune. Still, he wasn't surprised when the train stopped in the middle of the desert heading east. It was too much to hope they'd make it all the way without some kind of problem.

Without the air blowing in the windows, the inside of the metal passenger car grew uncomfortably hot. The last boundary left them in another steam engine, dressed in brown and tan. Red pulled the knives out of the box of supplies the pirates sent with them. The box started as a wooden chest. Then it turned into a leather bag. Before the last change, it was a briefcase. Now it was a wooden crate. The knives had stayed more or less the same all the way.

When cowboys came in, flashing guns in everybody's face and demanding money, Red stayed cool. They had money in the crate, but it was under fruit and bread. These desperados wouldn't want to take a box of food.

"Clean 'em out," the dust caked man barked in Red's face.

Red pulled a few coins from his pocket, leaving the fabric inside out to show he had nothing else in them. He kept his hands up.

"That's all you got?" the shorter, but much smellier man demanded. He used his gun to tip his hat back and then forward again nervously.

"Sorry," Red said. "We're poor travelers. We just have a little food to get us back home to Oklahoma."

"Poor folks sit in the back cars. Not up here with the rich folk."

Red shrugged. "That's all I have."

The cowboy stared at him a few seconds longer, "Don't make sense paying to sit with the rick folks, but dressing like a worker. You some kind of miner?"

"No, I just do books for a cattle ranch. They paid more for the seats because they had a good year for beef."

The cowboy scratched his cheek with the barrel of his gun. Red winced at the obvious lack of interest in personal safety. "Where'd you come from?"

Pete stayed quiet in his chair while the shorter, darker skinned bandit searched him. He pulled the key out of Pete's pocket. Along the way, it had become brass, with an Aztec calendar where the pirate skull used to be on the handle. "What's this?"

Red didn't like the shorter man's voice. More desperate, the stress indicated the man would be happy to shoot first and ask questions later. "Key," Pete said.

"Key to what?" he yelled. He squinted, searching Red and Dragon Star.

"A safe," Red answered, trying to diffuse the situation. "We just came from Los Angeles. A bank there keeps the money for our boss."

"So you took the cash there last time and bring the key back now?"

Red happily turned back to the taller, saner robber. "Yep."

"Which bank?"

"First American. Box 279. It's only a couple of blocks from the train station. The boss said the money wasn't worth anything now, but when all this craziness clears up it would be worth something again. Decided to keep the herd for a while, but wanted the cash off-site."

The desperados looked at each other and nodded. "If you tell anybody where we went, we'll make it our mission to find and kill you," the cowboy said with a smirk. Then they all worked their way out of the passenger car, mounting their horses and riding off to the west.

"That was close," Red said.

"How does he plan to find you if he didn't ask your name?" Pete asked.

"It was a bluff," Dragon Star said.

"Think he'll go all the way to Los Angeles?" Pete asked.

"Doesn't matter." Red leaned out the door trying to see why the train hadn't started up again. "We need to get this train moving before they change their minds." He saw several other people looking out their windows further back on the train. "What's taking so long?"

Pete yawned and lay back down. "I'm going to miss that key."

Red looked at Dragon Star and wagged his head. "At least they didn't get these." He jangled the big bunch beneath his shirt.

"Maybe we should go see what's going on," Dragon Star said, nodding toward the front of the train.

Red nodded. They both went out the door. Even though the boots Red had gotten at the last train station had decent soles, he could feel the burning hot sand through the sides when they sunk into the ground. Their car being close to the front, they only had to walk past the coal car to reach the engine.

A man's arm, clad in blue fabric and splattered with blood, hung out the open door. When he moved so he could see the body, he saw another lying over it. "Two more dead," he said. "Out of so many, it seems like it shouldn't keep bothering me."

"The others are only imagined," Dragon Star said. "These are here for us to see."

Red nodded. "What do we do now?"

"We drive the train."

Red looked at Dragon Star, conflicted. Normally he would revel in the chance to operate a train. Knowing he had to pull two bodies out to do it took a lot of the fun out of it. "If we wait, do you think another train will come along?"

"I don't know. But it might cause a crash."

Red nodded. He took a deep breath, grabbed the arm hanging out in front of them, and pulled.

Dragon Star took the job of shoveling coal, without asking or being asked. Once the pressure began to build, Red started playing with the various switches and throttles. He kept an eye on the pressure gauge, trying to get some kind of response from the metal behemoth. As the pressure rose he said, "That's enough coal. I can't figure out how to start it."

Dragon Star joined him. The pressure continued to build, despite their efforts.

Red pulled the chain hanging from the ceiling and blasted the train's horn. Noticing the pressure dip slightly, then continue to build after, Red decided he had no choice. Before the needle reached the red line on the right, he pulled the chain again and blasted the horn until their ears rang.

Venting some of the pressure, he returned to the controls. "Obviously we have to do this in order."

"Maybe this brake first?" Dragon Star asked. He squeezed the two handles together and pushed the lever away. A loud puffing sound heralded the engine jolting forward. As all the couplings back along the line of cars pulled tight, a loud ringing extended behind them. They both jerked forward when the engine slowed under the great weight behind and stopped.

"More on the throttle," Red said. He pushed the handle sticking up from the large, geared quarter circle. He felt the steam pressure straining the metal around them as it puffed out the sides again and began to turn the hundreds of metal wheels on the massive serpent.

They watched closely as the wheels began to turn. Maddeningly slow progress didn't encourage Red to add more. He didn't want to break anything, preferring to err on the side of caution.

A few more puffs out the sides forced the pistons turning the large drive wheels, moving the train a little faster each time. With each puff, the pressure on the gauge dropped. He asked, "More coal?"

Dragon Star grabbed the shovel, but Red put out his hand. "Hold on." The coal already burning, kept the pressure rising, then a big puff out the sides would drop it. Tense, despite the slow actions, they both watched the gauge dance up and down. Sometimes the needle gained for a few puffs, then it would drop faster. "This is tricky."

As the speed grew, the pressure equalized so the rise and fall kept the needle near the center of the gauge. Dragon Star threw a shovel of coal in to the only thing hotter than the sun beating down.

Red eased forward on the throttle. Only once they had the massive caravan moving did Red look outside to check if anything might be ahead of them on the tracks. With no window over the huge steam chamber, he had to lean out the side and feel the wind on his face.

Dragon Star tossed in more coal every few minutes, pressing black dust into the blood on the floor, diluting and covering it along the path between the engine and the car.

Long, tense minutes dragged into an hour. Red searched for water in vain. "I never realized how intense this job was. I always thought they just rode along with the wind in their hair, but it's really tricky."

Dragon Star nodded, pulling the whistle chain to ease the pressure after a recent rise on the gauge. "Do you know if there's a station near our destination?"

"No. There wasn't a train station in the small town."

"How will we know where to stop?"

Red laughed. "I guess we should stop at the next station."

Dragon Star leaned out the far side. "Do you know what those signs mean?"

"No," Red said. "But I saw a station in the distance."

"How long does it take to stop this thing?"

"Maybe we better start now." Red pulled back on the throttle. Dragon Star began blowing the whistle constantly. Still the pressure rose.

"There has to be another vent," Red said. "Nobody kept the whistle running so long."

Dragon star pointed to his ears and shrugged, continuing to blast the train's whistle. Red began looking for another dial or switch they'd missed. Toward the front, he found a lever hooked to a thicker chain. He pulled it. White steam belched with a roar into the clear blue sky, dropping the pressure by half in a few seconds.

Dragon Star let up on the whistle. "Or we could do that."

CHAPTER THIRTY-TWO

As they vented steam and slowly applied the brake, Dragon Star realized he enjoyed this work. Shoveling coal and watching the gauge felt like meditating with a singular focused mind. The controls to the train were simple, but they moved a massive vehicle of unimaginable momentum. Although he'd listened to Eugene talk about trains plenty of times before, Dragon Star never understood how incredible the machines really were. Eugene never made it off the base. He'd been killed soon after the Actuation.

A thrill went through Dragon Star as they neared the platform of the station. Red pushed too hard on the brake a few times, causing them to lurch forward a little. By the end, the hulking metal beast was barely rolling at all. Red vented more steam, so the puffing pistons stopped pushing. They coasted to an almost imperceptible stop. When Dragon Star looked back, he saw the last two cars were still hanging back past the dock.

Red pulled the steam vent all the way open, until the pressure gauge dropped to nothing, and ratcheted the tall brake lever on.

"We made it," Dragon Star said.

"But where are we?"

Dragon Star jumped down from the high engineer's platform and walked over to the back of the ticket booth where a carved wooden map with peeling paint hung from two hooks. The rough map showed the borders of California and Arizona extending below the southern tip of Nevada. Two other dots showed stations well into the other States. The top of the stylized map said, *Welcome to Laughlin, Nevada.*

When Dragon Star turned back, he saw several people cautiously exiting the train. He doubted many of them intended to disembark at Laughlin, but unless one of them wanted to drive the train, they would have to find their own way from here. He crossed the platform back to Red and called up, "This is the closest station."

Red checked the brake again before jumping down. Dragon Star noticed how much coal dust and soot caked their hands and clothes. He wiped the sweat off his forehead onto one sleeve, resting his other hand on the handle of his sword.

"Let's get Pete and get out of here," Red said. "I don't want to be stuck answering questions when the police figure out those engineers are dead."

Dragon Star nodded. They went to the first passenger car and Pete climbed down to meet them. "Here's the box," he said. "Nice work driving this antique toy home."

Dragon Star looked at Red and they nodded. Neither of them cared to explain what Pete obviously missed. Red sunk his teeth into an apple, carrying the wooden crate in one hand. They joined the trickle of people wandering out through the gate. Half a dozen passengers already assaulted the ticket booth with questions. The three of them continued walking off the platform on a dirt road heading north. Red knew it would take days if they had to walk where they were going. He wanted to keep going until they were far enough from the station to avoid involvement in the investigation.

"I'm surprised anybody's still showing up for work," Red said.

"Some people's jobs are their whole lives," Pete said. "I kind of envy them that."

"I'll never think of trains the same way again," Red said. "Whoever kept these running after the Actuation did us a huge favor."

"Eugene Templeton," Dragon Star said. "Dedicated House Monk."

Red thought a moment. "The spy thriller guy?"

"Makes sense," Pete said. "Lots of those books have scenes on trains."

"Still, it's surprising." Red stuck the apple in his mouth so he could switch the crate to his other hand. "I mean, this train stayed intact as it changed from a historical relic to a modern magnetic rail rider and then to this Steampunk contraption. I don't even want to know what it was when we went past San Francisco."

"It's the negotiation," Dragon Star said. He watched two men with huge goggles and shiny steel badges walk past them with purpose toward the station. Obviously, somebody found the bodies. "The Actuator looked into all their minds and arranged the world to fit all of them the best."

"It was never meant to do that," Pete said. "It was designed to work with one mind. They screwed it up with all their weird tests. They always talk about it like it's a person or something. But it's just a computer. It only knows the data we feed it. Having more than twenty people use it at once probably broke it. As far as the Actuator is concerned, all those people inside it were just one mind."

"Let's get off the street," Red said. He nodded at the sheriff now talking to the ticket booth operator behind them. Dragon Star saw the man point to the train. Both law enforcers pulled out guns with gears and parts too small to see from here and rushed through the gate to the platform.

"Where?" Pete asked.

"There." Red pointed to the telegraph station.

As the sun drooped over the mountains to the west, they walked into the shade of the small wooden building. It wasn't cooler inside. A man with a billed hat and elastic cuffs at the end of his white shirt looked at their mostly black clothes and stifled a derisive sneer. Dragon Star didn't care for his nasally voice. "Can I help you?"

"We need to send a message to a small town just north of here," Red said. He pulled a gold coin out of the crate.

The man's eyes went wide. "I don't have enough money to change that."

"Do you know the town?"

"How would I know who you want to talk to? If you run your finger up a map you'll hit hundreds of towns north of here." He turned to some papers he was organizing on his desk.

Red stepped forward, pulling one of the knives from the crate and tucking it into his belt. Then he set the crate down and stepped forward. "Well, you can either help us figure out the name of the town we're looking for, or you can send telegrams to every one of them. So if we're sending a hundred, you best get started now."

The man put the papers down and moved around the end of the desk to sit at the small telegraph there. He pulled a wire up with a plug and pointed it at a switchboard with two hundred holes it could fit in. "Do you have a name?"

Red looked at the others. "Cindy?"

Dragon Star nodded.

"Cindy Smith at the Steam Whistle."

"The Steam Whistle? I just got a letter from there. Wasn't from Cindy Smith, though. Just from somebody called 'X.'"

"Xenwyn?" Red asked.

"Don't know. Confusing telegram, though. Have no idea who to deliver it to."

"Can we see it?"

The clerk stood and moved behind the tall desk. He shuffled the papers he'd been holding again. "Here it is. It says, 'Red or D.S. Stop. Help. Stop. Come back to the Steam Whistle soon. Stop. Soldiers are taking over. Stop. X.' Nobody around here named Red or D.S."

"I'm Red." He took the paper and read the hand written message again. The clerk really had written, *Stop*, each time.

"Can you give us directions there?"

"No. But you got enough money there to hire a driver. My brother in law would be happy to take you."

Dragon Star decided he didn't really care for Steampunk. He sat next to Pete in the back of a wooden truck bed with no padding as the bizarre contraption bounced and rattled over rocks and potholes. Red sat in the front with the driver. A smaller version of a train's steam engine roared in front of the truck, ticking and sputtering. Unlike the huge, powerful train, this jalopy looked like an oversized child's toy, which seemed more likely to explode than to hold the pressure necessary to keep the metal wagon wheels turning.

"How far?" Pete asked.

Dragon Star shrugged. They were going just faster than walking speed. "At least the sun is going down." Pink and orange painted the west clouds. "Does it still hurt?"

Pete looked down at his chest, gently touching the wound. "Not much. Although this ride isn't doing it any good." He put his hands under his buttocks to substitute for a cushion.

Dragon Star thought about how Pete seemed pained whenever they talked about the past. He tried to never cause suffering. But in light of the importance of the subject to the fate of the world, he decided he had no choice. "So what happened to Arne and Agatha?"

"Can this thing go any faster?" Red complained to the driver.

Pete turned to look at Red, who had been worried constantly since Xenwyn's telegram. Dragon Star knew Pete just envied the soft chair. He wasn't the type to worry about other people very much. Pete clearly wanted to avoid this topic. Dragon Star continued to look at the older man's eyes until he finally took a deep breath and began to talk.

"I don't know. They went into the machine somehow."

Dragon Star blinked many times, trying to get a mental picture of what Pete said. The Actuator had a square base with key holes that changed at every Actuation to match the key made by the Machine Monk enacting the change. One key hole in the bottom right hand corner had been there from the first day. It never changed. Nobody knew what it was for or what the key for it might look like or do. *Perhaps that was from the Andersons?* A single person might fit inside it, but not two. Dragon Star tried to frame a question, but only said, "What?"

"The machine's transformative ability was part of the plan. It only had limited range at first. And nobody could possibly build a machine capable of transmuting the entire world. But Arne found a loop hole. He made the machine capable of remaking itself. So after he set it up, he used it first. It took tons of energy. Unbelievable amounts. The first step, as he explained it to me, was to design it to generate more energy on its own. Maybe it sucked energy out of the ground or something. I really don't know. He used it several times, each time teaching it to rebuild itself. He extended the range, improved the energy efficiency, and made it somehow self-sustaining. The way he explained it to me, it was a recursive process. Each time the machine expanded its own power according to his plan.

"Once he had it ready with enough power and range, he turned it over to Agatha. She had the whole utopia figured out. That was her part. He built the machine because he believed in her ideals.

"Anyway, I was there when it happened. The first few times somebody sat in a certain chair to use it. But with all the changes, she just had to be by it. She pushed the button and started talking in her mind to the computer. We watched for hours. Then, suddenly, the energy came out and changed the world.

"I didn't feel different at first. But Arne screamed. Agatha was gone. He started freaking out. He wrote the last page of the journal."

"About planning your place in the world?"

"Yes. Apparently, she didn't know that, and it erased her. Arne said it he had to fix it. So he went back and started talking to the machine again. But after a few minutes I knew it wasn't working. He started to cry. Sobbing like a baby. His mouth kept moving, but he wasn't talking out loud. I called to him. But after he looked at me and wiped away the tears, he just waved. Then he disappeared, too.

"I felt the white energy go through me once when she did it. I assume everybody in the world did. Then it went through me again when he did it.

Then the world was back the way it had been before and I never saw my friends again. For about five minutes, the world was a utopia, I assume. I never saw any of it to know. I didn't feel all warm and fuzzy inside. But that doesn't mean anything."

"Anyway, I tried to fix it. But I didn't know how to use the machine. It tried to start a conversation with me, but I didn't much care to be erased from existence. So I just left."

"Where did you go?"

"Ecuador. I had a brother who moved there when he retired. I had a passport already. So I hired a private boat under an assumed name to take me there and laid low for a year or so. But the government found me, of course. Once they found the Actuator, they came after me. They offered me life in prison or life on the base. But if I ever talked, the only choice would be life in prison."

Dragon Star nodded. "I've heard a similar story before."

CHAPTER THIRTY-THREE

As their vehicle approached the small town, rattling and hissing steam from several leaks, Red had an uneasy feeling. Although he'd only seen this town a few days ago, it felt like he'd been away a very long time. Everything seemed different. The square wooden building at the edge of town he recognized first, the Steam Whistle. He wished he'd left one of the airships behind now. The field west of the bar looked desolate.

With the sun almost gone, the twilight left the whole town gray and ghostly. Considering Pete's injury and only one weapon between them, whatever they did here against soldiers wouldn't involve a fight. Red had seen so many strange places recently, he couldn't believe anything in this small town would be so very bad. Then he caught himself and realized he only hoped it would be an easy problem. He knew better than to expect anything normal. He glanced at the letter, then said, "Hold on. Let's stop right here."

The driver looked at him like he was speaking Chinese, then shrugged and pushed the throttle bar in. As he pulled the brake, Red turned to Dragon Star through the open back window. "How do we want to approach this?"

"You think one of us should approach in secret?"

"You thought the same thing, didn't you? I don't know what we'll find there. But if soldiers have taken over, we might need somebody on the outside."

"I'll go."

"You sure?"

"You are the leader," Dragon Star said. "And your technique with the sword is terrible. It is like you are swinging a baseball bat around."

Red smiled. "You're the best."

Dragon Star nodded and mumbled, "A thousand words..." Then he jumped over the side of the truck and rushed toward the scrub brush off the side of the road.

"What about us?" Pete asked as the driver engaged the throttle and the car began popping and ticking forward.

"We drive up like we don't know anything is wrong, and hope for a simple resolution."

"Nothing about this is going to be simple," Pete said, catching a piece of dust in his eye and wincing.

"Not true. The train ride wasn't bad."

Pete rubbed his eyes, talking louder now that the steam engine was working harder. "And if things go wrong?"

"We do what we always do. We wing it."

"As a former vampire, I'm not impressed with this plan. Why are we even here?"

"For the rest of the Machine Monks, and Jon. Hopefully Jon is feeling better and he can help with a plan to take the actuator back from the dragon."

"Something tells me a handful of pseudo-nerds and another rogue cowboy aren't going to make up that difference. And what about the soldiers in that note?"

"I think we're about to find out."

Red turned back toward two men in bizarre military uniforms. They had more of the gear and hydraulic enhanced guns and wore a crisscrossing pattern of black leather with metal spikes across the shoulders. Both had dark lensed goggles pulled up so their eyes were unimpeded. Both had the beginning of a beard. Red rubbed his own chin, realizing it had been days since he shaved or showered.

"Stop!" called one guard.

The driver pulled on the brake and popped the transmission into neutral. "What's up?" he asked. Red hadn't talked to the driver much on the ride. However, he admired the man's casual tone in front of two nearly comic guards.

"Get out of the vehicle," the guard said.

"What's the problem? This is my car by rights."

"Not anymore." The soldier leveled a broad barrel with some kind of pressure tube behind it so it pointed at the man's face. "Get out."

Throwing up his hands, the man pulled the lever to open the door and stepped out cautiously. "I'm just the driver. These men paid me to bring them here. I don't have any beef with you guys and I haven't broken any laws I know of."

"We make the laws," the other guard said. "This vehicle is confiscated property of the Marshall. Wartime measures require all the resources we can garner."

"War?" Red couldn't believe it. "Who are you at war with? This small town's in the middle of nowhere."

"Not who," the first soldier said, spitting, "what. We're at war with the dragon just north of here."

"The dragon? You mean Commander Newell?" Red moved closer. With the sun mostly gone and no real light, he hadn't looked closely at the man's features. Now he saw a familiar square jaw and broad nose. "Yocum? Carl Yocum? I didn't recognize you. It's me, Red!"

The guard ignored Red's hand and left it unshaken. "I know who you are, McLaren. We've been expecting you. They told us you went after Pete. Where are Mack and Dragon Star?"

"They, uh, didn't make it," Red said. He'd never been much of an actor, but thinking about Mack bleeding out in his hands was enough to make him feel the words. He held it all in like a soldier would expect.

Yocum looked up and down Pete. "Looks like you made a bad trade. We could use a man like Mack."

"What's going on?" Red asked. "Where are Jon and the others?"

"They're being watched," the other soldier said.

Red examined him more closely now. The narrow nose and dark eyes were an easy giveaway. "Derrick Worth. Just last month we were playing poker. You took me for twenty bucks. Now you're going to take me prisoner?"

"This is war," Worth said. "Until we know if you are an ally or enemy, we have to keep you under observation."

"No, you don't!" Pete interrupted. "Who says you have to?"

"Marshall Ruiz," Worth answered.

"Marshall? His name's Luis. Head of security. He still owes me five bucks for the last time I did a burger run."

"Well he's the Marshall now. And he's declared Marshall law."

"Marshall law? There's no war!" Pete cried out.

"Until we get rid of the dragon and take control of that Actuator again, we are at war," Yocum said.

"That's what we want, too." Red pointed at himself and Pete.

"Then you might be welcome to join us." Worth signaled with the tip of his weird gun for them to start walking. "You, too, driver."

"I really don't have anything to do with this," the man said. "I'll just be taking my car and—"

"Freeze!" Yocum called. The man turned and ran. A hissing sound announced a thin shard of metal flying out the barrel and burying deep in the man's leg. He tripped and rolled, screaming out in pain.

"That's Marshall's property," Yocum said.

Worth prodded Red in the back with his weapon. Red had to grit his teeth and just walk forward. "I'm glad some of the soldiers made it out alive," he said casually. "How many are left?"

"A dozen," Worth said.

"Think that's enough to take a dragon?"

"Maybe, if we add you and Jon and a couple Monks in."

"Those guns won't work on the base," Red said.

"I know." Worth looked back, so Red followed his gaze. Yocum had the driver up on his feet. The driver, took a swing at him. Yocum put another shard through the man's chest and watched him crumple to the ground. Jumping in the car, Yocum started experimenting with the controls to get it moving.

Red turned away so Worth wouldn't see him gritting his teeth. Previously rational people were gunning down scared men in the streets. *More death? Where would this end? Could he work with people like this, even for a higher cause?*

When Worth prodded him through the door of the Steam Whistle, Red heard the rickety car go by outside with Yocum bouncing it over every pothole in the road.

"Red!" Xenwyn jumped up out of a chair and rushed forward. Red put his hands out and bent down to catch the one armed dwarf as she leaped up with enough force to tackle him. He let the energy turn him to the side instead, relieved that she still survived, he didn't even freak out about her weird appearance. Or maybe he'd just seen too much to care about anything so stupid anymore.

They hugged for several seconds. Red rather enjoyed it, letting himself forget about everything for a moment and just take a deep breath. Her wild hair and hard leather goggles scratched his face when she finally pulled back.

"I'm glad you made it back," she said, slightly embarrassed. Red thought it looked funny for a mech-enhanced dwarf to be blushing.

"I brought Pete."

"Where's Mack? Is Dragon Star here?" Cindy asked. She pushed her glasses up on her nose, hoping to change the focus and suddenly see them.

"They didn't make it," Red said. He stifled the guilt for lying about Dragon Star. They would forgive him when they knew it was in their best interest.

"What happened?" Xenwyn asked.

"The whole world is like this now," Red said. "Everywhere is different, but they're all brutal. Wolves killed Mack in the middle of the night."

"He would have preferred it that way," Cindy nodded. Red wanted to slap her. *How could they all keep believing this was an acceptable consequence?*

Pete said, "Hanna drank Dragon Star's blood. She bit me, too." He turned his neck to show off the pair of scars. "But Red got me out before—"

"The sooner we get the Actuator back, the better," Red said.

Xenwyn sat on a chair too tall for her legs. "Dragon Star wanted to kill Commander Newell."

Red looked around the familiar room. Despite Worth keeping post at the door, it felt empty. "Where's everybody else?"

"We moved Jon upstairs. Glass was with him, but she's probably asleep now." Cindy's eyes darted back and forth. "The others..."

"They didn't make it," Xenwyn said, echoing Red's words. "They took exception to the new regime and..."

"You shot them?" Red turned on Worth with murderous intent. "How could you gun down somebody you've spent the last five years with in cold blood? You were tasked with protecting the Machine Monks and you just killed them?" Red couldn't take any more of this. He felt a weight of horror settle on his shoulders. *We're already too late. So many people have died.*

"Not me," Worth said. "I wasn't around when it went down."

"But you're still working for them. You're still part of the problem."

Worth stepped forward, lowering his brow, "I didn't kill them, but if they got out of hand I would have, too. This is war, McLaren. And if you don't take orders, you receive corporal punishment." He leveled his weapon at Red's chest. "Now I suggest you think before saying things like that if you hope to gain the trust of Marshall Ruiz."

Red wagged his head. He could see Worth was just posturing. The soldier wasn't happy with how things had gone, but wasn't about to fight it at the cost of his life. He dedicated his life to following orders. Higher ideas weren't part of his training. Red wanted to strangle the brainless grunt. He even understood the irony. *What's the point? Were they all going to end up dead anyway?*

"Take me to Jon," Red said. He turned on his heels and marched toward the stairs, trying not to show his disgust.

"So, I see a bar," Pete said. "Do we at least get drinks here?"

"Come on," Cindy said. "I'll join you."

Xenwyn jumped up and rushed after Red.

When he entered the narrow hall upstairs, Red found the first door open. He looked in and saw Jon sitting up in bed.

"You used to heal faster," Red said. "Sure you're not getting too old for this job?"

"I'm so glad to see you," Jon said. The trademark bravado failed to support his low voice. "How was your mission?"

"Successful," Red said. He pulled the leather thong from around his neck and tossed the clump over to his boss.

Jon grabbed it out of the air, examining the three objects. "A key that's actually a key," he said with a smile.

Red smiled back. In this crazy world, at least one person understood.

Jon tossed the clump into a small drawer of the nightstand by his bed. "That makes five."

"I had it at four with Tina's wax seal stamp," Red said. *How could she be gone?*

"I forgot to mention I grabbed one of the keys before I went after Commander Newell. It's a syringe."

"From Eugene? That's going to be one crazy drug."

Jon nodded, keeping his eyes down. "We'll save it for celebrating."

"So what's the plan?" Red asked.

"I don't know," Jon said. "I thought we could work with the new *Marshall*, to get the Actuator back from the dragon. But I don't trust him now."

"You think he'll keep it for himself?" Xenwyn asked, stepping into the room.

They both looked at her for a moment before Jon continued.

"No. I think he's planning to use it to turn the whole world into his own military conquest."

CHAPTER THIRTY-FOUR

How could he use the Actuator to conquer the world?" Red asked. He could probably figure it out if he tried. But at the moment he was too tired and he just wanted to hear the answer.

"Because Actuations work in sets," Jon said. "The soldiers still alive and loyal to him worked that much out. Whoever sabotaged the machine chose a time when many users would be working together. Something we called a parallel Actuation. But we've run serial Actuation tests before, too."

"Of course," Red said. "That's how we ended up with that robot-dragon two years ago."

"That wasn't my fault!" Xenwyn said. "Brian went second and messed it up. He was supposed to fight the dragon with a spaceship, not transform it."

"Nobody's blaming you," Red said, but he saw Jon's jaw clench when he'd said it.

"The point is, the Actuator isn't offline. Anybody who gets control of it can still use it. The changes will just be on top of the world as it already is."

"Then it adds the new keyholes to the matrix on the control board, right?" Red asked. He already knew the answer, he wanted to clarify for Xenwyn's sake.

"Yes."

"That's why there has always been that one first key," Xenwyn said.

"We're not one-hundred percent sure," Jon said. "But we think it was from the Actuations the original creator did."

"But nothing in the world changed," Xenwyn said.

"We don't know that," Jon said.

"According to Pete, Agatha changed it and then Arne changed it back. So why would there be just one residual keyhole?"

"I don't know," Jon said. "Maybe if we talk to Pete some more we can find out."

"So you think Luis Ruiz wants to use the Actuator? He doesn't have any Machine Monks working for him."

"That's exactly it," Jon said. "He thinks if a *normal* person uses it, the world will go back to normal. No matter how many times we tell him otherwise, he has made up his mind. He says he wants to take it back so he can fix everything. But I think he's planning to change the world to be under his own personal control."

"So let him use it," Red said. "Without training he'll forget the last rule."

Xenwyn finished, "He won't make a place for himself in the new world."

"And he'll be sucked into the machine, same as Arne and Agatha Anderson."

"That's what happened to them?" Xenwyn asked. Her goggle-enhanced eyes were so wide that she looked like a giant bug.

"That's what Pete said happened."

"All this time Pete knew and never told us?"

"They ordered him not to," Red said.

"We need to talk to him now," Xenwyn said, moving toward the door. "We need to know more."

"No," Jon said, lifting one scarred hand through great effort. "We can't talk to him as long as guards might overhear us. We can't give up our only advantage."

"They need us for information about the Actuator," Red said. Suddenly his eyes were heavy and he couldn't think any more.

"You need some sleep," Jon said.

Xenwyn led him to a different room with an empty bed. Red fell into it and closed his eyes.

Dragon Star held the scabbard of his sword up with his hand tight where the weapon met the sheath so it wouldn't rattle as he tiptoed through the sandy brush. The mining boots he'd ended up with were heavy, so every twig popped loud enough to echo. He carefully chose soft sand or large rocks to step on as he moved away from the road.

He watched Yocum kill the driver and take the car. Then, he watched Red and Pete taken at gunpoint back to the inn. Now he had no idea what to do. He moved quietly, under cover of darkness, in a wide arc. He saw Yocum return and join Worth in guarding the door of the inn.

Working around the back of the buildings on the opposite side of the street, Dragon Star slinked toward the town hall. A few carriages and the uncomfortable steam car were all parked outside the building Yocum entered before. He found a nice copse of bushes with a view of the back window. He recognized Luis Ruiz, former head of security, pacing and talking. The man move like an engine inside him would overheat if he didn't vent the energy. His passion made him pace and gesture dramatically with his hands in a way Dragon Star had never seen before. Ruiz had always been a steady, unappealing person. He took his job deadly serious. Then at night, he drank himself to sleep. Since almost nobody off base even knew about the Actuator, Ruiz's job of guarding it amounted to doing nothing most of the time. Still, Dragon Star respected the vigor the man had always thrown into it. Now he marched back and forth with a passion. When he spoke, he threw out his arms or pointed to a map on the wall. Despite watching for a long time, he couldn't understand any of the plan being discussed.

Dragon Star found a rock and sat cross-legged atop it. He had a reasonable view of the window and a small amount of cover to keep him out of sight. Exhaustion overclouded his soul, weighing him down. Not just the physically sore muscles from shoveling coal and then riding on a bouncing torture device, but a gnawing sadness. He felt the end of their mission coming. He felt the nearness of the Actuator. He knew he couldn't suppress it any longer. Soon he would be at war... again. He hated the very idea with all his being. A lifetime of peace couldn't make-up for the suffering caused in one such battle. Just as a priceless Ming dynasty vase, protected for centuries, could be shattered irreparably in one second; soon his balance and inner harmony would be destroyed indefinitely.

It all proved his weakness. If he had come to a higher level of consciousness, he wouldn't be here. He would be alone, unaffected by changes to the world. Now he had a dark revenge to enact. He hadn't been naïve when he swore to kill Commander Newell. He knew it would have to be done. Having been through change after change, he knew the Actuator was only partly responsible for the Commander killing his students. She had been made into a dragon because it was the best reflection of her soul. And now, the only way to stop the profuse suffering all over the world, was to wrest control of the Actuator back from her. She would not give it up while she continued to live, whatever her form.

Dragon Star knew Red carried great sorrow for having killed Jackson, even to save a friend. Red's respect for life allowed Dragon Star to stand by his side through everything. Dragon Star knew hunting and killing Commander Newell would scar him for life, probably determining the form of his next life, too. This defining moment would prove he had failed to detach himself from emotions and suffering. It would justify why he did not deserve Nirvana.

Still, despite the cool breeze, Dragon Star felt a kind of peace. He didn't have inner peace now. He never would. The taint of the Actuator had denied it to him through the long years of service on the base. Now the poison of revenge would keep him just outside it. If she killed him first, it might improve his next life. Maybe then he'd be in a position to move to a higher state of mind. There were good odds, since she was a dragon.

As Pete sat next to Cindy at the bar, he knew all his womanizing had been a cover-up for a deeper need. He wanted validation. In the wake of Arne and Agatha, he'd been left with a hole in his heart. They'd always loved him. He only had them. He'd never had love. Being honest, he knew Hanna wasn't that love. But it slapped a Band-Aid on the bleeding wound for a moment to have a woman's affection. Somehow, deep down, that's all he believed he deserved.

"The only reason I never hit on you before was because I respected you."

Cindy pushed her glasses up as she watched Pete drink the foul smelling stuff. He'd seen her taste it and make a cute, wrinkled face. Then she pushed it away. Apparently, it didn't offend her enough to leave him alone with it, though. She gave him a pity laugh. "So if you start hitting on me now it'll mean you don't respect me anymore?"

"Touche." Pete swallowed the foul, but welcome alcohol. "I miss them."

"The Andersons?"

"Them, too. But no, I mean my crew."

"Crew?" He watched Cindy brush some wrinkles out of the sleeve of her pink cardigan sweater. He knew she was just being polite for conversation. She didn't have a deep interest in him. Still, he found he didn't care. He needed to talk.

"Pirates. They were guards at the castle first. Hanna bit me and turned me into a vampire. Then Dragon Star killed her. So her servants became mine for a little while. I could read their minds. It was so weird because I knew them. I mean I really knew them in a way I've never really connected with anybody but the Andersons."

Cindy nodded. When he said pirates, she had become genuinely interested. She wasn't a fan of historical fiction, but she had been Tina's friend and they'd talked about it a lot. "What was the ship like?"

"That piece of land was Tina's, right?"

Cindy smiled. "I know it's not historically accurate like the pirates to the south. But she always thought it would be a good place for it because during the gold rush people sailed up and down that coast with their finds. There was no real naval presence. Until the trains came through a crew of pirates could have made a good living there."

"So the trains weren't hers?"

"No. Those are Eugene's brain child. Except the Orient Express. But that's in Europe. So if you liked being with the pirates so much, why did you leave?"

"I had to. Red said they needed me to help with getting the Actuator back. And I have certain... information."

"You saw the key holes. You know what order they're in?" Cindy turned and slid a piece of paper and pencil over, eager to take notes.

"No. I didn't see that."

Her face dropped. "Red didn't see it either. Nobody who escaped got a good look at it."

"That's probably because anybody who stopped to look at it got eaten by the dragon," Pete said darkly. He filled the glass from the bottle on the counter. He didn't let Cindy's disappointment bother him. He'd been disappointing women for a long time.

"Does Red know this?"

"It didn't come up yet. But that isn't really why he needed me."

"There's more?"

"I knew the Andersons. I was there when they built the Actuator."

Cindy's mouth dropped open. Pete realized behind the librarian glasses and old-lady sweater, she really could be quite cute.

"You have to tell me," she said with the same sycophantic obsession as he'd seen in Dragon Star.

"It makes me sad," Pete said. "But maybe if you hold my hand I can get through it."

He hid his amusement as he saw the emotional gears in her head spinning fast until they jammed. He doubted any man had paid any real attention to this nerd. She'd dreamed of it, he assumed. But it had never been like this. Sitting in a bar, in a Steampunk territory, with a guy she'd never give two seconds to in normal circumstances, demanding the physical affection she always wanted to give, as a kind of payment for information she wanted—Pete guessed she would need days to sort out her feelings. He smiled when she reached out her soft, delicate fingers and put them into his hair covered, older hand. Now if he could just stretch the story out long enough to get her drunk.

"Have a drink," he said. "You're going to need it."

CHAPTER THIRTY-FIVE

"Where's Pete?" Red asked.

Cindy rubbed her eyes and put on her glasses from the nightstand. Red could see a wash of gratitude come over her face when she realized she woke up alone in the old cot. "I don't know," she said. She turned and sat up, still dressed in the same pink sweater. "We talked late. He said he missed his pirate crew. Maybe he went back to Oregon."

"How'd he get out? There are guards at the door."

"I don't know," she said. "When I left, he was asleep on the bar."

Red paced out into the hall and then back to her doorway. "How could he do this? After everything we went through to get him. Mack died for nothing..."

"And Dragon Star," she said with a sigh.

Red nodded, glancing down the hall to his left. "You said he went back to Oregon?"

"No. I said I don't know. He said he missed his crew. Anyway, it wasn't for nothing. Pete told me everything last night."

"Did he see the order of the key holes?"

"No."

Red wagged his head. "Jon didn't either. I guess it doesn't matter since we'll need them all eventually anyway. What about the other Machine Monks? Does he know where any of them went?"

"No. He said Saul and several others were definitely alive because they left the base together before splitting up. He also said Zack left with them. But we already know Zack wasn't part of the Actuation."

Red nodded. "Anything else?"

"He told me about the Andersons. It's sad."

Red didn't really need to know any of that right now. He could see Cindy fussing with the buttons on her sweater. "What's wrong?"

"I don't know," she said. "But I think Pete might have been responsible. You know, for all this." She pointed weakly with her finger in every direction and then used it to push her glassed up higher on her nose. "A few times he seemed to forget I was there. I heard him mumbling. I can't be sure, so I don't want to accuse him. But I think he said, 'Can't tell, it's too late now,' and, 'It's all my fault for showing.'"

Red thought this through. He'd seen enough drunk people blubbering or raging to know it usually wasn't a lie.

"He kept zoning out and mumbling those things. I tried to ask him about it, but he would just wave it away and go back to hitting on me."

Red nodded. He didn't know what it meant, but right now, it wasn't important. Whatever it meant, they didn't have the time to go after Pete now. He said, "Good job, Cindy. Thanks."

She had a big smile and looked at him over the top rim of her glasses. He suspected she felt like a spy.

Heading to the next room, Red opened the door. He saw Glass next to Jon's bed. Despite the larger man sitting up and eating, Glass looked sad. "Red, tell him he's not in any shape to go on the base and face the dragon again."

Red looked at Jon. "He wouldn't make a tactical error like that."

"But I need to be there to help, even if only in an advisory capacity."

"Or in case we need somebody for bait," Red said. Jon smiled. Red smiled, too. He hadn't been sure if he could count on Jon with so much melancholy before. Now he had some hope.

Glass began to sob.

"I'm just kidding," Red said. "Don't worry, once those soldiers turn back into orcs, we'll have plenty of bait."

"We already know they'll be useless against the dragon," Jon said.

"Pete's gone," Red said.

Jon nodded. "He'd be useless against the dragon, too."

"At least he told Cindy what he knew before he left."

Glass looked up, trying to put on a brave face. "Where'd he go?"

"We don't know. Oregon, maybe."

"We need a plan," Jon said. "We aren't going to take a dragon by force."

"I have a wild card," Red said. "But I'd rather not play it just yet."

Jon looked long and hard into Red's eyes. Red didn't flinch. He kept his face unreadable. He didn't win most of the poker games on the base for nothing. Jon eventually let it go. "Ideas?"

"We join the soldiers," Red said. "Agree to whatever stupid plan they come up with. Then once we're on the base, we break away and hide. While the orcs are drawing the dragon's attention we find her nest and wait there for her. Eventually she has to come back. When she's off her guard, we put an arrow through her eye.

Jon made a fist and rotated his arm to test his shoulder. "I could operate a crossbow."

"All the guns turn into them there anyway. We each round up a pair and position ourselves behind some cover—something better than a shield this time. When she settles in, we put a couple shots through each of those big yellow eyes."

"That's crazy," Glass said.

"Not really," Jon said. "We'll be off to the side. So even if she blows fire, it'll probably only hit one of us."

"So one of you will for sure die?"

"Not for sure," Red said. "We'll try to arrange to be behind cover."

"This is a terrible plan. So many things could go wrong with it. Why do we have to kill her at all?"

"It's our job," Jon said. "And people are dying all over the world."

"And we're the only ones who know what's going on. We're the only ones who have a chance."

Glass asked, "What about all the soldiers?"

"We can't save them," Jon said. "They're determined to die fighting the dragon, one way or another."

"They'll come up with some brilliant military plan," Red said. "But it won't work because they'll always rely on weapons."

"That's what you're doing," Glass said.

"No." Jon took her hand and looked into her eyes to try to reassure her. "We're relying on stealth."

"Against a dragon? You think you can sneak up on a dragon?"

"Of course not," Red said. "That's why we're taking the orcs."

"They're taking you, you mean. We're their prisoners."

"We let them think that," Jon said. "It's easier that way."

Glass buried her head in Jon's chest. He put his arm around her with difficulty. Red nodded after making eye contact and headed back downstairs.

Red was glad to see Yocum and Worth gone. The new guards, Whitmore and Tilu, seemed less agitated. Red had spent a lot more time with Tilu than the others. He regretted using that friendship now when he knew it amounted to luring the man to his death. He only justified it because these soldiers had made their choice to stand behind Ruiz. So it hadn't been Red's doing.

"Hey, Tilu," Red said with a head nod and smile. Red ran one hand through his dark hair to tame it after a night of sleep.

"Hi, McLaren." Laauli Tilu's voice revealed what his hardened Polynesian face wouldn't—deep tired from being up on guard duty all night.

"So this sucks," Red said.

"I know. I never thought we'd be on the opposite sides of anything."

"We aren't. I'm with you. I tried to tell them last night, but Yocum's wound up so tight he wouldn't listen. We came back here to take the Actuator back from Commander Newell."

Tilu nodded. "Good. That's smart."

"It's the only choice really. We're the only people who know about it. It's up to us to fix it." Red patted Tilu's shoulder. The bigger, but shorter man couldn't reciprocate because he had both hands on the incomprehensible gun.

"I don't think it can be fixed," Tilu said. "But, yeah. We need to try."

"So what's going on with Ruiz? He's calling himself Marshall?"

"It's so people around here understand he's taken over. When he tried to recruit them, most of them up and left. Probably only ten people still in this town, and they're all hiding in their houses. When we leave, it'll be a ghost town in days, I bet."

Red wagged his head. "It's a shame."

"It's those Machine Monks," Tilu said with venom. "They screwed everything up."

"No," Red said. "They were just doing their jobs. Somebody disabled the dampeners on purpose. That's who is responsible."

"If I find them, they will not have long to worry about it."

"I agree with that sentiment, but keep whoever it is alive long enough for questioning." He laughed. "So when is Ruiz planning to invade the base? When can I talk to him about the plans?"

"Plan's already made." Tilu turned to his companion, "Go tell the Marshall they're ready to talk."

The other guard turned without a word and marched off.

"Whitmore's not much of a talker," Red said.

"No. Lucky me. I got to spend all night enjoying his silence."

"Anything to eat around here?"

"Not likely. Ruiz has all the supplies locked up."

Red sat. Xenwyn came down the stairs, stomping her heavy boots. "What's going on? Where's Pete?"

"He took off," Red said. "We don't know where." She marched over and sat down at his table. Her hair stuck out in several places. She didn't even try to fix it.

"After all that?"

"He told Cindy everything he knew before he left at least."

"He could have told you that before and saved himself the trip."

"He wasn't in a talkative mood when I found him. Anyway, it doesn't matter. We've decided to join with the soldiers to attack the dragon."

Xenwyn took a deep breath. "I'm coming with."

"I don't think that's a good idea."

"I don't care what you think. It's my realm. I'll be tiny so I can hide. But I'm going with you."

Red reached over and touched her arm. "Okay."

A few minutes later Luis Ruiz marched through the door. Red stood up and pasted a smile on his face to cover his disgust. *Did this guy think he was Napoleon or something?*

"Red McLaren. Glad you made it back. My men tell me you're interested in joining us."

"It's a bit late to enlist as a soldier," Red said. "But I'll help you take the Actuator back from Commander Newell if I can. Jon, too. Although his injuries limit what he can do."

"Where's Pete?"

"We don't know. He took off last night."

Ruiz turned to look at Whitmore and Tilu with fire in his eyes. Whitmore held his gun up higher, as if it might deflect some of the wrath.

"Don't blame them. Pete's always been a slimy, little toad. He probably wouldn't be much good to us anyway."

"He's probably the one who did all this," Ruiz said. Red didn't detect anger in it. Clearly, Ruiz had adjusted to think of this as an opportunity. Red had to hide his disgust.

"No. Pete's not a stand-up guy, but he'd never sabotage the Actuator. First of all, he doesn't have the access or the technical knowhow. Second, he knew more than anybody the terrible consequences of a rogue Actuation."

"If he's not guilty, then why did he run away?"

"Probably because he's a coward," Red said.

Ruiz clenched his fists. "We have just twenty, then. Nineteen and a half since Jon's injured. It's less than I wanted, but we'll have to make it work."

"What's the plan?"

"You, Xenwyn, and Jon will take carriages through the main gates and split up. We'll come in with guns beforehand and spread out around the Actuator. When the dragon rises, to come after you, we'll catch her in the crossfire."

Red kept his face even. So this brilliant plan was to use the key hunters and Machine Monk as bait? What a surprise.

CHAPTER THIRTY-SIX

After a cold night on rocky ground, Dragon Star suppressed his hunger as he moved back around to watch the Steam Whistle from behind. He saw Luis go in to meet with Red. However, not knowing the outcome of that discussion, he had no idea how to act. He enjoyed the desert sunrise, meditating despite his sore muscles. Even though he no longer said his morning prayers, he felt the tug in his soul remembering the comfort they once brought him. He considered saying them again to pass the time, but it seemed wrong in light of his murderous path. He'd already plunged a stake into Hanna's heart. Commander Newell would get his sword. There was no balance or middle road in his future.

Concealed at a distance, Dragon Star waited in quiet until the sun drew higher. He saw people gathering several strange vehicles in the clearing to the west of the bar, including the steam truck they'd come in. The soldiers left and Dragon Star saw Red and Xenwyn bringing out supplies to the vehicles. They talked alone for a time. Then Xenwyn went in and Red began walking away from the inn, searching the trees and scrub brush beyond the field.

Dragon Star looked long and hard up and down the row of buildings. All their fronts had wooden facades, well aligned to the street. In the back, they jutted out in an uneven row. It would be difficult to detect any spy hiding there.

Once he felt sure he could see nobody, Dragon Star stood slowly and waved to Red. His friend changed course and entered the shady retreat.

"I'm so sorry I couldn't get to you sooner," Red said. He pulled three biscuits and a pear from his jacket. Dragon Star accepted them with both hands and nodded.

"I did not expect you to come at all. Does this mean you have made peace with Officer Ruiz?"

"He goes by Marshall now." Dragon Star nodded, refusing to utter the ridiculous title.

Dragon Star held up the biscuits, "Do you want to eat with me?"

Red smiled. "No. I've eaten." As Dragon Star broke and chewed the dry food, Red said, "The only liquid I could get was alcohol. So I brought some fruit. Sorry."

Dragon Star shrugged. Why should being dehydrated matter when they were going to fight a dragon?

"We're going out today. Ruiz's brilliant plan is to have us go in with the carriages to bait the dragon. Then the soldiers will catch her in a crossfire. Obviously, we aren't so excited about that plan. So we made some of our own. Instead, we're going to ditch the vehicles and sneak back to the dragon's nest. We think it's close to the Actuator. From there, we'll hide out on either side with crossbows. Once she finishes with the orcs and returns to roost, we'll shoot her in the eyes."

Dragon Star nodded. "Trading bait. Sounds like a good plan. What do you want me to do?"

"Wait until we get through the gate and the soldiers are set up on the outside. Then sneak in. If you can, round up another crossbow. Hide near the nest where you can get a shot at her. It's the only way we can think of that might actually kill her."

Dragon Star looked down and nodded, taking a deep breath. "Okay."

Red grabbed both of Dragon Star's shoulders and squeezed them for comfort. Dragon Star looked up. "I know this really sucks."

"She was my friend," Dragon Star said. It wasn't strictly true. Commander Newell had stayed aloof of everyone on the base, maintaining her superiority at all costs. But if any of them had been a friend to her, it was Dragon Star. He was the only one she joked and commiserated with. "Just like Hanna."

"I shot Jackson in the back," Red said, his own eyes heavy and his voice strained. "We had no choice. Just like we have no choice with Commander Newell. I believe if she were still herself and aware of the situation, she would order us to kill her."

Dragon Star nodded. "I just never thought I would have to do it again."

Red paused, tipping his head to the side. "You mean after Hanna."

Dragon Star wagged his head. "No."

"There was somebody before?"

Dragon Star took a deep breath. He'd held it all back for so long. He'd hidden behind teaching the Empty House Machine Monks, hoping to gain back some balance. Now he knew it had been in vain. His destiny had never been Nirvana. Whatever his fate, he knew they were on the brink. He had but one friend left in this world. So before he left it, he wanted that friend to know the truth.

"The reason I came to the base." Red nodded, listening intently.

"Military service is mandatory in South Korea. We are still at war with North Korea. They called a cease-fire, but there has never been a treaty. So every man at age nineteen is required to serve in the military for two years.

"I'd been studying tae-kwon-do for years. My grades were good, too. So I advanced through the ranks pretty fast. They stationed me at Dong-du-cheon, just below the demilitarized zone.

"By rank and luck, I was assigned as a liaison on the American army base there. Because English is such a necessary skill in Korean business, it was a coveted position. I made some friends among the American soldiers. I even started teaching them tae-kwon-do. I had all the prospects of a bright future. Some of the other Korean soldiers were so jealous they started accusing me of defecting to America."

Red listened, occasionally tipping his head to the side. "I've never heard you talk so much at once before." Dragon Star nodded, but didn't stop.

"Anyway, I was on guard duty one day at the bridge connecting the two countries across the DMZ. Both countries have guards stationed on their end of the bridge. I was in a nearby tower, with a view of the whole thing. Most of the time that job is pretty boring.

"While I was on watch, a man from North Korea broke past their line and started running across the bridge toward us. The guards on the north side started yelling. Then they started shooting. Our guards all dropped down and pulled out their guns. When the bullets did not stop firing, we began shooting back.

"I saw the defecting man jump behind a support column. The North Koreans started blowing whistles and calling for backup. They kept shooting at the man, determined not to let him go. As I watched our side trying to lay down cover fire, I realized we were a few seconds away from open war again.

"Then Kim-Han-Ju, one of my last Korean friends in the army, began crawling forward onto the bridge. He was tucked against one side where a few girders offered poor cover, trying to get to the wounded man. Our side began shooting at the enemy in earnest to protect our own, all the time calling for Han-Ju to come back.

"But the stupid guy just would not listen. He had it in his head he could help the escapee and he was not going to surrender.

"The North Korean soldiers became furious. They started moving out onto the bridge in formation, advancing across the DMZ. I couldn't believe my eyes. These people were willing to die to keep one man from escaping. I thought I was watching the end of the cease-fire. The sirens on both sides began to wail, calling both armies to alert. I knew thousands or maybe millions of people would die. With new technology, the two nearby countries could send rockets over the border with no way for anybody to stop them. With twelve million people in Seoul alone just sitting there in harm's way, a war now would be so much worse than the one decades before, which my grandfathers had fought in."

Red asked, "What did you do?" His voice held sorrow, indicating he had some idea already.

"I saw the escaped man on the bridge get shot and die. But Han-Ju didn't see it. He just kept crawling forward like he had lost his mind. More North Korean soldiers moved out, setting up formations on the end. Several fell over, shot by South Koreans. With the sirens blaring, we had maybe one minute before everything went too far. I knew there was only one way to stop it all.

"I took aim from my tower and shot Han-Ju in the back." Dragon Star felt tears in his eyes. He rubbed them for a moment.

"He stopped advancing. Then people stopped shooting. Everybody just held their positions for a long, long time. I watched a pool of blood spread out on the bridge beneath him. It seemed like forever before big wigs on both sides talked it through. They both sent out one soldier to drag their dead man back under cover of guns on both sides. Then the soldiers were pulled back and the gates on both sides locked. They left the blood on the bridge."

Dragon Star hated to relive the memories again. At the same time, it felt good to finally tell somebody. His Buddhist sensibilities told him to keep it to himself all these years, so he didn't spread suffering by the telling of it. But now, he felt a little better, as if Red could hold some of the invisible burden.

"Did they find out?"

Dragon Star nodded. "But there was never a trial. My American friends arranged it all. Before I knew it, I was being employed as a consultant for the U.S. Military, shipped to America to teach martial arts to Special Forces.

"Somehow I felt distanced from my country. I knew my family would have supported me, but I did not want them to have to bear the burden of my suffering. The new life was a good way to start over. I found other Korean immigrants and they helped me through the transition. When I heard about a job practicing to empty my mind, I was glad to apply. I wanted to leave all forms of war behind me. But peace was not my path."

Red hugged Dragon Star. "I know the feeling." He pulled back. "You did the right thing. With Hanna, too."

"I know. But the next one will not be."

"But it's the same. We're only doing it to prevent more death. I'm sure if Commander Newell were with us here, she would order us to kill the dragon even if it meant her own death."

"I know. That is not what I meant. This time when I kill, it will be for revenge."

Red let go, looking deep in his friend's eyes. Dragon Star could see the conflict there.

Finally, Red said, "I don't care why. If you need to be the one to do it, just pull the trigger first. But we'll be there, too. And if you take my advice, you'll let us shoot before you."

Red handed Dragon Star a weird looking pistol with external gearing around a metal pressure chamber. "Hopefully it'll turn into a crossbow on the other side of the boundary. I don't have any more to spare. With luck, we can fine more on the base. I put a huge duffel bag in the back of the truck. If you get in it, they probably won't notice you."

Dragon Star looked down at the ugly gun. Even meditation could not untangle the vortex of emotions battling inside him. They all led to the same ending, so he didn't try to quiet them. He channeled them. He remembered the advice he'd taught soldiers for over a decade. *If you fight in anger, you will lose. The cold strategy will always win, whether it is a bar fight or a nuclear war.*

CHAPTER THIRTY-SEVEN

Jon was surprised how quickly the preparations went. The surviving soldiers seemed to be the efficient ones. Ruiz had the vehicles ready in minutes. He sent soldiers to carry Jon down, but that would be stupid. If he was up to fighting a dragon, he could make his own way down. Testing each limb and joint as he rose from the bed, he felt only a few wounds crack open. Most had healed some. But they all still hurt. He'd had nothing but aspirin and alcohol to dull the pain this long. Now he just had aspirin.

He paused at the bottom of the stairs. "I'm fine," he assured the two guards and Glass who were following him awkwardly and standing on the wooden stairs above him. He wasn't fine. His head was spinning and his fingers kept twitching from the pain. When he made it through the front door, Jon felt grateful for a cool breeze, which seemed to carry some of the burning away. He slowly worked his way across the wooden deck in front of the bar and out to the field. Four strange vehicles of various sizes had been parked in the clearing. The largest looked like a nightmare bus.

Glass helped him lower into the driver's seat of an automobile that resembled a Model-T Ford, except with a pressure valve on the top of a steam chamber mounted on the back of the vehicle. Despite the black paint, the aluminum construction had gaps where various mechanical parts showed through.

Jon smiled to show he was fine, keeping his lips sealed over gritted teeth. Glass knew better she turned and ran to Ruiz.

"Please," Glass begged the shorter leader again, "Jon's not ready to go back in yet. He needs to heal."

"This is war. He's ready to make the sacrifice. Now you need to let him go." Ruiz marched over to his men. All sixteen of them were present, standing at attention in four rows of four. "At ease. This is our chance to save the world. You're all the best men I've seen. I'm proud to stand beside you today as we make history and usher in the next era of human history!"

The men cheered and hollered. They made a lot of noise, but Jon thought their small number diminished the effect.

"Now, on board." The men turned and formed a line to board the big brown bus. It had two pressure chambers in the front, sitting on top of a chemical fuel heater.

Cindy joined them amidst the commotion.

Jon turned to look for Red. If they had any hope today, it would be Red. Standing between a funny looking train-truck and a smaller vehicle that resembled a hybrid between a golf cart and a go-cart, Red watched Xenwyn. Somebody had given her leather gloves, which she pulled over the cyborg hand. Jon couldn't believe Red would still hold his crush on Xenwyn with her looking like the freak of the week. He knew Red was too nice to say anything before they went in and maybe died. If so, the uncomfortable situation never need be addressed.

"You ready?" Red asked.

"Time for the pre-mission meeting?" Xenwyn followed Red over to the small group. Jon couldn't look at her long. Between the knotted hair and weird prosthetic, he found her repellant in every way.

"We all know the *plans*," Red said, emphasizing more than one set. "This is our best chance to save the world. Despite everything, we're the only people left who even know what happened. The rest of the world is suffering out there. It's up to us to put things right."

"As much as anything can be right," Xenwyn added.

Jon suppressed a grimace as he tried not scratch a dozen places that itched so badly he felt sure they would drive him to insanity. As much as Jon liked Red, he didn't care for that speech. It wasn't even as inspiring as Luis Ruiz's. After a few seconds, everybody turned to him. So Jon decided to say something more.

"There is a dragon guarding the Actuator, cutting us off from undoing the changes that have plunged the world into chaos. That's not the biggest problem we face." He paused and waited for all of their faces to register surprise and then confusion.

"The biggest problem we face is letting go.

"The Actuator is just a manifestation of our many obsessions. People find little ideas to latch onto and they never allow anything to challenge them. Everybody thinks they have the best model of the world in their heads. We all walk around thinking we have a pretty good idea what's going on. And like everybody else in the world, we live our lives as best we can inside the simple constructions we have decided represent our truth.

"What's real? Is the way we see the world real? Are these ridiculous steam powered cars real? Is the dragon real? Or are we just seeing a warped image of real cars? How can any of us know if the models we build in our heads are anything like reality?

"We just grab some stuff out of the mix and claim it as truth. We find some fulfillment and hold onto it so tight that we'll never let go. These obsessions are our way of coping with the fear. We are afraid of the truth. We suspect it is huge and terrible, so we grab onto the first hand hold we can reach and never let go."

Jon wasn't usually the philosophical type, but lying in bed for so long, he'd had a lot of time to think about the situation. Now he hoped it would help all of them. "Is it wrong for somebody to obsess about science fiction and dream of a made-up world where aliens and space ships show humans advancing and growing? No. Is it wrong for Xenwyn to love the idea of magic and monsters defining heroes that rise above incredible barriers? No.

"What's wrong is our human frailty which lets our minds slip beyond the wanting. Our desires become our obsessions. And we reach to make our dreams true. It's human nature. We seek to make real the ideas we cherish. That's not bad.

"When Arne Anderson built this machine, it was to try and make the world better. When each of the Machine Monks used it to give life to a fictional world they loved, it wasn't bad. We are not the villains of this story. The only way it becomes wrong is if we hold onto those ideas and refuse to see what's real because of them."

Red nodded. "Like Mack."

Xenwyn, took a sudden interest in the ground beneath her heavy boots.

"We can make this right," Jon said. "But first, we have to see what's real. We have to let go of our obsessions. We have to let go of guilt and fear. The only way to win this is if we all see what is real.

"Commander Newell's mind was twisted by the Actuator long before her body was morphed to match. Our quest today is not to kill a monster. It's to set her mind free of the prison she put it in. The Actuator didn't do that. She did it.

"And we have all put our minds into prisons, too. We've built walls and bars to hold ourselves in a small world because it was comfortable and we didn't want to deal with the harsh, bigger reality. That has to end now.

"We are not going in to take back the machine responsible for our prisons. We are going to liberate our minds. Then we will be in a position to help the rest of the world. We have to do more than take back the Actuator. We have to fix the world.

"We locked everybody else in our prisons. We forced the rest of the world to see our escape mechanisms, our obsessions. Before we can free them, we have to free ourselves. And since Commander Newell is lost to it, we have to free her through death.

"We will bring her peace. We will bring ourselves peace. Only then will be able to bring the world some peace."

Red nodded somberly. "To peace, then." He put his hand out.

Xenwyn put hers on top of it. "To Peace."

The others joined in. Jon regretted it, but knew he had to show his solidarity with them. So he bit back the pain and reached his hand out through the car window. Then the group broke up.

"I don't care about the world anymore," Glass said as she grabbed Jon's collar. For an Untouched House Monk, it was a perfect sacrifice of her obsession. "I just want you to come back. You're my freedom and my peace now."

Jon looked into those beautiful blue eyes rimmed with tears. "I've loved you for so long," he said softly, not even trying to mask the pain. "I thought we had all the time in the world. I wanted to do my job. I thought the Actuations were so exciting. It was like touching the finger of God every time we played with the world. Now that we've been slapped, it feels like I finally woke up. I wish I could trade it all in and spend that time with you instead."

The tears rimming her eyes fell as Glass leaned in and gently kissed his lips, making him grateful his face was one of the only places on him not burned. Her cool tears tickled his skin. He put all his thoughts into the sensation of that kiss, ignoring for a beautiful minute the pain everywhere else.

As they walked away, Xenwyn had a close up view of Red's butt. She'd gotten sick of seeing people from that perspective lately. But with Red, she didn't mind as much.

She knew Jon was right. His words broke her heart. She'd given her love to all things fantasy, leaving no space for people. She'd tried to balance it, of course. But it was a lie. Like everybody on the base, she'd used the Actuator as an excuse to hide in her own fantasies and let real life pass by. It had been easier. It felt safer.

Now she knew better. Safe in prison was not a good trade. And look how much her false sense of safety had cost. She knew the state of the world wasn't her fault. But she had made the dragon.

They reached the space between the truck Red had come in and the smaller go-cart Ruiz had somehow scrounged up for Xenwyn. She regretted asking for Red's help now. Ruiz had the same plan all along. Once Jon healed he'd send the two of them in as bait. If she'd know that, she would have warned Red to stay away. One more example of her selfishness.

She'd known Red had liked her for quite a while. But it never seemed that important. There were plenty of guys on the base and Red just never measured up to her fantasy world. Now, the fantasy had betrayed her. Now she saw the idealism of a magical reality had blinded her. Red was the best hero on planet earth and she'd ignored him for a few minutes of unicorns and fairies. She knew down to the depths of her soul that she didn't deserve Red McLaren. He was noble and great, and she'd squandered her life in the pursuit of a phantom, which turned out to be evil.

He stopped and turned to her. She could see repulsion in his eyes. Before when anybody looked down on her ugly dwarfish form, she felt unfairly judged. She used to believe her soul was beautiful and trapped in this hideous body. Now she knew better. This disgusting body was better on the outside than she was on the inside. She deserved Red's scorn and his revulsion.

He opened his mouth to speak, obviously trying to think of something worth saying after Jon's scathing remarks. She reached one gloved finger way up and touched his lips before he said a word.

"Please don't," she said. "I'm sorry. I'm so sorry. You deserve the best this world has to offer. Don't say anything." Tears fell from her eyes and collected in the bottom of the leather goggles. As they fogged up the inside of the tinted lenses, she turned away. With her back to him she pulled them free and jumped into the small cart.

She knew when they crossed the boundary she'd turn into a fairy again. Ruiz didn't know that. But when it happened, she'd fly out of the steam cart and go draw the dragon out herself. She shouldn't be alive when so many had died because of her. Death was the only way to make restitution for the pain her obsession had caused. She knew Commander Newell couldn't resist chasing her in fairy form. She'd proved it before. Xenwyn would be the only bait and die so the others could kill the dragon.

CHAPTER THIRTY-EIGHT

s they bumped and puttered along the dirt road, Dragon Star felt bruises forming all along his body. Grateful at last to be moving so he could unzip the stinky bag he hid in and get some fresh air, he thought being killed by the dragon might be a welcome relief from his current hell.

He couldn't sleep or meditate in the chaotic and annoying bag. He just endured, trying to wiggle around so the softer parts of him padded the bumps. More than any other time in his life, he welcomed the change.

White. Hot. Radish kimchi and chocolate syrup. Sensations exploded in his mind, like fireworks blooming through his whole being, until the tendrils fell through cracks in reality and disappeared into an unseen dimension. Dragon Star always felt the touch of an unseen deity in the Actuations. The new physical laws and inflexible solidarity of the universe after a change left no evidence except a glimpse of the great cosmic machinery turning behind the scenes. Arne Anderson's machine tapped into the electronics of the universe, scrambling the signals like a computer hacker, so the manifested world came out changed by the parallax of one person's mind.

Grateful for a break from the pounding on his bruises, Dragon Star rolled back and stuck his head out farther. The small room effectively blocked out all light. Only a few small LED lights blinking on and off showed a small electronic control panel to one side. The even groan of engines and a faint buzz in the metal ground told him they were flying in a space ship. They'd finally entered Brian's sci-fi realm.

With little light, Dragon Star's eyes never adjusted. Instead, he squirmed in the tight bonds around him to free his hand. Unlike the large duffle bag he'd been in, his new confinement felt soft and flexible. While it would stretch to allow him to bend or squirm, he couldn't get his hands free to look for the zipper.

After he finally twisted his wrist, he could feel the strands of a thick fiber. It felt like it had been wrapped around him in layers. Suddenly, Dragon Star understood. In the cargo hold of a space ship, a cocoon bound him. He remembered Mack's insectoid alien form the last time they came through this land. He hoped he wasn't some kind of larval form of insect. In the dark, it wouldn't matter. If everything went well, they'd come out the other side of the territory without any problems.

Suffering from exhaustion and finally in a condition of warmth, Dragon Star let himself rest. He tried to keep his mind alert for sounds of intrusion, hoping the whole time not to have to figure out how to manipulate a giant bug-body.

A few minutes into his power nap, the change woke him. Thunder in his ears and lightning behind his closed eyes gave way to the burn of hot pepper paste and cheap ice cream.

In the darkness, he felt satin padding on every side. His knees were bent, the new container still too short for him. Light leaked in from a few cracks around the box lid above him, revealing a light blue fabric on all sides. Dragon star wondered what kind of box would be padded with... a coffin.

They had crossed into Xenwyn's fantasy. They would soon be at the base. Dragon Star pushed on the lid, finding it nailed shut. Panic began to fill him. He had to get out of this box before they arrived at the base or he'd be useless to help Red. Even worse, images of the dozen horse drawn carriages the dragon had smashed with only the tiniest effort ran through his mind. He'd be dead in a moment with no warning at all. Ironically, the coffin he was in would probably be smashed, so he wouldn't even get a peaceful resting place.

Shuffling around by inches, Dragon Star turned onto his belly and pushed up with his arms, smashing his back against the lid. He couldn't budge it. Then he wiggled back around, trying to pound on the lid with his fist. Using the most focused tae-kwon-do hits he could in the cramped confines still didn't help. He grabbed the sword at his belt, but had no room to draw it or use it as a pry bar. The gun Red gave him had turned to a crossbow, but it was too big to turn it upward. Twisting it around so it faced his head, Dragon Star realized panic now drove him to do stupid things.

He calmed himself and emptied his mind. He let the rhythm of the horses racing across a mostly flat road become the focus as he slowed his breathing. Once he felt his heartbeat slowing, he let the coffin come back into his mind. He imagined it from the outside, a wooden rectangle with soft lining. The top had been nailed on last, probably with six nails, including one at each corner.

Dragon Star rolled on his side and bent his knees so he could get his elbows up by his head. Leaving his knees sideways he twisted his torso so he was on his back with a whole head of space above him. Then with his elbows above his head, he pounded both fists in focused attacks. Continuing the steady hits until his triceps burned, he saw the crack above his head growing. Eventually the nails pulled up until he could wedge his fingers through the seam and push like an overhead press. Once the nails came up, he levered the rest of the lid and pushed it up into the air.

He stopped once the lid came free and lifted his head so he could see behind them. Red apparently had taken up the rear position. Nobody followed them. Pressing the lid higher, Dragon Star crawled out of the coffin and then replaced the lid. He stayed low in the hearse, grateful for a cover on the back of the wagon so he would stay hidden. Unfortunately, he couldn't see where they went.

Peeking sideways out of the back, he saw the long, crenelated stone wall surrounding the base. They were close. He needed to get out.

Turning so he climbed down facing the same direction as the cart, He took a deep breath before he jumped. Running forward to match the speed of the vehicle when he landed, each step jolted his body. After two steps, he knew he'd lost his balance and he pulled in to roll. Leaning to the side, he landed in dirt and desert grass instead of the stone pavers of the road. Except for landing hard on the side he'd bruised, he didn't think there was any serious damage.

Dragon Star stayed low in the bushes until he caught his breath. *This was not turning out to be a good day.*

Red felt the wagon bounce unnaturally behind him, and hoped Dragon Star would be okay as he tumbled onto the dirt road. Ruiz sat in the back of the lead vehicle, watching them like a hawk. This furious speed was ludicrous. Did Ruiz think they were going to catch the dragon unaware? They should have stopped far back and tried to sneak in. With luck the plan could still work after they all split up.

Red could still see the huge soldier transport pulled by eight horses in the lead. They had all turned to orcs again, their guns now huge crossbows which the green skinned monsters held up. Red watched one misfire into the sky and rolled his eyes. Ruiz, the biggest orc with metal plates on his armor and heavy axe, turned and began growling for the clumsy one to re-load.

Jon's carriage was the only normal one. It had two horses and an open car. Red could tell Jon suppressed a grimace. Coming before Jon healed completely really was a bad idea.

Xenwyn's cart had come to a stop a few seconds after they crossed the boundary. In Brian's territory, she'd been a squat robot again, driving some kind of hover drone. Then it turned into a pony with a tiny chariot behind it. As a fairy, she zipped away out of the cart and the animal just stopped trotting, distracted by the dry shrubs on the side of the road.

Just after Dragon Star disembarked, she zipped in the window and lighted on Red's shoulder.

"I'm so sorry," she said in a high pitched, whiney voice.

"This isn't your fault," Red said. "It's Ruiz's. But just stick to the plan. We can still make this work."

"No, I can't," she said. "I have to fix this. I'm the only one who can."

"Don't do anything rash," Red said.

Xenwyn leaned over and kissed his cheek. Even though she was tiny, Red felt an emotional jolt of electricity from her lips that spread over his whole body. Had she planned that when she became a fairy in the Actuation?

"You're the best man I've ever known," she said into his ear. "I wish I had seen it before."

"There'll be time..." He stopped when he saw her zip out the front of the carriage and over the castle wall. He wanted to hit something. *What is she doing?*

Ruiz came to a stop outside the gate. Red and Jon stopped their carriages. Red began to get out, but Ruiz the orc jumped down with one gnarled hand held out. "Just wait there."

A couple orcs came over to Red. One put his huge hand against Red's chest and pushed him back into the seat. "Hey, what's up?" Red asked.

"Just want to make sure," the orc said through snarls and grunts. Then the other one clapped a black iron manacle on Red's ankle and locked the other half of it to the metal frame of the carriage.

"I said I was on your side," Red protested.

They sneered a freakish smile. Then one of the orcs slapped the rump of the horse and the carriage lurched forward.

"I won't be able to get clear of the vehicle if she crushes it," Red said back to them. They just waved.

Red's carriage joined Jon's as they went through the gate. They pulled the horses to a stop as the orcs came through and pulled the gate shut, leaving their own carriage on the outside. They wrapped a chain around the metal grating of the gate, then fastened it with a thick metal lock using the same key.

"Stick to the plan," Ruiz said with a twisted grin. He indicated with his hands for eight orcs to begin marching along the wall in either direction. Before he joined the group on the east, he tossed one of his soldiers the key and said to Jon, "Give us a minute to get into position before you make any noise or movement to draw out the dragon."

Red saw Jon panting. His mentor probably didn't hear the orc's directions.

Suddenly the red-skinned behemoth rose into the sky above the test field where the Actuator sat. Red's horses began whinnying and stamping. Zipping around in front of the Commander Newell was the bright yellow light trail of a fast moving fairy.

CHAPTER THIRTY-NINE

M ove out fast!" Ruiz bellowed.

The orcs began waddling along each side of the stone barrier. Red pulled out his crossbow and set it next to him on the driver's seat so he'd be able to grab it quickly. He tugged at the shackle on his ankle, confirming it would be impossible to break free.

"Split up," Jon said. It sounded pathetic, but Red knew his friend would sacrifice himself to try and buy a little more time. It would be in vain. If they remained bound to these carts, their deaths would both come soon.

"No," Red countered. "We need to stay together until the last minute. Then if we split up, it might buy us both time."

Jon nodded. Red suspected at this point Jon would favor actions leading to an early death to cut short the pain. Red considered the various roads. They were as far from the dragon as possible now. There would be no advantage to leaving yet.

He watched the giant red reptile turn in the air, swiping back and forth with her long neck and occasionally spurting flames meant to destroy the annoying gnat Xenwyn made of herself. His stomach in knots, Red didn't know why Xenwyn turned suicidal. He just knew a single bolt from the crossbow by him would probably not be enough to save her, even if he could get up in the air to help her somehow.

The winged battle happened high above any of them now. The only thing worse than being trapped inside the castle wall to wait for the dragon, was feeling helpless to help Xenwyn. Time slowed, and each time the dragon twisted in the air and snapped those huge jaws, Red wondered if it would be the last moment Xenwyn's light would grace this earth. His heart nearly broke each time. He'd seen so many of their friends die. He didn't think he'd make it if he had to watch her die.

With the advantage of speed and agility, Xenwyn darted at the dragon's eyes and weaved around swiping claws. This dangerous game wouldn't last forever. The first touch from any of the dragon's weapons, even just a swipe from the tail, would snuff out Xenwyn's life forever.

Red's mind screamed for him to forget the plan and follow her. He wanted to spur on the horses and try to help. Maybe he could buy a short distraction for the little fairy he adored. Even as he held up the reins, he didn't snap them. He had nothing that would assist the tiny firefly as it zipped and braided around the death-dealing titan. If that small glimmer went out, he wouldn't restrain himself. The moment her yellow light stopped flitting through the sky, Red would charge in and join her in the bliss of final release.

At one point, the dragon chased Xenwyn near the rock wall to the east. They were close enough Red prepared to start the horses running. He paused when he saw several bolts streak up from below. Some missed. Some hit the dragon. However, the flying monster didn't show any sign of being hurt or even noticing the feeble attack. A spurt of hot fire blasted in that direction. Then the neck twisted to try and burn Xenwyn. *Had any of the orcs died?* Xenwyn turned north away from Red and Jon. Commander Newell pursued. *So much for Ruiz's brilliant plan.*

Engrossed by the action, Red almost didn't notice when a black iron key landed on the footrest with a clank. It took him a moment to figure out what had happened. Dragon Star must have gotten the key somehow. Picking it up, Red knew how. Greasy, black blood smeared on the handle of the large bow.

Red looked around to see if he could find Dragon Star, but the Korean had already disappeared. As he twisted the lock open and pried the manacles, Red knew where Dragon Star had gone. His friend now hunted the monster. Red wanted to join. He would prefer to face death side by side with his loyal friend. But he knew they would draw too much attention as a group. Easier to stay hidden alone.

Quickly jumping down from the hearse, Red moved over to Jon and undid the clamp around his friend's ankle.

"You going to be okay?" Red asked. Sweat beaded on Jon's forehead as he gasped irregularly for breath.

"I'm okay. Just stick to the plan." Jon looked down, as if he considered getting out to walk. Then he wagged his head. "I'll try to get closer with this wagon."

"The dragon will see you," Red said.

"I'll be careful." Jon smiled and spurred his team forward.

Red went back to his own carriage and released the brake. At least he could try to offer the dragon an alternative to Jon's big vehicle. He slapped his horse hard, commanding it to move down the road and into the main street lined with wooden buildings.

Red scanned the walls, unable to see any sign of the orcs. At least they wouldn't try to stop him. Rushing away with a crossbow over one shoulder, Red ducked into the shade of a nearby building. Suddenly the situation felt very familiar. *Isn't this how we started this whole mess?*

Red moved to the back of the buildings and began working his way toward the Dedicated House. He still had his crossbow. But he knew they needed a weapon with more kick. Xenwyn had told him where to find her key. If she could hold out long enough for him to get it, they might have a chance.

Dragon Star knew Xenwyn wasn't long for this world. Powerless to inflict harm on the demonic creature, the fairy was selling her life for a lot more time than he would have expected. However, unless she broke off and hid or flew away, Xenwyn would never last. Eventually, even by luck, Commander Newell would get the satisfaction of swatting the fly.

From hiding, Dragon Star easily tracked the orc with the key. It had been a simple matter of cutting the beast-man's hand so it dropped to the ground. The bumbling creature tried to shoot the crossbow one handed, missing its only shot. Dragon Star swiped the metal device and quickly raced back to the street to hide.

He tossed the key to Red, and moved back toward the armory.

Seeing the failed attempt by the orc guards to do any damage with their crossbows, Dragon Star dropped his own. They needed something bigger. He held out a faint hope that a sword, well placed, might do the trick. But he wasn't ready to bet his life on it. He wished he had time to change clothes. The medieval boots made it hard to move quietly.

Metal bars adorned the armory, one of the few buildings constructed of stone inside the castle wall. Dragon Star found it locked tight. Checking the dragon's position well to the east, he rushed to the shooting range next door. Except for the building being wood and the targets now being strapped to bales of hay, this building seemed about the same. He moved past the shooting lanes and found the connecting door to the armory. It was locked, too. But this door was wood. So he concentrated, letting out half a breath, then kicked it right next to the handle. In one glorious crack the door flew open, having torn the frame's inferior wood.

With only a few small windows high up, the dark armory felt like a good place to hide. Dragon Star didn't let himself relax, wondering constantly how long Xenwyn could keep up this dance on the brink of death. When his eyes adjusted, Dragon Star saw this building had changed. With spears, halberds, swords, armor, shields, and lances lined up in group on one wall, the more exotic morning stars, maces, and axes lined the other. He took a steel shafted pike with no barbs or frills on the end. The black, iron bar extended a good twelve feet to a single sharp point. Eventually he found what he'd come for. In a box along the outside wall, he found twenty bombs. He threw a wedge of flint and a torch on top of the box. Then he unlocked the door from the inside, kicked it wide open, and scanned the skies for any sign of the dragon. Seeing none, he hefted the heavy box and pike. Moving half as fast under great strain, he carried the thin wooden crate out into the sunlight and crossed the street.

Jon concentrated on moving in the right direction. He wanted to head to the clearing by the Actuator and wait for the dragon to finish what she started with the breath of fire. But he knew the crossbows weren't going to work. So he headed toward the Key Hunter's Office.

He didn't have the energy or strength to look for Xenwyn. He kept the reins in hand and when the horses needed it, he offered them a word of urging.

When they reached the office, he pulled back hard, feeling the bloom of pain on his arms and back. He set the brake and slowly shambled inside.

It hadn't been long into working as a Key Hunter before Jon realized some things would work no matter what change the Machine Monks enacted. Simple machines never changed because the Monks didn't think of them specifically. And even medieval people used them. Some pre-history peoples had them. So Jon had constructed a just-in-case weapon. One he knew would always work no matter what the Machine Monks dreamed up.

Opening the storage closet he kept it in, Jon could barely see the dusty contraption in the dark. Mounted on a wheeled trailer, even in his decrepit condition, he could lift the front and slowly pull it out into the road. Despite the metal frame and heavy machinery, the well-balanced mounting let him to move the device alone. The pain in his back threatened to black him out. But

Jon kept breathing and slowly eased the canvas covered device out where he could fasten it to the back of the wagon.

He had to rest before crawling into the driver's seat and slowly righting himself. Every move seemed to split more skin. Some of what oozed out to his clothes was blood. He felt sure an infection would be coursing through his veins soon. But he would take out the dragon before he died. Then Red would be able to put the world back. His one regret, Glass, kept popping into his mind. But Jon couldn't do anything about that now. One dead man and a broken heart were nothing in this world of horror and chaos.

He didn't pretend. He knew if the dragon didn't kill him, the infection would. Maybe he could at least see her face, kiss her once more before the end.

CHAPTER FORTY

ed saw Xenwyn getting a little slower. Instead of weaving and spinning in circles, now she only raced ahead of the dragon. In wide circles, she flew around the perimeter. She'd fall back to let the red monster get near, then race ahead, narrowly evading teeth and fire. When she circled over the orcs to the west, nine bolts flew up at the giant pursuer.

Some stuck in. Others bounced off. None had any effect at all. Then the dragon breathed fire down on them, almost as an afterthought, and continued her pursuit.

When she led the dragon over toward the east, only two bolts flew. Red hoped if people had to die, one of them would be Ruiz. Whatever else happened, that guy deserved to die first.

Red had a new leather jacket over the dark ages farming clothes he'd been given at the last boundary. He saw it in the closet next to the door of Xenwyn's apartment when he kicked in the door. He didn't know why Xenwyn had a jacket like the one he liked to wear, but he figured she wouldn't mind him borrowing it now. A little smaller than he preferred, it felt good. Mostly, he just needed pockets. He patted the breast pocket now as he moved across the grounds toward the machine responsible for everything. Xenwyn's magic wand key was still there. He lifted the crossbow up over his shoulder and rushed across the street toward the vast testing grounds.

A mile radius marked off the large, empty area they used to experiment on the Actuator. What had been high chain link fences with razor wire delineating the area, now had a stone wall around it with barbed iron spikes sticking up. The tall poles holding the dampener speakers had all changed into lookout towers. The failed dampeners were gone. They could never investigate them for evidence of the saboteur.

The main gate had become heavy wood. It stood ajar. The only other opening to the grassy flat circle was a broken section of wall to the west. Bodies littered the ground. Orcs and men had been decaying for over a week. Flies and rats still worked on the few bits of flesh clinging to the sun baked bones. The breeze carried the putrid stench of it all.

In the center of everything, unchanged, stood the Actuator. On a round foundation of concrete, the square base of the machine stood two feet high like a computer from a bad sci-fi movie. Behind that, a rectangle rose higher with bleeping lights, dials, and various oscilloscope readings. Although he couldn't see from this far, Red knew the top of the flat section in front of the base would have the key holes. Above the metal squares, a tall column had three small satellite dishes which projected the transformative signal. An antenna topped the machine. Red had expected that pole to act as a lightning rod.

Even from nearly a mile away, where the Actuator was little more than a spec, Red could see it perfectly in his mind. It had been the focus of his life for so long. Now it was the vehicle of destruction for the earth.

On this side of the Actuator, a large crater had been dug into the ground. Obviously, Commander Newell nested there. Red searched for any sign of rocks or bushes they could use for cover, finding none.

Watching the drama as the dragon chased Xenwyn around the perimeter of the base every few minutes, Red didn't know what to do. Before he decided, he saw Dragon Star walking up, carrying a box and a long stick. Red rushed over to help his friend. Taking the box, he led them both back to the wall.

"I do not think the crossbows will be enough," Dragon Star said.

"No. This will definitely help." Red set the crate of bombs insulated with hay down next to the gate. Then they both moved to wait in the diminishing shade of the perimeter wall.

Before either of them spoke again they heard a horse drawn cart approaching. The horses walked slowly, as if Jon lacked the strength even to spur them on. Red realized he was in pain when they bounced over the rocks too hard.

Jon halted the wagon before Red saw the trailer hooked to the back of the cart.

"Is that..."

"Uncle Joe," Jon nodded. Red remembered when Jon had commissioned this bizarre device and christened it. He'd forgotten all about the thing.

231

"Apparently we all had different plans," Red said.

"It became clear that the crossbows weren't effective," Jon nodded. "Nice jacket."

Dragon Star kept looking at the canvas pulled tight over a lump taller than any of them. "What's the new plan?"

Red smiled. "Still have the keys?"

Jon nodded, patting the lump of devices dangling under his shirt.

Red said, "We get Uncle Joe ready. Jon, can you man that on the move?" Jon nodded with teeth clenched. "Dragon Star, you're in the back with the bombs and the pike, in case the dragon makes a run at us. I'll drive.

"We head to the Actuator. With any luck, we'll have enough keys to be able to use this." Red reached in his jacket and pulled out a delicate golden rod with a star on one end.

"Xenwyn's key," Dragon star said.

Red nodded. "If we can get it to the Actuator..."

"Commander Newell won't be a dragon anymore," Jon finished. "It's a long shot."

"This is all a long shot," Dragon Star said.

Red put the wand back in his pocket. "If it doesn't work, we set up Uncle Joe and hide under the cart between the Actuator and the nest." He pointed to the crater just this side of the machine in the middle of the clearing. "We make our stand there whenever the dragon comes back."

The others nodded. Red put out a hand to help Jon. "Now get your old, useless butt out of my chair."

They pulled the cover off the trailer revealing an incomprehensible maze of gears, tubes, and springs. Out the back end, two rows of four tubes stretched a couple of feet at a slight upward angle. Uncle Joe had eight shots. Red helped Jon sit behind the device on a flat seat fastened to the trailer frame. Dragon Star could see handles allowing for a limited range of aiming, and several chains dangling down to act as triggers.

"It's made entirely of simple machines," Jon said proudly as he settled onto the metal seat behind it.

Dragon star used the flint to spark the torch. He set the pike down in the bed, partly sticking out one side. Then he held a round, black metal bomb up and nodded to Red.

Red gave the horses a little tap with the whip, deciding to start by using Jon's technique. Maybe if they went slow, the dragon would keep her attention on Xenwyn.

Red watched the dragon chase the little light around to the far side of the base. He could sense Xenwyn's exhaustion. She didn't even play the game of slowing down and speeding up now. She just kept flying in the wide arc. For the time being, the dragon was keeping up with her. If Xenwyn lost any more speed, the chase would be over. The testing ground was off to the west of the base. Xenwyn's path didn't lead this way.

When Red turned his attention back to the horses, he heard Dragon Star call, "Incoming!"

He whipped the horses to a run, then turned to see Commander Newell broke off the chase and was heading toward them. She was coming straight from behind. So at least Uncle Joe would get a shot at her.

Turning back to Dragon Star as the wagon bounced and rattled over the grassy bumps in the field, Red said, "Tell Jon to hand me the keys!"

Dragon Star relayed the message. With the wind now beating on them and the noise of hooves and wheels, Red couldn't hear the other talking. Finally, Dragon Star handed Red the leather thong, now with five keys on it.

Red held it along with the reins, whipping and calling for more speed from the horses. When the dragon bellowed behind them, the horses suddenly lurched with fear and moved even faster. Red knew they had only a mile to cross, but it felt like time slowed and they would never get there.

A loud *click* sounded and Red turned as Jon pulled one of the chains, launching the first needle-sharp spike from Uncle Joe. The feathered bolt flew true, but fell out of the sky just before reaching the monster behind them. He had to turn back to watch the horses, but he heard two more bolts launch. The dragon roared again. Red hoped pain motivated it.

Then the flying monster weaved to the right, flying alongside them, but out of range for a moment before turning and blasting fire sideways toward them. Dragon Star threw an unlit bomb above the jet at an angle so it dropped down closer to their enemy before exploding.

The giant reptile pulled away again, gaining altitude and flying to a position above them. When the shadow of the gargantuan fell over them, Red saw a tiny, yellow flame zip in from the side and land next to him on the driver's seat. Sparing a moment to look down, he saw Xenwyn breathing so hard it looked like her tiny chest would rupture. Tears glistened on her glowing face as her resting wings fluttered in the head wind.

"I'm sorry," her tiny voice said with the last of her energy.

"You were amazing," Red said.

"It's all over now. I just wanted to be by you at the end."

Red reached his free hand over and petted her frizzed hair and soft wings. "It's not over yet." He pulled out the wand. "Look, we're almost there."

Xenwyn lifted her head for a short smile, then passed out on the cushion. A bomb exploded above them, shaking the cart as pieces of shrapnel rained down.

Dragon Star cursed in Korean and shouted, "Come back here, coward! Take your medicine!"

The shadow flitted across them again, then another bomb exploded to their left. Red pulled on the reins as they neared the Actuator. But the horses refused to stop. Terrified by the dragon and the bombs, they ran like a stampede. The whole cart went past the Actuator at high speed.

Red grabbed the brake and pulled for all he was worth, but the horses knew the jaws of death were at their heels. Red tugged on the reins, trying to stop the manic animals. They only responded when the dragon hovered down in front of them, teeth bared.

CHAPTER FORTY-ONE

The horses nearly fell, turning and stopping with so much momentum behind them. Red yanked the reins for all he was worth, directing them left. Just as the glow of fire warmed up in the dragon's mouth, a black ball sailed through the air and landed right between her sword length teeth. The horses jumped from the explosion, gaining enough balance to keep running as Red turned them around. Once their blinders blocked the view of the dragon, they straightened up and headed the wagon and trailer back toward the machine.

This time Red bore down on the brake, not letting them build up so much speed.

Jon didn't wait for the smoke to clear. As soon as they headed back for the Actuator, he lined up Uncle Joe and pulled four chains at once.

When the dragon roared with pain, Red turned to see it spitting out metal shrapnel and ivory teeth. Several of Jon's spikes protruded from the monster's chest now.

Red hauled back on the reins, calling, "Whoa!" The hand with the thong of keys still pulled back on the brake. The horses strained against all the resistance, but failed to build up any more speed. Red glanced over Xenwyn's comatose body at the crossbow. If he couldn't stop the horses at the Actuator this time, he'd have to shoot one of them.

Two more bombs exploded, one on each side behind them. When Red looked back, he saw the dragon's wings had torn. Dragon Star had another black ball in his hand. Jon fired the last bolt. He aimed for the head, but the beast flapped hard, rising up and taking the bolt in the side of her long neck. Blood dripped from the neck wound, which didn't seem to affect her at all. At least the torn webbing of her wings slowed her down. But she still had the glint of murder in her yellow eyes.

"Jump!" Dragon Star called. He lobbed his last bomb, then dove off the side. Jon just tipped sideways and fell off.

Red didn't have time to think. On instinct alone, he grabbed the crossbow and Xenwyn. As he launched from the fast moving carriage, the full body of the dragon crashed down, crushing horses, cart, and Uncle Joe.

Pain shot up Red's side and back as he crashed to the rocky grass, thumping his head on the ground. He dropped Xenwyn and the keys, lifting the crossbow. Shaking from the adrenaline coursing through his body, he took aim at the giant reptilian head fifteen feet in front of him. In less than a second, he released the bolt on a perfect course for the linear black pupil of the massive, yellow eye.

The dragon blinked.

Metallic red skin dropped in front just as the bolt arrived. The tiny projectile rebounded off the tough hide and flipped harmlessly away into the grass. Red threw the useless crossbow next, bouncing the heavy device off the dragon's nose.

As the maw of the beast stretched open, preparing to strike like a snake, a black ball flew into the beast's gullet. Dragon Star tackled Red as the dragon fire and bomb shrapnel blasted from Commander Newell's throat. Searing heat grazed their backs until the long neck recoiled from pain and the concussive force of the bomb.

Red wanted to check the dimming light coming from Xenwyn's body. But Dragon Star said, "Run!"

Red grabbed the mess of keys and sprinted toward the towering Actuator. Dragon Star pulled his sword, taking a defensive stance and staring back at the coppery skin as it opened and revealed the yellow eyes.

"For Empty House!" the Korean cried. Then he charged.

Red reached the machine quickly. He looked down at the key holes searching for the familiar Saturn shaped hole that Xenwyn's key would fit.

He found it fourth down the line and smiled. Dusting off the five keys connected to the leather thong, he physically ripped the strap apart. The first hole was a black circle with a single block beneath it. He jammed Hanna's black key in and twisted. Nothing visible happened, but he heard an electronic moaning inside the machine as the power to that system surged and then cut off. Two more to go.

The second hole was a perfect circle, rimmed with brown. He lifted Cindy's wax seal stamp and shoved it in. When he turned it clockwise, he heard the same circuits whine and then drop off. *Looks like Pete's never going to get his pirate crew back.*

Just one more! Red looked at Nancy's medicine bag, Brian's RFE tube, and Eugene's syringe. None of them could possibly fit the third hole. It was a long thin card shaped opening like an ATM or... Red gritted his teeth and growled. Hitting the Actuator hard with his fist he cried out, "No!"

Dragon Star rushed forward, knowing every second he let the beast recover worked against him. As the wind from the tattered pumping wings helped clear the smoke, Dragon Star leaped up and stabbed with the elegant katana.

Aiming between two large plates on the monster's chest, he wedged the beveled tip in and thrust with all the force his legs and strong arms could generate. The sword slid sideways and up between the two layers a few inches, then stopped. Like Kevlar, the plates had some give, but he couldn't pierce them.

The great snake wound back, testing its damaged jaw by snapping it open and closed a few times. Dragon Star moved to the side, hacking at the coppery armor. A few small pieces of hard skin came off and clinked to the ground, revealing layers and layers of scales beneath.

The giant reptile flailed one arm, pulling the bolts free from her chest, Dragon Star plunged his sword deep into the closest hole.

The hard muscles resisted the blade. However, for the first time, the dragon noticed him. He yanked the sword free, realizing he hadn't even drawn her attention until now. It discouraged him. Still, he didn't fear death. He didn't even care anymore. He just wanted to buy Red enough time to hopefully shut down this fantasy realm and turn the commander back into a human.

Behind him, he heard Red scream out his frustration. At that moment, Dragon Star knew they had failed.

Surprisingly, he didn't even have to try. His mind, in perfect meditation already, accepted death happily. It was the only way to escape this new horror they had unleashed on the world. Dragon Star realized, the only lucky people since the great Actuation were the ones who died at the beginning. The people who lived were the unlucky ones.

Still, he had sworn revenge. So he would die trying.

When the huge hand swiped at him, Dragon Star knew he could never withstand the blow of so massive an appendage with claws like knives. So he jumped out of the way. As it whooshed by, he spun and sliced with his katana.

The dragon roared and pulled back, clutching her hand to her chest. *So I can hurt her.*

He pressed the new advantage, leaping into the air and brought the sword down hard on her rear foot. He sliced through the hard webbing as she used her great legs to launch into the air. Quickly out of his reach, the dragon spun around.

They both knew all she had to do was crash to the ground on him. His sword might prick her, but it would never cut deep enough into her body to kill her. And he couldn't possibly jump far enough to get out of the way.

Too far from the Actuator to get there in time, Dragon Star ran for the wreckage of the cart.

Cringing with anger, Red scanned the field. Jon and Xenwyn had fallen. He watched Dragon Star jump into the twisted mess of the cart as the belly of the dragon crashed down.

The thunder seemed to stretch for minutes. Red felt his whole soul break as he watched his last friend crushed beneath the weight of a titanic monster. This was the one death he couldn't endure. He felt his own will to live ebbing away. Then he heard the dragon screaming.

Whimpering and shaking, the titan wiggled her wings, but couldn't invest enough strength to fly. Red leaned around the Actuator to get a better view. Writhing in pain, she stepped back twice, swiping uselessly at her belly with both forearms.

A trail of black ichor ran down her ventral plates. When he took two steps forward, Red saw the end of the pike sticking out about a foot.

The behemoth continued to stumble and retreat. So Red rushed to the twice-crushed rubble. Pulling away two boards, Red found his friend curled up next to the pile of gears that used to be Uncle Joe.

Still breathing, but wincing in pain, the Korean asked, "Did I get her?"

Tears fell from his eyes. He wasn't happy or sad. Just beyond his ability to hold it all in. "Yes. But she's not dead."

He turned to see the dragon nipping at the protruding metal bar with her mangled face. She chose that moment to look up and see Red. Her reptilian visage twisted into a murderous expression and she began hobbling forward. Alive or dead, Red knew she would not let them have her hoard.

"Get up," Red said. He grabbed Dragon Star's good hand and stood, pulling his friend free of the mess.

Then he picked up the blue silk handle of the katana and handed it to Dragon Star.

"What is that?" Dragon Star asked.

Red looked down. In his other hand, he still held the wand. Suddenly he started to laugh. The realm key looked like a child's toy. It all suddenly struck him as terribly funny.

"I should have brought Brian's RFE instead," Red said. "I'm sure it's just as useless."

Dragon Star lifted the sword, keeping his crushed hand in a fist at his waist. "I want you to run away now."

Red looked up at his friend. "What? No. Never. I'll stay with you to the end."

"This is not about loyalty," Dragon Star said. "I think she has a fatal wound. But it could be weeks or months before she dies. You need to be there to take possession of the Actuator when she does."

"Then come with me."

"She will catch us. I can barely move anyway. Just get the keys and go. When she dies, you can come back."

"What about Jon and Xenwyn."

"Take Xenwyn. I will try to protect Jon if I can."

"I can't watch you die."

"There is no time," Dragon Star said, stepping forward to intercept the slowly advancing dragon. "I can only buy you a few seconds. Run!"

Red took a few steps toward Xenwyn. When he saw her glowing body, he realized something he'd been forgetting. This was her fantasy realm.

And he had a magic wand.

When he turned, Red saw Dragon Star dodge a feeble blast of flames, swiping with the sword at Commander Newell's hand. The sword hit one of the claws and clanged as it bounced off.

Red lifted the wand and pointed the gold star on the end at the dragon. *How does a magic wand even work?* Gritting his teeth and holding the wand so tight it shook, Red scrambled to remember anything he knew. The monster's tail spun around and caught Dragon Star unaware with a row of spikes, knocking the man to the ground.

Red cried out, "Go! Magic! Abracadabra!"

Nothing happened. The great enemy reached back with one claw, ready to smash and cut Dragon Star into oblivion.

CHAPTER FORTY-TWO

Desperate for anything to save his friend, Red imagined something shooting out of the end of the stick he held. Somehow, his psyche touched the wand and he felt his mind pull a mental trigger.

Suddenly a cold blast launched from the tip of the gold star, leaving traces of snow on the hand holding the rod. A huge block of ice formed around the dragon's arm, holding it back so she couldn't crush Dragon Star.

The Korean rolled over, crawling for his sword. The dragon raised her spiked tail, preparing to smash it down and destroy her prey.

Red shot another blast out the end of the wand. Ice encrusted the tail, holding it in place.

Commander Newell lashed out with every possible appendage. One at a time, Red blasted each one until the weight of the massive frozen blocks rolled her body forward. With only her neck and head free, the dragon began bobbing back and forth like a giant snake, snapping with her ruined jaw. Red blasted it, too. With a heavy crystalline muzzle weighing down her long nose, the ice block stopped her breathing and welded her head to the ground.

He slowly moved forward, wand at the ready. Exhausted and wounded, the dragon lacked the strength to break the massive blocks of clear ice.

Dragon Star slowly rose, sword in hand, and turned to face the beast. She began breathing fire, melting the block on her face to a puddle. Red prepared to shoot another blast of ice. "Move back, I can't get a shot."

Dragon Star ignored the warning, thrusting the sword down between the dragon's eyes. The first hit didn't sink in. The second either. But with each thrust, chips of scale and bone fell away. Muffled growls from deep in the monster's throat escaped as a rumbling moan. Again and again the Korean hacked and poked with his sword. As the puddle grew around Dragon Star's feet, a swell of fire burst from the sides of the ice, freeing the monster's face. Recoiling its neck, the head began to rise with great chunks of ice still clinging to frills and bearding. Before it lifted two feet, Dragon Star thrust the sword through.

The skull broke with a loud *crack*, which echoed in Red's ears. Dragon Star leaned forward and pushed with his whole body. The sword slid in, scraping against bone and scales. Smoke leaked through the hole. Then the dragon's head twisted and fell to the ground, splashing in the puddle of water.

Red ran forward and caught Dragon Star before the man fell to the ground. Helping his friend out of the bloody mud, Red moved them both away so they could sit on the grass.

Breathing hard, they watched in silence as the sun began to melt the big blocks of ice around the limbs of the prostrated dragon.

Leaving his friend to his dark meditations, Red checked on Jon and Xenwyn. They were both unconscious, but breathing. As he crouched over the glowing yellow fairy, he lifted his head to see six crossbows pointing at him. A circle of orcs, all with ugly and angry green faces, caused him to raise his hands without a word from them.

"Well done," Ruiz said. "The ability to improvise when plan A goes awry is commendable in a soldier."

"If I'm one of your soldiers, why are your men pointing their weapons at me?"

Ruiz snorted through his pig nose. "We don't trust you to remain loyal for the next phase of our plan."

"Now? You're going to mess with the Actuator now? Don't you want to talk to some Machine Monks about how to work it first?"

"They lie," Ruiz said with wide, murderous eyes. "This is my chance to fix the world and I won't wait. And I won't let you or anybody else ruin it."

Two more orcs led Dragon Star at weapon's point over to join Red. Red laughed. If they had a clue, they would have known they should have spent six of their men on Dragon Star. He was by far the most dangerous of the pair. "You don't know how to use the machine," Red said. "It takes years of training. You can't just walk up and work it."

"That's what you two are for. You're going to turn it on, or whatever you do, so I can use it. If you disobey or try anything stupid, you'll die on the spot. Do I make myself clear?"

"Don't worry about us," Red said, "there's plenty of stupid here already." Could it really be possible they had defeated a dragon only to die at the hands of trigger-happy orcs? Obviously, the world was already messed up, long before the Actuation.

The manic smile fell from Ruiz's monstrous face. "Go!"

The circle of foes parted on one side, leaving only a space for them to move toward the Actuator. They put their hands down as they walked. One glance told Red that Dragon Star's sword remained stuck in the fallen creature's forehead like an extra horn.

When they reached the large machine, Red quickly covered Brian's resonant frequency emitter, Eugene's syringe, and Nancy's medicine bag with his hands, slipping them into his pockets when nobody was watching. "It won't work," Red said. "We don't have the rest of the keys." He pointed demonstratively at the rows of key holes on the top of the base.

"Don't try to trick me," Ruiz said. "I don't care about all that. I'll just work right over the top of them, projecting a new change to mix with what's already out there."

"You can't," Dragon Star said. "You don't have the training. The only way you could do that is if you were familiar with all the existing realms. There are still twenty variations of the world out there. You have to understand each one before the machine will let you change them."

"Aim!" Ruiz called. The orcs pulled the butt of their crossbows tight against their shoulders, peering with their ugly eyes across the deadly bolts resting in front of high-tension string.

Red could feel the touch of the Actuator in his mind. He knew it was a psychic tendril from the machine. The Machine Monks connected through it to start the Great Conversation. Red had been trained to ignore it. The machine wouldn't enter an unwilling psyche.

Dragon Star felt the caress of temptation like the finger of a seducing woman. As he stood in the hot sun, exhausted and in pain, the desire to connect to the Actuator still filled his mind. He knew how. He'd done it so many times. Like each of those times before, he automatically emptied his mind, the first step for Empty House Monks.

The moment he snapped to his meditation, the stress and guilt of killing Commander Newell washed away. Dragon Star had expected it to haunt him for the rest of his life. But now he realized it was barely a buzz in the back of his mind. He remembered shooting his friend on the bridge. He remembered stabbing Hanna in the heart. But while those memories brought shame and regret, pushing his sword through the dragon's brain didn't.

He didn't have time to contemplate the implications right now. He realized he'd placed all his hope in killing the dragon and not left any desire for what could happen after. He was a ship without an anchor, drifting in the breeze.

Yet even as the Actuator tried to lure his mind into the intoxicating escape of an Actuation, Dragon Star found he still had one thing to hold onto. He had Red. His only friend left in the world, and Red needed his help now. Perhaps there was one person still worth dying for.

"Stop!" Dragon Star said. Several orcs grunted their disapproval at yet another delay in bloodletting.

Ruiz held up his hand. "You're ready to help me?"

"Yes." He made eye contact with Red and winked. Worry crossed Red's face, but then trust. Red slightly nodded his support. Dragon Star said, "There's one more key."

Red's eyes went wide.

"I don't want to die," Dragon Star said. He could hear the false notes in his own voice as it fell a little flat. He was a terrible liar. But one look at Ruiz showed it wasn't obvious to everybody. "Red has one more key."

Ruiz stepped forward. The two closest orcs lowered their weapons so they couldn't shoot him accidentally. "Show me the key."

Red reached inside the breast pocket of Xenwyn's black jacket and pulled out the gold wand.

"Cute!" Ruiz laughed. "You don't expect me to believe that turns on the machine." Several orcs chortled, making Dragon Star worry they might fire the crossbows accidentally.

"No. But it will shut down the fantasy realm we are in now." Dragon Star put his hands out to indicate the dragon and the medieval citadel. "Then you can use the Actuator."

"Give it to me," Ruiz said.

Dragon Star hoped Red would not mistake the plan now. He said, "Show him what it does."

Red nodded. Then he blasted Ruiz with a block of ice.

Dragon Star jumped to the side, tackling Red just as a barrage of crossbow bolts flew over them. Two lodged in the frozen block encapsulating Ruiz. Without it, they would have been fatal. One of the orcs fell as a stray bolt impaled him.

The closest orc dropped the useless crossbow and pulled out an axe. Red blasted that one, too. Jumping up, Red began pointing the wand in every direction. With wide eyes and unarmed bows, the orcs turned and ran.

Dragon Star stood as he watched the green pig-headed soldiers waddle as fast as they could across the grassy clearing. "They are so dumb. You could have shot them all as they retreated."

Red grimaced. "I've had enough of shooting people in the back for a while. Looks like you got your revenge."

Dragon Star nodded. "I thought I'd feel worse." He pulled his crushed hand in closer to his waist, ignoring the pain.

"Maybe when the adrenaline wears off?"

"It is off. I just feel numb."

"You should feel like a hero. You slew a dragon!"

"Yeah." Dragon Star smiled. As long as he lived, he knew nobody else would ever believe it. "What do we do now?"

Red wagged his head until they both turned to look at Jon.

Rising slowly, he hobbled over to them, clearly wincing in pain at every step. When he finally reached the Actuator he said, "That's some good work, you two."

"But now what?" Red asked.

Jon looked at the order of keyholes on the waist high platform in front of the readouts and controls. "We need to turn off the fantasy realms, obviously. You have that key already."

Red put the wand back into his pocket. Despite the heat of the sun, he wasn't about to take off the black jacket. "Yep. But there's a problem." Red pointed to the third keyhole, between the two he'd turned and the fourth one for the wand.

Jon stared at the third hole for a few seconds, as if he couldn't or wouldn't let himself comprehend the meaning of it. Red ran his finger up and down the thin slit and said, "It's for an electronic key card."

Jon finally allowed understanding to settle in. "Saul."

Dragon Star said, "Wait, do you think he's on Mars?"

"I don't know if the Actuator can reach Mars," Red said. "But we've all seen Saul's actuations. If he's made it to Cape Canaveral, he'll be on a space ship headed to Mars already."

"And he'll have the key with him," Jon said darkly.

"Until we get it back, we won't be able to do anything else," Red said.

"Looks like I'm going to Florida," Jon said.

"You're not in any shape for that."

Dragon Star nodded. "I'll go."

"No." Despite his weakened condition, Jon's hardened voice left no question of his decision. "I can heal on the trip there. We'll radio Saul and tell him to stop the ship and turn it around. If he won't, I'll go after him. You two can start recovering the other keys. We know the order now. So you can start looking for the next ones down the line. When I get back, we'll shut down a lot more realms."

"Okay," Red agreed. He stepped down from the concrete base and walked over to Xenwyn's body, still lying prone in the grass.

Dragon Star followed him. "Maybe she would heal better if we took her across the boundary."

"No," Red said. He lifted her fragile form in two hands. Dragon Star could see a huge chunk of her side missing. Apparently, the dragon had managed to connect once, tearing part of her abdomen completely away. She was still breathing. "Any other form, she would bleed out in seconds."

"What about as a robot?" Dragon Star asked as pity for this small helpless form filled him. He didn't let it show, but he was glad to feel an emotion. "Maybe in the sci-fi land we can fix her with wires and circuits."

Red took a deep breath, holding back tears. "I don't know."

THANK YOU FOR READING

Curiosity Quills Press

http://curiosityquills.com

Please visit http://curiosityquills.com/reader-survey/ to share your reading experience with the author of this book!

JAMES WYMORE

Tall tales and imagination filled **James Wymore**'s formative years as he moved around the American West. Constantly in pursuit of a gateway to another world, he failed to find a literal door to another reality. However, he learned to travel everywhere fantastic through writing.

As an adult, James voyaged to other continents, where new philosophies and cultures fed his desire to see life from different perspectives. He then immersed himself in studying nature, in the hopes of finding a loophole. Along the way, he continued creating stories about alternate worlds like the ones hiding just out of sight.

James finally settled in the Rocky Mountains with his pet wolf, Kilgore, and started publishing his work. With three books and six short stories in print after just one year, he celebrates the best supernatural portal he's found so far—the mind.

Search with him at http://jameswymore.wordpress.com

AIDEN JAMES

I began writing stories roughly sixteen years ago, after pursuing a career as a singer/songwriter in Denver and later in Nashville. My writing career could've been a brief one, as it started one night when it was my turn to read a bedtime story to my two young sons. Rather than read the 'Mouse birthday book' for the umpteenth time, I began a ramble about a mystical world parallel to our own, a world where sinister creatures sought to take a little boy into their hidden lair... forever.

My first critical reviews from my young audience were mixed. My youngest child, Tyler, was enthralled about the magical place I created, and eagerly awaited more. However, my oldest, Christopher, thought it was the dumbest tale he had ever heard! Luckily, my wife, Fiona, listened nearby. She thought the idea had potential, although she kept that fact a secret until the following spring, 1997. When she suggested I create a fuller blown version of this story, it marked the beginning of my love affair with writing stories.

I wish I could tell you that the experience has always been a glorious progression, where crafting characters, incredible landscapes with captivating plots, and surprising twists was easy. Far from it. It took nearly three years for me to complete my first novel--based on the bedtime story to my boys who by then were young teenagers—and another two years to decide if I liked it enough to show it to anyone else. Signed to a small independent publisher in 2004, *"The Forgotten Eden"* in a previous version was released to small critical acclaim in 2006. But the book found only a very limited audience, so the search for that elusive 'bigger' audience continued.

While pursuing a bigger book deal for my paranormal adventure series, *The Talisman Chronicles*, of which "The Forgotten Eden" and "*The Devil's Paradise*" are the first two of five installments, an itch to dabble in something a little different hit me. A ghost story, and one dealing with a murdered teenage girl who waited nearly a century to enact her revenge became my next creation. Completed in 2007, "*Cades Cove*" was my second release on Kindle, last August. The sequel to this ghost story soon followed in September, entitled "*The Raven Mocker*". But, I'm getting a bit ahead of myself, so allow me to fast-forward to July 2010, when my good friend J.R. Rain talked me into leaving the elusive NY book deal treadmill, and try something new: ebooks. Specifically, ebooks on Kindle, Nook, and eventually other outlets such as Sony and the Apple IBook store.

I just mentioned the releases for both "Cades Cove" and "The Raven Mocker". But before those books were released on Kindle, there was another—my very first ebook: "*Deadly Night*". Released in July 2010, it is the first installment of what promises to be a unique and exciting ghost hunting series. Based on a fictional exaggeration of Fiona, and me "Deadly Night" is a mixture of 'now' and where we were 20 years ago as ghost hunters (and in my hard-hitting' days as a Nashville rock n' roller).

"*The Vampires' Last Lover*" was my first release specifically written for the Kindle and Nook audience. One that pushed the personal envelope for me, the story was written from a female perspective. Like Stephen King, when he wrote "Carrie" so many years ago, my wife provided precious insights into how women view the world around them, and in particular, their true perspectives on males—something I'm sure would surprise most of us guys. Anyway, as the first installment for my new "*The Dying of the Dark*" series, the story brings a fresh perspective to the vampire genre, focused on what it means to be unique and alone, both for the living and the undead, and how self sacrifice for the good of others remains the most noble aspiration for all creatures—above and below our beloved earth.

Flash forward to summer, 2013.

The book business and my career have evolved since I released "The Vampires' Last Lover" at the end of 2010. Two more vampire installments in The Dying of the Dark series have happened since then (*"The Vampires' Birthright"* and *"Blood Princesses of the Vampires"*), and a fourth book is possible for 2014. Deadly Night has spawned a sequel (*"The Ungrateful Dead"*). Meanwhile, my most successful series to date, *"The Judas Chronicles"* started in the spring of 2011 and has seen four bestselling installments published (*"Plague of Coins, Reign of Coins, Destiny of Coins, and The Dragon Coin*). There will be five more books in this series, which will likely reach its conclusion in mid 2015.

Earlier this year, I embarked on a joint publishing venture with Curiosity Quills Press. To date, we have four brand new series in operation, along with coauthored books to continue The Talisman Chronicles and The Dying of the Dark Vampires. The first series is coauthored with *Michelle Wright*, and is entitled *"The Judas Reflections"*. Much more meditative than The Judas Chronicles, we are taking the immortal Judas Iscariot back in time with each new book. It is an interesting perspective, since as he moves backward through time, his personality and soul show less and less likeable characteristics, as compared to the Judas Chronicles. This series promises to be a lot of fun, and the first two installments (*"Murder in Whitechapel"* and *"Curse of Stigmata"*) are available now.

But there so much more, beginning with *"The Serendipitous Curse of Solomon Brandt"*, co-authored with *Lisa Collicutt*, and set for release in late July. A tale about the true nature of good and evil revolves around a wicked plantation owner in Savannah, Georgia and an unusual Hoodoo curse. This will be followed by a fun science fiction series co-authored with *James Wymore*, entitled *"The Actuator"*. Lots of genre bending that effects the physical world—literally. Following this is serialized supernatural thriller in pint-sized installments called *"Mind's Eye"*, coauthored with *Grace Eyre*.

Curiosity Quills is also handling the remaining installments for the Talisman Chronicles. The last new project for this year is the long awaited book 3 from that series. I am happy to announce that *"Hurakan's Chalice"* will be available sometime in September.

That brings us up to date. My commitment to you all remains the same... to create the finest stories my imagination can concoct. And, as always, I want to hear your thoughts. We share this journey together, and I aim to please!

Peace and love always,

Aiden

Aiden James resides in Tennessee with his lovely wife, Fiona, their two sons, Christopher and Tyler, and a feisty terrier named Gypsy. An avid researcher of all things paranormal, he still spends time visiting haunted locales throughout the Deep South. Please visit his website: http://www.aidenjamesfiction.com

A TASTE OF...

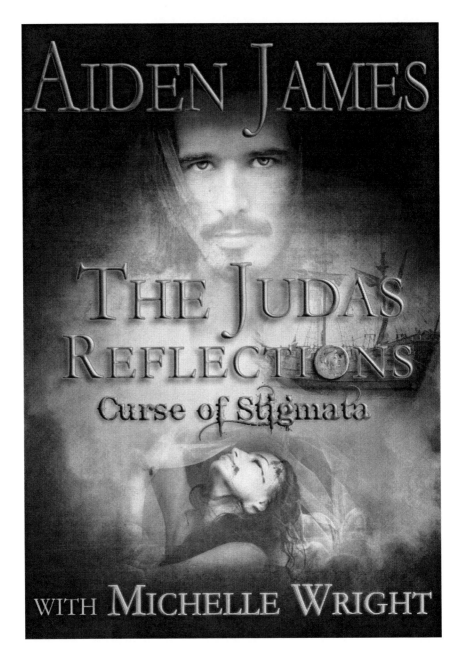

AIDEN JAMES

THE JUDAS REFLECTIONS

Curse of Stigmata

WITH MICHELLE WRIGHT

CHAPTER ONE

From now on, let no one cause me trouble,
for I bear on my body the marks of Jesus.
Galatians 6:17

A wise man once told me when I found myself in a personal mire, "From crisis comes opportunity." It seemed impossible to believe I'd find it in the bowels of hell, aboard the ship Vestibule, which rocked violently from side to side as the weather deteriorated. I felt nausea rising from the pit of my stomach. Having already lost control a few times, causing me to run to the closest side of the ship to vomit was especially embarrassing. Since I perceived weakness as an unwanted liability for an immortal, I did everything I could to be strong.

Captain Van de Velde, of Dutch nationality and burly in stature, claimed he was a direct descendant of Nordic Vikings who took no prisoners when it came to seasickness. He followed suit, convinced it to be a personal attack on his abilities as a Captain, never mind the weather. In the ten days I'd endured the perilous journey, I watched two able-bodied seamen receive six lashes apiece for vomiting.

Not a pleasant sight, yet I remained ambivalent as to what happens with a paying passenger such as myself, if I unexpectedly lost control of my stomach contents. All I wanted to do was get from A to B with no stops in-between. Crossing an ocean in such conditions was frightening, and naively, not anticipated.

"How much longer do I have to endure the endless waves throwing us around like rag dolls? Above or below deck it's all the same. I'm tired of it, Judas. I want to disembark!"

The voice of Isabella rang in my ears, a reminder of her overbearing, annoying personality. Apart from her prowess in bed, she held little attractiveness for me. Physically, she was stunning. Her dark Spanish complexion and sultry eyes a magnet of appeal. For the rest, I had the misfortune of being on the end of her fiery Latin temperament too many times.

"If you want to know when we'll be in calmer seas, I suggest you ask the Captain. I'm no expert, so do not try to make me one."

I hoped, in vain, she would leave me be. When I embarked in the port of Santander, I intended to deliver her straight into the bosom of her family without my presence. Her irksome habit of calling me 'Judas', knowing I go under the name of Emmanuel, was infuriating. Certain she did it with deliberation; it provided another justified reason to leave her to journey on to mama and papa in their palatial country palace.

"You are nothing more than a selfish, boring man who brings me no pleasure. I am not happy, I cry endless tears, yet you ignore me, your heart is frozen!"

Unprepared for a grand altercation on deck, I snubbed her continued tirade and made my way below deck to the cabin, and peace and quiet. But I was not afforded the luxury. Isabella followed in hot pursuit.

"I have been dragged through Italy and Sardinia, not to mention Egypt and the Sudan looking for those stupid coins. I have been rained on, parched from thirst in deserts and covered in dust from cities of filth. For what? For nothing... You failed to find anything. A fruitless search."

"I don't recall breaking your arm to make you follow me. You chose to come along. Now you think it fair game to attack without provocation an innocent man who is doing what he has to do, searching for something important. Holland was tolerable, I thought. Or was that also a hardship?"

"Tolerable? You are indeed delusional, I had to play the little mouse woman while you went about your business!"

My Spanish wasn't perfect. At times, I wish I knew less when she attacked. Ignorance indeed would be blissful.

As the tall ship creaked and rolled with unrelenting waves, Isabella and I made passionate, angry love, if you could call it that. I, for one, did not enjoy it. My mood, coupled with mild seasickness, didn't make for a pleasurable experience. I was glad when it was over and she left for her cabin, leaving me alone, *finally*.

I expected her to get out the rosary beads. Something she did, as she liked to pray hard for her sins. I often had to bear this scenario as she pleaded to be forgiven in the eyes of God. Meanwhile, she raged at me with the guilt of her immorality.

"I curse the day I met you Judas Iscariot!" was thrown at me with alarming regularity.

I was to be met at the port by one Juan Garcia de Moguer. A Basque acquaintance I had the fortune to meet many years ago, he was now to be my guide through the Pyrenees Mountains. Whispers, via Juan, had reached me by letter on good authority that a coin or two lurked within reach. *My* coins, and they were in the possession of a certain shepherd who lived with his daughter and goats high on a mountaintop just across the border in France. It truly defied belief as to how someone of such low standing had come across such fortune, or misfortune, as the coins are cursed. However, I didn't doubt Juan's intuition and knowledge. Once I'd arrive in Spain, leaving Isabella where she belonged, on the road to her family in Aragon, Juan and I would make our way. If successful, then all will be revealed. If not, I will regale a tale or two of how I trekked the French Pyrenees on the cusp of winter and survived. There was nothing to lose.

I was expected for dinner, not a culinary delight. Ship food being rather basic, most often consisting of beef stew with a hard biscuit.

As I'd failed to make Isabella's allotted time, there came the predictable knock on the door.

"Dinner is served, Master Ortiz. Your fellow passenger, the young lady, is asking why you have yet to join her."

The cabin boy had appeared on Isabella's demand. Too irritated to come herself, she sent a messenger. It reminded me again, of how foolish I'd been to stumble across such a woman and embark on a relationship. My carelessness trapping me for seven torturous months, I had failed once more to realize beauty most often is only skin-deep.

Isabella was born into a wealthy family of olive growers who'd preened and pampered her since birth. Well-traveled with a host of suitors, her father had taken a business trip to Rimini with Isabella for company. He hoped for her to form a union with Count Redditi of Florence, a wealthy landowner linked to Italian Royalty. Isabella Rosana Montez disliked him on sight, claiming he was too effeminate for her taste and smelled of garlic.

The ill wind of fate blew when I attended a dinner given by the Count in his regal estate on the shores of Lake Como, where I hoped to find business connections, not a desert storm in the shape of a woman.

An ample bosom enticed me as it squeezed from the bodice of a scandalous dress. Her sense of humor intoxicated me into a fever while her sensual lips worked their magic, inviting me to kiss her passionately. By the end of the evening, we'd slipped into the gardens to make hurried passionate love behind a tree. I had easily snared the twenty-three-year-old Spanish beauty and, without conscience, corrupted her. The next step was to fool her family into believing she was to be a travel companion for my fictitious sister. This enabled me to happily drag Isabella from one land to another, bedding her at every opportunity.

Now, reluctantly, I made my way to dinner and the sight of a woman I could no longer endure. The food remained uninviting as we continued to hit rough seas and my stomach churned. Isabella was more than settled as she tucked into mutton stew, long slender fingers tearing at the bread. By her mood, it seemed our argument was forgotten. She was once more on fire.

"I expect to see you in my cabin when you've eaten... have you washed since this morning? You know how I despise dirty men," she advised.

"I've washed, but as for joining you, that I'll debate."

Isabella constantly vied for an hour or two of passion, more than three times a day. Unable to control her urges, she'd be a challenge for any virile man. I was never weak in matters of sex, but even I wasn't immune from saying no. She was *exhausting*... sometimes.

"If you don't come to me, then I will shirk you for the rest of the voyage. I don't jest with you. There is always a cabin boy or seaman, if I become desperate!"

"Which one? I thought you'd already been through them all," I replied with suspicion, hoping the assumptions were out of place.

I stopped listening to her enraged response by thinking of my upcoming meeting with Juan and our journey to the Shepherd, holder of my coins. She mattered not, and the only thing we could agree on was we both wanted off the ship, badly. Aside from our happy union, the unstable weather hindered our journey from Holland. There were constant altercations between the Captain and his first mate creating continuous tension that Isabella only worsened.

I had left Holland in good spirits, riding high after securing a lucrative business deal in a country of great wealth. Exporting clocks to Japan, I'd purchased a thirty-three percent stake into an established export company in De Hague and expected a nice dividend at the end of the year. A growing priority to search for the coins, funds were needed in order to travel freely whenever necessary. I'd amassed a fortune as the centuries passed, and liked being wealthy. It brought respect in business and social circles, funded on-going education and new skills, and drew women aplenty. There would be many more after Isabella, as they come and go.

"The moment we dock I am sending you on your way," I told her, now. "Your travel expenses will be offset by me. Our time together is over my dear, this is my conclusion." As blunt as I could be, unfortunately, I failed to see the spoon fly across the table and hit me in the eye. An embarrassing moment for me, it also pained our fellow passengers.

"I will despise you for the rest of my life!" she cried out. "You are dishonorable, corrupted, and repulsive! I will make sure everyone knows who lies underneath your thin disguise of a gentleman. What kind of man are you to disown me like this? *Heathen!*"

"The sooner we're off this ship and you are on your way to Aragon, the better. I am done with you Isabella… you are a disgrace!"

We ate in stony silence, neither inclined to continue in the fray, while the swaying ship forced us to hold tight to our bowls. Isabella would return home with her morals intact as long as she continued with the web of deceit, never daring to disclose my true relation to her. I, in turn, would do nothing to discredit the family name by revealing the true nature of their daughter. I had *some* decency.

"I will be delighted to lose your company, a man who fails to satisfy a woman's needs is a man not worthy of my attention," she whispered in my ear as she swayed past, the sound of her petticoats rustling. Less than one day from port, it would soon be over.

I went up on deck, my mood soured, the rainy night air uninviting.

"That woman has the look of an angel and the soul of a beast," said a sailor as he finished rigging. He placed his calloused hands firmly on my shoulders.

"I'm aware of the beast in her, when we arrive in Santander we go our separate ways, I've made it perfectly clear," I replied.

"Good choice, mate. I've had her and I'm not the only one. She can't get enough. One night it was, right here on deck with a high wind lashing. She came up on deck and enticed me. I've never known a woman like her… so insatiable."

I was an immortal, forced to live under an assumed name as I ploughed my way through an ever-increasing troubled world hoping to find resolution. Yet, for all my struggles, I never took myself for stupid. Now, I admit to it. Shamefully, while I slept, my man-sick woman was beating down the cabin doors of sailors and passengers alike.

I didn't confront the sailor for his role in this. She was not to be fought over, an unworthy human who didn't deserve my attention. I thanked him, and for the remainder of the voyage avoided my wayward woman at every opportunity.

Knowing all along that it would end acrimoniously, I never imagined she'd betray me. Something told me to watch out when our relationship extended beyond one night. Now it looked like my intuition was right all along, despite ignoring it. I should have listened. Isabella wasn't the first poison dart through my heart. I was luckless with women, my choices often abysmal. Seeking only the wildest vixens with a passion for living on the edge always came with a price. *Time to reflect, Judas.* Immortality did not equal irresponsibility, so says The Almighty to my heart…

The morning of our arrival in the port of Santander was a welcome relief; I could finally dispose of the excess baggage.

"I expect you to make immediate arrangements for my journey home," she demanded as we stood on deck watching the coastline come into view. "And, I want to be spared the humiliation of waiting unchaperoned on the dock with my luggage. Men will think me a woman of immoral intent."

Knowing what I did of her escapades, I found her comment especially amusing. What kind of Jezebel would describe herself as nothing more than a pious nun type character to the outside world while leading a life of lustful debauchery? Only Isabella. Unable to look at her, I chastised myself for initiating anything more than a sexual dalliance needed to fill a lonely night or two.

A cabin boy collected my trunks while eager passengers chatted excitedly, as they waited to dock and continue with their journeys.

We'd all suffered varying degrees of seasickness, and I for one, was relieved to have two feet firmly on the ground. Summer passages were always more agreeable. As the dock came closer, I preferred to keep my own company, disregarding comments from all and sundry, including Isabella.

A chilled wind ripped through my heavy cloak as we left the ship for the exposed dock. Santander had changed little since the second half of the 15th century when I last graced its sandy shores. Back then, a large project was underway, an extended dock reaching to the foot of the castle. Apart from Castilian wool exports, profitable in the 12th century, there was little to entice me to stay these days.

Isabella had come ashore, her cap and cloak fastened tight against the cold. A woman who read books, spoke fluent Latin, Italian and French, who could hold her own in any situation, now appeared very lost. Meanwhile, I looked everywhere for Juan, expecting him to come bounding forward to greet me. But he was nowhere to be seen.

"Where is the horse and carriage to take me to Aragon?" Isabella asked.

"When you see Juan, then you'll see the carriages. Woman, can you not have patience for once in your life?"

"I'm not you, drifting through countless centuries with no concept of time. I have only one life. Maybe I'll follow in my family's footsteps and die young. I make the most of what I have. Patience is not always a virtue for us lowly mortals."

She had a point. Her mother died very young, as did her older sister and uncle. For once, we agreed on something, I had an advantage. When first I confessed my immortality to Isabella, she balked and wasn't amused. As the weeks passed, she began to slowly accept what she'd been told, although she remained slightly unsure and madly intrigued, telling me numerous times she found it wild and strangely exhilarating.

"You hope finding your coins will redeem you in the eyes of Jesus, our Savior and the Lord God. Perhaps you'll even be forgiven for your terrible sin against him. I, on the other hand, *cannot* forgive you!"

I ignored her, wishing Juan would hurry. I amused myself by watching the fishing boats come in, one after the other, bringing their catch to eager buyers. The dock was busy with passengers embarking, and locals arriving to buy something to go in the pot. Depending on the catch, in a few hours the sea air would be tinged with fragrances of the region. Oil and garlic, grown in the rich soil, would complement fish frying in the pan. Judging by the amount of shellfish on offer, I anticipated the smell of Cantabria's sherry to invade my nostrils, enticing me to stay just a little longer.

I searched endless faces for Juan, his beard a trademark. Our last encounter, on the shores of Lake Como, was one of frivolity. He arrived drunk and provided non-stop entertainment for all of the Count's guests, including myself. Later on in the midst of my travels, Juan urged me to follow him here at my earliest opportunity. There had been one or two delays while he searched for the precise whereabouts of the Shepherd, while I waited patiently.

We'd met seventy-five years earlier, by pure chance on my travels through Cataluña. I was delighted to find a fellow immortal who lost his right to mortality in 1492 by betraying his fellow soldiers in a battle against the Moors. His fatal mistake? Giving vital information to the enemy in return for payment and getting caught. The Moors were evicted and Juan was hung. Convinced his punishment was to put things right in the world, no matter how long it took, he wandered the earth in a saint like fashion spreading goodness. Apart from one weakness, left over from his mortality, alcohol, he would surely be perfect. The more wine he drank on our first meeting, the more he told me how much he dreamed of redemption. I suspected he had a long wait but did nothing to burst his bubble. The mortal he had been was changed, and he loathed any form of betrayal he came across, while clinging each century to his beard and optimism. I worried what his thoughts would be if I confessed the truth about Isabella?

While considering this, out of the masses he emerged, heading in our direction. I caught his attention while Isabella deliberately sighed with impatience and stamped a foot.

"Finally, he's here and I hope he's secured my carriage. I have a long journey ahead and need to be on my way," Isabella demanded, coldly. I dismissed her, more focused on making sure the night would be spent in peace and quiet.

"My good man." Juan came to me, his arms outstretched. "You've arrived safely having battled the winter sea. It's so good to see you!"

"We're in one piece, although the journey was not without peril. I take it you've arranged a carriage for Isabella?"

He smiled, glancing at her only briefly. She turned her head defiantly. Fortunately, I had written to Juan explaining some of my predicament with Isabella. Now I depended on his good nature to make the best and safest arrangements possible for her return home. Regardless that she deserved worse, I am not a man to abandon a helpless female to an unknown fate.

A dock boy transported my trunks to an inn close by and willingly returned for Isabella's, who coldly refused to pay him for his trouble. "I have to take care of myself first," so said the woman whose family had amassed a fortune.

Finally, the moment came when I could help her into the carriage paid for by me, without argument. Juan gave her some food for the journey. There was no gratitude.

"I wish you a safe journey," I said. "Our time together is over, but I want you to know I'm sorry for what went wrong on my part, I hope you see the problems from your side also."

"I was a victim of your selfish evil ways. Such evil I have never experienced, I hope you rot in hell because Jesus will reject you in Heaven. Now I must go home to confess my sins and never touch another man. I will become a nun."

"Farewell Isabella," I replied, ignoring her dramatic nonsense. "I will send your father the bill of expense for the carriage, and explain how you single handedly managed to bed the entire crew whilst I slept." Knowing she would scream wildly and bang her fists on the window as the carriage took off, I dismissed her with a slight of my hand. I had no intention of communicating with her father, and only needed to have the last word.

Finally free, I followed Juan to a warm and inviting Inn. It was a good feeling to be back on dry land and not rocking to and fro. As I sat warming myself before the fire, I sent lingering thoughts of Isabella deep into the embers, distracted by the innkeeper who served us two spiced red wines, so hot it burned my tongue. The familiar feeling of tissues regenerating soon followed.

"You are fortunate, Emmanuel," observed Juan. "If only my weak stomach could respond so graciously." He laughed. The sorcerer's spell that could not relieve a host of physical maladies did enable second sight. Juan could sense conditions in others as well as events to come. Eternal life on earth was the prize, to which we commiserated often.

"I will sip it slowly my friend," I said. "Now tell me everything you know about the shepherd."

Juan leaned back in his chair, tipping it slightly so it rocked. "As you know, my close confidant, Dario, a man of great knowledge and an intrepid explorer, is certain he's seen the coins," he began. "Two of them with his own eyes. The shepherd wanted to know their worth, curious of their age and value. His daughter, a young girl apparently wild like an animal, tried to convince Dario the coins glowed when she stared at them. He disbelieved her, but was sure the pieces were extremely old. He recently made another climbing trip to the Pyrenees where he met with the shepherd again. Dario believes the coins belong to you, he only asks for a small finder's fee."

"If your friend is correct, this will be an easy task of recovery. Two coins in one swoop—an attractive reason to take a risk." I chuckled. "I'm no great mountaineer, but I'm willing to learn, and more than willing to compensate the man."

"Then we'll have a wonderful evening of fine food and good wine. Tomorrow morning the carriage will be here to take us across the border to France. Dario will be waiting at an agreed location. He's a trusted mountain guide."

It sounded too good to be true, coins falling into my lap. The trick would be either to steal back what is rightfully mine, or barter a price. The idea of a purchase reeked of self-punishment, seeing as it was payment I was given for the ultimate betrayal.

"I will remain optimistic." I smiled, relishing Isabella's departure.

The evening was pleasant, indeed. A wonderful shellfish platter, fried sardines, freshly picked tomatoes and olives soon arrived. Juan was delightful company, and I could not think of a better person to accompany me on such an intriguing journey. Somewhere high up in the Pyrenees lay two coins, necessary to redeem my soul. But to retrieve them meant an encounter with a shepherd and his seemingly deranged daughter. I couldn't wait to meet them.

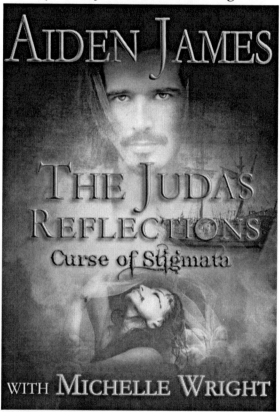

A TASTE OF...

THEOCRACIDE

JAMES WYMORE

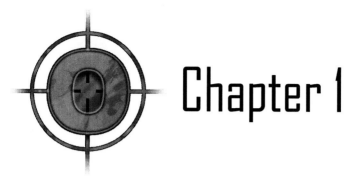

Chapter 1

Undying Emperor Turns 240

Millions of Americans tuned in to watch the celebration yesterday as the Undying Emperor turned 240 years old. Fireworks filled the sky after independent scientists did blood tests again to verify the age and DNA of our immortal leader. Almost one thousand people physically came to the White House for the party of the year. Several of the most famous bands played while the Emperor danced with the newest First Lady.

"His youth and vitality are a miracle which blesses us all," said Bishop Americanhorse, the new Religious Advisor on the Undying Emperor's cabinet. Bishop Americanhorse recently replaced the late Bishop Peoples, who died after serving as the Religious Advisor on the Undying Emperor's cabinet for over thirty-six years. The appointment was part of the birthday celebration, which lasted for hours, available via live computer vid to every American, anywhere in the world.

One soldier in the Undying Emperor's service overseas said, "It brought tears to my eyes. Knowing a living God chose to walk among us and guide us makes me proud to serve the same great man my father and grandfather fought for."

Police arrested a few online protestors after they tried to set up chat rooms to petition the government to end American involvement in the war. One police officer said, "It was really pathetic. There always has to be somebody who just can't let people be happy and enjoy life. We will deal with these heretics quickly. We were just glad their actions were futile because so few people joined their protest."

The Undying Emperor closed the festivities with an inspiring speech. "This occasion is a celebration of our solidarity. It is through unity of purpose that this country grew to greatness, and with continued unity I will carry us not just another two hundred forty years in to the future, but another two hundred forty thousand years."

With 96% of the country tuning in, this represents the most watched program in history.

Willing his feet to remain silent, Jason Hunt concentrated on the ground as he weaved between the outstretched claws of the tree branches. The lens on his computer helped him see despite the heavy blackness of night. He deliberately lifted each foot higher to avoid rocks and roots, which looked deceptively flat on the computer projection screen wrapped around his face like glasses. He controlled each breath so the tiniest sounds would not give away his position to the people hunting him.

He recognized the welcoming gesture of a large tree with wide branches ahead. He slipped around it, quietly leaning his heavy pack against the trunk and pressing in so the tree would support his weight, letting him rest.

Risking his own safety for a moment, Jason did a quick check on each of his companions. Jason knew he couldn't help them now, but as he rested here, he just wanted some reassurance they weren't dead yet. He had to suppress the desire to talk to them, and the desire to hear their voices. It would be suicide to speak aloud now. The men chasing them were in the Army of the Undying Emperor. They would not hesitate to shoot for an instant.

Jason winked his left eye, engaging the user interface of the computer. The computer then tracked his eye movements as he raised the sensitivity of his microphone to maximum. The speakers inside each earpiece of his glasses began to hum as Jason strained to detect the faintest sound within thirty feet. Hearing nothing, he lowered the volume, then then pulled the glasses off the front of his nose so they hung below his chin. Nobody ever removed their computer.

He stared into the dark sky, waiting patiently for his eyes to adjust to the near pitch black. Only a tiny sliver of a moon illuminated the forest tonight, with enough brownish smog wafting on the air to block out any starlight. The pollution filtered the crescent-shaped spot of moonlight behind layers of brick-red silk. Jason's father had always said something about the moon having turned to blood, but Jason never understood what that meant. Right now, he had to exploit the small advantage. His pursuer would never remove the computer.

Eventually his eyes could distinguish the gray of the trees through the darkness. Jason quietly peered around the edge of the trunk serving as his fortress, and scanned the woods. He traced the ground and every silhouette with precision; searching for any abnormality. His heart leaped when he spotted the steel toe of a black combat boot poking out from a tree trunk about forty feet away. The computer would never recognize it as anything more than a rock.

Jason pushed his glasses back into place, remaining as behind his tree as he could so the light from the glasses would not give his position away. The projected light temporarily night-blinded him. Jason had to ignore the blur from the tears to blink up his computer screen, selecting the tree serving as cover for his enemy. Immediately, a dim red glow highlighted that tree from all those around Jason. Then, he returned to the main program. He would be able to easily find this tree from any angle.

A predatory smile pulled at Jason's mouth. He loved the moment when the game turned; when the hunted became the hunter. He knew his quarry—the highest-ranking R.O.T.C. cadet in the university. In another year's time, the cadet and his team would be fighting, and most likely dying, in the service of the Undying Emperor. Therefore, the cadet took this game very seriously. For him, this game equated to more training.

For Jason, this game represented freedom. If he didn't have a scholarship, he would have paid to play. His father had been training him all his life, but Jason never appreciated the value of the training until he started playing tag.

Whenever two undefeated teams played against each other, the stress of the game escalated. Adrenaline pushed them to the breaking point. Whoever won would go on to represent the University against other teams at the state level.

Jason pitied his opponent as he silently slid a mock-grenade out of his pack, recalled his memorization of the trees, and squeezed the grenade. It wouldn't really explode, of course. It would just send out a scrambling signal which all the nearby computers they wore would register as an explosion. Light and noise would fill their senses. Gauging the distance carefully, Jason tossed the grenade in a wide arc. Before it hit the ground, he jumped out and started running behind it.

He clasped his hands together with one forefinger pointing forward and the other curled as if around an imaginary trigger. The computer, recognizing the virtual gun, pulled up red crosshairs to indicate the target. In a real war, their backpacks would have large guns mounted on electrical motors, which automatically followed the crosshairs.

The enemy peeked out when he heard Jason's footsteps. He took a wild shot before he saw the grenade and reversed to dive the other direction. Jason pulled his glasses down on his nose and peered over a small line above the top rim. As expected, white dots and rumbling noise filled the screen for a few seconds. It temporarily blinded his opponent, who started shooting wildly in every direction, hoping for a random hit.

Jason carefully leaned around the tree. Estimating where the cross would land, he pulled an imaginary trigger. His computer showed the image of a bullet hitting exactly where the crosshairs indicated.

"No!" The young man's voice roared in anger. His glasses flashed red; indicating his death in the game. "You would have killed yourself with that grenade, too!"

"This isn't war," Jason said with his slightly higher, but much more composed voice. "This is a game; different strategies."

Jason Hunt pocketed the used grenade and quickly stalked away from his victim. He heard cries of cheating fade as he carefully blended back into to the wood. Jason smiled because the noise covered the sound of him quickly climbing two limbs up into a great ash tree.

Time for another tactic nobody else ever used. His father taught him to do the unexpected. Exploit the expectation of common actions in those who never do anything extraordinary. People didn't climb trees any more. Most people didn't leave their houses for months on end. Fewer had the physical strength or manual dexterity required to climb a tree.

Jason leaned back into a perfect saddle and clasped his hands again to pull up the crosshairs. The defeated cadet still ranted. Predictably, his temper tantrum drew two of his team members. In the deep night, the faint glow of the computer glasses through which they viewed the world made an easy target. It radiated like a tiny lighthouse beacon. The fourth member of their team must have been defeated already. Jason grinned as he lined up the shot on the furthest enemy and fired. One second later, his glasses showed two people flashing red.

"What?" The newest camouflage clad arrival cried in confusion. "I'm dead!"

The last young man in the clearing tried to jump for cover. The moment his body hit the ground, his glasses began flashing red, too.

Jason jumped down from the tree quickly. He wanted to keep as many of his tactics as possible from becoming public knowledge. Even though his night vision glasses flashed a green border around the forest scene, indicating victory, he moved back into the woods and started making his way around the grouping of defeated foes.

Accepting defeat, they began searching the forest for their enemies. Jason froze and pretended to be hiding on a rock behind a cluster of quaking aspens. Jason had been all too happy to choose this park after having won the right to select the battlefield. Most of the people in the game had not set foot in a real forest before, giving Jason's team a huge advantage.

One of the opponents spotted him and pointed him out to the others. Jason waved, but he didn't move closer. A flashing black arrow on the screen indicated the direction to the rendezvous point so both teams could meet before starting another game or ending the session. Jason waited. He didn't want to be alone with three opponents. In a few minutes, the rest of his team emerged. Like Jason, they all wore black from head to foot. Then, he stepped out and walked over to meet the group.

"That shouldn't count as a win," the opposing captain barked. "That would never happen in a real war."

Jason's team ignored the indignant grunt. They had each scanned the stats for the game and saw Jason scored three hits. Once again, he was the hero.

"So awesome!" The shortest member of Jason's team was positively delighted with the win. The team called him Boss. Despite his clumsiness, they kept him on the team for his contagious enthusiasm. He was the only member of Jason's team "killed" today, but he took one of their enemies out first. An exceptional personal victory like that made him cheer. "The Snow Cats are undefeated!"

"It's not a win," the cadet persisted. His team stood in line behind him now, refusing to concede. Obviously, they all wore the same military uniform, and their enormous egos would not let them admit defeat. "You can't run up on your own grenade without dying."

Jason put his hand out to stop his short comrade before Boss said something to turn this into a fight.

"Dead men don't call out to their team, revealing the position of their enemies either."

"That's not…" The cadet stopped short. His team would not hesitate to back his hypocrisy, but the realization of it took some of the fire from his heart.

"We'll play again if you want," Jason said. "But if we beat you next time, you have to concede two wins."

"And we get to be the team who puts Regiment 21 out of the varsity championships," added Skipper, another of Jason's group. It would mean a great deal more humiliation for Regiment 21 than losing just once to an undefeated team.

"No deal," the cadet replied. Since he did all the talking, Jason assumed he was a higher rank than the rest of his team. The others hung on his words, as if waiting for the signal to attack.

The last member of Jason's team, Temple, took a turn. "Then we have no choice but to submit the video to the judges and let them decide if your claim is valid."

Jason winked his left eye. He quickly called up a video feed of the cadet's ravings about unfairness, which had accidentally lured his teammates out into the open. He used his hand to touch virtual controls only he could see hovering before him in the air. He cut the segment and pasted it into a file. Then he sent it out so all the players in the gathering could watch it simultaneously.

The cadet's posture slumped. He finally realized he had brought about the demise of his entire team. Without a word, he winked his controls up and touched the imaginary concede button in the air. "This is not over," he growled. "One way or another, it's not over."

Jason's team cheered and laughed while the neo-military group turned and marched away. Jason regretted making an enemy. In his heart, he hoped this would teach the cadets no strategy was good enough to keep them alive in war. Signing up to serve in the military of the Undying Emperor amounted to suicide. Something told him these cadets had gone too far to question it now.

"We're going to state!" Boss crowed. They all clapped each other on the back and began talking at once.

Suddenly the reverie quieted with the return of the opposing captain. His hands, posed as a gun, pointed straight at Jason's heart. His manic face snarled beneath a real swivel mounted machine gun.

Skipper tried to step forward and speak, but the wild-eyed soldier quickly shifted his aim. Instantly the electric servomotors repositioned the gun so it pointed straight at the young man's heart. Then he snapped his hand and the gun above him back toward Jason. Jason's team, hands in the air, stepped back instinctively from the insane captor.

He said evenly, "It's not just a game."

The story continues in…

Theocracide

By James Wymore

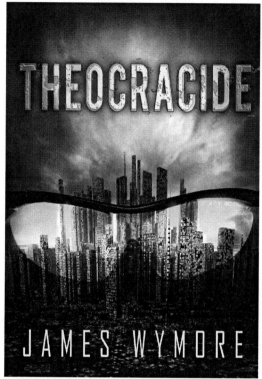

Available Wherever Books are Sold

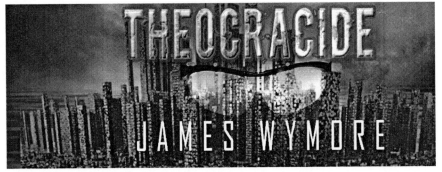

Theocracide, by James Wymore

In a time when Americans live isolated lives behind computer glasses that mask the harsh reality, Jason is forced to abandon this rose-colored fantasy as an unwilling part of his father's plan to assassinate the Undying Emperor. With aliens invading the world and his sister dying of an incurable flu they brought, he is pulled from his perfect life with an amazing new girlfriend and plunged into a dark game of intrigue and conspiracy against the most powerful people in the world. Is there any way to regain the respect of the girl he loves after committing Theocracide?

The Judas Reflections: Murder in Whitechapel

by Aiden James & Michelle Wright

Emmanuel Ortiz holds an ancient and dark secret: his real name is Judas Iscariot. Forced to walk the earth as a cursed immortal, Judas' disguise as Emmanuel does little to ease his eternal loneliness.

But when the brutal murders ascribed to Jack the Ripper in poverty-stricken Whitechapel, London in 1888, he recognizes the bloody signature of killing that speaks to the unholy talents of a fellow immortal... an enemy from long ago.

The Serendipitous Curse of Solomon Brandt

by Aiden James & Lisa Collicutt

The soul of Solomon Brandt, an evil plantation owner murdered by his slaves, has been safely contained by the Hoodoo circle over his burial site. But construction work has disturbed the seal, and the essence of Solomon emerged at last into the modern world – but forever changed.

Will the Hoodoo priestesses that imprisoned him give Solomon a chance at redemption? A chance at true love? A chance to find himself again?

Will the good in him triumph, when his soul's evil side comes knocking?

The Forgotten Eden, by Aiden James

A brutal murder of a noted archaeologist and teacher at the University of Alabama. Jack Kenney, close friend of the late professor are abducted by the FBI, held against their will in a secret holding facility.

The agency's interrogations become increasingly violent, until Jack gains a welcome reprieve when Special Agent Peter McNamee arrives from the FBO's Richmond office. He befriends Jack and gains his trust, drawing upon a similar supernatural event from his own youth. Jack leads Peter on an extraordinary roller-coaster ride involving a mystical and deadly realm located in America's Deep South…

The Judas Reflections: Curse of Stigmata

by Aiden James & Michelle Wright

The immortal Judas Iscariot (known by his alias, Emmanuel Ortiz) is hot on the trail of two precious coins believed to be part of the bounty once paid to him for betraying Jesus Christ.

Traveling thousands of miles across the world's grand open waters with fellow immortal, Juan Garcia de Moguer, the captivating Rachel, and a ruthless Dutch pirate slave trader named Captain Dirk Chivers teaches Emmanuel an important lesson about himself.

How far is he willing to go to get what he wants?

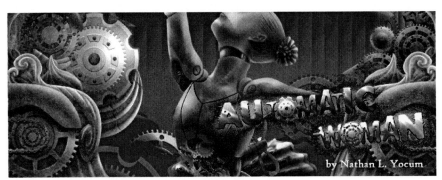

Automatic Woman, by Nathan L. Yocum

There are no simple cases. Jacob "Jolly" Fellows knows this.

The London of 1888, the London of steam engines, Victorian intrigue, and horseless carriages is not a safe place nor simple place... but it's his place. Jolly is a thief catcher, a door-crashing thug for the prestigious Bow Street Firm, assigned to track down a life sized automatic ballerina. But when theft turns to murder and murder turns to conspiracy, can Jolly keep his head above water? Can a thief catcher catch a killer?

CPSIA information can be obtained at www.ICGtesting.com
Printed in the USA
BVOW04s1852200214

345549BV00002B/3/P